He finished his drink and stood up, his mouth twisted into a bleak little smile. He looked a little drunk. 'I'm going to fix her wagon, Bobby. I know just how to do it and I'm gonna fix it good. And I think I know how I'm gonna get me onto that movie of yours, too.' He gazed around, spotted the waitress and waved at her. 'Hey, you have such a thing as a phone in this place?'

I watched him lurching away towards the phone at the back of the room and wondered why, among all the events of this curious evening, there was one comparatively small thing that bothered me most ...

Barry Norman is the author of numerous books, mainly about film and film stars, including *100 Best Films of the Century*. *Death on Sunset* is his tenth novel.

*By the same author*

FICTION
The Matter of Mandrake
The Hounds of Spaeta
A Series of Defeats
To Nick a Good Body
End Product
Have a Nice Day
Sticky Wicket
The Birddog Tape
The Mickey Mouse Affair

NON-FICTION
Tales of the Redundance Kid
The Hollywood Greats
The Film Greats
The Movie Greats
Talking Pictures
Barry Norman's Good Night-in Guide
(*with Emma Norman*)
Barry Norman's Family Video Guide
(*with Emma Norman*)
100 Best Films of the Century

# DEATH ON SUNSET

## Barry Norman

ORION

An Orion paperback
First published in Great Britain by Orion in 1998
This paperback edition published in 1999 by Orion Books Ltd,
Orion House, 5 Upper St Martin's Lane, London WC2H 9EA

A CIP catalogue record for this book
is available from the British Library

ISBN: 0 75281 736 1

Printed and bound in Great Britain by
Clays Ltd, St Ives plc

This is a work of fiction.
Names, places, characters and incidents are
either products of the author's imagination
or are used fictitiously.

*For Harry and Charlie*
*with all my love*

# 1

It was the ski mask that bothered me. The rest of his gear – quilted anorak, black polo neck sweater, ski pants, gloves and fleece-lined ankle boots – seemed reasonable enough. It was January in New York and what with the chill factor and all it was about forty degrees below zero out there. Only we weren't out there; we were on the seventh floor of a very smart, very expensive centrally heated hotel on the Upper West Side and as I stepped out of my suite into the plush carpeted corridor I had no qualms at all about facing the immediate elements with a totally naked face.

So what did this fellow need with a ski mask, up here in the warm, and, come to that, the Cleveland Indians baseball cap with the peak pulled low over his forehead? If it hadn't been for the mask I might not have looked at him twice, just nodded, murmured 'Good evening' and gone on my way, minding my own business. But I did look at him twice and the second time I noticed a couple of other things that bothered me. For instance, as I stepped out of my suite he was stepping out of the one next door and I knew he didn't belong there. That suite was occupied by the Legend – Virna Newport, the green-eyed goddess of the screen (hey, come on, these aren't my words: I'm just quoting from the film posters) who was once the biggest movie star in the entire world. And as I knew from only casual observation her taste in room mates ran to the young and the lissom rather than tall, broad-shouldered and obviously mature males like the man in the ski mask.

And then I noticed another thing: as he closed the door to the suite with his right hand the Saks 5th Avenue carrier bag in his left hand gaped open to reveal what looked like a chunky, velvet-covered jewellery case. Embossed on the top of it, gold letters against the midnight blue velvet, were the initials 'VN'.

I said, 'Excuse me.'

He turned and grinned thinly at me. Hazel eyes and a lot of white teeth were all I could see because the ski mask blanked out everything else. 'What?' he said, irritably.

'Well, not to put too fine a point on it, what exactly are you doing with Miss Newport's—'

And then he shoved me hard in the chest and, while I was still reeling backwards, turned and ran down the corridor towards the lifts. I bounced off a wall, recovered my balance and set off after him, and I was even gaining on him as he turned the corner towards the elevator station.

I think I'd have caught him, too, but as I skidded round the corner he glanced back and with a strong, wristy underhand delivery hurled the Saks bag at me. If he'd thrown it at my head or chest I could have caught it or knocked it to one side and carried on but he threw it hard and low and it cracked agonisingly against my right shin.

I yelped, stumbled and fell and while I was still on my hands and knees the fellow in the ski mask reached the lift and the door opened to disgorge an elderly man and woman.

They toddled out, smiling and chatting. Ski mask burst between them, hurling them both in different directions, leapt into the lift and pressed the button. By now I was up again and ready for the chase but the dazed and staggering elderly parties got in my way. First one bumped into me, then the other and by the time I had shoved them both aside and reached the elevator it was too late.

The old man, stout and silver-haired like a US senator, said, 'Jesus Christ, what the fuck's going on here?'

I ignored him, grabbed the Saks bag, ran back to my suite, picked up the phone and hit the button for reception.

A male voice, polite and bland, said, 'Yes, Mr Lennox, may I help you?'

'There's a man coming down in the elevator,' I said, 'dressed like he's taking part in the Giant Slalom. Whatever you do, stop him.'

The bland voice said, 'You should have called earlier, Mr Lennox. A guy dressed like that just went through the lobby like Carl Lewis on speed. He's either at Columbus Circle or way down the West Side by now. Why did you want us to stop him?'

'I think he tried to rob Virna Newport. Hold on.' I took the box out of the Saks bag. It was a jewellery case all right. 'Yep, he did. He tried to steal her jewels. I think you'd better call the police.'

'Ah, shit!' he said and hung up. I lay back on the bed and took a deep breath. Carl Lewis? Where had that young man been living these last few years? Hadn't he ever heard of Linford Christie or Donovan Bailey?

# 2

'SO THAT'S ALL you can tell us, huh?' the cop said. I was on the couch in the sitting-room part of my suite; he was squeezed into an armchair, his fat legs crossed, his paunch resting on his knees, his notebook resting on his paunch. 'Aside from the ski-ing outfit and his height – six-one, six-two maybe? – all you know is he had hazel eyes and a lot of teeth.'

'Well, the usual American number,' I said. 'Whatever that is.'

'Par' me?'

'What I mean is, he showed a lot of teeth and they were very good. Very white. You know?' I just have this theory that Americans have more teeth than anyone else in the world, or maybe they simply have wider mouths.

'Yeah, well,' the cop said. 'Good teeth, why not? We take care of our teeth over here. I was in Europe last year – the wife has family in Poland? – and what I noticed, you Europeans have lousy teeth. Hey, no offence – yours are fine. I'm talkin' most Europeans, know what I mean? Their teeth are terrible. Maybe they smoke too much, I don't know.'

I braced myself, waiting for the customary American lecture on how smoking, and secondary smoking in particular, was responsible for every known disease on the planet from lung cancer to athlete's foot but then he lit a short, fat cigar and I relaxed.

'You don't mind?' he said.

4

'Please,' I said, and meant it. I've never smoked myself but that's because I used to be a professional fighter and boxing and smoking don't really go together. I have no objection to other people smoking, though. In Britain I reckon the National Health service would have collapsed years ago if it weren't for the taxes smokers paid and since they tend to die earlier than other people it's the non-smokers who really benefit from their habit. Besides, I reckoned the emissions from this cop's car would probably do me far more harm than any number of cigars he smoked in my presence.

The police had arrived impressively soon after my call to the hotel's reception desk. No doubt the mention of Virna Newport's name had something to do with that and with the rank of the investigating officers. The man sitting opposite me, a shortish, chunky person almost as broad as he was high and with thin black hair and a fat black moustache, was a lieutenant. In the next suite, talking to Virna Newport, was a woman sergeant. Various other cops of lesser rank were roaming around the hotel looking tough and grim and probably wondering what they were supposed to be doing there since the unsuccessful burglar was long gone.

I had told my cop everything I could remember and then gone over it again at least twice and now he said, 'What you did, trying to stop that guy, that was something. Don't you know that in this town the bad guys carry knives, shooters, machine guns even? You coulda been killed.' He shook his head. 'Boy, you were stoopid.'

I said, 'Oh, thanks. Next time I'll just trot on ahead, shall I, and make sure the elevator's waiting for him?'

The cop put his notebook away and rocked himself back and forth in the chair, preparatory to propelling his rotund body into an upright position. 'Everybody's a comedian,' he said, sourly. He struggled finally to his feet, punched in a room number on the telephone and when whoever it was answered said, 'You finished there?' He listened for a moment, then grunted, 'Okay, I'll send him in.'

He replaced the handset, relit his cigar and said, 'You ready for this, Lennox? This could be your big opportunity. This could be the first really great day of the rest of your life. The Legend wants to say thank you. In person.'

Actually, I'd already met Virna Newport. I'd been introduced to her – quite unmemorably, no doubt, as far as she was concerned – the previous night at the gala opening of a swanky new restaurant on the Upper East Side. I was there, representing my two London partners and myself, as serious backers of the enterprise. This was what we did, really: we invested, we speculated, we bought low and sold high and we kept a close eye on the trends. And in this sybaritic age hardly anyone was trendier than the celebrity chef, the guy who emerged sweating from an apprenticeship in a hotel kitchen to open his own establishment and be fawned upon by food writers who, such were the curious standards of the time, became hardly less celebrated than the chef himself.

There was money to be made from these cooks, so long as you avoided paying their exorbitant prices and ate in more reasonable places, and when one of them, in whose very successful London restaurant we had wisely invested, decided to open a sister establishment in New York we were happy to invest in that, too.

The grand opening of Rick's Café – the chef was a hopeless movie buff – had taken place the previous night and I had been among those present, on behalf of our own little consortium, which consisted of me, a solicitor and a stockbroker. For them the consortium and the investments we made were a sideline, a nice little earner which augmented their already considerable incomes from their day jobs; for me it was much more important. Basically, it was what I now did, the way I earned my living, and I wasn't complaining. It was a very nice living indeed.

The owner of the Manhattan hotel in which I was staying also had money in Rick's Café, which was why I'd been given a suite at a very competitive rate. And Virna Newport was one of a number of stars, past and present, who had been flown in to ensure that the launch did not pass unnoticed by the media.

She had arrived swathed in emerald silk with diamonds in her hair and ears and wrapped round her wrists and throat and, as the final touch – the accessory that completed her ensemble – wearing on her arm a dark, svelte young man with a profile like Rudolph Valentino and a pout like Kim Basinger.

As a minor partner in the restaurant I had been among those presented to her. I had said, 'How do you do?' and she had smiled faintly, said, 'Good evening,' and walked on. As an encounter it was hardly one for the memoirs.

A young black woman, the police sergeant who had been taking her statement, let me into the Newport suite, the honeymoon suite by the look and size of it.

She hitched her bag onto her shoulder and said, 'Okay, Ms Newport, you got my card there. Anything else you remember just call me.' Then she gave me a pretty smile and left.

Virna Newport, in a long black dress with a high collar, was stretched out on a scarlet chaise longue; the svelte young man was at a table on the far side of the room, using the phone. Through the open bedroom door I could see a huge, heart-shaped bed which, to be fair to the management, was the only truly vulgar piece of furniture in the suite.

She said, 'Mr Lennox, isn't it? My saviour.' There was irony in the voice and the slight smile that went with it. The famous green eyes studied me thoughtfully above the rim of a chunky goblet that contained ice cubes, a slice of lime and a lot of colourless liquid that could have been water, though I doubted it. 'Come and sit here.' She curled her legs up to make room for me on the chaise longue. When I sat down her stockinged feet pressed lightly against my thigh.

She was well into her fifties but even close up she was still beautiful, if a touch Rubensesque by modern standards. Of course, according to the tabloids she'd had more cosmetic surgery than Michael Jackson but if so she had obviously gone to the best because the only real signs of ageing were in her neck and hands. There's not a lot you can do about the neck and hands and hers looked fifteen years older than her face and particularly those remarkable eyes and the thick, dark almost auburn hair.

She took a sip from her drink and gave me that ironic smile again, only now it seemed less ironic than coquettish. 'You were very

7

brave,' she said softly and rubbed one small foot along my thigh. I moved a little further away but the foot followed me.

'Yes, well,' I said, 'the lieutenant reckoned I was stupid.'

'Oh, no. Reckless, perhaps, even a little foolhardy but not stupid.' Another sip, more like a gulp this time. 'Thank God I wasn't here when the thief broke in. I wouldn't have known what to do.'

I nodded towards the svelte young man, jabbering away on the phone. 'No doubt your friend would have come to the rescue.'

She laughed as if the idea were genuinely funny. 'Darren? Somehow I don't think so. He's not built for fighting. Other things maybe but not fighting ...' She gave me another of those ironic smiles.

'So where were the two of you when the robbery happened?'

'Downstairs, having cocktails with the owner of this place. That nice young sergeant thinks the thief must have known that, got hold of a key from someplace – a master key, a skeleton key, whatever – and just walked in here. And then you came along – Sir Galahad.'

The irony again and she was beginning slightly to piss me off. I didn't want sobs of gratitude for what I'd done but equally I didn't want to be treated like the comic relief who comes on in the second act to provide a few laughs.

Darren put the phone down and came over to us. He rested his hand possessively on Virna Newport's head and glowered down at me. 'Who's this?' he said.

She knocked his hand away with a sharp flick of her fingers. 'This is Mr Lennox, Darren. Get him a drink. He'll have the same as me.' Darren moved sulkily to the cocktail cabinet against the wall, put ice, lime, some tonic and a lot of vodka into a goblet and handed it to me as though in an ideal world it would poison me.

'Thank you, Darren,' she said. 'Now go downstairs to the bar and get yourself a drink. You don't have to pay – just sign for it.'

'Go down . . . ? What, are you crazy? We got every drink in the world right here, why should I go to the bar?'

She sat up straight and I took the opportunity to remove myself from the chaise longue and moved to an armchair a few feet away.

From the slight frown that briefly creased her flawless forehead I gathered she was not too pleased about that.

'Darren,' she said, purring like a dark marmalade cat, 'you didn't hear what I told you? Clear the wax out of your ears and listen good. Go down to the bar and buy yourself a drink – and do it now.'

No, Darren, I thought urgently, don't do it, son. Stick around here where I need you. But I wasn't paying his rent and I hadn't bought his cashmere sports coat and any telepathic message I was sending either didn't get through to him or was simply ignored. He glared at me and there was an icy hatred in his dark eyes that belied the softness of his pouting mouth.

'Well, all *right*,' he said, 'but I won't be long. One drink, that's all.'

When he had gone, she said, 'Well now, Mr Lennox ... No, I can't keep calling you Mr Lennox. What's your first name?'

'Robert,' I said. 'Well, Bob. Or Bobby. That's what my friends call me.'

'Can I be your friend, Bobby?'

Oh shit, I thought. She's not old enough to have been in movies with that kind of dialogue. But I just gave her a weak grin and said, 'Of course, you can, er, Virna.'

She held her glass out to me. 'You want to freshen up my drink, Bobby?'

I took it from her, went to the cabinet and threw in a lot of vodka along with very little tonic. It wasn't a case of trying to get a woman drunk so that I could have my will of her but trying to get her so sloshed that she couldn't have her will of me which, immodest though it may sound, was what I suspected she was after.

I went behind the chaise longue and handed the glass to her over her shoulder. She had curled up her legs again so that the space beside her was ready for me. I pretended not to notice, picked up my own drink from an occasional table and resumed my seat in the armchair.

I said, 'A bit rash of you, wasn't it, to leave all that jewellery in your room? Practically an invitation to a thief. Everyone knows you're not exactly short of a diamond or two. I mean, there was a line in the paper this morning that said you have the best collection of jewels outside the British royal family and a few oil sheikhs.'

'Elizabeth Taylor's probably got more than me,' she said, frowning.

'Yes, well, aside from Elizabeth Taylor.'

She patted the space beside her. 'Why don't you sit here, Bobby?' she said softly.

'Yes, right,' I said, staying where I was, 'but listen, what I don't understand about these jewels of yours is why you did it. Why did you leave them just lying around in the room? You really were taking an awful risk, you know.'

She heaved an exasperated sigh, as if the subject were beginning to bore her. 'Bobby, they were copies, fakes. That guy must have been an asshole if he thought I'd keep the real things unguarded in a hotel room. You just risked your life for a load of paste, sweet thing.' She patted the space beside her on the chaise longue again, more peremptorily this time. 'Now come and sit beside me. I want to get to know this handsome English cavalier who came to my rescue and I want to figure out a really appropriate way to thank him.'

I looked at my watch, wishing fervently that Darren would come back from the bar.

And then the door opened and a maid came into the room, wheeling a trolley with fresh towels and stuff. She saw us both, stopped and said, 'Oh, sorry. I theenk nobody in room so I . . . So sorry, so sorry.'

Newport said, 'Get out.'

She wasn't talking to me I knew but I took the maid's arrival as my cue anyway and leapt up. 'Virna, I'm sorry but I have to go. Sitting here, talking to you, I just lost track of the time. I'm late already, there are people waiting, I ... Look, I hate to drink and run but I really have to rush.'

She said, disbelievingly, 'What? *What*?' I didn't wait to study the look on her face, just shook her hand, mumbled something about it having been a great pleasure to meet her and ran out.

I'm not saying the maid came in just in time to save my honour but

I'm pretty damned sure she spared me the trouble of having to fight
for it.

# 3

DONOVAN TURNED LEFT off Kensington High Street, swung the white Corniche round a corner or two and drove into the underground car park. It was a fine spring evening, unseasonably warm for London, but at eight p.m. on a Monday night it was nearly dark and the area was pretty quiet.

The car park was half full of cars but empty of people except for Donovan and me. The fumes of petrol and urine hung heavy on the air and our footsteps rang loudly on the concrete floor as we headed for the exit. I'm always wary in places like that at night when there's nobody around.

Not always wary enough, though.

I was just saying, 'Good spot for a mugging, this,' when three young punks – one black, two white – stepped out from behind a pillar. They were all about twenty years old, dressed in grubby sweaters, jeans and trainers and each of them had a knife in his hand.

'Let's 'ave yer wallets,' the black kid said. He had dreadlocks and a Rasta hat and he sounded slightly bored, like someone going through the motions of a job that had become routine. His accent was south London.

'Fuck off,' Donovan said.

A gleam of interest came into the black kid's eyes. This was not the reaction he'd expected or, I imagine, usually got. 'D'you 'ear that?' he said to the two white punks. 'Man told us to fuck off.'

'Fuckin' liberty,' said one of the white kids.

'Get out of my way,' Donovan said. 'I'm a busy man. I haven't got time for all this crap.'

The black kid grinned and jabbed playfully at him with his knife, a carving knife with a long, thin blade. 'Gutsy old bastard, incha?'

'Not so much of the old.' Donovan is getting on a bit but he doesn't like to be reminded of it, certainly not by snot-nosed yobs with knives. 'Now are you three wankers going to piss off or do I have to get nasty?'

The black kid, still grinning, made another little pass with the knife. Donovan watched the blade carefully but he didn't move.

'You don't say a lot, do you?' the black kid said to me.

'No. Strong, silent type, me.'

'Gutless wonder, you want my opinion, bloke your age hiding behind an old geezer like this.'

'Nowhere else to hide,' I said calmly. At least I think I sounded calm, though I didn't feel it. In truth, I wondered what Donovan thought he was playing at, not because there were three of them against the two of us; that didn't bother me particularly. But the knives made a difference.

'Quit fuckin' around, Joey,' one of the white kids said. 'Let's just get their wallets an' things an' get out of 'ere 'fore anyone else turns up.'

The black kid nodded. 'Yeah.' He jabbed the knife at Donovan again and with his free hand made a beckoning gesture. 'Come on, gents, let's 'ave it then. Everything you got. Turn out your pockets.'

'You must be bloody joking,' Donovan said. 'I wouldn't give you the droppings from my nose, bunch of little turds like you.'

The black kid's look changed. Up to this point he had been kind of amused; now he wasn't. Donovan was making him look bad in front of his mates and he was growing angry.

'Don't be a cunt all your life, Grandad,' he said. 'Either you give us your stuff or we take it and if we take it you get hurt. We got knives and we know how to use 'em.'

Donovan shook his head stubbornly.

'I don't know,' I said, 'maybe we should listen to them. If you look

13

very carefully you'll see he's telling the truth – they really do have knives.'

Indeed all three of those knives were now pointing at us, the white kids weaving theirs to and fro in the air presumably in imitation of some half-arsed stunt they'd seen on a video. Donovan glanced at me, shrugged his shoulders and gave a sad little sigh.

'I suppose you're right,' he said. 'They do have knives.' He looked at the black kid as if seeking permission for what he was about to do and then slid his hand slowly inside his jacket. 'Only, the thing is, I've got a gun.' And he pulled it out. It wasn't a very big gun but to my – I admit it – relieved eye it looked quite big enough.

'Fuckin' 'ell!' said one of the white punks.

To give him his due the black kid took it well. He seemed vexed rather than scared. 'Now you done it,' he said to Donovan. 'Now I'm really going to cut you up.'

'I don't think so,' I said. 'I think the smart move would be to drop the knives and walk away.'

There was a pause, Donovan aiming his gun at the black kid's chest, the three muggers still pointing their knives at us. 'Joey?' one of the white kids said. 'Better do as he says, eh?'

'Nah,' said Joey. 'He won't use that.' He looked back at Donovan. 'You won't use that,' he said, confidently.

'You could be right,' Donovan said, 'or, on the other hand, you could be wrong. As it happens you're wrong,' and he shot him.

Well, I say shot him but in fact the bullet grazed the back of the black kid's knife hand and carried on across the car park. The echo of the shot drowned the noise of the knife falling from Joey's hand onto the concrete floor.

'You fuckin' bastard,' Joey said. He watched the blood flowing from his hand as if he didn't believe it.

'I must be out of practice,' Donovan said. 'I meant that to go through your wrist. Maybe I'll do better next time.' He aimed the gun carefully at the black kid's groin. 'Left bollock,' he said. 'I'll be generous and try and leave you the other one. Well, you don't need two. Nobody needs two.'

One of the white kids said, 'Joey, for Chrissake let's get out of here. This old bastard's fuckin' mad.'

And then they were gone, running through the cars towards the exit on the far side, the black kid sucking at the wound on the back of his hand.

Donovan put his gun away. 'Any idea what happened to that bullet?'

I pointed across the garage. 'Blew up the front tyre of that Merc over there.'

Donovan looked and nodded. 'Oh, well, I expect he's insured. You weren't a lot of help there, were you?'

I raised my hands. 'Hey, I had every confidence in you, Sundance.'

He snorted. 'You didn't even know I had a gun.'

'True. But then you're always full of surprises. I knew you'd think of something. Shall we go and eat?'

'Might as well.' And we strolled out into the street above, two well-dressed gents on their way to a nice dinner at a smart restaurant and at ease with the world.

'I liked that black kid,' Donovan said. 'He had a lot of style. Pity we didn't get his full name. I could have found work for him.'

# 4

What I should tell you about Donovan is that he's a crook, but when I say that I don't even begin to tell the half of it. In many ways Donovan is *the* crook. Hardly any big criminal enterprise goes down in London without him being in control of it or at least having a very large piece of it. Except drugs. Donovan doesn't touch drugs. He had a nephew once who overdosed on heroin and since then he has regarded drug dealers as the lowest of the low, the scum of the earth. Well, everyone has to look down on somebody and he looks down on the drug merchants.

Sometimes he's insufferably smug about it, presenting himself as some kind of altruist. 'If I'd done what everybody else does,' I've heard him say, 'if I'd said, "Right, sod it, if I don't sell drugs someone else will," there's no telling how rich I'd be today. But that's the whore's justification, isn't it? Besides, I watched young Ronnie die and, I'm telling you, hanging's too good for the bastards who got him hooked on that stuff.'

Of course, you might think that a criminal who doesn't deal drugs couldn't amount to much in the present climate but that's because drugs get all the publicity. There's an awful lot of other crime, in a sense clean crime, that passes pretty well unnoticed, often because it's either undetected or because the victims – institutions like banks, for example – would be too embarrassed to want the public to know about it. That's the kind of crime Donovan controls and has done for many years. He's good at it, too, very good. He has no criminal record; he has never even been arrested, and if that's partly due to the fact that he owns a lot of policeman it also has much to do with his lack of enemies.

I'm not saying Donovan doesn't make enemies; he makes plenty but somehow, one way or another, they tend to die before their time. And when they die they generally pass unmourned because they're all criminals like him and, if they're drug dealers, worse than him. Donovan offers no violence to what he calls 'civilians', only to what he calls his 'business competitors' and not then unless he believes them to be seriously out of order.

All this, though, is only part of the picture; the other part shows Donovan the legitimate businessman, for he also runs a large number of strictly honest and very lucrative commercial enterprises. *That* Donovan – the impresario, the entrepreneur, the chairman, the managing director, the CEO – has a reputation for scrupulous fairness and is much respected in the City and even in the loftier social circles. He is noted for his generous donations to charity and to one of the major political parties. It's even been suggested he might be given a knighthood and I expect he will eventually. He wants one, I know that, and in the end it's just a matter of agreeing the price with the political party of his choice.

But, sure, when you get right down to it, Donovan is a crook and I like him a lot. I've known him since my father died when I was a boy and my mother took me to live in the south London street where she and Donovan grew up and where, at a precociously early age, he started to build his empire. None of us lives there any more because the planners moved in ages ago, ripped out the terraced slums and replaced them with high-rise slums where the people live in less dignity and comfort than laboratory rats and turn on each other like rats as well.

These days it's a nasty place, the Street, and maybe the law-abiding would say it wasn't a lot better when I lived there. Because of Donovan it was, after all, the hub of nearly all the major criminal activity in south London. But at least in my time we didn't fight and rob and mug each other. We reserved all that for outsiders, not that I was ever involved in that kind of activity. My father, a good-looking man with crisp dark hair and a naturally athletic build but very little brain to speak of, had been a small-time crook who died broke and my mother, a very intelligent lady, always wanted something better for me.

It was thanks to her that I went to university and it was thanks to her, or anyway Donovan's interest in her, that he became a sort of surrogate father to me when I was growing up. I've never been quite sure how close their relationship was and in any case it's nobody's business but theirs. But I suspect there was a time when they might have married if it hadn't been for Donovan's criminal activities.

Life with my old man had put my mother off crooks or at least off the idea of having them in the family. She was far too bright to believe that crime didn't pay – well, we all know it does, don't we? You just have to look about you, look at big business, look at politics. But she didn't want it around the house; she didn't want to live with it. Luckily for us both I'd inherited my father's looks and build but my mother's brains and, to a large extent, her principles, so I'd never found it difficult to resist Donovan's blandishments when he tried to persuade me to enrol in his firm, learn his various trades and take over when the time came.

Like I said, I'm fond of Donovan – but I don't want to *be* Donovan.

# 5

Donovan got his cigar going nicely, waved away the smoke that had gathered in a cloud around his head and took a sip of his brandy. 'Something I want you to do for me, Bob,' he said.

I topped up my coffee cup. 'Thought there might be.' Donovan was always a generous host but this had been a particularly excellent dinner even by his standards. 'Nothing comes free these days. What is it? You want me to rob a bank for you? Kill somebody?'

He shook his head impatiently. Sarcasm never goes down well with Donovan. 'I want something like that done I got experts only too happy to oblige. No, this is different. Legit, of course, I wouldn't be asking you otherwise, but right out of the ordinary.' The cigar between his teeth pointed at me like the barrel of a sawn-off shotgun and he squinted thoughtfully along its length. 'How do you fancy being a film producer?'

I put my coffee cup down. 'So it's come to this, has it? You've gone into the porno movie business. Dear, dear. I always thought you had more class than that. Not a lot of class, of course, but more than that.'

He spluttered indignantly. 'Porno! Bleedin' porno? You been listening to me, Bob? I told you – this is legit. I'm talking a thirty-million-dollar Hollywood production here, big stars, classy director, everything. I want you to be the associate producer.'

I leaned across the table towards him. 'Donovan,' I said, slowly and carefully, 'I'm not a film producer. I've never even been in a film studio. I don't know anything about film producing.'

'So what's to know? Listen, have you looked at screen credits lately? Some films have more producers than they got stars. You reckon all those people know what they're doing? Do they hell. Some of 'em are there because the studio owes them, some of 'em because they're sleeping with the leading lady. Or the leading man. You get a movie with five, six, seven people claiming some kind of producer credit and you can bet your life there's only one, maybe two, doing any real work.'

This was Donovan speaking, Donovan whose interest in the movies, as far as I knew, extended no further than ripping off hundreds of thousands of pirate videos of whatever was the latest hot-selling Hollywood blockbuster, penny-ante stuff to him that merely helped lubricate the wheels of his business and launder some of his money. I said, 'How come you're such an expert all of a sudden?'

'Because I'm going into the movie business, aren't I? The real movie business.'

I took a moment to let this sink in. 'You mean, you personally are backing this thirty-million-dollar Hollywood epic? With your own money?'

He snorted derisively. 'Don't be bloody daft. I've got a percentage of it, that's all. Me, the studio and my partner, we're all in it together.'

'Your partner?'

'Yeah, my partner.'

'An American partner?'

'As it happens, yes.'

I took a deep breath. 'Don't tell me, let me guess. His name ends with a vowel, right?'

Donovan relit his cigar. 'Matter of fact it does. Matter of fact both his names end in vowels. You know him, actually. Well, you've met him. It's Carlo – Carlo Minelli.'

He was right, I had met Minelli – a few years back when I was in California trying to work out why someone had hired a hit man to kill an old friend of mine. The introduction had come via Donovan but though Minelli had been helpful to me I hadn't liked him.

'I knew it,' I said. 'You're in bed with the Mafia and you want me to crawl in beside you.'

Donovan spread his hands beseechingly. 'Bob, Bob, you've got it all wrong. It's not just Carlo. I'm talking about one of the major studios, MCF – Maestro Consolidated Films, strictly kosher outfit. This isn't a Mafia operation.'

'Oh, no? And I suppose Minelli isn't Mafia either.'

'No,' Donovan began and then hesitated. 'Well, he is, yes. But, see, this movie hasn't got anything to do with that. It's all above board, trust me. Carlo and me, we've both set up production companies, so clean you could eat off 'em. And we're putting them together to go into this co-production.'

'So where did the money come from?'

Donovan was silent for a bit. 'You don't want to know that, Bob,' he said softly.

I folded my napkin and laid it neatly beside my plate, the way my mother had taught me. 'Well, thanks for the dinner,' I said. 'It's been a most interesting evening.'

As I got up he reached across and took hold of my arm. 'Sit down, Bob. Please.'

I did, reluctantly. He said, 'Thanks.' Then he played around with his cigar and the matches again and said, 'All right, I'll level with you. There is a little bit of laundry work going on here. I'm not saying the money's dirty, you understand, but I must admit it would look better for a wash and brush up. But the thing is, there's quite a lot of it. I'm talking millions here, you understand? My share, that is.'

'Heck of a gamble,' I said, 'putting that kind of money into something as dodgy as a movie.'

'Not really. If the film does well I'm laughing. Even if it doesn't, even if I only get my money back, I'll still be better off than I am now because it'll be different money, all clean and tidy, and the way the thing's set up, what with video deals, TV deals, airline deals and all that, I can't do worse than break even.'

'So why do you need me?'

'I want you to go out there, to Hollywood, and look after my interests. I want you—'

I held up my hand. 'Hang on a bit.' I called the waiter over. 'I think I will have a brandy after all,' I said. 'The way things are turning out here I feel I'm going to need it.'

When the drink had come I said, 'Right. I go to Hollywood, pretending to be a producer—'

'Associate producer, actually. Means sod all but sounds good.'

'Okay, associate producer. So I'm out there, hanging around the film set and looking after your interests because why? Because you don't trust the studio, or you don't trust Carlo Minelli?'

'Oh, I trust the studio all right. My lawyers have got those buggers trussed up like an oven-ready chicken. And I trust Carlo, too.' He paused. 'Most of the time anyway. But then I thought: well, Hollywood's a long way from home, where's the harm in having someone there to keep an eye on things?'

I said, 'Are you proposing to send a small army with me? I mean, I'm not exactly equipped to take on the Mafia on my own, you know.'

He shook his head sadly. 'Bob, on my life it's not going to be like that. I just want you to keep your eyes open and make sure everything's above board, see that Carlo's not costing me money by padding the payroll with his own people, that sort of thing.'

'All right,' I said. 'Worst case scenario – I find out Minelli's screwing you. What do I do then?'

'Just tell me. I'll deal with it.'

'You can't just deal with someone like Minelli. He's not only Mafia, he's very big Mafia.'

'I know bigger and some of them owe me. Look, don't worry, Bob, this is only a precaution. I'm not expecting trouble. Carlo knows better than to try to screw me. I want you there just in case, all right? Look, there could be all kinds of legitimate problems – one of the stars doing a moody, the film going over budget or over schedule, anything. And I just want my own man there to tell me fast so I know exactly what's going on.'

I let that go for the moment. 'What exactly does an associate producer do then?'

Donovan, the instant expert, considered his answer carefully, wanting to give me the full picture. 'Like I said, fuck all, really. See, there's someone called a line producer does all the hard work. Then there's the overall producer, or maybe a couple of 'em, who probably put the deal together in the first place. These're the only ones who really have to know how to find their own arses in a dark room. Far as I can work out, the most associate producers have to do is keep an eye on things and report back to the producer or the studio, only in this case not. In this case he reports to me.'

'And, of course, you're not the producers, you and Minelli?'

Donovan looked aghast. 'Christ, no. Our names never get mentioned. What – I should announce the fact I'm in business with Carlo Minelli? Are you mad?'

'So who is the producer?'

'Studio nominee. What he'll do, he'll sort out all the day to day problems with the cast, the director, the writer and like that and look after things for the studio.'

I thought about all this. 'The movie business seems pretty full of people keeping an eye on things for other people, doesn't it?'

Donovan nodded. 'Lot of money involved, lot of scope for wastage, skimming and downright thieving.'

'So if you and Carlo aren't officially connected with this production what's the explanation for my presence?'

'Easy. You're looking after the interests of one of the studio's financial partners – like I said, a respectable British company. Look, Bob, it's not hard work I'm asking you to do here. I know blokes would give their eye teeth for the job.'

'So why me? Why not one of them?'

He took his cigar out of his mouth, laid it carefully in the ashtray, took a sip of his brandy. 'Because you're the only one I can really trust. Most of my blokes are as loyal as you could expect because I treat 'em right. But I couldn't be sure, not absolutely sure, that if push came to shove they wouldn't sell me out to Carlo. With you I can be. First place, you don't need the money; second place, you're a friend – not a member of my firm. Plus, you look presentable, speak nice, know which knife and fork to use, don't pick your nose in public and never take a lady's knickers down without saying please.'

I thought it over. 'Well, there is all that,' I admitted, modestly.

And besides, by this stage I was getting interested. This is the age of the movies, after all. Maybe not quite as much as the 1930s and '40s were, but far more than the succeeding decades. All right, film hasn't exactly won its battle with television but it's fighting it on equal terms. Satellite and cable channels and even the networks fill their schedules with wall-to-wall movies; people, young people, use their sets mostly as slots in which to stick a video of a recent cinema release; in Britain the TV companies have gone into film production in such a big way that they've more or less replaced the studios that died in the 1960s.

Robert Lennox, film producer. I liked it. It had a nice ring to it.

I said, 'Lot of casting couch work involved, I expect, being an associate producer.'

'There'd better bloody not be,' Donovan said, grimly. 'I'm not having you shoving up the budget, hiring a bunch of little tarts.'

'You never know, I might find a new star for you. A lot of the big ones served their apprenticeships on their backs. I mean, early on even Marilyn Monroe was one of the starlets studios hired to give visiting firemen a work-out.'

'Is that right?' Donovan asked, interested.

'So they tell me.'

'Well, well.'

It was the money – where it came from – that really bothered me, though, and I said so.

Donovan made an impatient gesture with his cigar. 'Grow up, Bob. You think there's never been dirty money in the movies before? You think Lucky Luciano and Meyer Lansky sent Bugsy Siegel out to Hollywood back in the thirties for the good of his health?'

'I thought they sent him to start up big-time gambling in Las Vegas.'

'That came later. The Mafia's been into movies since day one. The Depression era, who do you think bailed out some of the studios –

and I'm talking major studios here – when the banks were closing their doors? The movies are big business, always have been, and where there's big business there's dirty money. Trust me.'

On that I did. Donovan would know.

'Doesn't make it right, though,' I said.

He sighed. 'Look, Bob, I'm not asking you to steal for me. I mean, it's dead ironic, really. I'm asking you to be as honest as you can because you're just about the most honest and law-abiding citizen I know. I wanted a villain in there I just have to walk into my office and go eenie-meenie-minie-mo. But I don't want a villain. I want a bleeding straight-arrow boy scout like you.'

I gave him the benefit of the doubt and assumed he meant that as a compliment. 'Tell me about the studio then. What's the connection? Does Minelli own it?'

'No, but they owe him. That's why we're doing the deal through them. Couple of years back they had a big, big picture on the stocks – and I mean really big, hundred million bucks give or take.' He mentioned the title: an action-adventure epic, loads of special effects, violence, stunts, movement, sex, lousy script – the usual crap. It cleaned up at the box office largely because of its star, a young, macho hunk who was then and still is one of the golden boys of Hollywood. Women smell testosterone in the air and go wobbly at the knees at the mere mention of his name.

'Anyway,' Donovan said, 'it made a lot of money, which MCF really needed right then. Only it nearly didn't happen because some dumb rent boy tried to put the black on the studio. Had some tasty pictures of himself and the star getting up to all kinds of naughties in bed.'

I was astonished. 'You mean he's gay? Every girl's dream lover is gay? But he's got a wife and a kid.'

'Lavender marriage.'

'But she's gorgeous. The wife is absolutely, bloody gorgeous. I have fantasies about her. Are you telling me she's gay, too? Please don't tell me she's gay, too.'

Donovan brushed the interruption aside impatiently. 'I don't know what she is, except I know she was nobody till she married him and now she's rich and famous. All right, maybe she is a dyke or maybe she swings both ways, battery and mains. Maybe he's the same. I don't know and I don't care. Maybe she's really straight down the line hetero and is just playing the beard. Anyway, this rent boy tells the studio, pay up or I'm selling my story to the highest bidder. Arsehole thought he had them over a barrel.'

'He wasn't far wrong,' I said. 'If one of the tabloids had got hold of a story like that the picture would have been dead and so would the star.'

Donovan nodded. 'True. Only what the prat didn't know was that the bloke who runs the studio, Anthony Florence – Tony Flo – grew up with Carlo Minelli. His name was Antonio Fiorentino in those days.' He watched slow comprehension dawn on my face and nodded again. 'That's right. Carlo took care of it for him.'

'What happened to the rent boy?'

'Nobody knows. One of life's little mysteries. Just disappeared one day and was never seen again. Occupational hazard of whores, I suppose. Anyway, it all worked out nicely. The actor will do anything for that studio now and the studio will do anything for Carlo.'

'So he's in your movie, is he – the rent boy's friend?'

Donovan shook his head. 'Wrong type,' he said, wise old movie mogul that he had suddenly become. 'We needed somebody more physical, more sort of dangerous like. So we got Michael Rialto.' He beckoned to the waiter to bring more coffee. 'Besides, Carlo has a hold on him and all.'

'Ah,' I said. 'Silly of me. I should have realised. But … Not a bad choice, I suppose. Rialto's big at the box office.'

Donovan cradled his brandy glass in his hands. 'So what do you think?'

There was one thing I was still wondering about. 'Okay. Minelli wants to get into the movie business and after what you've told me I can see why he'd do it with MCF. What I don't see is how you come into it.'

'Carlo and I have done a lot of business together over the years.' He held up his hands. 'Not drugs, of course. Well, you know that. If he wants to move drugs that's up to him. Nothing I can do about it. But he knows better than to try to involve me. On other matters though, some of it legal I might add, we've been able to scratch each other's backs very profitably and, well, I done Carlo a big favour a while back. He was in a spot of bother, I helped him out and he was grateful. So when this movie deal came up he offered me a piece. Studio's putting up most of the money, Carlo's putting up most of the rest, I'm taking up the slack. It's quite a lot of slack, I got to tell you that, but like I said unless the movie's a total disaster I can't really lose.'

I nodded. 'And I'm there to make sure it's not a total disaster.'

Donovan made a small, impatient gesture with his right hand. 'You've not been listening to me, Bob. I don't want you to *do* anything. I just want you to keep your eyes open and let me know if things look like going bad. Anything smells a bit iffy, you let me know and that's all. I take it from there. I mean, how bloody difficult can it be?'

I thought back over the conversation. 'A little while ago you mentioned money and how I didn't need it. What sort of money were you talking about that I don't need, me being an associate producer and all?'

Donovan named a sum and I uttered a little 'Wow!' of appreciation. 'That much? They really give that kind of loot to glorified dogsbodies in Hollywood? And you're happy to pay it?'

He snorted derisively. 'Me? No, not me. Your fee comes out of the studio's end. So? What do you say?'

I tried frantically to remember everything I'd ever heard about the movie industry and ... 'Points,' I said. 'Do I get gross points? Do I get a percentage of everything that comes into the box office?'

Donovan snorted again. 'Course not. Gross points is what I get, what Carlo gets, what the studio gets, what the star gets. How else do you think we're going to make our money back? You like, I'll get you nett points and much good may they bloody do you.'

'What are they then?'

'Nett points are a percentage of the profits, after all the costs have been cleared. Only, funny thing is, very few movies ever get into profit. Officially. A film costs fifty million, okay? It earns five hundred million worldwide so it's got to be in profit, right, even allowing for the fact that taking into account advertising, publicity, distribution, bank loans, the cut the cinemas take and other incidentals it has to clear three times the production cost before it makes a penny. You with me?'

Of course I was. Basic arithmetic is one of my strong points. 'Three times fifty million is a hundred and fifty million, so it's three hundred and fifty million in profit.'

Donovan smiled grimly. 'You'd think so, wouldn't you? But you'd be wrong. The *real* genius in Hollywood, the real imagination and invention, the real creativity comes in the accountancy. The kind of movie I just mentioned, the kind costs fifty million and takes five hundred million, never turns a profit. End of the day it's always in the red and the poor suckers with a percentage of the nett end up with fuck all. So, you want nett points, I'll give 'em to you. Have as many as you like.'

I poured more coffee to give myself time to think. 'No casting couch work you say?'

Donovan eyed me solemnly. 'That's right, except in your own time.'

'And no profit share that means anything?'

'Right again,' he said, nodding.

I sipped the hot, fresh coffee, put my cup down and stared thoughtfully at the ceiling. 'So all I get is the fee you just mentioned?'

Another nod. 'That's about the size of it. That and a per diem, all your living expenses paid.'

'How about an extra ten thousand quid?' I said. Donovan was right: I didn't need the money but on the other hand I've never believed in selling myself cheaply.

He looked a little startled at first – after all, the sum he had originally mentioned was not unimpressive – but then he smiled, faintly. 'If that's what it takes.'

'Well, you're not paying, are you? MCF is.'

'Right. So you'll do it, will you? As a favour to me?'

I waved his cigar smoke away with a languid movement of my right hand. 'I'll think it over,' I said.

# 6

THE CALL CAME through just after six. A man's voice. 'Mr Lennox?'
I admitted it.

'Mr Minelli would like to see you. Tonight. Ten o'clock. He'll send a car.'

Pretty damn cool, I thought. Too pretty damn cool. 'Tell Mr Minelli I'm busy.'

'No, you're not.' He sounded amused. 'Give you a word of advice, Mr Lennox. You're never busy when Mr Minelli calls. Remember that and you could live a long and happy life. Ten o'clock then.' And he hung up.

I was staying at the Bel Air Riviera Hotel because, yes, I'd accepted the job Donovan offered. Not because of the money; he was right – I didn't need it, attractive though it was. Curiosity, wondering what it would be like to hang around a film unit, was a more potent factor. That and friendship, the knowledge that if I asked a favour of Donovan it would be done and I could hardly do less for him. You don't necessarily have to approve of your friends but if they are your friends the least you can do is support them.

So there I was living it up at the Bel Air Riviera where the daily rate for one of the elegant individual bungalows was more than most of the world's population earns in a month but what the hell, I wasn't paying – the studio was. This was Hollywood (I use the word generically to mean the film business) where a man is what he earns, what he drives, what he wears and where he stays, and so long as he seems rich nobody cares how he got that way. I was an associate producer, for heaven's sake, attached to a thirty-million-dollar movie and associate producers don't stay in motels on Sunset Strip or fleapits in West Hollywood if they want to be taken seriously. They stay at the Bel Air, or the Bel Air Riviera, or the Beverly Wilshire or the Beverly Hills Hotel. I could have stayed in any of those but I had chosen the Bel Air Riviera because it was unlike most of the others: more spacious, more relaxed, spread out over acres of immaculately tended lawns and flower-beds, quietly self-confident and more like a Mediterranean than a Californian hotel. The people who stay there don't care who knows they're in town because they have the clout to make their presence felt any time they feel like it.

Except me, of course. In movie-land I had hardly more clout than the bell boy who carried my bags to my bungalow.

That had happened in the late afternoon of the day before the phone call from Minelli's man, who, naturally, was quite right – I wasn't busy at all. Who would I be busy with? I didn't know anyone in town except Linda Kelly, an actress who had lived with me in London before she became a big movie star, and Rex Poorboy, a film director whom I'd busted in the mouth the last time I saw him, causing him to lose at least one tooth. Now they were married to each other and somehow I didn't think they'd exactly welcome a call from me.

So that day, my first full day in Hollywood, I'd spent my time settling in.

I'd rented a car – a soft-top RX7 because a Mercedes would have been too obvious and a Porsche too flashy – and driven down Sunset Boulevard to the Pacific Coast Highway to look at the ocean and then back all the way to Hollywood to have lunch at Musso and Frank's, a restaurant and bar that has been going for half a century and more and is therefore so ancient as to be regarded locally with the same kind of reverence the English accord to Stonehenge. And after that I'd gone back to the hotel and sat by the pool, reading the latest Elmore Leonard. My tan was already coming on nicely.

At ten o'clock the car arrived, this year's model Cadillac driven by a man in a grey suit who looked as if he had bought his moustache and hairpiece second-hand from Burt Reynolds. Apart from confirming my identity he didn't say much. Actually, he didn't say anything on the short drive to Minelli's house, which was also in Bel Air and occupied the whole top of a hill.

I'd been there once before and remembered it quite well – the ten-foot wall all the way around the estate, the electronic gates and the muscular goons in the gatehouse who patted you down to make sure you weren't trying to smuggle in a howitzer for a kamikaze hit on their boss.

The driver led me into the house, through the foyer with its ankle-deep Oriental rugs and the oil paintings of other people's ancestors to a living-room about forty feet square with a lot more rugs on a glowing parquet floor and settees and sofas and love-seats and armchairs and drapes and stuff, all in soothing pastel shades as if the whole thing had been designed by someone who found that bright colours hurt his eyes.

Carlo Minelli rose from one of the armchairs to greet me. It was some years since I'd seen him but he didn't seem to have changed. Late forties, a little more than medium height, thick chestnut hair coiffed and teased. A good-looking man, lean, fit, tanned and trim and yet more than trim. His body had the hard look of someone who worked out every day with a zealous personal trainer.

'Lennox,' he said, shaking hands. 'The prizefighter. You're still looking pretty damn good.' He said that with the appreciation of a man to whom physical fitness was probably some kind of religion and an ounce of surplus fat an obscenity.

There was someone else in the room, taller and younger than Minelli – closer to my age – but also fit and hard-looking and handsome in a dark, swarthy way.

'Let me introduce you guys,' Minelli said. 'Bobby, this is Rico Agnelli. Rico, Bobby Lennox, though I guess I don't need to tell you about him, right?'

'Yes, you do,' Agnelli said, unsmiling. 'I never heard of him.'

'What?' Minelli managed to look a little surprised. Then ... 'Oh, sure, I forgot. You don't follow the fight game do you, Rico? Well,

Bobby once fought Willie Slate for the middleweight title. Lost on points but put up a hell of a fight. Tell him, Bobby.'

Minelli stepped back, a glint of amusement in his eyes. I knew what was going on. They were putting me in my place, making it clear that I was not only the new kid in town but a pretty unimportant new kid at that.

I could have told Agnelli quite a lot of things. I could have told him that when I came down from university I went back to boxing, at which I'd been a schoolboy champion, because teaching – the only other thing I was qualified for – was driving me mad. I could have told him that I'd won an Olympic bronze medal and then turned pro; that I'd retired as middleweight champion of Great Britain, Europe and the Commonwealth and that my fight with Willie Slate, who was probably one of the best six middleweights who ever pulled on a protective cup, for the undisputed championship of the world was not only my last but landed me in hospital with a broken jaw and cracked ribs. But I didn't tell him any of this because I had a pretty shrewd idea he knew it already.

So all I said was, 'Yes, I fought professionally. I was good, too. My problem was, Willie Slate was in a whole different class.'

Minelli watched me thoughtfully, appraisingly, as if I was doing better than he'd expected. 'Yeah, but that was then and this is now,' he said, 'and now Bobby is Donovan's boy.'

'Donovan's representative,' I said. 'On this occasion anyway.'

'Representative, sure,' Minelli said, smiling faintly as if we were simply discussing semantics. Boy, representative – what did it matter? It was all the same to him. Minelli was a man who owned people and so long as they never forgot that he owned them he didn't care what they called themselves. 'But what we gotta remember, Rico, he's kind of a loose cannon. He only works for Donovan when it suits him, am I right, Bobby?'

I nodded.

'I gotta tell you, Bobby ...' Then he interrupted himself. 'Hey, what kind of a host am I? I haven't even offered you a drink.' He clicked his fingers. 'Rico. A glass of Krug for Bobby and get me one, too, will you? Hell, get yourself one. Let's all have a drink.'

And that put Agnelli in his place, too. Minelli was letting me know that just as, to him, I was simply Donovan's boy, Agnelli was simply his boy, the one who did the menial jobs when occasion demanded. Agnelli walked over to a side table where a couple of bottles of champagne nestled in ice buckets and poured drinks for us all. He served Minelli first and then came back with his own glass and mine.

'Krug,' Minelli said. 'The best.' He raised his glass towards me.

'Yes,' I said. 'I've drunk it before.'

He frowned at that but what had he expected? That I'd roll over in gratitude? Or that I'd fall back in open-mouthed admiration that he knew the difference between Krug and Californian domestic? He shook his head a shade irritably and picked up where he had left off.

'I have to tell you, Bobby, I'm a little uneasy about a guy like you. I mean, what is it with you and Donovan? You don't work for him except when you feel like it? So you don't owe him allegiance, you don't owe him loyalty, maybe you don't even owe him respect. And yet you're the one he sends out here to be his man on our movie. Now why do you figure that is?'

I finished my champagne. It was as good as Minelli had suggested it would be, so I went over to the side table and poured myself another glass, holding the bottle aloft to see if anyone else wanted a refill. Nobody did.

'Well, the fact is,' I said, 'you're quite right. I don't owe Donovan any of the things you mentioned – loyalty, allegiance, respect. I don't *owe* him any of those because he hasn't bought them off me. But in special circumstances, like now, I give them to him instead because he's a friend and he's wise enough to know that loyalty and stuff that are given are worth a lot more than loyalty and stuff that are bought and paid for.'

Minelli was very still for a moment. Then ... 'You hear that, Rico? He's saying his respect for Donovan is worth more than your respect for me. What do you reckon?'

'Fuck him,' Agnelli said, angrily.

Minelli nodded, smiling faintly. 'Oh, maybe I shoulda told you, Bobby. Rico is my guy on this movie. You two are gonna be working together, except Rico doesn't have a title, associate producer or whatever. The people who need to know he's around know he's around but otherwise he's kind of anonymous.'

Agnelli and I looked at each other, sizing each other up. What he saw was what I look at in the bathroom mirror every morning – dark hair and eyes to match, the hair just beginning to be flecked with grey as forty approached, pretty regular features, a six-foot frame that would weigh in around the super-middleweight limit these days but still didn't carry any fat if I could help it. What I saw was a tough, dangerous-looking man and not one to be taken lightly.

'Hey,' Minelli said, trying to ease the tension that had crept into the room. 'No problem. You're gonna be good friends. In fact, we're all gonna be good friends unless somebody makes trouble.'

He stepped up close to me and slapped me lightly across the cheek. Not all that lightly, though. 'You won't make trouble, will you, Bob?' he said.

'I will if you slap my face again,' I said.

He half-raised his hand, then paused, looked at it, grinned and let it fall to his side. 'It's okay, Rico. It's cool.' Agnelli had moved up beside him, glowering at me. 'You're some independent-minded son of a bitch, you know that, Bobby? Donovan told me you were and he wasn't wrong.'

He walked away to put his glass down beside the champagne bottles on the side table. 'I'm sorry I didn't invite you for dinner tonight, Bobby,' he said. 'I would've only I had Pete Jordan here. You know Pete?'

'I know who he is. The Governor of California.'

Minelli nodded. 'Right. And the next president of the US of A.' He smiled at me. 'I own him. All of him.'

'I'd heard that.'

'And you heard right.' He smiled again, looking straight at me, allowing me time to absorb this knowledge of his power. Then he clapped his hands together and said, 'Okay, time for you two guys to get to know each other. What are you doing tonight, Rico?'

Agnelli looked surprised. 'What? Well, I was going to Lou's, get a little action.'

'Good idea. Take Bobby with you, show him a good time, treat him to some of that old-fashioned Californian hospitality.'

'Hey, Carlo, gimme a break. Some other night, what do you say? I got—'

'Take him with you,' Minelli said, softly but firmly. 'Tell him about the movie, let him know the score. And find him somebody nice.'

Agnelli hesitated, then shrugged resignedly. 'Okay, whatever you say. Is it all right I get Charlie to drive us?'

Minelli nodded.

'Come on,' Agnelli said and made for the door.

As I moved to follow him Minelli put his hand on my elbow and turned me towards him. 'I think you and I will get along okay, Bobby,' he said quietly. 'I think Donovan chose good sending you. Only, you want to stay healthy, don't ever threaten me again. You hear what I'm saying?'

And then he let me go and smiled and waved as I followed Agnelli out to the car.

# 7

'You got some fuckin' nerve,' Agnelli said, 'talking to Carlo like that. I've seen guys disembowelled for less. Would you really have hit him?'

I shrugged. 'We'll never know, will we, unless he slaps me again.'

'Tough hombre, huh?' A slight sneer in his voice.

'Not really. I was just establishing the ground rules. I work for Donovan, not for him. If Carlo wants to hit you, that's fine with me. He can do what he likes with his own property just so long as he realises I'm not his property.'

'Watch your mouth,' Agnelli said.

Charlie the driver had turned left along Sunset Boulevard, going eastwards, and soon he turned left again, climbing into the hills towards Mulholland Drive, where he made yet another left. The view from up here was breathtaking. Down below us the lights of Hollywood and Los Angeles, whites and blues and greens and reds, glittered like the decorations on a million Christmas trees, burning up enough energy to run a small country. From this distance, at night, LA looked beautiful; close-up in the daytime it gave urban sprawl a bad name.

'Where are we going?' I said.

'Lou's,' Agnelli said. 'Nobody told you about Lou's?' He laughed. 'You hear that, Charlie? Mr Lennox doesn't know about Lou's. Boy, has he got a surprise coming.'

Charlie grunted. I saw him grinning at me in his rearview mirror but neither he nor Agnelli said anything else and a few minutes later we approached the entrance to a sprawling, three-storey house, brightly lit and standing back from the road in a fair bit of ground. There were several other cars ahead of us going the same way, big expensive cars, Mercedes, Cadillacs, a couple of Rolls-Royces and one or two sporty Jaguars, Ferraris and Porsches.

Valets in white shirts and black trousers took most of them away to find parking but a favoured few, including us, drove straight in. Three very big men in white tuxedos stood at the gate checking names against the lists on their clipboards.

Charlie rolled down the nearside rear window and one of the tuxedos peered in. 'Your names, please, gennle ... Ah, Mr Agnelli. Good to see you again, sir. Go straight on in.' He stepped aside and put another tick on his clipboard.

'Gonna be some action tonight, Charlie,' Agnelli said. 'Party night.'

I said, 'Will someone please tell me—'

Agnelli put his finger to his lips. 'All in good time, Bobby.' His mood had lightened as we got closer to the house. 'I just want to see your face as you go through that door.'

Charlie pulled up at the front steps to let us out. Disco music blasted out of the house and light seemed to blaze from every window.

Agnelli straightened his tie, smoothed the lapels of his midnight blue suit. 'You ready for this?' he said. 'Then come on,' and he led me into a big, wide living area, all done in white but with little in the way of furniture – a few sofas and armchairs, one or two occasional tables. There were no carpets or rugs on the polished wood floor.

Twenty or thirty men stood around, drinking, talking close to each other's ears to make themselves heard over the music. Some were quite young, a few pretty old, but most were thirty- or fortysome-things. Men in tuxedos or suits or sports jackets, men in designer jeans and silk shirts, men in dark glasses, men with gold chains around their necks and medallions nestling in their chest hair. Waiters moved around dispensing a variety of drinks.

All this I noticed but most of all I noticed the women. I had never seen so many beautiful young women in one place before. They came in every colour from blonde to brunette to redhead; from peaches and cream to California tan, from milk chocolate to jet black. They wore mini-skirts or tight, tiny shorts, silks and linens and gossamer-light dresses that flowed and swirled as they moved and showed off the long legs and the bodies that had been toned and honed and rounded and firmed in a hundred health clubs and aerobics classes.

Glossy of hair, bright of eye, teeth sparkling, they clustered together in small groups, animated and excited, chatting, smiling, laughing in anticipation of whatever adventures the night might hold. And the men watched them, sizing them up, making their choices.

Agnelli said, 'Well, what do you think?'

'A whorehouse,' I said.

A female voice behind me said, 'I prefer to think of it as a MAW house.' As Agnelli and I turned she said, 'Good evening, Rico. Aren't you going to introduce me to your friend?'

She was in her late forties, as tall and slim as any of the younger women in the room, dark hair slightly curling, a white, knee-length shirtwaister dress and a single row of pearls around her neck. She looked like the chatelaine of some stately home in the Cotswolds.

Rico kissed her effusively, aiming at the mouth but getting the right cheek instead as she turned gracefully away from him. He said, 'Bobby, I want you to meet Lou. This is her house. Lou, this is Bobby Lennox.' He paused. 'He's a guest tonight of Mr Minelli.'

'Ah, then he's doubly welcome.' She held out her hand and I took it, mumbling 'Thank you' and 'How do you do'.

'English as well,' she said. 'In that case you're triply welcome, Mr Lennox. The English have such nice manners. All my girls say so.'

I said, 'I didn't quite catch your meaning just now. You said something about—'

'A MAW house, yes.' She smiled fondly at her stunning flock of chattering birds of paradise, some of whom were beginning to pair off with the men. 'It's an acronym for Model-Actress-Whatever. That's what these girls are, Mr Lennox, most of them. One day

39

they're running around barefoot in, I don't know, Hard Nipples, Georgia, and the next they're in Hollywood and they're going to be movie stars. Only it's very, very difficult to become a movie star so they become models, actresses, whatever instead. And when the modelling and acting jobs grow hard to come by the whatever becomes increasingly important. It pays the rent and something more and occasionally one of my girls will get really lucky, meet a movie star, or a rock star or some industry honcho who's just shucked off his fourth wife and is looking for something young and sweet and tender.'

'You want young and sweet and tender this is the place,' Agnelli said, nodding.

'And these movie stars, rock stars and the rest,' I said, 'what do they do – set the girl up in an apartment?'

'Or marry her,' Lou said. 'Some of the smartest young matrons in Beverly Hills met their husbands in this very room. Only in America, Mr Lennox, only in America.' She held out her hand to me again. 'Still, I mustn't waste your time with all this conversation. I'm sure you have other things in mind.' She looked me up and down and nodded in what I took to be approval. 'I don't think you'll have much difficulty finding somebody very nice and very suitable.'

Agnelli said, 'Lou—'

She patted him gently on the arm. 'I know, Rico, she's here. I'll send her over. Enjoy yourselves, gentlemen.' And she moved serenely away across the room.

Agnelli and I watched her for a bit and then watched the younger women instead.

'See anything you like?' Agnelli said. 'If you do, I'll have it gift-wrapped and sent to your room.'

'Difficult to choose between them. Is it always like this here?'

He shook his head, grabbed a couple of drinks from a passing waiter and handed one to me. The glass was not glass but plastic. Agnelli said: 'Surprised you, huh? Well, things can get kind of wild around here later on and Lou doesn't want to spend tomorrow morning clearing up broken glass.'

We both sipped. The wine was okay, nothing special.

Agnelli said, 'It's usually a little quieter than this. Like I said, it's party night, invited guests only, actors, rock musicians, studio executives. You'll probably recognise a few people.'

Girls drifted past us in a swirl of long legs and smooth bare shoulders, wafting exotic scents, smiling, looking friendly and outgoing rather than sultry and seductive. The music changed from hard rock to smoochy love songs and conversation became a little easier.

I said, 'How much do they earn – not for modelling or acting but for whatevering?'

'A thousand bucks. And you don't pay the girls, you pay Lou.'

'*How* much?'

'Don't worry. For us it's free. It's always free for Carlo's guests.'

'Oh, I see. This is his place.'

Agnelli shook his head. 'No, it's Lou's. But Carlo takes an interest. He's one of the reasons Lou never gets busted, him and a whole bunch of judges and cops and politicians who do what Carlo tells them. What you gotta understand—'

But I never did learn what it was I gotta understand because a vision in pale silk had just draped herself around Agnelli's neck and was kissing him fiercely on the mouth. He lost all interest in what he had been saying to me and started kissing her back with equal fervour. They were pressed so close together you couldn't see daylight between them.

When finally they released themselves from the Velcro that seemed to be fastening their lips together, he said, 'Terri, hey. Where you been these last couple weeks?' His voice was softer than I would have thought possible.

'Ah, Rico. I've been ... you know, I been so busy. But I missed you, honey, I really did.'

They kissed some more, tenderly this time.

I moved back a step to get a better look at her. Eurasian, half-Chinese probably; tall enough in her heels to match my and Agnelli's six feet; hair so black and glossy that it almost shone blue as the light struck it; wide, dark almond eyes; olive skin and the kind of calendar-girl figure that no woman in this room would be without.

They carried on nibbling each other for a bit and then she said, her eyes widening, 'Is it true what they tell me? You're doing a movie? *You* are doing a movie?'

He kissed the tip of her nose. 'Yeah.' He smiled. 'Don't tell everyone, though. I got my reputation to think about.'

'But, honey, it's great! We can work together. There's got to be something for me in—'

He stopped her with another kiss. 'We can talk about that later. Right now we got other things to talk about, don't we? Let's go someplace quiet and—'

Suddenly he seemed to remember that I was there, lurking in the background like – and given the setting the concept wasn't too inappropriate – a spare prick at a wedding.

'You gonna stand there gawping all night?' he said. 'What are you, some kind of faggot? There's a million girls over there, go find yourself one. Give Terri and me some privacy, for Chrissake.'

'Is he with you, honey?' Terri said, 'Won't you introduce us?'

And maybe he would have done but right then there was a slight commotion, an excited buzz at the door and a whisper went round the room: 'Michael Rialto's here.' The excitement wasn't too surprising. There were certainly other actors among those present and I had even recognised a couple of them, including a plumply avuncular-looking fellow who had won a best supporting Oscar a couple of years back. But Rialto was easily the biggest star in the place. After all, he pulled down ten million dollars a picture (plus points, of course) and each of his last two movies had grossed more than two hundred and fifty million dollars. You want a star, this was a star because you can't argue with figures like that. His presence alone gave the evening the cachet of an A-list party and made all the other guests feel better for being there.

He was dressed in black – black silk shirt and black silk slacks. The hair on his head was black and the hair sticking out of his shirt was black. He stood just inside the room, glowering, a pair of beefy minders standing a pace or two behind him. He was talking amiably enough to Lou, so the glower probably didn't mean much. As far as I could remember from the few films of his I had seen it was his only expression – a surly downturn to the mouth and a slight but permanent frown as if he was either very short-sighted or the business of thinking made his brain hurt. Women loved him because he was tall, broad-shouldered and athletic, and looked nasty.

'Our star,' I murmured.

And then Rialto gave Lou a big hug and said in a voice that carried across the room, 'Okay, Lou, where is she? Where's the slope? How many times I gotta tell you that whenever I come in here she's mine?'

He looked around the room, said 'Aha' and walked straight over to where Rico and Terri were still standing with their arms around each other's waists.

'Terri, baby, there you are.' He pulled her away from Rico and started massaging her buttocks with his right hand. 'And Rico, how nice. You been keeping her warm for me.'

Everyone was watching and a couple of the men giggled nervously. Rialto seemed to enjoy the attention. He pulled Terri closer to him and said, 'But I'm here now so you can take the rest of the night off, Rico. You won't be needed any more, my man.' And he slapped Agnelli on the cheek, much as Minelli had slapped me.

Agnelli did nothing. He just stood there, his face expressionless, staring not at Rialto but past him.

'Hey, lighten up,' Rialto said and slapped him again. 'It's a party, for Chrissake.'

And still Agnelli did nothing, said nothing.

'Mother of Mercy,' I murmured aloud, 'is this the end of Rico?'

Lou, who had come up unnoticed beside me, said softly, 'No, but it will be if he does anything stupid.'

Rialto, still holding on to Terri, stared at Agnelli as if genuinely puzzled. 'What is it with you, man? Pre-menstrual stress or something?' A few more people giggled. Rialto shrugged and turned away, pulling Terri along beside him. 'Some guys, what can I tell you? Come on, honey, we got things to do upstairs.'

Agnelli still stood there motionless as Terri hurried by, not looking at him.

One of the minders, following behind their boss, wanting to get in on the act, deliberately nudged Agnelli's hand, the one with the drink in it. The plastic glass tipped backwards and spilled red wine down Agnelli's trousers.

'Aw, gee, Rico,' the minder said, mock-apologetic, 'I'm so so—'

And that's as far as he got because Agnelli suddenly moved. His elbow cracked viciously into the minder's face, his knee came up into the man's groin, doubling him over. As the man bent, squealing, Agnelli grabbed him by the back of his head with both hands and brought the knee up again into his face. I heard the man's nose crack as Agnelli pushed him away.

Rialto, aware of the kerfuffle, turned, the frown more puzzled than it usually was.

'Hey, Michael,' Agnelli said. 'You should teach your monkeys some manners.' And then he stormed out of the house.

'Oh, hell,' I said. 'There goes my lift.'

Lou took me by the hand. 'Come with me,' she said. 'I'll find you someone nice to talk to and then later, if you like, we'll get you a cab.'

# 8

In the end she didn't introduce me to anybody. She was going to. She was even leading me across the room in the direction of a matched pair of long, lithe blondes who were standing together like languid daffodils, when she suddenly said, 'I'm sorry, Bobby, please excuse me. There's somebody—' and she dashed away.

I didn't feel up to accosting the blondes so I stopped and watched her. She seemed to be hurrying towards a slender young man who was beckoning urgently from a doorway on the far side of the room. I couldn't be sure but I thought it was Darren, the gigolo who had so grudgingly poured me a drink in Virna Newport's suite, what, a hundred years ago? Several months anyway.

I took another glass of wine and waited for Lou to come back but she didn't, so I went out onto the porch and accosted one of the bouncers standing there.

'Any chance you could call me a cab?' I said. I saw the beginnings of a grin breaking out on his heavy face and before he could utter a word I said, 'And if you say anything like "Okay, you're a cab" I'll break your arm.'

He carried on grinning anyway, looking at me with admiration. 'I was gonna say that. You know? I was actually gonna say that. I've always wanted to say that. How did you know?'

'Just psychic, I suppose.'

'Gotta be. Okay, I'll get you a cab.'

I spent the ten minutes that elapsed before the taxi turned up out on the porch watching the ebb and flow. More men and more girls arrived, the men sweaty and excited but trying to disguise it, the girls cool and elegant, hiding behind that hauteur women adopt when they're surrounded by rampant men and are not entirely sure of themselves. A few couples left, clinging to each other, no doubt seeking greater privacy than Lou's house offered.

And I went home to bed. By myself. Pretty wimpish, really. I'd been given the run of the candy store and I hadn't sampled anything. One day, I thought, when I'm lonely I'm going to regret this; I'm going to remember the delights I could have savoured and hate myself for passing them up. But not that night. That night I was glad to be out of there.

I took a sleeping pill to counteract the jet lag that usually, when I fly to California, has me awake at four a.m. full of life but with nobody to play with. As I nodded off I was wondering why Agnelli had let himself be humiliated like that.

The next day I drove to the studio. It was one of the few still left in Hollywood as opposed to Culver City or Burbank or Century City. The area and the businesses around it were pretty run-down – small factories and nondescript commercial enterprises either making or wholesaling cheap clothing or furniture and looking not so much eager for trade as desperate for it. Most of the restaurants thereabouts were diners or fast food joints, Chinese and Thai to go, but the bar opposite the studio gates looked clean and prosperous and I noted it down for future reference.

The gates themselves were rather majestic, huge and wrought-iron and arched, set in a high, white wall and proclaiming Maestro Consolidated Films in fancy gold metal work. This was one of the older studios, aged but still imposing, built some sixty years ago and dominating its run-down neighbourhood as a reminder of the days when Hollywood the place rather than the generic term was both exciting and glamorous.

The jobsworth on the gate checked my name against his list, directed me to the administration building adjoining stage one, raised the barrier and let me in.

The entrance to the redbrick admin building was also wide and imposing and bore above its lintel the name of some 1940s producer who had made a lot of films there. As I went in Tom Hanks came out and said 'Hi' as he passed me. What a nice man, I thought, and then as I walked up the stairs to my second-floor office I thought: what are you talking about? The man says 'Hi' to you and you automatically assume he must be nice? Get a grip.

The second-floor corridor was wide and carpeted, its walls lined with pictures of stars and posters of films that had been made at the studio from way back when till the present day.

My office was halfway along. Not as luxurious as I had hoped but reasonably impressive. The desk was early American repro and not bad, the chair behind it leather and padded and comfortable. Carpet on the floor, a few more posters on the walls. Bookshelves, empty, a TV set and a word processor; a fridge, also empty except for some designer water; a couple of armchairs and a settee that was not quite wide enough or long enough to serve adequately as a casting couch. I didn't run to my own private bathroom but I did run to my own secretary, a middle-aged mouse with thick glasses and a grey bun who sat in a little office of her own attached to mine.

Some of the secretaries I had glimpsed on my way down the corridor wouldn't have looked out of place at Lou's the night before but I obviously wasn't important enough to qualify for one of them. Not that I was complaining. Margaret, the one I had, seemed efficient enough and perceptive, too. When I asked her to bring me a copy of the script she brought, unasked, a cup of coffee as well.

I thanked her, said that would be all for the moment and, as she was leaving, asked, 'By the way, what's Tom Hanks like?'

She smiled fondly. 'Tom? Oh, he's very nice.'

'Good,' I said. 'I thought he must be.'

On my desk Margaret had left a list of the office numbers and phone extensions of the rest of the film's production staff – the real producer, the director, the line producer and one or two others. Rico Agnelli's extension was on a separate sheet of paper. I called a couple of people to introduce myself but nobody seemed to be in that

47

morning, so instead of shooting the breeze, chewing the fat and generally schmoozing I settled down to read the script.

*Death's Head Dangling.* Very violent, very sexy, loads of action – or anyway movement – an invincible hero, a ballsy heroine, a sadistic villain, a smattering of good one-liners. It was exciting, empty, vacuous, illogical. A typical Hollywood thriller. If you haven't seen it I should tell you that Michael Rialto – the hero, of course – was a maverick crime fighter, somewhat loosely attached to the Los Angeles police force, who went up against a criminal Mr Big, an American drug baron so powerful that even the Colombian cartels were in awe of him. The heroine, the partner Rialto naturally despised at first but then grew to love, was played by Annie Klane, Hollywood's latest hot blonde and not, I thought, a bad actress. Martie Culper, once a romantic leading man but now in his middle age a solid character actor, was the heavy. A press release which Margaret had attached to the script declared that 'an exciting announcement' about a 'sensational addition to the cast' was to be made at a launch party the following evening.

I buzzed Margaret. 'What's this "sensational addition to the cast" all about?'

'I can't tell you, Mr Lennox.'

'Yes, you can. I'm the associate producer, for God's sake. You can't keep secrets from me.'

'No, no,' she said, flustered. 'I mean I can't tell you because I don't know. Nobody does except Mr Charleston and Mr Proctor.'

These were, respectively, the real producer and the director and they weren't in the studio that morning.

'Okay,' I said and read the script again. It was no better and no worse the second time around. A solid, professional piece of work untouched by inspiration.

I had just finished the re-reading and was wondering what to do with the rest of the day when Agnelli came in. 'I told your secretary we don't wanna be disturbed,' he said.

I sighed and leaned back in my chair. 'Pity. I'd been rather hoping for some kind of disturbance – Michelle Pfeiffer bursting in, perhaps, panting that she couldn't live without me any longer or—'

'Shut up. I have to talk to you about last night.' He sank into an armchair and glared at me. It didn't faze me. In my days in the ring I was glared at by experts. 'Nothing happened last night.'

I shrugged. 'Fine. In that case why are we talking about it?'

He took a cigarette from a gold case and lit it with a matching gold Zippo. 'You tell anybody about last night?'

I stared thoughtfully at the ceiling. 'Let me see now. I told the waiter at breakfast, I told the girl on the hotel switchboard, I told the kid who sold me the *LA Times*, I told a panhandler who accosted me on my way to the car. Who do you think I might have told? I don't know anybody here.'

'Good. Let's keep it that way.'

I said, 'Why are you sounding off at me? A whole crowd of people saw what happened, or what you say didn't happen, last night. How about them?'

'Most of them don't know who I am and the rest are too smart to go around talking about it.'

I studied him carefully. 'Who exactly are you, Rico? What's your real connection with Minelli?'

He hesitated. 'Let's just say I take care of things for him, okay?'

'Ah. So getting slapped around in public would be bad for your image.' I held up a hand to stop what was clearly going to be an angry interruption. 'All right. But before we decide that nothing happened last night let me ask you about what happened last night. Why did you beat up the monkey and not the organ grinder? Rialto was the one who walked off with your girl and slapped your face.'

There was no ashtray in my office so he flipped his still glowing cigarette butt into a wastepaper basket. Luckily it was metal and luckily there was no paper in it.

'Rialto is family,' he said.

'What, your family? A cousin or something?'

He grunted irritably. 'Not my family – Minelli's family. I don't mean his business family either, I mean literally. Michael's married to Carlo's niece.'

That came as a surprise. I didn't know Minelli had a niece and I said as much.

49

Agnelli nodded. 'Very few people know, so that's something else you better keep under your hat, you know what's good for you. Carlo has a sister, just one, name of Maria, got religion when she was about twelve. She hated the family business. Carlo's old man, her old man, ran things then. I think Maria hated him, too, and Carlo. When she was old enough she ran away to Canada. Most people who ever knew she existed think she died years ago. But what she did, she changed her name, married a surgeon in Vancouver and had a kid, a girl, Angela. Carlo hasn't seen his sister, maybe hasn't even talked to her, in years. Angela he does see. Nice kid, he likes her. But, just so you know the score, it's not common knowledge that they're related. Hardly anybody knows and they both think it's better kept that way. They been in touch since Angela graduated from college and moved to LA. She got a job with some publicity outfit, met Rialto and married him. That was, what? – two, three years ago.'

I thought it over. 'What does Carlo think about that?'

He shrugged. 'Family is family and he doesn't want his niece to get hurt. That means nobody hurts Rialto either, understand? Especially since he likes Rialto, too. He likes the way Rialto brown-noses him.'

'And that's why the monkey got the beating, not Michael.'

'Yeah,' he said quietly. 'Just a little warning, let Michael know what I can do I set my mind to it. Like they say, what goes around comes around and one day, who knows? Angela could grow tired of him and if she does Mr Rialto and I are going to have a little get together.'

I took a moment to digest all this information. What I seemed to have got myself into was a Mafia-backed movie, overseen by a Mafia enforcer and starring a Mafia godfather's nephew-in-law. I began to wonder whether I was going to like the film industry as much as I had hoped.

'Meanwhile,' I said, just to get everything clear, 'what does Carlo think about his niece's husband hanging around in whorehouses?'

Agnelli made a dismissive gesture. 'When he was married Carlo was the same. A man has certain needs. He understands that. Michael just has to understand certain other things: not to let Angela know what he's doing and never, never to shame or humiliate her. He also has to remember that when you're an outsider married to the mob, you stay married unless the mob wants to divorce you.'

'Interesting. But what about a woman, a wife. Does she have certain needs, too?'

The idea seemed to appal him. 'She better not. To a guy a lay is a lay. It's nice, it's over, you go home and you forget it. But to a woman a lay is different. To her it's important.'

'I see. Women keep their emotions between their legs, do they?'

'You care to put it like that, sure.'

Well, it was a point of view but less interesting to contemplate than the situation between Agnelli and Rialto – two men both deeply interested in the same woman, or at least I assumed they were. Potentially a very explosive set-up.

I said, 'That girl last night – Terri was it? – she's obviously important to you. Did you know that Rialto was seeing her, too?'

'I'd heard. She had two lines in his last movie. That's where they met, that's where it probably started. And I guess it was Michael told her I'm involved in this picture because it's certainly not common knowledge.'

'What are you planning to do about all that?'

He got up and walked to the door. 'I'm working on it,' he said, and then he left.

I sat there for some time staring at the door and hoping for Rialto's sake that his wife never grew tired of him and that if she did his minders turned out to be better equipped for the job than they'd seemed last night.

# 9

I HAD LUNCH alone in the studio commissary. The food was very good and the restaurant itself would not have been out of place in Beverly Hills. Elegant, spacious, cool, well-kept indoor plants dotted here and there, a lot of glass walls green-tinted to keep out the sun. If this was the way movie honchos lived I thought I might enjoy being an associate producer.

Back in my office I asked Margaret to track down Bill Charleston, the film's producer, and Richie Proctor, the director. She called back a few minutes later to say they'd been out scouting a location that morning and were now in conference, not in the studio but at Proctor's own office on Sunset Boulevard.

'Shall I call them for you?' she asked.

'No, just give me the address. I'll go and surprise them.'

Well, I was bored with reading the script and there seemed nothing else for me to do at the studio. Besides, I wanted to meet Proctor. He was an Englishman, a Londoner who had worked in television and then made a reputation for himself with a couple of remarkably good low-budget British films, comedy-dramas which were sharp and sophisticated and, unlike most low-budget British films, had universal themes.

Hollywood had snapped him up about twelve years ago since when he had moved into a much bigger and more expensive league. He had made seven or eight movies there, dramas mostly, some of them adapted from novels and plays. Those I had seen I had liked a lot. He had flair and humour, and though occasionally saddled with mega-stars who would have had difficulty acting out a charade, he invariably produced good performances from them. He had never before made a thriller, though, and I was curious to know what had attracted him to a glitzy potboiler like *Death's Head Dangling*. I also wanted to find out about the 'exciting announcement' that was to be made the next day. After all, as associate producer I reckoned I ought to know these things.

Proctor's office, or rather suite of offices, was in a ten-storey building on Sunset Strip with its own private underground parking area. With a ten-dollar bill I talked the attendant into letting me leave my car there and went up to Proctor Productions on the eighth floor.

In the front office a young woman in a white shirt and jeans was scowling at a word processor, her profile towards me. Dark blonde hair that curled inwards at the nape of the neck and hung in an untidy fringe over her forehead, a good straight nose, dark eyes with very long lashes and a generous mouth. She didn't look up as I shut the door behind me, just hit a couple of keys on the qwerty board and said, 'Yes?'

'I'd like to see Mr Proctor please.'

'Would you now? Well, he's in conference.' She hit another key, looked at the screen, said 'Shit!' and swivelled in her chair to direct the scowl at me.

I gave her my best smile because she was worth it. She was slightly less than beautiful but a lot more than pretty, largely because of the animation in her face and the intelligence in her eyes. I've always found intelligence in a woman more erotic than anything else, though she seemed to be well-equipped with all the other erotic stuff, too. 'I'd help you with that thing,' I said, pointing at the word processor, 'but they always make me say "Shit!" as well.'

She leant back in her chair and looked me over, slowly and carefully. Then, suddenly, the scowl was gone to be replaced by a smile. It was like dawn breaking. This was one of the great smiles, an amused smile, a friendly, intimate smile. She'd been very attractive even with the scowl but the smile was several hundred per cent better.

'Why do you want to see Mr Proctor?' she said. Her voice was soft and easy to listen to, with the slightest trace of a southern accent.

'I just thought I'd introduce myself.'

The smile faded but only slightly. Reading between the lines I thought she was quite glad I was there but not so glad about why I was there, or why she assumed I was there. 'What have you got?' she said. 'A script? An outline? A synopsis? Leave it on the desk, I'll see he gets it.'

'No, no, I'm not trying to sell anything. Mr Proctor's in conference, I know that. He's in conference with William Charleston and I want to say hello to both of them. My name's Bobby Lennox, I'm the associate—'

'I know who you are.' The smile had gone completely now.

'On the whole,' I said, 'I think I preferred the scowl.'

'What?' she said blankly.

'Of course, I liked the smile best of all but even the scowl was a lot better than all that naked hostility you're directing at me right now. What did I say?'

'You said your name. I think you better leave now, Mr Lennox.'

I shook my head. 'No. I came here to meet two men I'm supposed to be working with and that's what I'm going to do.' And before she could get up I had walked past her and through the door at the far side of the room, leaving her squawking 'Hey!' and then 'Shit!' again as she banged her knee against the desk.

I had guessed right. The door led directly into Proctor's office, much bigger than the one I had just left. The light was dim in there because the venetian blinds had been pulled down to keep out the sun. Proctor and another man, Charleston obviously, were at the end of the room, sprawled in armchairs with their backs towards me. There was a table between them and on the table were a couple of tumblers and a quart of Jack Daniels, nearly empty. Neither man noticed me come in.

Proctor was saying, 'It's not right, Bill, you know it's not right. You know that, Bill, don't you? It's just not right.' The words were slurred and he was clearly very drunk. I noticed that smashed or not he hadn't lost his London accent.

Charleston said, 'For Chrissake, Richie, will you cut it out? Doesn't matter whether it's right or not we're stuck with it. There's nothing we can do.' Charleston was not drunk.

I said, 'Gentlemen, I'm sorry to interrupt but I thought it was time we all met. I'm Bobby Lennox.'

Proctor waved his glass, slopping bourbon over his shirt. 'See what I mean, Bill? Here's another of 'em. Fucking Mafia hoods all over the place like, like …'

'Fleas on a dog?' I suggested helpfully if unoriginally.

'Yeah, fleas on a bloody dog. Lennox, is that your name now? What was it before you changed it? Roberto Linguine was it? Roberto Oregano? Bill, Bill, what are we doing working with these scumbags? Can you tell me that, Bill? What are we doing working with these—'

Charleston said, 'Richie, for God's sake shut up.'

Proctor shook his head vigorously. 'No, Bill. No, no, no, no, I'm not going to shut up. Let them shut up, all these fucking Mafiosi, let them shut up. Let them all just piss off.'

'Richie, for the last time, I'm warning you—'

'No, you're not 'cause I don't give a shit. Wassamatter with you, Bill? We used to be artists, Bill, you and me. We made two, three good pishers together, bloody good pishers, Academy Award nominations and everything and now look at us. Working for the fucking Mafia, that's what we are.' He waved his glass at me then held it to his lips and drank deeply. 'People like him and his mate wossisname, Rico Angelo or whatever he calls himself. Scumbags. What are we doing, Bill, you and me, working for people like that?'

Charleston got up angrily, shouting. 'Right, that's it. I'm outa here. As a matter of fact I was never here at all, okay? I never heard any of this.'

I said, 'Wise decision.'

The door behind me opened and the girl came in. 'Is everything okay, Richie? I heard like a row going on.'

Proctor finished refilling his glass with straight bourbon and took another long gulp. 'Everything's fine, Lucy, just fine. I was, I was just telling Bill what a load of scumbags old Lennox Linguine and his mates are.'

Charleston said, 'Okay, hold it right there. That's enough. I don't need all this shit. You're out, Richie, you know what I'm saying to you? I'll get a new director. As of right now you're off this movie.'

I said, 'No, he isn't.'

Charleston turned his anger on me. He was a big man, going bald and running fast to fat. 'Who the fuck do you think you're talking to? I'm the producer of this movie. If I say the director goes, he goes. I make one call to Tony Flo and Proctor's history. He'll—'

'Never work in this town again,' I said, nodding. 'Only you won't make that call. Because if you do I'll make a call of my own – to Carlo Minelli. I'll tell him how I came in here and found you badmouthing him and what's more I have witnesses. Don't I?' I said, turning to the girl.

She hesitated just for a second then nodded vigorously.

'You bitch,' Charleston said. 'You goddamn bitch.' And then to me, 'You're bluffing.' He sounded confident enough but he was beginning to sweat.

'I might be,' I said. 'All it takes to find out is to make your call to the studio boss. But if I'm not bluffing I don't think Richie Proctor will be history, I think you will.'

He looked bemused now rather than angry. 'Why are you doing this?'

'Because I don't like you,' I said. 'I don't know why, just one of those irrational things. So I think, Bill, you got it right the first time. You aren't here, you never were here, you didn't hear a thing.'

He said, blustering, 'You're making a big mistake, you know that? You cross me, you're making a big mistake. Huge.'

'Sure,' I said. 'I know – I'll never work again in this town either. Hop it now, Bill, and keep away from telephones.'

He went out and the door slammed behind him hard enough to shake the partition wall.

There was a longish silence, then Lucy said, quietly, 'Why did you do that?'

I jerked a thumb at Proctor, who had somehow contrived to fall out of his armchair and was lying with his legs stretched out and his eyes half-closed. His head and shoulders were propped against the front of the chair and he had spilt bourbon all over his groin. 'I like his work and it seems to me that if this film of ours is going to be any different from a million other Hollywood movies it'll need a very good director. That's one reason anyway.'

Proctor opened both eyes and squinted down at the wide wet patch on his cotton trousers. 'Bloody hell, I think I pissed myself.' He looked around the room, said. 'Where'd ol' Bill go? Lucy, where'd ol' Bill go?' Then he looked at me. 'Wass he doing here? Bloody Mafia goon, wass he ...' His eyes closed and he fell asleep.

I said, 'Is he often like that?'

She shook her head. 'No. Usually he hardly drinks. I've never seen him like this before. I think, I think everything kinda got on top of him.'

'Yes, I'd rather gathered that.' Proctor was snoring loudly, spittle gathering at the corners of his mouth. 'Don't you think we'd better get him home?'

She looked at him doubtfully. Proctor was not much more than medium height but he was plump and probably outweighed her by about fifty pounds. 'Do you think you could help me? I'm not sure I can manage him on my own.'

I pulled the drooling, protesting movie director to his feet and slung him across my shoulder, being careful not to stagger or show too much sign of strain, thinking to myself even as I did it: what are you playing at, you adolescent clown, showing off your muscles in front of the pretty lady? 'Lead on,' I said, trying not to pant.

She showed the way out of the back of Proctor's office and along to a rear elevator and pressed the button for the basement garage. 'You could put him down now,' she said as we got in. 'Lean him against the wall.'

'No, it's fine.' Actually it wasn't fine at all but I was pretty sure that if I put him down I'd never be able to get him back on my shoulder again and he sure as hell couldn't walk.

We laid Proctor on the back seat of his car, a big white Mercedes, with his head propped up so that if he vomited he wouldn't choke himself to death. Lucy thanked me and said, not sounding too certain about it, that she thought she could manage now.

'Nonsense,' I said. 'You'll probably crack his skull dragging him out of the car.' Actually, I didn't want her to leave me and not merely because of the sudden proximity, the way our hands had touched as we manoeuvred the dead weight onto the seat, or the disturbing smell of the light but musky scent she wore. It simply happens that way sometimes; you meet somebody and for some reason, probably chemical, you instantly decide you want to know her better. So it was with this Lucy. Besides, I'd had a lonely day and I wanted someone to talk to.

So I got in the car with her, she driving, I in the front passenger seat. As we moved through the heavy late afternoon traffic on Sunset she introduced herself. Lucy Lane, Proctor's assistant and not, as I had assumed in my male chauvinist way, his secretary. She had been with him for four years and was obviously very fond of him. She kept glancing anxiously back to reassure herself that he hadn't fallen off the seat or otherwise damaged himself. Next year, she said, he was going to direct a low-budget independent film that he had written and she would produce it.

'He's an angel,' she said.

I looked at the snoring, snorting piece of human wreckage in the back and said, 'Yes, well, if you say so. You know him better than I do.'

'He is,' she said fiercely. 'He's just about the nicest man I know. I love him.' She looked at me coldly. 'What would a person like you know about nice people anyway?'

I couldn't really think of an answer to that, so the conversation rather died as we came down from the hills and turned left along Ventura Boulevard. Serves you right, I said bitterly to myself. You never check, do you? You never ask the right questions. So now you're stuck, aren't you, helping this woman to haul her rat-arsed lover back to their lair and much good will it do you.

As we drove into Encino the silence had gone on long enough to feel uncomfortable and for want of anything else to do or say I suddenly pointed to a side street on our right, a street of nondescript houses and apartment blocks, and said, 'Linda Kelly used to live down there.'

'Really? Wow. That was before she made it, right?' A touch of warmth had crept back into her tone and expression. 'You know Linda?'

'She lived with me for a while. In London.'

'Did she?' She looked at me with greater interest now, clearly not having marked me down as the kind of man Hollywood screen goddesses would be inclined to shack up with. 'That was also before she made it, right?'

I sighed acknowledgement.

'You know her husband?' she asked. 'Rex Poorboy, the director?'

I nodded.

'He a friend of yours, too?'

'Not really. The last time I met him I punched him in the mouth and kicked him in the balls.'

'Good.' She grinned enthusiastically. 'Great. Everybody should kick him in the balls. He's a total asshole. I can't imagine why she married him.'

'Neither can I. Especially when she could have married me instead.'

She took a hand off the steering wheel and patted me sympathetically on the knee. I liked that. Even knowing about her and Proctor I liked it. 'I'm sorry,' she said.

A couple of minutes later she turned left into the fashionable side of Encino where the houses were bigger, more expansive, much more expensive. Proctor lived on a corner site a couple of blocks from a small estate that had once been owned by Michael Jackson. Proctor's was a large single-storey ranch-house with a shingled roof and a lot of shrubs and flowers in the front.

Lucy pulled up outside the garage and together we manhandled the director out of the car and into the house, me walking backwards and holding his head and shoulders, Lucy hanging on to his legs and giving directions. These led us to a huge, airy bedroom with pink and white carpet and curtains and a king-sized bed with a canopy.

We pitched Proctor onto the bed where he lay on his back, still dribbling and snoring. I took off his cotton jacket, shoes and trousers and unbuttoned his shirt a little more. The bourbon had soaked all the way through to his underpants. They looked disgusting.

'I'm not touching those,' I said firmly.

'Hell, neither am I.' She pulled a sheet over him, wiped his mouth with a tissue from the box on the bedside table and kissed him fondly on the forehead. 'I guess all we can do now is let him sleep it off.'

I followed her back into the hall, closing the bedroom door behind us. Lucy offered me her hand. 'Thank you,' she said. 'I'm really, really grateful. I don't know what I'd have done without you.'

I said it was nothing, anyone would have done the same, and hung around awkwardly. I very much wanted to stay but there hardly seemed much point.

'Do you want me to take you back to your car?' she asked.

'Well, I could get a cab if you'd call one for me.'

'No, no, I'd be glad to take you.' She hesitated. 'Would you like a drink? I mean, despite that object lesson in there about what alcohol can do to you?'

'Yes,' I said. 'I'd like a drink very much.'

She took me through the house to the back yard where, apart from a few flower-beds and a small lawn, most of the space was taken up by a pool and Jacuzzi area. It was pleasantly warm and sunny out there, peaceful, too. 'Wait here,' she said and went back into the house.

I took off my jacket and sat at a poolside table shaded by a sun umbrella. A few minutes later she came back with a bottle of Chardonnay, glasses, peanuts and taco chips. I uncorked the bottle, filled the glasses and handed one to her. She raised it solemnly in my direction.

'Richie and I have a lot to thank you for,' she said. 'If it wasn't for you we'd both be out of work right now. The way you handled Bill Charleston there, I was, I was really impressed.'

I shrugged modestly as if it was all in a day's work for a tough guy like me.

'There's something been bothering me, though,' she said. 'When you told me why you kicked Bill out of the office, you said "That's one reason." Was there another?'

I chomped away at a mouthful of peanuts, swallowed and said, 'Yes. I don't like the Mafia any more than Proctor does.'

'What?' She put her glass down carefully and leaned towards me, the dark intelligent eyes studying me intently. 'But you're one of them, you're with them.'

'Only in a manner of speaking,' I said. 'Actually, I represent the British side of the partnership, a man named Donovan. I'm just here to see he doesn't get screwed.'

'How did he get involved with people like Carlo Minelli?'

I hesitated. 'Yeah, well, Donovan is, well, he's not as bad as the Mafia but he's into organised crime, too, I have to admit that.'

'I see. So the only real difference is that you're a London gangster as opposed to an American one.'

I shook my head. 'No. I … Oh hell, I suppose this is going to destroy my street cred entirely but I'm not even a criminal. I grew up with Donovan, he's like a surrogate father to me. But I don't have anything to do with his business, I don't work for his firm. I'm just doing him a favour.'

'Is that the truth?'

'Yes.'

I got the intent searching look again. It went on much longer this time and then she nodded, as if she'd made an arbitrary decision, said, 'Good,' and reached across the table to kiss me. Just a peck on the cheek but nice, her lips cool and soft. Then she put her hands behind her head, leaned back in her chair and smiled up at the sky. 'You know something? Maybe I'm crazy but I believe you. And you know something else? It makes me feel so much better, knowing you're not one of the bad guys.'

I refilled our glasses and gestured vaguely around us, happy that she'd divorced me from the bad guys and not wishing to go any more deeply into my exact position in case she lumped me back in with them. 'This is a very nice place you have here.'

'What?' she said, frowning.

'You and Proctor. It's a very nice house you have—'

Surprisingly, she began to laugh. 'Me and Richie? Me and ...? God, I wish Barbara could have heard that.'

'Barbara?'

'Richie's wife. Didn't you know? They've been married for ever. They're famous for it round here. Well, notorious, I guess. In this town you're married three years, it's like celebrating your silver wedding. You get long-service medals and everything. But Richie and Barbara have been together twenty years, maybe more. She and the two kids are in London right now, visiting with her family.'

Suddenly I began to feel that the evening was turning out okay after all. She said, 'What on earth made you think that Richie and ...? Aha, because I know my way around the house, right? And because I said I loved him. Well, I'm an old family friend and I do love him but only like a big brother.'

I started to say something but she just carried on. 'So the next question is: do I have somebody else? Do I have a husband, or a boyfriend, or a lover or, to be politically correct here, a significant other? Isn't that a lulu – significant other? Isn't that romantic? Close your eyes, think hard and tell me what you suppose a significant other looks like.'

I did as she told me. 'Earnest,' I said. 'The kind of person who buttonholes you at a party to tell you how fast his new car can get from nought to sixty.'

She nodded enthusiastically. 'Right. So I never had one of those.' The smile faded and in a much quieter voice she said, 'I did have a lover, though, until a little while ago.'

'But then you broke up?'

She topped up both our glasses. 'Nope. He was shot dead.'

'Oh, my God.' I wondered how it had happened and then stopped wondering because the possibilities were too numerous. Hereabouts, for heaven's sake, you could be shot dead for trying to overtake on the freeway. So to save time and speculation I asked Lucy outright: 'How did it happen?'

'An argument over territory.' She paused. 'Ironic, isn't it? My friend worked for Carlo Minelli. And now, in a different way, so do I. Anyway, some idiot down in Long Beach tried to move in on

Minelli's interests there. My friend and a few other guys were sent along to let him know this wasn't the smartest move he ever made, there was some shooting and my friend and one or two other people got to be dead. Fade to black. The End.'

'I'm very sorry,' I said.

She shrugged. 'Yeah, so am I. You could say he was a worthless piece of goods and you wouldn't necessarily be wrong but he was my worthless piece of goods and that made him important.' She sipped moodily at her wine. 'Actually, it was pretty well over between us. As lovers, I mean. I was still fond of him but not like before. He was getting too possessive, too jealous, a bad trait in a man, in anyone, I guess. But, anyway, it's because of him that I know who Rico Agnelli really is and the connection between Minelli and Tony Flo at Maestro Consolidated. He told me a lot of things he shouldn't have done.' She sighed. 'I guess he was a blabbermouth and so am I. I was the one told Richie about the Mafia connection on this movie. I was just trying to warn him, let him know the score. I had no idea he'd go ballistic about it.'

'I'm glad you told me,' I said. 'I was getting a little worried. Nobody was supposed to know about Minelli or Donovan but so long as Richie keeps his mouth shut from here on in, I suppose there's no real harm done. I don't think Charleston will be any trouble but if he is, let me know and I'll go and frighten him again.'

She gave me the same slow appraising look she'd given me when I walked into her office. 'You know, I really believe you could do that.' She put her glass down, propped her elbows on the table and her chin on her hands and leant towards me. 'Okay, now it's your turn to answer the questions. First up, do you have a wife, or a girlfriend, or a lover, or ...'

I told her, truthfully, that I had none of those things, not even an insignificant other. I told her about the Street and Donovan, about my years as a prizefighter and about my present occupation as a businessman, small-time entrepreneur or whatever you want to call it.

At one point in the evening we interrupted the reminiscences to drive to a Chinese take-away on Ventura Boulevard. We even got some food for Proctor but he was still comatose, so we ate his share, too, and drank another bottle of his wine.

There were some things I didn't tell her. I didn't, for instance, tell her that I had once killed a man, a sadistic piece of scum who had brutally raped a girl I was in love with and was threatening to do it again. Somehow I suspected that a confession of murder would damage my new reputation as one of the good guys.

We ate and drank and talked out by the pool until nearly midnight, looking in on Proctor from time to time to make sure he hadn't strangled himself with the bedsheet. We compared notes about our childhoods – mine in a crime-ridden London slum, hers in a quiet suburb of Atlanta, Georgia – about parents and university and even school. We discussed the books and poetry, the films and music that we liked, the food we preferred. Okay, we weren't in total agreement: she loved Brussels sprouts and I hated the things but I didn't feel this was necessarily insurmountable in a relationship.

Just before midnight she yawned and stretched and said that some people around here had to work the next day and it was time for bed. She would stay at Proctor's house – in one of the guest bedrooms, she added with a mischievous grin – get him up in the morning, and make sure he was fit for work. I said this sounded like too big a job for one person and I'd be only too happy to help, but by then she was already organising a cab for me.

'He'll take you to your hotel,' she said. 'You can't collect your car tonight, you've had too much wine and I don't want you killing yourself on the way home.'

'You like me!' I said, excitedly. 'You really like me!'

She laughed. 'Sally Field at the Oscar ceremony, right? 1979, something like that. But, yes, I do kinda like you.'

And when the cab arrived she proved it with a kiss that fell short of intimate but was more than friendly, the classic interested but uncommitted first-date kiss.

It could have meant much or it could have meant little but I tasted it on my lips all the way back to Bel Air.

# 10

THEY WERE WAITING for me as I walked back to my bungalow at the hotel. One of them was big and heavy, about 230 pounds, much of it beergut. The other was shorter, lighter, younger and sporting muscles rather than fat.

They loomed out of the darkness on either side of the brightly lit porch and confronted me, side by side, on the walkway.

The big one jabbed me in the chest with a forefinger the size of a salami. 'Hey, you, Lennox. We gotta little message for you.' Moonlight glinted on the knuckleduster on his right hand.

The younger one chuckled, a noise like God knows what flushing down a toilet. 'Oh boy, do we have a message for you!'

The big one jabbed me again, hard enough to make me stumble backwards a step or two. 'Message is, Lennox, get the fuck back to London and stay there.'

The younger one said. 'Enough already. Let's just do it.' He had a short, leather-covered cosh in his hand.

I said placatingly. 'Look, please, I don't understand. Can't we just talk—'

The big man swung at my head with his right fist. Amateur, I thought, ducked under the blow and kicked the younger man savagely just under the left kneecap. Because he was lighter and fitter I had marked him down as potentially the more dangerous of the two. He gave a yelp of agony and clutched at his leg and while he was still yelping I backhanded the fat one in the mouth with my right fist and then hit him in the throat with a straight left.

The smaller one was hopping around on one leg so I kicked him just under the right kneecap as well and this time he screamed and fell face forward onto the ground. The big one was making painful gurgling sounds and clutching his throat. I took his mind off whatever problem he had up there by sinking my right deep into his stomach, turned and kicked the younger one in the ribs. He gave another scream of pain and then, to my surprise, he started to cry.

I knelt beside him, took a handful of his long, bleached-blonde hair and tugged his head back. 'What do you two jokers think you're up to?' I said.

His sobs were now alternating with sharp moans as I tugged his head further and further back. I glanced across at the fat one. He was on his knees, still holding his throat and vomiting.

I stood up, put one foot in the small of the younger man's back and took his hair in both hands. 'One more tug,' I said, 'and your neck will break.'

Tears, snot and saliva were streaming down his face. 'You smashed my knees,' he wailed. 'You smashed my fuckin' knees.'

'Well, I hope so,' I said. 'But look on the bright side: once your neck is broken you're not really going to give a shit about your knees, are you?'

'Please,' he said, 'please don't hurt me no more.'

'Dear me,' I said, 'where on earth do you people come from – Rent-a-Nerd?'

'The studio.' He pronounced it 'stoodio'. 'MCF, Maestro Consolidated? We're on the security staff? Mr Charleston said—'

'Charleston. Well, well.' I had clearly underestimated Bill Charleston. 'He said what?'

'He said we was to rough you up a little, scare you off. You know? He didn't say why. He gave us a hunnert bucks. Each.'

'Wasn't enough, was it?' I was feeling pretty cocky now. You'll think I'm just bragging but honest, cross my heart, I hadn't been too worried at any point. As soon as they started talking to me I knew I had a chance. Professionals wouldn't have done that; professionals would have just grabbed me and beaten me unconscious. Then maybe, when I came round a bit, they'd have talked to me.

'Where's your car?' I said. The fat one was showing signs of getting to his feet so I clumped him hard on the back of the neck and he sighed heavily and fell onto his face again. I turned back to his friend. 'Where did you leave your car?'

He hesitated. 'I dunno.'

'What do you mean, you don't know?'

'Somebody brung us here. I dunno where he parked.'

And then Rico Agnelli strolled out of the darkness, hands in trouser pockets, cigarette in mouth. 'Pretty good, Bobby,' he said. 'Pretty damn good. You can let him up now.'

I let go of the thick blonde hair and stepped back. Agnelli kicked the younger goon not too lightly in the chest.

'You and your friend,' he said, 'go down to the main gate and wait for me there.'

The man sobbed and moaned again. 'I can't walk.'

'You better be able to fuckin' walk or I'll blow your brains out right here. Now go.'

The two men got up, slowly and painfully and, clutching each other, hobbled away towards the gate.

'You really smash his kneecaps?' Agnelli asked.

'No. They'll be a little sore for a day or two, though.' I brushed some dust off my trousers. 'What's this all about, Rico?'

'Ask me in for a drink and I'll tell you.'

I took him into my bungalow and poured Scotch for both of us. What with the wine and all this was getting to be a big drinking night for me.

Agnelli raised his glass to me. 'You handle yourself good, Bobby.'

I shrugged. 'Those two were hopeless.'

He conceded that. 'Yeah, well, I'd sent a couple of my boys it might have been different. Only, my boys prefer knives and shooters and it coulda got messy. Nobody wanted that.'

'So what did they want?'

He held his whisky up to the light and admired the golden glow. 'Charleston wanted you scared off. He called me tonight, told me about Proctor sounding off and how you stepped in and then he asked what I thought he should do. Should he call Tony Flo, get him to call Carlo? I told him that could get heavy, for him as well as other people. So then I asked what alternative he had in mind and he told me about these two guys on the security staff, said they'd taken care of one or two problems for him in the past. I told him to send them over here. Then I thought, no, wait, I'll *bring* them over here, see how it turns out.'

'And how did you hope it would turn out?'

He held the whisky goblet to his mouth with both hands and looked at me over the rim. 'Tell you the truth, Bobby, I hoped they'd beat the crap out of you. I didn't want you to get hurt, y'understand, not really hurt. That's why I came, make sure it didn't get out of hand. I just wanted you hurt enough so you'd realise it's not too smart to toss Minelli's name around in conversation, even as a threat.'

I nodded. 'So now what? Are you going to go along with Charleston, get Proctor thrown off the film? Because if you do I'll have to get Donovan involved and—'

'Donovan wouldn't go up against Minelli,' he said.

I smiled at him, a shade patronisingly. 'Donovan would go up against anybody,' I said. 'Trust me on that.'

He thought it over, sucking on his cigarette. 'Yeah, well, it won't come to that. There's no way I'd let Charleston fire Proctor. The money we're paying him we couldn't get another director half as good.'

That surprised me but I tried not to show it. 'So now what? You tell Charleston to keep his mouth shut and his head down and Proctor carries on?'

He nodded.

'Have you told Minelli about all this?' I said.

'Hell, no. Carlo's got enough problems right now. He doesn't need to worry about some fuckin' movie.'

'Problems?'

He got up to go. 'You haven't been watching television tonight?

68

Well, read the paper tomorrow morning. I think you'll find it interesting.'

# 11

MINELLI DOMINATED THE front page of the *Los Angeles Times* the next day. A warrant had been issued for his arrest on three counts of accessory to murder. The warrant, which hadn't actually been served because neither the FBI nor the Los Angeles police had been able to find him, related to a recent gangland slaying – 'execution' was how the *Times* described it. Two men, known members of the Minelli crime family, as the newspaper put it, were already under arrest, charged with the killings which, so it was alleged, had been ordered by Minelli himself.

That was the hard news. The rest of the story was given over to a catalogue of Minelli's known and assumed activities – the prostitution, the gambling, the drugs, the numbers and the rest. There was also a list of apparently legitimate businesses in which he was thought to have an interest. I was relieved to find that *Death's Head Dangling* wasn't included among them.

There were photographs and brief descriptions of some of Minelli's known criminal associates but Agnelli's name wasn't mentioned. Neither was there any reference to Angela, Minelli's niece, nor to Michael Rialto.

But, sure – Agnelli had been right: Carlo Minelli certainly had problems. Whether or not they would affect the movie – and me – only time would tell.

I had woken early with a slight hangover, thanks to last night's booze. So, to punish myself for such over-indulgence, I went for a long, hard run down to and along Sunset Boulevard, then worked out for half an hour and finished off by swimming a mile in the pool. After that, to reward myself for undergoing the sheer boredom of all that running and swimming, I had a big breakfast and sunbathed beside the pool while I finished off the Elmore Leonard. It's a dirty job being an associate producer but, like they say, somebody's gotta do it.

In the late morning I took a taxi to Proctor Productions to collect my car. Neither Proctor nor Lucy was in. The secretary who now occupied the outer office said they were off location scouting somewhere but would certainly be at the studio for the launch party that evening.

'What's this special announcement they're making tonight?' I asked her.

She looked surprised. 'Don't you know, Mr Lennox?'

'I wouldn't be asking if I did.'

'Well, I'm sure I don't know either,' she said.

I drove to the studio and went in search of Charleston's office. A look of mild dismay crossed his secretary's face when I told her my name and she said he wasn't in. Nice try but I could hear him on the phone in the next room. I grinned amiably at her and moved towards the interconnecting door.

'He's not to be disturbed,' she said.

I gave her my other grin, the wolfish one I borrowed from Robert Redford, the one he used as the Sundance Kid when, just before the knife fight, he told Butch Cassidy he'd be glad to avenge him in the unfortunate event of the other fellow winning. 'Oh, I'm not going to disturb him,' I said. 'I'm just going to scare him shitless.'

In the event that was unnecessary. Charleston was scared shitless before I got into the room. He was bent down behind his desk, clinging to the edge with both hands and apparently trying to make himself as small as possible.

'Where are your two friends?' I said.

His voice was little more than a whisper. 'Hospitalised. Both of them.'

I walked across and slapped him lightly across the cheek. It was very contagious, this Mafia habit of slapping people. 'You didn't do what I told you, did you? You went behind my back. Tut, tut. You've been a naughty boy, Billy, and you know what happens to naughty boys. They get beaten and they end up in hospital, too. But if they're very, very naughty they sometimes get beaten so badly that they bypass the hospital altogether and go straight to the morgue. Am I getting through to you, Billy?'

He nodded.

I said, 'So now you know there's no future in telling tales to Tony Flo or Carlo Minelli, always assuming you can find him, which seems to be more than the FBI can do. And I imagine you also know that Rico Agnelli's not going to help you. So what I suggest, Billy, is that from now on you try awfully hard to be a good boy. Keep your nose clean, go about your business and make sure you're very nice to Richie Proctor and Lucy Lane. Do we have a deal?'

He nodded again and I gave him the Robert Redford grin and left him. I wasn't particularly proud of myself, bullying a man like that, but at least now he knew where the goalposts were and that he would try to move them at his peril.

As I came out of Charleston's office I ran into Agnelli in the corridor.

'I saw the paper,' I said.

He put a finger to his lips. 'Let's go for a walk round the lot. You never know who might be listening.'

We left the administration building, walked down the main street of Dodge City, circa 1880, went past sound stage two, strolled through part of Greenwich Village and ended up in Smalltown, USA. None of these sets was being used just then.

'Minelli seems to be in a pretty tight spot,' I said.

'With the FBI?' He shrugged. 'Nah. The guys they arrested would keep their mouths shut if you pulled their toenails out one by one. The other guy, the one turned state's evidence, trying to get himself into the Witness Protection Programme, we know who he is, we know we can get to him. He's never gonna testify. But with the rest of the families, sure, Carlo does have problems. Number one, he's been careless to let things get this far with the Fibbies. Number two, the other families don't like all the publicity. It's bad for everybody, gets the cops all worked up and eager. Everyone suffers. So, things get any worse, Carlo could be in real trouble. People might even decide to replace him.'

'Where is he now?'

'Out of town. Out of the country, you want the truth. But it won't be for long.'

I wondered whether I should make an anonymous call to the FBI, tell them their prime witness's life was in very considerable danger. But they'd probably sussed that out already and were doing the best they could to make sure the man testified and then vanished into anonymity somewhere in the middle of America.

Agnelli said, 'You tell Proctor about Carlo's connection with the movie, my connection with Carlo?'

'Me? Of course not. I'd never even met the man till yesterday afternoon and then he was smashed out of his mind.'

'Somebody told him.'

I peered into the window of the Smalltown drugstore. There was nothing to see except the wooden slats holding up the storefront and, behind them, more wooden slats holding up the front of some other building on another set. 'Hard to keep secrets in the movie business, I imagine.'

Agnelli said, 'As far as the rest of the world is concerned I'm an independent businessman. No connection with Minelli. Carlo and me have worked hard keeping it that way.'

'No arrests, no convictions?' I said.

'Right. So who told Proctor?'

'Search me.'

'Then I'll just have to ask him.'

I said, 'Leave him alone, Rico. All right, he shot his mouth off yesterday but he was drunk. Now he knows better. He won't say another word, I promise you.'

He lit a cigarette and looked at me thoughtfully. 'Who are you protecting, Bobby – him, yourself, or somebody else? Somebody's been talking out of turn, I have to know who it is.'

I shook my head. 'No, you don't. Believe me. Nobody's going to say anything to anybody.'

He blew out a big cloud of smoke, stared at me for quite a long time and said, 'I'll tell you something, Bobby. It wouldn't be pleasant if it came down to you against me. We're in different leagues, you and me. Sure, you were good last night with those two guys but they were comedians. I'm not and you better remember that.' Another cloud of smoke, this time a smile behind it. 'But for the moment, okay, I hear what you're saying. I'll leave Proctor alone.'

We started walking back towards the admin building. A bunch of extras in western gear were drifting into the main street of Dodge City. Cameras and lights were being set up. We walked past Wyatt Earp and then Doc Holliday, talking urgently into mobile phones.

I said, 'A thing that puzzles me: how did Minelli get mixed up in a film production in the first place?'

Agnelli grinned. 'Three reasons. One, he was born and reared in this town. The movies are in his blood, deep down he's a fan. Two, he's been aware for a long time that this is as good an industry as any for laundering money. You put dirty money in, you take clean money from the box office. Three, he kind of inherited a four-million-dollar script.'

'Come again?'

From a safe distance behind the movie cameras Agnelli stopped and watched as Wyatt and Doc put away their phones and went into a huddle with their director. Doc's girlfriend, Big-Nosed Kate, was sitting on the stoop in front of the Main Street saloon with her skirt up around her thighs to catch the sun while she read the *Hollywood Reporter*.

Agnelli said, 'You notice the name of the guy who wrote *Death's Head*? John W. Byass? Highest paid writer in the movies. Ever. Four studios were bidding for *Death's Head* and four million was the opening offer.'

'And Minelli bought it?'

He laughed. 'Carlo doesn't buy, Carlo takes. See, Byass likes to gamble. He likes Vegas, he likes Carlo's casino there but he's a lousy gambler, never knows when to quit. Few months back he was into

Carlo for close to two million dollars. So Carlo calls him in, asks how he's planning to pay. Byass says he can't pay, he's got no money. So Carlo says, "Okay, how's about collateral, assets?" Byass says he's got this house, nice one in Malibu, half paid for. Carlo says he doesn't want half a house, he doesn't need half a fuckin' house, what else has he got? Byass says, "Well, there's this screenplay," so Carlo says he'll take it. Guy says, "Hey, wait a minute. It's worth four mill, conservative estimate." Carlo says that's great, four mill is what Byass owes him if you include the vigorish.'

'Include the what?'

'The interest,' Agnelli said, patiently. 'So Carlo takes this hot screenplay to Tony Flo at Maestro and they make a deal. Couldn't be sweeter. Tony agrees the script is worth five million, so that's Minelli's contribution to the movie, and it's all clean money, right down to the last nickel.'

I thought it over. 'Byass must be well pleased,' I said.

Agnelli smiled thinly. 'Byass is so mad he's running up walls. He's broke and he's lost his screenplay. But look at it this way: he can always write another one and he couldn't do that if he was dead. Which was his alternative, he hadn't given *Death's Head* to Carlo.' His phone began to ring. 'Excuse me,' he said with unexpected politeness and dragged it out of his pocket.

'Yeah, Bill,' he said, covered the mouthpiece and muttered, 'It's Charleston.' I nodded. Agnelli said, 'Bill, what is your problem? Huh? What is your fuckin' problem? You gave it your best shot last night and it didn't work, so accept that and get off my fuckin' back. I don't wanna have to tell you again. It's over, okay? It's—'

I didn't hear the rest. I went to my car and drove back to the hotel to prepare for the launch party that evening. I was half a mile from the studio before I remembered that I still had no idea what the exciting announcement was going to be.

# 12

ACTUALLY, IT DID turn out to be a bit exciting, partly because of what it was and partly because of the typical Hollywood hype with which it was made.

The party, on stage one at the studio, was warming up nicely, loads of booze and pizzas and fingerfood from Spago. The media were there with their cameras, tape recorders and notebooks. The cast and the chief production people had all turned up, Annie Klane looking gorgeous in a dress so tight she must have been squeezed into it with a piping bag; even Tony Flo, the head of the studio, put in an appearance, graciously receiving homage from his underlings. Charleston was there, too, but he kept well away from me.

Agnelli introduced me to Michael Rialto and his wife, Angela, a small woman, as dark as her uncle but a lot prettier. Rialto didn't recognise me from the night at Lou's. No reason why he should, I suppose. There, as here, he was the star and I was simply one of the extras murmuring 'Rhubarb, rhubarb' in the background.

He was polite enough but too conscious of himself and of being the centre of attention for my liking. His wife seemed all right, though, chatty and natural. I made small talk with her while keeping an eye on Agnelli and Rialto, Agnelli cold and formal, Rialto seemingly puzzled by the other man's attitude and the fact that his own famous charm wasn't working. Probably it hadn't occurred to him that slapping a man in public and walking off with his girl wasn't necessarily the best way to endear himself.

Lucy led Proctor over. He and I shook hands and I kissed Lucy on the cheek. Because Rialto was there cameras were flashing all around us. Rialto turned his back on them and brought the charm to work on Proctor. 'Hey, Richie, at last we get to work together. Man, I'm so excited about it I can hardly wait.'

'Me, too,' Proctor said, but not as if he really meant it.

Rialto said, 'Rico, you know this guy's work? Well, sure you do. But I gotta tell you, he's up there with the best. No shit. Right up there with the very best.'

Tony Flo joined the group. A shortish, solidly built man in a double-breasted white suit, navy blue shirt and pink tie. He looked more like a Mafioso than Agnelli did. Immediately he embarked on an anecdote concerning a trip he'd recently made to a casino in Las Vegas with someone in the movie business I had never heard of. Proctor and Lucy smiled and so did I. Well, it seemed only polite, though it wasn't a particularly funny story, since the whole point was that Flo and his mate had apparently lost enough money at blackjack to support about ten families for three months. Agnelli stared into the distance, not bothering to hide his boredom. He didn't have to. Because of his connection with Minelli he knew that Tony Flo needed him more than he needed Tony Flo. Angela Rialto chuckled delightedly, though the slightly baffled expression in her eyes suggested that she didn't really understand what she was hearing.

His tale over, Flo looked at me and said, 'So, Bobby, you a gambling man?' His mouth smiled but his dark brown eyes were cool and calculating.

'No,' I said piously. 'When I feel the urge to throw money away I throw it in the direction of a charity.'

He nodded amiably enough but somehow I had the feeling that I'd failed an important test.

'Pity,' he said, put his arm round Rialto's shoulder and took him and Angela away. Agnelli said, 'See you around,' and went off in the opposite direction.

Proctor gave me a shy, hesitant look. 'I don't know quite what to say to you,' he said, grinning a little sheepishly. 'I mean, yesterday afternoon … I want to apologise for what I said, the state I was in. Lucy told me what you did. I don't know how to thank you.'

'You don't need to,' I said. 'Us Brits have to stick together.'

'You can say that again. Especially in this company.'

'Yes, well, you could thank me by not making remarks like that in public. That's how the trouble started in the first place.'

'Right.' He nodded. 'Mum's the word, eh?'

'Exactly. Sobriety wouldn't be a bad idea either.'

He held up his glass. 'See this? Orange juice, plain, good old OJ, as harmless as the first jury said O.J. Simpson was. I won't touch anything stronger till the movie's over.'

Agnelli came by hand in hand with Terri, the Eurasian girl from Lou's. She wore something very short that showed off her remarkable golden legs and she exuded a raunchy sexuality. Lucy, her thick, dark blonde hair slightly tousled as if she had been running a hand through it and looking both beautiful and elegant in a simple, sleeveless white shift, studied her coolly.

Agnelli paused long enough to introduce the girl. Terri Chin, model, actress, whatever. She shook my hand warmly and said, 'I remember you. You were at Lou's with Rico. He didn't introduce us.'

'I know,' I said, with polite regret. 'You've no idea how disappointed I was.'

She giggled and Agnelli led her away. Lucy drew back from me a step or two. 'You go to Lou's?' she said. 'You hang out in cathouses? Well, well.'

Somebody came over and took Proctor away, talking to him earnestly. In movie-land everybody talks earnestly even if they're only discussing what to eat for lunch.

'No, no,' I said. 'I was simply there as an observer.'

'An observer? What, are you some kind of voyeur? Is that how you get your kicks?' She seemed very disappointed in me but oddly enough I found that encouraging.

'You don't understand. I didn't even want to be there. Agnelli took me. He was ordered to by his boss. I left as soon as I could.'

'Yeah? All those gorgeous whores and you weren't even tempted?

Oh, I bet.' She watched Terri's undulating hips as Agnelli, his arm now around the girl's waist, took her across the room. 'Were they all as gorgeous as her?'

'A lot of them were,' I said, watching, too.

'Huh,' she said, tartly. 'Then maybe you should have stuck around a little longer. You might have got lucky.'

'Luck hardly enters into it. At Lou's you just point at what you fancy and pay for it. It's about as romantic as buying an Egg McMuffin. I'm much, much happier standing right where I am.'

She smiled faintly at that. 'Oh yeah, then why are you looking at Terri?'

'I'm not.' And indeed I wasn't. What I was looking at was Agnelli, his hand now resting on Terri's right buttock, introducing her to Mr and Mrs Rialto and Michael Rialto pretending he had never met her before. A little bit of revenge for Agnelli perhaps but I didn't think it would satisfy him. Not in the long run.

Suddenly a voice rang out through a microphone. 'Ladies and gennulmen, your attention please.' At the far side of the sound stage a studio publicity man in a white tuxedo was standing on a dais, the microphone on a stand in front of him. Behind him there was a golden curtain with stars all over it. 'Ladies and gennulmen, this is the moment we've all been waiting for, the moment when Maestro Consolidated announces the last, truly vital, piece of casting in its exciting thirty-million-dollar production of *Death's Head Dangling*. Now I'm gonna keep you in suspense just a little longer as I ask the film's director, Richie Proctor, to come up here and make the announcement himself.'

Proctor shambled onto the dais. He was the kind of man who always shambled, the kind who could walk out of Armani or Cerrutti in a brand new made to measure suit and look as if he had already slept in it. He said, 'Right, well, yeah, this is a great moment for us all. The role we're talking about here is of what the French call a woman of a certain age and when I tell you who's going to play it, I think you'll be amazed.' He said all this in a loud mumble with very little conviction. I saw the PR man frowning at the lack of enthusiasm and hype. 'Ladies and gentlemen, I ask you now to welcome a star,' Proctor glanced across at the PR man, shrugged, and went on, 'a truly, truly great star, one of the greatest stars in the whole history of Hollywood, a lady whose name is synonymous with glamour in the movies and we are very, very lucky to get her. Ladies and gentlemen, Miss Virna Newport!'

The golden curtains opened and there was Newport in a full-length dress no less golden but without the stars. She stepped forward onto the dais with her arms held aloft and everyone gave her an ovation. As if on cue – what am I saying? Of course, on cue – Rialto and Annie Klane and Martie Culper and Bill Charleston bounded onto the dais and joined Proctor in embracing her. Then, more slowly, oozing dignity, Tony Flo stepped up and for a moment he and Newport stood on opposite sides of the little stage with their arms outstretched to each other before moving forward into an enthusiastic clinch. There was another ovation.

Lucy and I were separated after that, she going off to keep an eye on Proctor as the interviews broke out and newspaper writers, stills photographers and a bunch of multi-toothed TV reporters with hair and smiles lacquered into place moved in on Newport and the rest.

I stood around passing the time of day with various strangers until the publicity bit was done and the media had packed up its tent and left.

At that point the party was pretty well over, most of the food and drink gone, though a few studio people were still milling about. I was looking around for Lucy, thinking of asking her to dinner, when a voice said, 'Bobby! Bobby Lennox!' and Virna Newport hurled herself into my arms and landed a smacking great kiss on my mouth. There was a strong smell of whisky on her breath.

To say that what she had done created something of a stir is a considerable understatement since the other remaining guests couldn't understand why the great star was wasting all this enthusiasm on a nobody like me. But she told them.

'Gather round, everybody,' she said, in a voice guaranteed to hit the back row of the upper circle, if there'd been an upper circle on stage one. 'I wanna tell you about this wonderful man.' She had one arm tightly around my waist and with the other hand she was stroking my face. I noticed the boy Darren glowering at me in the background.

Newport said, 'This is the man who risked his life to save my jewellery. Yes, he did. In New York. Isn't he handsome, isn't he beautiful? He used to be a boxer, did you know that? Bobby Lennox. I think I'm in love with him. Isn't that great – the prizefighter and the lady? They should make a movie.'

A voice in the crowd said, 'They already did.'

Virna Newport directed a thin smile at the speaker. 'I know that, stoopid. I'm saying they should do a remake with me and Bobby.' Grammatically, of course, she should have said 'with Bobby and me' but she was hardly going to give me top billing. She wrapped her arms around my neck, giving me another of those long damp kisses, and over her shoulder I caught sight of Lucy, glowering as intently as Darren.

Then Lucy turned away and Darren came up and tried to pull Newport off me. 'Virna,' he said, 'we gotta go.'

Without releasing me she pushed him firmly away. 'Uh-uh, Darren. *You* gotta go. Like now. Go home to momma, go where you like but keep away from the hotel.' I realised that she hadn't simply been drinking, she was close to being drunk. 'Bobby's gonna take me home. Hey, you hear that, everybody? Bobby's gonna take me home. He could be the new love of my life and you heard it here first.'

So then she hit me with another of those whisky-sodden kisses and I tried to push her away but I suppose to onlookers who had probably drunk nearly as much as she had all my wriggling and shoving might easily have been mistaken for sexual ecstasy.

This time her tongue succeeded in forcing its way into my mouth and I was just wondering whether I might dampen her ardour by biting it right off when a well-dressed but slightly dishevelled man shoved his way through the crowd, pursued by a breathless security guard, tore Virna Newport away from me, shook her as if she were a dusty carpet and said, 'You bitch, you fucking bitch!'

# 13

HE WAS A tall, extremely handsome man, late fifties but in very good shape, with a thick mane of dark hair that was flecked with grey but probably not as much grey as nature had intended. There was something oddly familiar about him.

Then somebody said, 'Oh God, it's Greg Harrison,' and I recognised him. An actor who, when he was young and pretty, had starred in three or four nondescript movies without ever making much impression. Later he moved on to character roles, supporting parts in other people's films, but just lately there hadn't been too many of them and until recently he had been best known as Virna Newport's constant escort, all tan and teeth, holding her arm at premières, charity events and the like. Not much of a job for a grown man, really, but in the last few months he seemed to have lost even that and the boy Darren had taken his place.

Now here he was shouting at Newport and Newport was shouting back and the boy Darren was getting in on the act, too, hammering ineffectually at Harrison's back.

Newport glanced around wildly as if in search of a potential saviour, of which there were quite a few muscular specimens about. 'Tony!' she yelled. 'Tony, do something!'

But the chosen one, Tony Flo, didn't look too happy. He even looked a little surprised to have been selected and just stood there, flapping on the spot, shaking his head, and it was Rico Agnelli who broke it up. He grabbed Darren by the collar and sent him spinning into the crowd of a dozen or so onlookers. Then he stepped between Harrison and Newport and with his hands on their chests shoved them apart.

Newport let out a scream of outrage. 'How dare you touch my breasts!'

'Shut up, both of you.' Agnelli said. 'Fuck do you think you're doing, making a scene like this in public?'

Harrison, his face as white as was possible for someone so deeply and permanently tanned, his voice shaking with rage, said, 'That bitch promised me a part in this movie. She promised me. She said she'd talked to Tony Flo and, and what's his name, the producer, Charleston. She said it was all fixed and now my agent tells me there's nothing. Nobody's contacted him, nobody knows anything about it.'

Agnelli said, 'Is this true?'

Newport drew herself up disdainfully. 'Of course not. He's lying.'

'You're the liar,' Harrison yelled. 'You're the fucking liar, you bitch.'

Agnelli stepped up close to him, his face and voice oozing quiet menace. 'Cool it, okay? Just cool it. We'll sort this out.' He glanced up, spotted Charleston standing anxiously at the back of the small crowd and beckoned to him. 'Bill, c'mere.'

Charleston trotted obediently over, mumbled, 'Hi, Greg,' but wouldn't look the man in the face. I glanced around for Lucy and Proctor but there was no sign of them.

Agnelli said, 'Bill, you heard all that. Did Virna or Tony Flo say anything to you about getting Harrison on the movie?'

Charleston shook his head. 'Just Greg's agent. He called this afternoon, asked when the contract was coming. I had to tell him I didn't know what he was talking about.'

Harrison started shouting again but Agnelli laid a finger on his lips. 'Hush. I don't want to hear another word. You're not on the movie, you never were on the movie, you never will be on the movie.' He crooked a finger at the security man. 'Get him out of here.'

Then, at last, Tony Flo piped up. 'Okay, everybody, show's over.

Let's all have another drink and forget about it. And I mean forget about it. I know everybody here and if you all want to continue working at this studio nobody, nobody, says a word about this to the media. Am I making myself clear?' From the subdued murmur from those around him it seemed he was.

The security man took Harrison firmly, though not roughly, by the arm and led him away. I gave them a few seconds' start and followed. At the gate the security man said, 'I'm sorry, Mr Harrison, I hate to see you thrown out like this but what can I do?'

'It's okay, Larry. You're only doing your job.'

'You all right, Mr Harrison? You want me to get you a cab?'

'No. My car's just down the street.' He strolled quickly away. I caught up with him as he was about to unlock an old but well-kept Cadillac and tapped him on the shoulder.

He whirled angrily, his face still white around the mouth and nostrils. 'What do you want?'

I said, 'I'd like to buy you a drink.'

He stared at me suspiciously. 'What for?'

'I'm curious, that's all. Just wondering whether you've given up moonlighting as a burglar.'

'What?'

'New York,' I said patiently. 'Back in January. Virna Newport's famous jewels. Surely you can't have been so busy you've forgotten.'

He studied me some more, then nodded slowly. 'Oh, right. It was you, huh?' He grinned, as if at some not too pleasant memory. 'That night I was mad as hell at you. But now ... I'm glad you were there. Serve the bitch right. So where we gonna have that drink?'

I took him to the bar opposite the studio gates. It was only about eight o'clock but the place was quiet and we found a booth at the back well away from any other customers.

When our drinks had arrived Harrison said, 'How'd you know it was me?'

'The eyes, the mouth, the general build. I thought there was something familiar about you as soon as you turned up tonight.'

'You were there, huh?' He jerked his head in the approximate direction of the studio. 'At the party – you were there?'

I nodded. 'I'd like to know about that, too.'

'Yeah?' Suspicion had crept back into his voice. 'Well, first off just who are you?'

So I told him who I was, associate producer of the movie and all that, though I left out any mention of Donovan or Minelli. He said, 'You're not working for the cops, are you?'

'Absolutely not.'

He nodded, unconvinced. 'Are you sure you're not wearing a wire?'

I gave him a heavy, exasperated sigh and opened my jacket. 'You want to cop a feel? Reassure yourself?'

He stared into my face for a moment or two, then grinned slightly. 'Nah. I guess I've seen too many movies, been in too many movies.' He took a big gulp of his drink and, apparently satisfied at last, said, 'All right, where do you want me to start?'

'With the jewel robbery. I imagine that was set up as some kind of insurance scam.'

He looked impressed. 'Clever of you – Bobby did you say your name was? Very clever. Yep, that's exactly what it was supposed to be ...'

It had been Newport's idea, he said. She had been strapped for cash; she was always strapped for cash, not in the way most people are but in the way the very rich can be when their income no longer quite matches an extravagant lifestyle. She had homes in Connecticut, New York and Florida, all acquired as the result of several lucrative divorces. But her most recent allotment of alimony was not quite what she had expected, she hadn't made a film in five years, and the residuals from her earlier pictures were beginning to dry up. Meanwhile, her homes cost money, her servants cost money and her clothes cost money.

So she had hit on the idea of stealing her own jewellery, not her real jewellery of course, although, in fact, there was less of that left than people believed. She had already sold the odd bit here and there to tide her over the occasional cash flow problem but the insurance company didn't know that. If the 'robbery' had succeeded Virna Newport would have lost, as far as the insurers were concerned, upwards of three million dollars' worth of diamonds, emeralds, sapphires and other assorted baubles. And if I hadn't been around it would have succeeded. Harrison would have taken the jewellery box and dropped it in the East River and Newport would have given the acting performance of her life when she got back to her room and apparently found all her precious stones gone.

'Why did you agree to do it?' I asked.

'I needed money, too. I was on a percentage.'

'But why did she ask you? Why not Darren? He seems to be the current boyfriend.'

Harrison sneered into his gin and tonic. 'She doesn't trust Darren. He's just a whore. Listen, practically all her grown-up life I've been the one she turned to for help whenever she got into trouble.' He grinned wryly. 'I thought if I did this for her I could ease Darren out, make things like they used to be. I mean, Jesus, she owed me. She still does. Who was there, holding her hand, drying her tears, wiping her nose between husbands two and three, and three and four, and four and five?' He tapped himself on the chest. 'Me, that's who. It was only after husband five that she started getting restless, looking around for someone new to run her errands for her.'

'What about between husbands one and two?'

He looked at me quizzically. 'What did you say you were – associate producer on this film? For somebody in the movie business you don't know a lot, do you? I *was* husband one.' He shook his head, a touch sadly. 'Well, it was a long time ago, I guess. We were both young and I was a star then. A kind of star, anyway. And she was just about to become the hottest property in Hollywood. Soon as that happened she tossed me into the trash can and took on husband two, some billionaire real estate man.'

He communed moodily with his gin for a bit. When I thought he had been indulging his private grief long enough I said, 'But you didn't go away?'

'No. When the second marriage started breaking up she came to me for comfort and that kind of set a pattern.' He shrugged. 'I'm her personal doormat, I guess, her family size box of tissues. She's a greedy, selfish bitch and all her life she's used me.'

I didn't ask the obvious question. I didn't have to because he asked and then answered it himself.

'Why'd I let her do that? Because I loved her. Still do. And from time to time she's been good to me, taken me places I could never afford to go or nobody would ever have invited me to and helped me get work when my career started going down the toilet. She swore she'd get me a part on this *Death's Head* movie, a kind of goodbye gift, make up for the fact that she didn't want me around any more.' A little gleam came into his eye. 'I suppose there's no chance you could—'

I shook my head firmly. 'Sorry. I simply don't have that kind of clout.'

He sighed. 'What I expected. So, okay, next thing – what are you going to do about that "burglary"? You gonna tell the cops?'

'What's to tell? No crime was committed. Nobody stole her jewels, nobody submitted a fake insurance claim. I have a question for you, though – what are you going to do about Virna Newport? Are you going to leave her alone now?'

He finished his drink and stood up, his mouth twisted into a bleak little smile. He looked a little drunk. 'I'm going to fix her wagon, Bobby. I know just how to do it and I'm gonna fix it good. And I think I know how I'm gonna get me onto that movie of yours, too.' He gazed around, spotted the waitress and waved at her. 'Hey, you have such a thing as a phone in this place?'

I watched him lurching away towards the phone at the back of the room and wondered why, among all the events of this curious evening, there was one comparatively small thing that bothered me most.

# 14

THE BEDROOM IN the Spanish-style bungalow was big, soft, opulent – a woman's bedroom. The woman herself sat by the dressing-table, painting her toenails. Her white, silk robe had fallen open to reveal the full length of one long, shapely leg.

The two men, one tall and lean, the other short and running to fat, came in through the wide French windows that opened onto the patio and the pool area.

The woman hardly glanced at them. 'What do you two comedians want?' she said. She carried on painting her nails, the tip of her tongue protruding slightly from the corner of her mouth.

'That's nice,' said the tall man.

'Very nice,' said the short one.

'I mean, what kinda welcome is that?' the tall man said, elaborating.

'No kinda welcome at all,' said the short one.

The woman ignored them. She was working on the third toe of her left foot.

'You gonna talk to us at all?' asked the tall man.

'Just a couple words even – like "Hello, how ya doin'?" something like that,' asked the short one.

The woman leaned back, stretched, dipped her brush into the varnish bottle. 'I suppose my husband sent you,' she said.

'Who else?' asked the tall man.

'Sure wasn't your boyfriend,' said the short one.

The woman looked at them sharply. 'Cut to the chase,' she said. 'What do you want?'

'You notice she's not scared of us?' asked the tall man.

'She should be scared,' said the short one.

'You figure she's not scared because she's just stupid?'

'Could be. Does she look stupid?'

'Hard to tell. You look into her eyes, the lights seem to be on.'

'Yeah,' said the short one, 'but that don't necessarily mean anybody's home. The lights could be on to scare off the burglars.'

The woman finished painting her little toe and stretched out her leg the better to admire the small splashes of blood red on the end of her pretty foot. 'You guys kill me,' she said.

'What we're here for, lady,' said the tall man, and shot her three times in the face.

'Cut,' said Richie Proctor. 'Print it.' He hauled himself up from his chair beside the camera, a canvas-backed chair with his name boldly inscribed upon it. 'That was good, children, very good, but I'd like you to do it one more time. I think we need more gun.'

An assistant standing beside him said, 'More guns, you need more guns?'

Proctor shook his head vigorously. 'Not more guns – more gun, a bigger gun. The one he's using looks like a bloody pea-shooter. I want a big gun like what Clint Eastwood used in *Dirty Harry*. A Magnum, that's what I want, a bleeding great Magnum, the sort of gun you'd shit yourself as soon as someone pointed it at you. And I want a silencer on it, too. I like that pop-pop noise a silencer makes.' He rubbed the back of his neck with both hands as if to soothe away tension. 'All right, reset, everybody. We'll go again soon as the new gun arrives.'

Early afternoon on the first day of shooting and the *Death's Head* unit was on location at some millionaire's house just outside Santa Monica. They'd rented it for six weeks, planning to use the gardens, the pool and a few of the rooms for scenes in the movie. The cost was exorbitant but still a lot cheaper than building sets in the studio.

They'd been setting up the bedroom scene, rehearsing it and

working on it since morning. I'd arrived just after lunch as they were doing the second take on the master shot. Once they'd got that done to Proctor's satisfaction he'd start on the close-ups.

I wandered across to him. 'How's it going?'

'Oh, fine. Bit slow but it always is on the first day when you're all getting to know each other.' He rubbed the back of his neck again. 'Hey, that was a funny old business last night, wasn't it, Greg Harrison turning up like that. What was it all about? Nobody ever said anything to me about having him on the picture. Wouldn't want him anyway. He's not an actor. He's a bloody cardboard cut-out.'

I looked around at the small army of technicians, carpenters, electricians, props men, assistant directors, second and third assistant directors, make-up men and women and said, casually, 'Where's, er, where's Lucy?'

'Doing stuff in the office. I think she's a bit upset with you after the way you shoved off last night without a word to anybody.'

'I came back to the party. I had to go and talk to somebody but I came back. I looked for her but she'd gone. So had you. Perhaps I'd better go and see her, explain what happened. You don't need me around here and—'

And at this point uproar broke out beside the swimming pool. I looked across at the source of all the shouting and hollering – everybody did – and couldn't believe what I saw. Virna Newport and Greg Harrison were treating us to a reprise of last night's verbal punch-up.

Proctor said, 'Yes, I bloody do need you. Charleston's not here and you're the only producer on site. Go and sort it out.'

'Me? Why me?'

'Because that's what producers do, even if they're only associate producers.' He gave me a powerful shove in the direction of the row. 'Go get 'em, boy.'

Reluctantly I started pushing my way through the crowd. Newport had just slapped Harrison's face; he had slapped her back and now she was weeping with rage and pummelling at his chest. Through the tears she was screaming, 'You can't do that, you bastard. It's my life, it's *my life* ...'

Harrison yelled back. 'I can't do that? You wanna bet? I'm already doing it, been planning it for months. You're finished, you hear what I'm saying? You're finished.'

Newport looked around for help and, as luck would have it, spotted me. 'Bobby!' she yelled, 'stop him, please stop him!'

But in fact Proctor, who was probably pretty accustomed to tantrums on movie sets, had already solved the problem himself. He had dispatched a couple of burly security men who were now advancing purposefully in our direction and Harrison, seeing them, took off, running across the lawn and around the side of the house towards the road.

The fact that he had gone did not, however, satisfy Newport. She clutched my arm fiercely and said, 'Get him, Bobby! Stop him! He can't do this to me. It's my life, not his.'

I said, 'Stop him? How? Why? I don't even know what's going on.'

She shook her head, looking genuinely distressed. 'He told me he would do this. He called me this morning ... I didn't believe him. I laughed at him ... And now he comes here ...'

Proctor, who had eased up alongside me, muttered, 'I think you'd better go and talk to him, Bobby.'

I let out a yell of frustration. 'Talk to him about what, for Chrissake? Talk to him where? I don't know where he's going, where he lives.'

Newport muttered the name of a hotel, a room number. 'Please, Bobby, talk to him. Tell him he mustn't do this awful thing.' She was sobbing now, both hands to her face.

I looked at Proctor over the top of her head and we shrugged hopelessly at each other.

'I think you'd better go and find Harrison,' Proctor said. 'Sort it out with him. You're not going to get any sense out of her.'

Well, he'd got that right, I thought. Newport, still weeping, was being led away to her dressing room by a couple of make-up girls.

Proctor and I exchanged a couple more shrugs. 'Go on,' he said, 'see what you can do.'

'All right,' I said, resignedly, 'all right,' and went off to find my car, thinking that if this was what the film business was about I could have made a seriously bad career move.

# 15

I TURNED UP from Santa Monica onto Sunset and slowed down as I passed Proctor's office building, tempted to swing into the basement car park, invest another ten dollars and go up to make my peace with Lucy. But then I thought, no, later. Duty called, though what I was going to say to Harrison or even what I was going to talk to him about I had no idea.

I looked at my watch. Nearly four o'clock. I'd give Harrison forty-five minutes, an hour top whack, and then go back to Proctor Productions. I wondered what Lucy might like to do that evening. Go to a film, perhaps, or a theatre if we could find one that wasn't playing an Andrew Lloyd Webber musical. My own fancy was for dinner in a good restaurant followed by a drive to her place or mine to continue the getting to know you process that had started so promisingly two nights ago.

So, okay – forty-five minutes, I thought, that's all you get, Harrison. An hour? Forget it.

Harrison's hotel was not far from Sunset, just off La Cienega and close to the Beverly Centre. A pleasant, comfortable-looking place, neither big nor small, nothing grand nor ostentatious. You wouldn't get stars staying there, only wannabes and usetabes.

I checked the room number Virna Newport had given me and thought about calling it on one of the house phones, then decided not to. There was no guarantee that Harrison was in, of course, but if he was I didn't want to give him any opportunity of avoiding me. Much better to go up, bang on the door and confront him with the problem – whatever the hell the problem was – right there and then.

I took the lift to the third floor where a bunch of tourists was waiting – four Japanese and a young couple, probably honeymooners, with the bloom of the Midwest on their cheeks. The young woman was saying, 'Oh, honey, I can hardly believe it. We're in Hollywood, we're actually in Hollywood. It's so exciting.'

I felt like telling her not to get too worked up. There's really not a lot to see in Hollywood except tat and tackiness, but I didn't say anything. Why should I rain on her parade? Hollywood itself would do that soon enough.

The Japanese, chattering animatedly to each other, were probably saying much the same things as the girl, but I didn't say a word to them either.

They all got into the lift and when they had gone there was silence on the third floor.

Harrison's room was to the left as you came out of the lift, at the far end of a winding corridor. There was no sound from any of the rooms though trays containing the remains of room service lunch had been parked outside a few of them and presumably some kind of activity, possibly involving consenting adults, was going on behind the locked doors.

The thick beige carpet muffled the sound of my footsteps as I walked up and knocked on Harrison's door.

No answer, though I was pretty sure he must be there because the door was slightly open. I gave it a push and went in.

Harrison was lying on the floor at the foot of the bed, his eyes wide open and staring at the ceiling. The handle of a knife protruded from his throat and there was blood all over his shirt and on the carpet around him.

I stood there for a moment, shocked into immobility, my hand still on the door handle. Then a strange, awful sound came from Harrison's lips and his right hand twitched.

I ran across the room and knelt beside him.

And something very hard, wielded with great force, smashed across the back of my skull.

# 16

I'VE NO IDEA how long I was unconscious, though I do remember drifting in and out of partial awareness, as if I were floating up from the bottom of a swimming pool, briefly glimpsing the clear blue sky then sinking again into the dark, dark depths.

In those comparatively lucid moments I could feel various things happening to me: people pulling at me, hands fumbling in my coat pockets, someone – probably more than one person – lifting and carrying me none too gently, to some other place, people talking urgently to me, although I had no understanding of what they were saying.

When, eventually, I rejoined the rest of the conscious world I was lying on a bed in what was clearly a hotel room. I was aware of a dark coverlet beneath me, of what seemed to be a still life of a fruit salad on the wall opposite me, of a relentless, unbroken, throbbing pain in my head. For a moment the light hurt my eyes and I closed them again, groaning.

A man's voice said, 'So you're awake, huh?'

I squinted along the length of my body in the direction of the sound. There were two of them, sitting in little straight-backed armchairs at the foot of the bed. They weren't in uniform and they weren't flashing badges at me but they didn't need to. Even in my groggy condition I could recognise policemen when I saw them.

The older one said, 'You ready to talk now?' He didn't sound friendly.

I started to nod, thought better of it as a blinding flash of pain streaked through the back of my skull, and croaked at him instead. 'Yes.'

'Lennox, right? Robert Lennox, a.k.a Bobby. Some kinda movie producer.'

I croaked again, my hand shielding my eyes from the sunlight filtering through the blinds on the window. 'Very good.'

'A couple calls was all it took. You ready to tell us what happened?'

The older, white, man was doing the talking; the younger, black, one beside him appeared to be taking notes.

'Who are you?' I said.

The older man produced a shield and held it up. Given the state I was in and his distance from me I couldn't have read it even if I had wanted to. I took it on trust, although for all I knew it could have identified him as Deputy Dawg.

'Detective First Grade Carlton,' he said. 'LAPD. This is Detective Third Grade O'Malley.'

'I suppose he must be what they call black Irish,' I said and giggled faintly. All right, it was a pretty feeble joke but then I wasn't at my best.

'What?' said Carlton. I said nothing, just lay back and closed my eyes again. I was beginning to feel very sick.

After a bit Carlton got back to the questioning. 'So what happened? Why did you kill him?'

'Why did I what? I haven't killed anybody.'

'Oh, really? You taken a good look at yourself lately?'

I moved my head gingerly, carefully, so that I could examine myself without my head splitting apart. There was a copious amount of blood, drying fast, all over my jacket and shirt. From the absence of pain anywhere below my neck I assumed it wasn't my blood. I must have acquired it after I was hit and had fallen across Harrison's body.

'I just found him,' I said. 'He was dead already. Dying, anyway.'

97

'Oh, yeah? Know what we think? We think maybe there were two of you did it and the other guy crossed you up, left you to take the rap.'

'That's bullshit,' I said with such vehemence that my head jerked and I groaned again.

Carlton got up and came to stand beside me. Grey-haired and neatly dressed with the smell of hamburger and onions on his breath. 'Your head hurt?' he asked, sympathetically. 'I could find ways to make it hurt worse.' He sat down on the bed heavily enough to make the mattress bounce and start the daggers shooting in my skull again. 'Listen to me, Lennox. We know about you, we know about Harrison. We know he used to be Virna Newport's boyfriend and we know you just took over the job.'

'Don't be daft,' I said. 'She's practically old enough to be my mother.'

He nodded, accepting that. 'But she's rich, too. The world is full of lonely old broads but there's no such thing as a lonely old *rich* broad, just like there's no such thing as an unattractive old *rich* man.'

'I don't even like her,' I said.

'You don't have to like 'em to fuck 'em,' he said. 'Not when they're rich.'

'What can I say to persuade you? I'm certainly not interested in her body and I'm not interested in her money. I've got money. I'm rich enough already.'

'Nobody's ever rich enough,' he said. 'You'd been a cop as long as I have you'd know that. So come on, Lennox, tell us what happened. Who was the other guy?'

It was a nightmare. Unbelievable. Surely they couldn't really think I'd done anything more sinister than discover the body. And yet, ludicrous though it was, they seemed to have me marked down as the prime suspect. Me and some mysterious accomplice.

He bounced around on the bed some more, smiling a little as he heard me moan. 'Look at it this way, Lennox, you got two choices: either you talk to us here in the comfort of this nice room or we take you down to the station and sweat it out of you.' He took a deep breath, shaking his head slowly to let me know how patient he was being. 'Okay, let's take it from the top. You come up here, you and the other guy, you knock, you ring the bell, whatever. Harrison lets you in and then what? Which of you used the knife? And why?'

I said, 'It wasn't like that. I was alone, the door was already open, Harrison was on the floor with the knife in his throat, I went to him and then somebody—'

Relief came suddenly and from a quite unexpected quarter. The door opened and Rico Agnelli stepped into the room. O'Malley, the hitherto silent cop, turned sharply in his direction.

'Get out of here,' he said.

Agnelli ignored him and looked across at Carlton. 'Jeremiah,' he said, 'tell your boy to step outside for a minute.'

O'Malley leapt furiously to his feet. 'Tell his what? Tell his *what*?'

Carlton said, placatingly, 'Frank, give us a moment, will you? Please.'

O'Malley glared at him in disbelief. 'What are you saying, Jerry? You want me to leave? You want to talk to this asshole alone, without me?'

Carlton nodded, unhappily. 'Yeah, Frank, that's what I want.' He didn't look at his younger partner.

O'Malley glanced at him, looked longer at Agnelli who was leaning against the wall beside the door, arms folded across his chest, everything about him from his expensive haircut to his dark, lightweight Bejan suit and handmade shoes exuding the arrogance of money and power. Then he looked back at Carlton and shook his head, slowly, scornfully. 'It's like that, huh?' he said and went out.

Carlton said, 'Frank, hey, Frank—' But his partner had already gone. To Agnelli he said, 'Jesus, Rico, you have to do this? I didn't want the kid to know.'

'Time he learned the facts of life,' Agnelli said. 'Don't worry about it. We'll find some way to cut him in.' He sat down in the armchair O'Malley had vacated and lit a cigarette. 'You had a doctor look at Mr Lennox yet?'

Carlton said, not too confidently, 'Well, yeah, sort of. I mean, not like a thorough examination.'

Agnelli nodded. 'Okay, so here's what's gonna happen. I got a doctor and a team of paramedics waiting in the corridor to take Mr Lennox to hospital, which is where he belongs, and you won't raise any objections, right, Jeremiah?'

Carlton said, 'Hey, hold on, Rico. The guy's a suspect—'

'Oh, yeah? You found him with a smoking gun in his hand, did you? Or not a gun because Harrison was, what, knifed, was it? You found Mr Lennox with the knife in his hand, is that right?'

Carlton looked unhappy. 'Well, no. Truth is we haven't located the murder weapon yet.'

Agnelli dragged thoughtfully at his cigarette. 'Let me see if I can follow your thinking, Jeremiah. You're thinking Mr Lennox walked up to Harrison, stabbed him – where? In the throat was it? – stabbed him in the throat, went away, got rid of the knife, came back to the room and coldcocked himself across the back of the head to give himself an alibi. Is that what you're thinking?'

Carlton shuffled his feet. I wished he wouldn't because he was still sitting on the bed and his movement made the mattress jerk around and kickstart the shooting pains in my head. I began to wonder dazedly whether the killer had hidden the murder weapon in my skull. Carlton said, 'Rico, it's not like that. There coulda been an accomplice. Hey, we just started this investigation. We gotta cover all the angles.'

Agnelli stood up, stubbed out his cigarette. 'Okay, so here's an angle for you to cover. The toy boy, Darren whatever his name is, Virna Newport's latest gigolo. Everybody knows he hated Harrison, because Harrison used to have his job. And he hates Mr Lennox, too, because Newport seems to have taken a shine to him. So unless you find the knife somewhere close by with Mr Lennox's fingerprints all over it, here's an idea you might consider: Darren has a fight with Harrison and kills him. Then before Darren can get away Mr Lennox comes into the room. Darren steps out from behind the door or wherever, slugs him across the head and takes off. Go find Darren and you find the killer.'

He opened the door, ignoring O'Malley who was lurking balefully outside and beckoned to someone out of sight along the corridor. 'Okay, doctor, you can come in now.' To Carlton he said, 'We're moving Mr Lennox to hospital. I take it you have no objection, Jeremiah. There's nothing more you want to ask him?'

Carlton shook his head.

'In that case get out.'

Belatedly showing a flash of spirit Carlton said, 'You got some nerve, Rico. I just wanna see your face, hear how loud you crow the day your boss goes down for murder.'

Agnelli flashed a thin, cold grin at him. 'You guys got as much chance of convicting Minelli as Bill Clinton has of passing a virginity test. Go.'

Carlton went and as the doctor and a couple of paramedics with a stretcher took his place in the room Agnelli said to me, 'Just as well for you that Jeremiah is one of ours.'

# 17

THEY TOOK ME to the Cedars of Sinai hospital only a few blocks from the hotel. A private room, teams of doctors and nurses. Scans, X-rays, examinations so thorough that they'd have shown up anything from a fractured skull to multiple brain damage, haemorrhoids or terminal halitosis.

Fortunately, I didn't have any of those things. What I did have was a case of concussion. The doctor said I should stay in at least overnight, maybe longer, and I didn't demur. I know of too many fighters who got knocked out in the ring and either didn't go to hospital at all or discharged themselves too soon and suffered terrible consequences. Not that I myself was ever knocked out; the only person who ever beat me up was Willie Slate and even he didn't hit me half as hard as whoever had cracked me across the back of the skull.

So, no, I wasn't going in for any heroics like insisting on getting up and walking out. If medical opinion thought I should stick around the hospital for a while, until they were absolutely sure I was clear, then I was happy to go along with it.

I slept for several hours and when I woke up, already feeling much better, Lucy was sitting beside my bed, reading a magazine.

'Hi,' I said in a voice weaker than was strictly necessary because I wanted her sympathy.

She held up the magazine. 'You bring this in with you?' she asked, suspiciously.

It was a soft-core porn job, pictures of women with enormous breasts and groins bushier than the Amazon rain forest. 'No,' I said, indignantly. 'Of course not.'

'Well, I found it in the cupboard right by the bed, so what was I supposed to think? Guy who hangs out at Lou's, just watching, not even touching, is capable of any depravity.' She looked me over, though less tenderly than I would have liked. 'How are you feeling?'

'Nice of you to get around to that,' I murmured.

She produced that wonderful, dawn-breaking smile again. 'Hey,' she said and leant across to kiss me on the mouth. It was only a quick, gentle, sisterly kiss but even so I could feel my temperature soaring.

'More,' I said hoarsely when she pulled away.

'Later,' she said. 'Maybe. First, tell me about Harrison.'

I told her. There really wasn't a lot to say.

'You had no idea what the fight with Newport was about?' she said. 'And he didn't tell you? Didn't tell you who killed him either? I mean, he didn't go like this,' she put both hands to her throat and started croaking at me, 'he didn't say, like, "Richie Proctor did it. Aaargh!" ' She slumped sideways in her chair.

'No, he didn't,' I said. 'And if he had I'm pretty sure he'd have done it better than that. I don't know how good an actor he was but he had to be better than you.'

She sat up primly and smoothed her skirt down till it nearly reached her knees. 'Okay, that's the way you wanna be, screw you. I don't have to sit here making like Florence Nightingale, you know. You want another kiss, ask one of the regular nurses. She'll probably have you arrested for sexual harassment and serve you right.'

I grinned at her because there wasn't anybody I wanted to see more right then. 'So what's new,' I said. 'Agnelli told the police Darren probably did it. Have they arrested Darren yet?'

'Nope. Couldn't find him. He's disappeared along with about three thousand dollars Virna Newport had lying around her hotel suite. The cops are all eager and quivering to find him, Agnelli's spitting mad, Charleston's trying to hide, Richie's telling everybody to fuck off and the world's media are outside waiting for you to make a statement.'

'Oh, shit,' I said.

She inspected the fingernails on her left hand, giving them rather more attention than I would have thought they were due. 'They seem to think you and Newport are an item, that everything happened because Darren went wild with jealousy. That the way it was?'

I groaned. 'Not you, too. Has everyone gone mad? I can't stand Virna Newport. She makes my flesh crawl.'

She studied me thoughtfully. 'Is that true?'

'Cross my heart and hope to die.'

She nodded. 'Yeah, but is that just the way you are with women generally? I mean, a voyeur like you. Maybe every woman makes your flesh crawl. What I'm saying, can you name any woman – just pluck one at random – who doesn't have that effect on you?'

I stared up at the ceiling. 'One woman. At random. Who doesn't make my flesh crawl. That's a tough one.'

'Come on, come on,' she said, impatiently. 'It can't be that tough.'

I took a deep breath. 'Well, apart from a couple of acknowledged movie sexpots, who might there be? Oh, I know. Yes, of course – you. You do a lot of things to my flesh but you certainly don't make it crawl.'

'Good,' she said and patted me approvingly on the hand, while I checked my flesh. Nope. It didn't give the slightest indication of crawling.

'Now then, here's the set-up,' she said. 'They're having a press conference here, in this hospital, sometime tomorrow, whenever the doctors say you're up to it. Bet your life Newport will be here, playing the tragic heroine, the *femme fatale* that men kill each other over. Harrison's dead, Darren's gone, so she'll be climbing all over you, making like you're the new man in her life. Is that okay with you?'

'No, it's not.'

She grinned wickedly. 'Well, you better get yourself prepared.' She stood up and hitched her bag over her shoulder.

'Where are you going?'

'Home. I have things to do.'

'No, stay here,' I said. 'Stay with me. There's plenty of room.'

'In that bed? Two people? No way, not unless one was on top of the other all night.'

'So?'

She stared down at me gravely. 'Don't you think maybe you're taking an awful lot for granted?'

I felt my cheeks reddening because, of course, she was right, but before I could say anything a nurse came in to minister to me. Lucy smiled, kissed my forehead and murmured that she'd see me tomorrow. The nurse watched us grimly from the doorway.

'This is way past the hour for visitors,' she said.

Lucy moved away from the bed and, as she went out, handed the porno magazine to the nurse. 'You really shouldn't give him stuff like this to read,' she said, disapprovingly. 'It's sent his temperature way up.' Then she winked at me and was gone.

The nurse looked at the magazine, shuddered and looked at me, even her uniform bristling with starched contempt.

'It's not mine,' I said. 'It was in the cupboard. I didn't even know it was there. Honestly, it's not mine.'

But I knew she didn't believe me.

# 18

THE HARRISON MURDER was big on the front page of the *LA Times* and featured strongly on all the TV breakfast shows. Toe-curling stuff it was, too, certainly as far as I was concerned. With Harrison dead the row at the studio party had inevitably leaked to the media so now I was confidently identified as Virna Newport's mysterious new suitor, the catalyst who had caused Darren – Darren Carmody was his full name apparently – to crack, kill Harrison and probably try to kill me, too.

Everyone had marked Darren down as the culprit, guilty until proved innocent, but nobody knew where he was. All that was known about him was that he had been born in Arizona twenty-six years ago, had worked as an actor in television in New York, then come to Hollywood and played small parts in one or two films before gaining wider publicity as Newport's most recent escort.

So far all attempts to trace his family, if any, and dig more deeply into his background had failed. But the media weren't too bothered about that. In their view the kid had done the crime and eventually the police would find him, therefore they'd be able to have their fun with Darren later. Meanwhile, they had on their hands the juiciest Hollywood murder mystery since the O.J. Simpson case, and there was a lot of salacious mileage to be gained from the presumed love quadrangle involving Newport, Harrison, Darren and me. And I, having found the body and been assaulted myself, was the main focus of interest.

The prizefighter and the lady gag featured prominently, of course. On one of the television shows some twerp with a moustache like two hairy caterpillars mating reminded viewers of the 1933 movie with Myrna Loy and Max Baer to prove that life imitated art. All over the place there were run-downs of my boxing career, with particular emphasis, naturally, on the beating I had taken from Willie Slate. There were even photographs of me during that fight, fortunately taken in the early stages before my eyes were closed, my nose was spread and my lips swelled up like a Hollywood sex queen who had overdone the collagen implant.

Bill Charleston, Richie Proctor and the studio had done their best to play down any suggestion of a relationship between Newport and me, denying any knowledge of such a thing and insisting that the reason for the murder was a total mystery. None of them knew much about Darren either and Virna Newport had, by all accounts, been 'too overcome with grief' to make any kind of statement last night but had promised to rectify that today. This was not a prospect that filled me with anything resembling joy.

As I was finishing breakfast the studio's chief publicity man turned up. I recognised him from the studio party as the one who had called on Proctor to announce the addition of Newport to the cast. He asked how I felt and I said I was fine, which was reasonably close to the truth. My head still ached but otherwise I didn't seem to have suffered any damage. He said he was happy to hear that but it would be better if I led the media to assume that I was still feeling groggy. That way if I happened to contradict myself at the press conference he could step in, claim that I was unwell and bring the proceedings to an end. I was happy about that bit, less happy about what I was expected to say.

'Okay,' he said, 'here's what we've all agreed. The row between Newport and Harrison – the second row, the one on location – wasn't a row at all, it was just an argument about how they were going to play their big scene in the movie together. Artistic temperament if you—'

'Hang on,' I said. 'Which big scene was this? He wasn't even in the movie.'

'Right, yeah, well, for the purposes of this press conference he was going to be. Tony Flo and Bill Charleston have issued a statement saying that, contrary to any rumours floating around, they were delighted to offer him the part of the police commissioner. There is such a part, okay? We haven't actually cast it yet but the character does have a big scene with Newport. So, far as the media knows, Harrison was to play the role. He and Newport argued about it, he stormed off and you, as the associate producer on the spot, went after him to calm him down, found him dead and got hit on the head. End of story.'

'Well, all right,' I said, doubtfully. 'I suppose I can go along with that. Nothing about me being the new man in Newport's life, though, right?'

He shrugged. 'Unless you want to play it that way. From our point of view – great. It's good publicity. I mean, we play it right it's all good publicity, Harrison's murder, everything. In this town, if you know what you're doing, you can make anything work for you. I mean, you can get caught by the police taking a blow job from a hooker on Sunset Boulevard and, you handle the media right, you still come up smelling of roses. It's up to you.'

I said I most certainly didn't want to play it that way, he shrugged again and said it was okay with him and he hoped the media would believe me but, of course, a lot depended on Newport. I asked anxiously what she was going to say and he said nobody knew.

'All I've been told,' he said, 'is that she's going to arrive here about half an hour into the conference and make a statement. Right now we can only hope it's the same statement the rest of us are gonna make but who knows? The one thing that's for sure is that she's planning a grand entrance.'

I was still worrying about that an hour later when a team of nurses wheeled my bed down the corridor to a large conference room occupied by television crews, photographers and print journalists from, it seemed to me, all over the world. Actually, there was no need for me to be in bed, or to have such a huge bandage round my head.

I'd been up and showered and shaved and walked around my room with no harmful effects but the PR man and the two assistants, who had turned up later, were agreed that a bandaged man in bed would be in greater control of a press conference than someone who looked as if he was fit enough to go to the gym for a sparring session.

So I lay back on my pillows, wearing an unnecessary turban of bandage, did my best to look weak and wan and stuck to the official script. The media didn't like it. They wanted sex, they wanted dirt, they wanted lurid confessions about my amorous affair with Virna Newport. Television reporters thrust their microphones, their tans, their teeth and in some cases their tits in my face and asked how long she and I had been together.

I said, 'Look, I don't really know Miss Newport. I've only met her three times.'

A bored newspaperman in the front row said, 'That broad has *married* guys she's only met three times.'

A cute Hispanic girl from Channel 7 smiled disarmingly and said, 'Mr Lennox, we understand Miss Newport will be coming here any time now to make a statement about your relationship. Wouldn't you like to tell us something about it before—'

From the back of the room a prematurely bald young man with a weasel face said in a sharp London accent, 'Here, Bobby, what are you doing pretending to be a film producer?'

And that, curiously enough, was the question I'd been dreading most because I really didn't have a plausible answer. Vague explanations about representing a British consortium that was in partnership with an American consortium that was in partnership with MCF simply wouldn't be enough. The one thing neither Donovan nor I had considered when it was agreed that I should go to Hollywood was that I might be tossed, willy-nilly, into the limelight.

I was just wondering whether right now might be a good time to be overcome by my injuries and throw a dramatic faint when the grand entrance that the studio PR man had predicted duly happened.

The double doors at the back of the room were flung noisily open by some young male flunkey; there was a pause, crackling with anticipation as everyone turned to look; and then, slowly, slinkily, she came in. Alone. No entourage. Just her.

With all the art that conceals art her hair was framed loosely, softly, perfectly around her lovely, oval face. Her make-up was immaculate, just enough around the eyes and the lips, the merest brush of colour on the cheekbones. Her figure was not so much flattered as enhanced by a simple navy blue dress which ended halfway down her thighs to reveal long, smooth legs whose curves were accentuated by the high-heeled pumps on her slim, elegant feet.

She smiled enticingly at the assembled media persons and then strode swiftly down the aisle to where I lay, wide-eyed and propped up against the pillows, in my hospital bed. She stopped, just for a moment, with her arms half outstretched towards me and then, 'Darling,' she murmured and kissed me on the lips.

I didn't hesitate for a moment. I returned her kiss with a passion that made her gasp with surprise. Then, gently, I held her away from me and gazed deeply into her eyes.

'Lucy,' I said, 'oh, Lucy. I've never been so pleased to see anyone in my life.'

She leaned forward to kiss me again, murmuring so that only I could hear, 'Virna Newport's on her way. We'd better keep this up for a while. You reckon you can stand it?'

'It could be hard,' I murmured back, gently biting her ear, 'but I think I'm up to the job.'

'Easy, feller, easy,' she said, a shade breathlessly, and we carried on nuzzling each other while the photographers and the TV cameras moved in on us. And while they were doing that Virna Newport came into the room.

Only, at first, nobody noticed her.

She just stood there, looking like she'd spent at least two hours in wardrobe and make-up and surrounded by a small entourage of young men and women who did God knew what to make her life easier. And nobody, except me, even realised she was there ...

... until one of the newspapermen, curious enough to wonder what I was looking at over Lucy's shoulder or why I should even bother to look over Lucy's shoulder, happened to glance behind him. 'Christ,' he said, 'it's Virna.'

And then they all turned and got up and moved towards her.

Virna Newport stood perfectly still for a long moment while she glared at me with bitter loathing. And then she swept out of the room again and, to my intense relief, the assembled media ran after her.

Lucy said, her cheek against mine, 'Have they all gone?'

'Yes, but don't move. They might come back.'

She chuckled and sat up. 'Did I do good or did I do good? After that little scene nobody's going to believe you're Virna's boy. So I reckon that makes us quits. You saved my job and Richie's and I've saved you from a fate worse than death. Unless, of course, you were just lying there, longing for Virna to come in and—'

'No way. You were brilliant. You look brilliant. Those media people, did you see their faces? The men were looking at me with naked envy.'

'Oh, right,' she said, amused. 'And how about the women?'

'I didn't care about the women. I didn't care about any of them. I was too busy enjoying the moment.'

The PR man came back. 'You're on our movie, right?' he said to Lucy. She said she was, told him who she was and what she did. He said, 'Well, I got news for you, Lucy. Virna wants you off it. She's outside right now, spitting blood. No, actually, tell you the truth she's giving a press conference on the hospital steps and spraying charm like a scattergun, but at *me* she spat blood. I have to tell Tony Flo either you go or she goes.'

Lucy said, 'Oh, shit. Shit!'

He shrugged. 'What the hell did you expect? You sweep in here and upstage the biggest diva in Hollywood. Virna was supposed to do the romantic love scene by the bedside, not you. I'm real sorry, kid, but soon as Tony Flo gets to hear of this you're history.'

Lucy bit her lip angrily. 'Now what, goddamn it? This is what I get for playing the good Samaritan?' She turned accusingly towards me. 'This is all your fault, Lennox. So do something. I saved your ass, now you save mine. I need this job. Richie needs me to have it.'

I thought it over and what I thought was that she was right. Proctor obviously felt happier with her around and besides, and more importantly, I felt happier with her around. I said, 'Proctor has a cellphone, yes? Call him, let me talk to him.'

She nodded. 'Okay.' She took a phone from her handbag, dialled a number, waited a long time for an answer, then said, 'Richie, it's me. I've got Bobby Lennox here. He wants to talk to you.'

I took the phone from her and said, 'Look, Richie, this is the set-up. I'll tell you how it came about later but what everything boils down to is that Virna Newport wants Lucy fired from the picture. The studio publicity man ...' I looked at him enquiringly.

He said, 'Arthur.'

I said, 'Arthur, right. Arthur, the publicity man, says Newport's delivered an ultimatum – either Lucy goes, or she does. What? Okay, I'll hand you over to him.'

I gave the phone to Arthur who said, 'Yeah, Richie, what a fucking mess, huh? Yeah, that's right what Bobby told you. What? Oh, Jesus, don't say that. Richie, don't say that to me. No, Richie, please, I—'

He flicked off the phone and tossed it onto the bed, rubbed his hands through his dark, thinning hair and glared bitterly at Lucy. 'You know what he just said? He said if you go, he goes. Isn't that great? Two days into the movie we got one dead body, a killer on the loose and no director and you know who they'll blame? Me. They'll fire me, that's what they'll do.'

I plucked the silly, useless bandage off my head and threw it on the floor. 'You have a number for Rico Agnelli? Good. Get him for me.'

I took hold of Lucy's hand and squeezed it reassuringly, while Arthur flicked through a notebook, tried several numbers and finally handed the phone to me.

As succinctly as I could I gave Agnelli a run-down on what had happened that morning and the threats Newport was making.

He said, 'Christ, couldn't you have just screwed the stupid broad, kept her happy?'

'No, I couldn't, not in any circumstances and besides that's not the problem now. Thing is, are you prepared to let Proctor go, find a new director?'

'No. Proctor's got a loose mouth but he's good at his work.'

'What if Newport insists?'

He thought about that. 'Newport needs the part. She hasn't made a movie in years.'

'Excellent,' I said. 'Then what I suggest is that you get onto Tony Flo and tell him to do whatever he has to do to keep Newport happy but also to make it quite clear to her that nobody gets fired.'

'What makes you think I can do that?'

'I've seen you with Tony Flo. He's nervous of you.'

Agnelli chuckled. 'You don't miss a lot, Bobby. Okay, I'll do it, but tell me this: are you putting me to all this trouble just so you can get into Lucy's pants?'

'That's not the sort of question you should ask of a gentleman,' I said primly.

Agnelli chuckled again. 'Right. What I thought. Okay, I'll fix it with Tony Flo. Just one thing, though: ask your girlfriend if she ever went out with a guy called Mickey Meo.' He hung up.

To Lucy and Arthur I said, 'Crisis over. Everyone can relax. Agnelli is going to tell Tony Flo to tell Newport she can go and take a running jump.'

'He can do that?' Arthur asked, anxiously.

I nodded. 'He can do that. Don't ask me how but he can do it.'

'What about Bill Charleston?'

'A word of advice to you, Arthur. Charleston isn't anybody to worry about. If you have problems come to me and if I can't handle them Agnelli will.'

Arthur said, 'Jesus, what am I doing in this crazy, fucked-up business? Why don't I grow up and get a real job?' He went out.

To Lucy I said, 'Did you ever know a man named Mickey Meo?'

She nodded. 'He was my friend, the one I told you about – the guy who got shot.'

# 19

LUCY WENT BACK to work soon after that while I stayed around the hospital for a few precautionary tests. The doctors congratulated me on my speedy recovery, Arthur arranged for the studio to pick up the medical bills and I walked out in mid-afternoon with nothing much to show for my misadventures except a sore skull.

A young woman accosted me outside the hospital while I was waiting for my taxi to arrive.

'Mr Lennox?' she asked. She wore large round spectacles and flat-heeled shoes and was power-dressed in a grey suit. She had a briefcase in her hand. A lawyer maybe, an ambulance chaser eager to get me to sue somebody on account of that crack on the head.

She said, 'I'm Jane Baker?' The question mark in her voice suggested I might be about to argue the point. 'From Marcus and Lowe? The publishers?'

'Yes?'

'I was wondering if I could talk to you, ask you a few questions. About Greg Harrison's book?'

'What book?' I said. The taxi drew up and I moved towards it.

'Please,' she said. 'If you could just spare me a few minutes. I don't know who else to ask.'

I made an instant decision. 'Hop in,' I said.

She hesitated. 'Where are we going?'

'To my hotel. It's okay – I'm staying at the Bel Air Riviera. You can't get much more respectable than that.'

We both got in, I told the driver the address and he headed up towards Sunset. 'What's this all about?' I said.

Ms Baker sat as far from me as she could get, her back straight, her briefcase on her lap and her hands folded on top of it. She was quite a good-looking young woman with a nice figure. No make-up and a touch mousy as to the hair. In a Hollywood movie she would have played the demure secretary who suddenly turned up with a blonde rinse and a soft perm, lipstick and a tight, low-cut dress, causing her previously unobservant boss – with whom, of course, she was hopelessly in love – to gasp, 'Why, Miss Baker, you're … you're beautiful!' Life, however, is not a Hollywood movie and in the cab she stayed mousy, possibly because she wasn't hopelessly in love with me or possibly because she had reason not to think much of men anyway.

She said, 'I'd rather not talk about it right now.' She gestured towards the cab driver. 'It's a somewhat delicate matter.'

So all along Sunset we talked about the weather (which we agreed was fine), where she had come from (New York that morning) and the multi-million dollar houses we were passing (which she thought were very nice). It was largely a one-way conversation – most of it going from me to her and very little coming back. After a while it made my head ache and we spent the last ten minutes of the ride in silence.

When we arrived at the hotel she declined an invitation to talk in my room, looking at me as though I were some moustachio-twirling villain from a Victorian melodrama intent on ravishing her. In the end we settled on a secluded table by the pool, far enough from anyone else to discourage eavesdroppers but close enough to civilisation for her screams to be heard if lust should suddenly overcome me.

Once our order had been delivered – coffee for me, a low-cal cola for her – I said, 'All right, what can I do for you?'

She took a deep breath, straightened her back even more and said, 'First, I think I'd better fill you in on the background …'

And the background was this: Greg Harrison had approached Marcus and Lowe early last February suggesting they should publish his memoirs. The initial response was lukewarm. Marcus and Lowe, being hard-headed publishers, had wondered why anybody should give a damn about the memoirs of an unsuccessful movie actor. But then Harrison had promised them the full, unexpurgated version, which would include every intimate detail of his, and other men's, dealings with Virna Newport. At this point M & L began to take notice. It was a known fact that another firm had offered Newport a vast sum of money for her own ghosted autobiography and Marcus and Lowe were quick to realise that, for a far smaller amount, they could scupper their rivals by getting all the juicy stuff from Harrison. A deal was swiftly struck and Jane Baker was appointed as Harrison's editor.

'I imagine,' I said, 'what that meant was that in the end you were actually going to write it?'

She nodded. 'We worked quite closely together for a few weeks but then he got guest spots on a couple of TV shows and had to go to places like Montreal and Chicago. While he was away he would speak everything he could remember into a tape recorder and send me the tapes at the end of the month.'

'What sort of stuff was he delivering?'

'Well ...' There was more hesitation and a bit of frowning before she nodded firmly, as if she had finally convinced herself that what she was about to do was the right thing. 'Perhaps you'd better listen to this. It's a record of the first meeting between Mr Harrison and me and it's what convinced Marcus and Lowe to offer him a contract.'

From her briefcase she took a small tape recorder, set it up and pushed the play button. The tape began with her clear, businesslike voice establishing the date, time and place of the meeting. Then Harrison talked a bit about his own career before saying, 'Okay, okay. What you really want is the dirt on Virna, right? Well, I can dish it, believe me. The thing is ... no, hey, wait up. I'm not going to give you any details now. I mean, why should I give you something for nothing? Let me just tell you this, whet your appetite. First off, Virna's not nearly as rich as everyone believes. Yeah, sure, she has some jewels, a couple of houses, but after her last marriage she walked away with a hell of a lot less than everyone thought.'

A prim interruption here from Jane Baker: 'That's very interesting, Mr Harrison—'

'Greg.'

'Yes. Thank you, er, Greg, but I don't quite see—'

Harrison again, a sour note in his voice: 'Bear with me for a minute. When we were both seventeen we made our first three movies together. It worked for her, not for me. I never really made it as an actor. Sure, I'm well-known but these days I'm well-known for having Virna wear me on her arm like an extra sleeve. Forty years now, give or take, I've been part of her life. Between and during all her husbands, I was there. I know her eating habits, her drinking habits, her drug habits, her sex habits. I know where all the bodies are buried. I know the men she screwed, the boys she screwed, the girls she screwed. I've lived her fucking life as much as she has. God knows, I've hardly had a life of my own or a career of my own. Everything I've done practically has been through her, for her, because of her.'

Baker: 'And, of course, you were married to her.'

Harrison, on an even more sour note: 'Yeah, right. And you know something? The one time I was totally out of touch with her was the eighteen months we were married. I made two movies in Europe, she made one here and another in Japan, and by the time we got together again she'd divorced me.'

Baker: 'Since you've been so close for so long did you never think of writing your memoirs together? After all, it sounds as much your story, a shared story, as hers.'

Harrison: 'You'd think so, wouldn't you? I suggested it to her but Virna's not one for sharing. I don't mean she's all that tight with her money. She's helped me out often enough through the bad times, which have been most of the time. I have to give her that. But when it comes to the big pot, she wants it all for herself. And for her, this book, this unexpurgated, Virna-Newport-tells-all autobiography she's supposed to write is the big pot. That's why I was telling you she's not so rich as people suppose. Way she's set up financially right now the book's the main thing that's going to provide her with a pension to support her old age. And she ain't gonna share it with nobody. When you get right down to it, she's probably the most ruthless, self-centred bitch the world has ever seen.'

Baker: 'Well, yes. From what I've heard of her, I suppose she does rather come across like—'

Harrison: 'Hey, watch it. I won't let anybody talk about her like that. Nobody talks about her like that except me and you know why?'

Baker: 'No.'

Harrison: 'Because I love her.' A pause on the tape, a silence broken only by the sound of someone – presumably Harrison – drinking. Then ...

Baker: 'But nevertheless you're prepared to tell everything you know about Virna Newport, the bad as well as the good?'

Harrison: 'You bet.'

Baker: 'May I ask why?'

Harrison: 'Because, like I said, it's my life as much as hers. Because I'm getting old and I'm up to here in debt. And because, well, because she dumped me and I want to hit her where it hurts, right in the wallet. She's got this toy boy. I ... I didn't think it would last but a couple of weeks ago I tried to do something for her and it didn't work out and she told me it was over between us. For ever. No slow walk into the sunset for her and me. For her, yeah probably, but with someone else beside her, not me. I've never seen her so mad. Icy. So I figured, what the hell – she wants to tell her story, fine, but I'm gonna tell mine first and I'm gonna tell it all. Screw her.'

There was more sound of drinking, then Harrison again: 'So that's the deal. You people get the whole works, nothing held back. But we gotta work fast before Virna gets her book out.'

Baker turned the tape recorder off.

I said, 'Why did you play that to me?'

She took the tape out of the machine and put everything neatly back into her briefcase. 'To establish my bona fides. I thought it was only fair.'

'Uh-huh. And when Harrison started spilling the beans, for publication, did he deliver as promised?'

'Oh, yes. The book would have been a sensation. The woman's sexual habits alone ...' She shuddered in a genteel sort of way. 'But unfortunately he didn't deliver enough. When we were working together I was able to devise a kind of shape for the book but then he had to go away. He sent us tapes he made in March and April, which were fascinating but meandered rather a lot. There was no kind of chronological order in them. After that he wasn't able to do much in May because he was working on a TV show in Chicago, but I know he had nearly finished another tape because he told me so on the phone only a few days ago.'

'And what happened to that?'

She sipped cola through a straw. 'I don't know, Mr Lennox. That's why I approached you. You were the one who found him dead, or dying was it? Anyway, I wondered whether you had noticed a tape recorder in his room. I've tried to contact the policemen dealing with the case but so far without success. So I thought that perhaps you could—'

'Hold on.' I thought back, remembering how I had gently pushed the already open door, gone into the room, seen the body, glanced quickly around and ... 'Yes, there was. There was a tape recorder on the bedside table. One very much like yours. That's what reminded me.'

She nodded. 'Yes, well, we provided him with an identical model.' My news had caused her to brighten considerably. She even offered me a cautious little smile. 'I'll try the police again.'

It was early evening now and if the sun hadn't quite gone over the yardarm in southern California I reckoned it was bound to have done so somewhere in the world. 'May I offer you a drink?' I said. 'A real drink. You know – wine or hard liquor, grown-up stuff.'

She shook her head firmly. 'That's very kind but no thank you.' She fastened her briefcase preparatory to leaving. The little smile had long since vanished and her lips were set once more in a tight, wary line.

I said, 'You don't like men much, do you?'

'If you are talking about men in general, experience has taught me not to, Mr Lennox. But, to pre-empt what I imagine will be your next question, no, I am not a lesbian.'

Actually, that wasn't going to be my next question. It didn't seem to be any of my business. I said, 'Still waiting for Mr Right to come along, eh?'

Her lips curled disdainfully. 'If you wish to put it like that.'

'And when he does come along he won't be a lot like me, will he?'

She stood up, brushing her hand over her hair. 'No, Mr Lennox, he will not. I believe you used to be a prizefighter and I find it impossible to understand how a man of your apparent intelligence could have been involved in anything so barbaric as boxing.'

I shrugged. 'Well, you had to have been there.'

She held out her hand and I took it. She had a good, strong handshake. 'Thank you for your help and please don't get up. I'll ask the girl on reception to get me a cab.'

As she walked away, her stride not exactly mannish but business-like and deliberately unseductive, I called after her. 'Let me know if you manage to find the tape recorder.'

She stopped and glanced back. 'Very well. But why should you be interested?'

I shrugged at her. 'I don't know. I just have this feeling that you're going to be out of luck.'

# 20

LUCY CALLED ABOUT seven o'clock. I'd been trying to reach her ever since Ms Baker had left me but I kept missing her. She asked how I was and I told her that apart from a bump and a cut on the back of a generally tender head I was in terrific form.

'What are you doing tonight?' she asked. 'Do you have a date?' I was pleased to note that her tone suggested I better not have.

'Well, naturally I have a million offers,' I said. 'Us associate producers have starlets climbing all over us. I don't know whether to have three of them come over or, bearing in mind my slightly weakened condition, simply restrict myself to two. The doctor suggested I should cut down.'

'Yeah, yeah,' she said. 'Well, just stay right where you are. See you in an hour.'

In fact it was closer to eight thirty when she turned up and then, dammit, she had Richie Proctor with her. They arrived in a chauffeur-driven limo bearing two bottles of wine and a take-away feast from Greenblatt's, the deli on Sunset. They had cold chicken and pastrami, turkey and shrimp, coleslaw and pickles, potato salad and Russian salad, mustard and mayonnaise and three different kinds of bread.

Lucy swept everything off the table in my sitting-room and laid out the food. 'I brought pastrami because I know you like it,' she said.

'How do you know that?'

'Because you told me. At the studio party, remember? You took a sandwich and said, "Pastrami, I love pastrami." You didn't think I was listening?'

She had greeted me with no more than a peck on the cheek, maybe because Proctor was there. I wanted more. I wanted her, alone. I didn't want Proctor; I didn't even want the food. I wanted to talk to her, to tell her that I wasn't really taking anything for granted but that anything she granted I was ready to take. Proctor, happily ignorant of how unwelcome his presence was, bustled about, uncorking the wine.

'Got to give this stuff a break,' he said, 'let it breathe, flex its muscles.' He held a bottle up to me. 'Ever had this before? Comes straight from Francis Coppola's own vineyard in Napa Valley. Francis sent me a crate of it for my birthday last month. You'll like it, I promise you.'

Just before we sat down to eat Proctor took himself off to the bathroom. I waited till the door closed behind him, then turned to Lucy, my arms outstretched towards her.

'What?' she said.

'Come here. I want to hug you.'

'No way,' she said. 'What makes you think we're on hugging terms already?'

'The way you kissed me in the hospital. I was hoping—'

'That was an act of charity,' she said, 'to save you from Virna. It doesn't give you hugging rights. Besides, Richie will be back any minute.'

'Why did you bring him?'

She shrugged. 'He wanted to come.' She looked at me with amusement. 'I didn't see why he shouldn't. He arranged the car, bought all the food ...'

At which point Proctor returned from the loo, nodded approval at the meal laid out on the table and busied himself with pouring the wine, sniffing and tasting it and making appreciative snuffling sounds. 'Okay, let's eat,' he said.

The food was good; so was the wine. As we ate we talked – first, inevitably, about Harrison's murder and why Darren should have done it. And after that I told them about Ms Baker and the Harrison memoirs, which would now never be finished unless the missing tape turned up. And when we were through with all that we talked about progress on the film which, according to Proctor, was going amazingly well. Of course, they'd only been shooting for a couple of days but already, he said, they were a minute ahead of schedule.

'A whole minute,' I said. 'Fancy that.'

Big mistake. Lucy frowned as if I had disappointed her and Proctor waved his fork and said, 'Listen, my friend, while I tell you something about the movies. If you're making a feature, especially this kind of feature with loads of action and special effects, you're doing very, very well if you get three minutes of usable film in the can each day. Well, so far we're doing that and better, so don't knock it. If we can only carry on this way we'll come in ahead of schedule and under budget.'

I hadn't known any of this stuff and it obviously showed because Lucy said, mischievously, 'Hey, you can't expect too much from these Mafia guys, Richie. What the hell do they know about the movies?'

For a moment Proctor looked embarrassed. 'Shut up, Lucy. I've already apologised for all that. I was hoping Bobby might have forgotten about it.'

'I have,' I said. 'It'll never be mentioned again. But now explain something that's been puzzling me – why are you doing this film? I wouldn't have thought it was your kind of thing at all.'

There was an awkward silence before Proctor grinned ruefully and said, 'Well, if you must know, it's the only solid offer I've had in two years.'

'What? Why? You got an Oscar nomination only, when was it, last year.'

He nodded. 'Yeah, but that film did zilch at the box office and so did the two I made before it and I got an Oscar nomination for one of those as well. Forget any crap about art, Bobby – in Hollywood, movies are a business. If your pictures make money, doesn't matter what they're like, you're the flavour of the month; if they don't, people literally cross the street to avoid saying hello to you. That's happened to me a lot these last two years. In this country I get great reviews. The critics think I'm some arty-farty intellectual European director, but great reviews aren't the same as bums on seats.' He chewed moodily on a pickle. 'Tell you the truth, I'm pretty nearly broke. This film hadn't come along I'd have had to sell my house.'

Lucy looked shocked. 'Richie! I had no idea things were that bad.' He patted her hand and smiled sadly at her.

'I know, love, but it *was* that bad and it doesn't really get much better. I took this picture for not much up front but quite a few points. If *Death's Head* is a hit, I'm laughing; if it bombs I'll be looking for work directing daytime soaps on TV.' He looked across at me and said, 'I thought you'd have known all that, being the associate producer.'

'Yes, well, I'm not exactly your regular, run-of-the-mill associate producer, am I?'

He smiled, more of a grimace really. 'I hate being in this position. I've been going around like I was walking on eggshells, scared of offending anybody in case I got fired.'

Lucy said, leaning back to look at him, 'I should have noticed. I thought it was because things have been going pretty well so far that you weren't as bloody-minded as you usually are on a movie.'

'Yes, well, you can only afford to be bloody-minded when you're confident, not when you're in a position of weakness.'

I poured more wine for all of us. 'Actually, Richie,' I said, 'you're in a much better position than you think. You probably don't know this but, despite what I told him, Bill Charleston went to Agnelli and tried to get you booted off the film but—'

'He what?' Lucy said and sprang up, angrily. 'He actually did that? He actually—'

'Yeah, but it's okay. Agnelli told him to forget it because he knows we got Richie at a bargain price. He also knows that we couldn't get anybody else half as good for twice the money. So the way I see it, Richie, you're in pole position here. Agnelli and I are on your side, which means Carlo Minelli is, too, wherever he may be. Charleston can't hurt you and neither can Virna Newport because she needs the work as much as you do. So if you're happier being bloody-minded on the set, go ahead and be bloody-minded. Only thing is, if you try it with me I'll punch your lights out.'

Proctor raised his glass to me. 'Thanks. I appreciate that.'

Lucy got up and came over to me, giving me the hug I had asked for earlier except that it was just one of those sisterly jobs. It was nice enough, certainly, and I revelled in the feel and smell of her as she wound her arms around me, but a quick squeeze and a kiss on the top of the head were considerably less than I wanted.

That, however, was destined to be my ration for the night. A little later Proctor said, 'I'd better be going. Early start tomorrow. Lucy, will you be okay if I take the car and—'

'I'll come with you,' she said.

'No!' I said. 'No. You don't have to go.'

'Yes, I do. I have an early start tomorrow, too.' She gathered up her handbag and denim jacket and headed for the door.

'Damn,' I said.

'What?'

'You know what.'

She looked me over with that amused smile again. 'Yes, I think I do.' Proctor had gone on ahead and there were just the two of us in the doorway.

'Lucy?'

'Yes?'

'I know I'm making a fool of myself here,' I said, 'and though I don't particularly like that I can live with it if—'

'If what?' She was standing so close it was almost an invitation. Almost, but not quite.

I sighed. 'If I can be sure I'm not totally wasting my time.'

'Well, that's for you to find out, isn't it?' she said and hurried after Proctor.

I followed, wanting to say more, not wanting the evening to end on this frustratingly enigmatic note. But when she caught up with the director she slipped her arm through his, turned, smiled and waved goodbye and didn't look back as they walked towards the car park.

I watched them out of sight, sighed again, and began retracing my steps. The path led me past Virna Newport's bungalow, which was of precious little interest to me right then except that just before I got there the door opened and Newport stepped onto the porch. She looked around very carefully, then turned and beckoned to somebody inside.

And Darren came out to join her.

# 21

FOR A MOMENT I was too surprised to move, just stood there watching as he said something to her and moved forward as if to kiss her. She pushed him away, none too gently; he hesitated a moment and then he was gone, into the darkness on the other side of the bungalow.

I couldn't see which direction he had taken but instinctively I turned and ran back towards the car park. There was no sign of him, no sign of anybody except a couple of the yellow-jacketed attendants. Nobody had driven in or out, they said, since I was last there waving goodbye to Lucy and Proctor. I hung around for a few minutes, then went to look for Darren in the hotel grounds and, wouldn't you know it, I'd only gone about fifty yards when I heard a car start up. I raced back in time to catch a glimpse of him, lit briefly by one of the lamps around the car park, at the wheel of an open black Porsche. If he saw me he gave no sign.

Immediate pursuit wasn't even an option because my own car keys were in my room. I started back in that direction, changed my mind and knocked on Virna Newport's door. She opened it almost immediately.

'Goddamn it, what is it *now*?' she said irritably, and then, 'Oh, it's you.' She wasn't pleased to see me.

I said, 'What was Darren doing here?'

Her reactions were quick, I had to give her that. The look of consternation in the famous green eyes came and went so fast that I could almost have imagined it. 'Darren?' she said. 'You mean Darren Carmody?' The note of incredulity in her voice would alone have been enough to get her into acting school. I was almost convinced myself. 'You can't be serious.'

I gave her a gentle round of applause. 'Very good, Virna. Now, what was he doing here? I saw him come out, I saw him drive away.'

She gave me another bit of her repertoire, the trick where she draws herself up to her full height and looks the offending male full in the eyes with icy dignity. It's one of her specialities; you've seen her do it in a dozen films. 'I'm afraid you're mistaken,' she said. 'Nobody has been here all night. And now if you will forgive me ...' She started closing the door but I leant one hand on it and pushed.

'Don't be stupid, Virna. What are you protecting him for?'

She said, 'I don't like you, Mr Lennox. You made a fool of me at the hospital today, so if you don't get off my porch right now I'll call security and accuse you of sexual harassment. Okay?'

She started closing the door again and this time I let her do it. I'd no more think of sexually harassing Virna Newport than I would Baroness Thatcher, but if push came to shove, her word against mine, who would believe me? And if I called the police to tell them Darren had been around, her word against mine again, who would believe me? The smart thing to do, I told myself, was go to bed and forget it.

I went back to my room, put on a coat, picked up my car keys and returned to the parking lot. One of the Mexican yellow jackets said, 'Some guy, he drive off soon after jou go. Black Porsche, right? Thees the guy jou lookin' for?'

'Which way did he go, did you notice?'

'East on Sunset, goin' fast.'

I gave him five dollars, climbed into my Mazda and drove away, turning east onto Sunset. Though it was midnight there was quite a lot of traffic about but then there usually is. Hollywood and Beverly Hills are notoriously early-to-bed towns but their roads are busy twenty-four hours a day. Insomniacs perhaps, people passing through, or bloody-minded non-conformists who were damned if they were going to get an early night just because Bruce Willis and Arnold Schwarzenegger did. I had a mental image of such non-conformists driving aimlessly around and sneering at the idea of so-called tough guys who were tucked up in bed with a mug of cocoa by ten o'clock every night.

By the time I reached Mulholland, however, the traffic had thinned considerably. There was very little street lighting up here and most of the illumination came from the big movie-star estates, which even so looked unapproachable and unwelcoming. I imagined Jack Nicholson in one of them, doing whatever Jack Nicholson did at midnight, and the now gargantuan Marlon Brando in another, probably tucking into a late night snack of a dozen hamburgers.

There was a fair amount of toing and froing at Lou's, though not as much as there had been the first time I was there. This, presumably, was just a business as usual, as opposed to a party, night. I drove into the entrance and was stopped by the security man on the gate.

'Help you, sir?'

'Yes, I'd like to see Lou.'

'She expecting you, sir? I ask because I don't think we know you.'

'No, she's not expecting me. Just call her and tell her Bobby Lennox would like to talk to her. It's very important. I simply have to get in there.'

'Yeah?' He looked down at me curiously, hugging his clipboard. 'I sympathise with you, sir. There are times all of us think what we need most in the world is a piece of ass but, sir—'

'I'm not talking sex here! Listen, I didn't come to this brothel to argue with the bouncer. I want to talk to the madam. So call her.'

His veneer of politeness, which had never been any thicker than the facing on a piece of repro furniture, now vanished completely. 'Get outa here, buster, before I stuff you up the exhaust pipe of your little toy car.'

I took a couple of deep breaths while I controlled my impulse to leap out of the driving seat and jab him half a dozen times on the nose. 'Look, I'm going to give you one more chance to save your job. Call Lou and tell her Bobby Lennox is here, the same Bobby Lennox who came a couple of nights ago with Rico Agnelli. Tell her I very much want to talk to her. Do you think you can manage that?'

It was Agnelli's name that did the trick. I couldn't imagine why I hadn't mentioned it in the first place because it worked wonders. The security man said, 'You a friend of Mr Agnelli? Why didn't you say so? Hold on a minute.'

He stepped away from the car, murmured into his walkie-talkie and waved me through. 'Have a nice night, Mr Lennox.' The politeness was back but, I don't know, I didn't get the impression that we could ever really become bosom friends.

Lou was waiting for me at the door. 'Nice to see you again, Mr Lennox. I understand from Hughie down at the gate that you're really eager for some action. I must say I'm a little surprised. You didn't strike me as being that impetuous.' She tucked her arm into mine and led me into the house. There weren't as many girls as there had been on my previous visit but those who were there were just as gorgeous and the men around them looked exactly like the earlier lot, giving the curious impression that they had been there all the time.

I said, 'Sorry, Lou, but I'm not here as a customer.'

'Client, please,' she said, with a little moue of distaste.

'Okay, but I'm not here as a client either. I want to talk to Darren.'

She took her arm away and stepped back, her expression both cold and wary. 'I'm sorry but I don't know what you mean. There's nobody called Darren here.'

'Oh, I think there is, Lou. He was here the other night, wasn't he? And I saw him again, about an hour ago, talking to Virna Newport at the Bel Air Riviera. My bet is that this is where he came after that.'

'I'm afraid you're mistaken, Mr Lennox. I don't know anyone called Darren.'

I took another of my deep breaths, not to control anger this time but to sort out my thoughts. 'Lou, I … Well, look, I'll be straight with you: I admit I'm still mad at him for cracking me on the head—'

'He did not!' Then she blushed and bit her lip, angry at herself.

I raised an eyebrow, quizzically I like to think. 'Yes, well, be that as it may. What I want you to understand is that I have no intention of turning him in. I think he should do that himself. I don't want to get involved with the local law any more than I imagine you do. But I do want to talk to Darren.'

She stared into my face for what seemed like a long time and then shook her head. 'No.'

I stared back at her, nodding slowly. 'In that case all I can do is play the honest citizen and make an anonymous call to the LAPD, tell them I saw Darren here this evening.' As the beginnings of a confident smile started on her lips, I added, 'No, wait a minute. A couple of days ago all you'd have had to do was phone Carlo Minelli and the police would have sat on their hands. But Carlo's not around any more, remember? And I seriously doubt whether Rico has the kind of clout Carlo does. So if I made that call the very best that could happen to you is that the cops would be crawling all over the place, taking names and maybe arresting people. Do you want that?'

With a small movement of her head she gestured back towards the bouncers at the door. 'Those guys could make sure you never got anywhere near a telephone, Mr Lennox.'

'True. But as soon as one of them takes a single step in my direction I'm going to start screaming at your girls and clients over there. I'll scream that I saw Darren in this house tonight. I'll scream my name as well. I'll scream my local address and telephone number. I'll scream Virna Newport's name and the studio's name and—'

'All right.' She cut me off with an impatient gesture of both hands. 'You've made your point.'

I said, earnestly, 'Trust me, Lou. I mean you no harm, I promise. I mean Darren no harm. I simply want to talk to him. I have a large bump on the back of my head that gives me a personal interest in this matter. I just want to know why he did what he did and what, if anything, he did with the tape recorder—'

'What?' She looked puzzled.

'Never mind. I'll ask him.' I stopped and waited while she made her decision. She looked around at her whores, her whatevers, and their johns, at the bouncers on the door, and then she looked back at me and nodded.

'Very well. Come with me.'

She led me around the big, white room, into the hallway at the back, up a sweeping staircase and along a wide corridor. As we approached the room at the end she called out, 'Darren, it's me. I've brought someone to see you. It's okay, honey, don't get nervous.'

There was no answer from inside the room but she didn't seem to expect any. She rapped on the door with an elaborate pattern of knocks, a code of some kind, and after a moment, a key was turned on the inside and the door was drawn open. She gestured to me to follow her and went in.

It was an office-cum-study, hers I supposed, and very businesslike. A big desk with a computer, a few upright chairs and a sofa. Three or four pictures on the walls, bookshelves containing, as far as I could tell with one quick glance, several tomes on tax law. There was no sign of Darren but that was because he'd been behind the door which, once Lou and I were in the middle of the room, he closed and locked.

I turned to look at him. He had a gun in his hand and he was aiming it at me. There were dark smudges under his eyes and his usually immaculate clothes were crumpled and none too clean. He said, a note of mingled incredulity and despair in his voice, 'Mom, what did you bring him here for?'

She said, 'Darling, there was nothing I could do. He already knew you were here. But he won't hurt you, I promise.'

'The fuck he won't. Don't you understand? This is the guy who turned Virna against me. He's the reason I'm in all this shit.'

I said, 'No, I'm not. I have no interest in Virna Newport. None. And I'm not helping the police either. They'll find you eventually, we all know that. They don't need my help. I just want to know what it's all about. Why you killed Harrison and whether you took the tape recorder and why and—'

Darren said, 'I'm getting outa here. Mom, I don't want to talk to this guy. I don't know where the fuck he's coming from anyway. I'm leaving.'

'Darren, please!' Lou said, wailed really, and stumbled towards him. He grabbed her round the waist with one hand while, with the other, he kept the gun on me.

'Mom, listen to me. I want you to take this gun. I want you to point it at him for ten, fifteen minutes after I leave the room. You understand? If he tries to follow me, shoot him. Will you do that, Mom?'

She said, 'Darren, oh, Darren please, maybe you should talk to him. Maybe he can help you—'

'No way, Mom, no way. Now, please, will you do as I ask?'

She gave a little moan of despair, then nodded. He handed her the gun. 'Two hands, Mom, hold it with two hands. He makes one suspicious move, shoot him, doesn't matter where, anywhere you can hit.'

And then he was gone and the door had closed behind him. I made one tentative move and Lou said, 'Don't. I will shoot you if I have to.' Her voice was unsteady but her aim wasn't.

'I know,' I said and sat down, slowly and carefully, in one of the upright chairs. She moved away, still pointing the gun at me, until her back was against the door. The grief and anxiety in her face made her seem a lot older than she had before.

'Darren and Mom, eh?' I said. 'Well, well. That explains a lot.' I crossed one leg over the other and she jerked the gun at me.

'Keep still. I know how to use a gun. I live in California, for Chrissake. Every woman in California knows how to use a gun. It's called survival. I'll try not to kill you but if you attempt to go after Darren I'll shoot you someplace.'

I held up my hands. 'I believe you,' I said. There was no point in going after Darren anyway. Already he had too much of a start on me. 'So he's your son. Do many people know that?'

She shook her head. 'Hardly anyone. He wants to be an actor, a movie star, and he could do it, too. He's handsome enough, talented enough but I … we … I thought it wouldn't exactly help him if people knew his mother ran a whorehouse.'

'A MAW house,' I said, seeking to ingratiate myself.

She made an impatient gesture with the gun. 'The hell with that. Whatever these girls choose to call themselves they're still whores and this is a whorehouse. It's no kind of starting place for a boy who could be the new James Dean.'

'James Dean was gay,' I said. 'Is Darren—'

'No!' There was vehemence in her voice. 'Don't look at me like that.'

I'd had no idea I was looking at her in any particular way. All I was trying to do was look harmless and unthreatening. But she said, 'People like you, you think that because I provide the girls and you only use them I must be dirtier than you. You think I like what I do? I do it because there's money in it and I need money to give Darren his chance in life. He's all I've got.'

'Okay, okay.' I made placatory gestures with my hands. 'I understand that. I sympathise. I come from poverty, too. But what I don't understand is what turned Darren into a killer.'

'He's not a killer,' she said. 'He's not a killer. He's not, he's not.'

And suddenly she began to weep, so helplessly that she slid down the door until she was sitting on the floor, her hands over her face, the gun abandoned beside her.

I went over and held her, making soothing noises as she buried her face in my shoulder. And we were still sitting like that, gently rocking back and forth, when we heard the police sirens.

# 22

IN FACT, THERE was just the one siren, cut off very quickly, but not before it was obvious that the car was coming in this direction. It sounded to me like a warning rather than an announcement that a bunch of gung-ho cops was about to raid a den of vice. So whether Minelli was around or not, it seemed that there was still at least one person in the LAPD who, for whatever reasons, had Lou's interests at heart.

'I didn't tip them off,' I said.

'I didn't think you did.'

'So what happens now?'

She stood up, smoothed her dress and did a quick repair job on her make-up. 'It'll be okay. We have enough time. My guys know what to do.'

I hoped she was right because being arrested in a police raid on a whorehouse and turning up in court the next morning to pay a fine or whatever would decidedly not be good for my street cred. As for how Lucy would react I didn't even like to think.

'Come on,' Lou said. 'Don't worry.' She took a deep breath, closed her eyes for a moment and from somewhere summoned up a calm, confident smile. I had to hand it to her. This was a very worried woman but to look at her now you wouldn't think so. She was still a little pale but otherwise she was the epitome of the gracious hostess.

The police, a dozen of them, were already at the door by the time we got downstairs. Three cars, rooflights flashing, were drawn up at the foot of the stairs leading to the porch. The cop in charge, a trim, elegantly dressed black man, stood at the entrance to the big salon, scowling at the sight which presented itself to him.

Thirty or forty people, roughly equal quantities of men and women, stared back at him in polite surprise. Soft music was playing in the background and a few couples stood in the middle of the room as if they had been interrupted while dancing. Others sat around in pairs or small groups with drinks in their hands. Bottles, glasses and trays of canapés and hors d'oeuvres were arranged on half a dozen tables. I attached myself unobtrusively to a band of four or five men standing around a table and tried to be invisible, hoping the black cop wouldn't notice me.

Lou glided elegantly up to the assembled law. 'Lieutenant Brown, what a surprise. Is there a problem?'

'What's going on here, Lou?' Harry Brown said. He hadn't changed much since I last saw him; still tall and lean and quietly sure of himself. If he looked rather more prosperous than the average cop it was because, as I happened to know, he had done favours for people like Carlo Minelli.

She shrugged. 'As you can see, it's just a private party.'

He did some more scowling. 'Yeah, it is now.' He glanced back over his shoulder and jabbed a forefinger at one of the cops behind him. 'Casey, go wait in the car. I'm gonna have your ass for this.'

Casey, a balding man with a heavy Irish face, gave him a look of offended innocence. 'What did I do, lieutenant? I didn't hit the siren on purpose. It was an accident. Ask any of the guys.'

'Go wait in the fuckin' car. Now.' He turned back to Lou. 'Who are all these people?'

'Friends. Friends of friends. Just my guests.'

'Right. And if I looked upstairs this minute I wouldn't find any of your "friends" snorting coke or screwing each other's brains out in the bedrooms, would I?'

'Certainly not, lieutenant.'

He shook his head slowly. 'Yeah, well, this isn't a vice raid anyway. We have reason to believe Darren Carmody is in this house.'

136

Lou said, sounding puzzled, 'Darren who?'

'Carmody, the guy who killed Greg Harrison. Come on, Lou, you know who I mean. His mug shot's been on all the TV stations every hour on the hour.'

'Well, you are quite wrong, lieutenant. There's no such person here. But if you don't believe me please feel free to take a look, anywhere in the house or grounds.'

Harry Brown reached behind him and scratched absent-mindedly at his left buttock. 'Yeah, well, since we're here ...' To the men behind him he said, 'Okay, go look for him.'

The cops fanned out to search the house. Brown said, 'They're not going to find him, are they?'

'Of course not.'

'No. Tell you the truth, Lou, I never thought they would. It sounded crazy to me from the start. Anonymous tip-off, killer hiding out in a well-protected whorehouse. Didn't sound like your kind of scene. But, Jesus, I'd have loved to come in here and caught your "friends" with their dicks in places they shouldn't have been. Oh, well, guess I better go join the search party.' He gave the assembled company another scowl, then did a double take. A slow grin spread across his face.

'Well, well,' he said. 'Bobby Lennox, what are you doing here?'

Reluctantly I walked over to him. 'Hello, Harry.'

Lou said, surprised, 'You know each other?'

Harry nodded. His grin had taken an ironic twist now. 'Oh, sure, we kinda helped each other out a couple years back. That right, Bobby?'

'Pretty well, I suppose.' It had been a curious business that led to a lot of death and though Harry Brown had cleared the matter up the purist might have thought his methods left much to be desired. In particular his habit of reserving his best police work for the highest private bidder, Carlo Minelli for example, rather than the LAPD might well have been considered unorthodox.

He gave me the ironic grin again. 'So what are you doing here, kid? I wouldn't have figured you as a guy who got his kicks in whorehouses. I'd have ... Aha! Of course. Carlo – he's the connection, right? You know Carlo, Carlo knows Lou and he sent you here.' Then the grin vanished to be replaced by a hard, thoughtful look. 'Well, now, that's quite a coincidence we have here. Darren whacks Harrison, you find the body, Darren hits you on the head and the very night we get a tip that Carmody is hiding out in a whorehouse who should be there but you. You care to have a shot at explaining that?'

I said, 'I don't know who hit me, I don't know where Darren Carmody is, I don't know who gave you what tip-off. But, yes, Carlo introduced me to Lou and I'm here as a guest of hers. That's it, end of story.'

He kept the hard, thoughtful look on me. 'Why do you suppose it is, Bobby, that every time you come to LA shit happens?'

'I dunno. Nature of the city perhaps.'

'Yeah, maybe. Or maybe not.'

The other cops started drifting back into the room, shrugging resignedly. 'Waste of time, loot,' one of them said. 'There's nothing here.'

Harry Brown said, 'Okay, round 'em up and head 'em out.' To me he said, 'You gonna be around a while, Bobby? If so I'll know where to find you. Meanwhile, I guess you know where to find me. Anything you feel you want to tell me, just give me a call. Any time.'

'I'll do that.'

'Good.' He went over to join the other cops assembled by the door. Lou followed and offered them drinks but Harry Brown refused on behalf of them all. His men looked disappointed; they looked as if they would have been perfectly happy to stay on and sample the booze and maybe a few of the girls as well.

One of them sidled up to Lou as Brown stamped off to his car. 'Okay if I come back later, join the party? I mean, everything would be on the house, right, this being a private function and all?'

Lou smiled sweetly. 'I'm so sorry. Everyone was just about to go home when you boys turned up.'

'Yeah, right, just my friggin' luck. Another time maybe?'

'Maybe.'

Everyone gave the police a good twenty minutes to get clear of the area and then began to pair off and drift away. A little thing like a police raid wasn't going to keep these people from the serious business of the night.

Lou said, 'That Lieutenant Brown, is he a friend of yours?'

'I wouldn't say that but I think we understand each other.'

'He's a useful man to know.'

'So I've discovered.'

She slipped her arm through mine and walked me to the door. 'Thank you for not telling him Darren was here tonight.'

'Yeah, well, maybe that was a mistake. The longer Darren's a fugitive the worse it's going to be for him. He really ought to turn himself in, you know.'

Lou said, 'Why? He didn't do it. Bobby, I know he didn't do it. He's my son.'

'Of course he is. But look at it this way: somebody's son did it.'

Rico Agnelli woke me at ten that morning. From the sharp way he cut through my drowsy burbling as I clutched the receiver under my chin I gathered the phone must have been ringing for some time.

'You always sleep this late?'

'I had a heavy night.'

'Well, now you got a heavy day coming up. Get your ass to the studio. Fast. Tony Flo wants to see us.'

'Trouble?'

'You could say that.'

'What sort of—'

'You'll find out soon enough. Just get here.'

I was puzzled. Within the Agnelli–Flo relationship it was very clear who had the clout and it wasn't Tony Flo. And yet Agnelli had seemed worried.

I shaved, showered and dressed and persuaded one of the waitresses in the restaurant to let me have a large coffee to go. I was still sipping it when I walked into Agnelli's office. It didn't make him happy.

'You stopped for coffee? You lie in bed half the day and then you stop for coffee?'

'I needed it. It gives me a kick-start in the morning.'

'Well, get rid of it.' He took the polystyrene mug from my hand and threw it in his waste basket. 'Come on.'

I followed him obediently out of the room. He said, 'That stuff kills you, you know.'

'Is there anything that doesn't? Lead me to it and I'll drink that instead. Rico, what is all this about?'

'You'll see.' He led the way up the stairs to Tony Flo's office, a vast, almost palatial spread that made mine look like a broom cupboard. Flo was sitting behind an enormous glass-topped desk, or rather he was hunched over it in a posture that exuded anxiety. Opposite him, in a leather armchair, sat a tall, slender man of about sixty. What he exuded from the top of his beautifully coiffed silver hair to his glossy hand-made shoes was wealth and power. He was tapping his fingers impatiently on the glass top. As Agnelli and I came in Flo jumped up, releasing some of his tension on us.

'Jesus, you guys took your sweet time.'

'My fault,' I said. 'I stopped for coffee.' Flo's eyes widened as if he couldn't believe what he was hearing. Beside me Agnelli took in a sharp, angry breath.

The silver-haired man turned towards me. He didn't get up. 'Him I know,' he said, pointing at Agnelli. 'So you must be Lennox.'

'That's right. And you are?'

Again that look of disbelief from Tony Flo. 'This is Mr Baldock,' he said. 'Charles Baldock? He owns the studio.' There was a note almost of reverence in his voice. In Hollywood people who actually own movie studios, as opposed to merely running them, are known to walk on water.

I looked at Baldock with some interest. I'd read a piece about him in the *New York Times* after I'd accepted Donovan's proposal and was doing a little research into the people and the studio with whom I was about to be associated. According to the *Times* Baldock had made his money from supermarkets, real estate and asset-stripping. Just how much money nobody quite knew because he had covered his tracks well. But he was assumed to be seriously rich since only a seriously rich man could afford to buy a film studio. That he had done so had rather surprised Wall Street. Hitherto he had kept himself pretty much in the background, quietly amassing money, and his move to centre stage was even more surprising than Ross Perot's had been in politics. But suddenly Baldock had begun to live a high-profile existence, giving and attending the swankiest parties, getting himself invited to the White House and turning up at first nights with a succession of female movie icons on his arm. It was as if, after labouring rewardingly but anonymously for so many years, he had decided to burst out of the financial closet, declaring that he had arrived, that he was somebody, that he was hungry for his share of the limelight. In America there's no better way to do that than through some form of show business.

Now he said, 'As of thirty minutes ago, which is when you were told to get here, you two are off the movie.' He looked up at me. 'You've just had your last coffee break on my time.'

Agnelli said, 'You can't do this.' Unlike me he didn't seem at all surprised by Baldock's announcement, but then I supposed Tony Flo had already warned him.

Baldock crossed one well-trousered leg over the other, taking care not to disturb the almost lethally sharp creases. 'I've just done it. I won't have a bunch of Mafiosi running around in my studio.' For a moment I was a little disappointed that he said 'Mafiosi' instead of 'guinea hoods' but perhaps he didn't remember *The Godfather* as clearly as I did.

Agnelli said, 'Carlo Minelli is not going to like this.'

Tony Flo, leaning on his desk top and looking more anxious than ever, said, 'That's what I was trying to explain. That's what I told you, Char ... Mr Baldock.'

Baldock waved both arguments aside. 'Minelli is history. The FBI has him by the nuts, we all know that.'

'So how do I fit into this?' I asked. 'I don't work for Minelli. I don't have anything to do with the Mafia.'

He grinned at me, a nasty little grin. 'Really? What about this guy you do work for, this Donovan? You telling me he has nothing to do with the Mafia either?'

Agnelli again. 'Shut up, Bobby. Let me handle this.' To Baldock he said, 'It wasn't for Minelli, this studio would have gone down the toilet two years ago. You still owe him.'

'I told him that, too, Rico,' Flo said, eagerly. 'That business with the rent boy, Mr Baldock? You remember how Carlo fixed that little problem for us?'

Baldock said, frowning, 'I'm becoming seriously unhappy with your attitude here, Tony. What I think you should remember is that I employ you to run this place for me, not to act as a mouthpiece for the mob. You don't want the job I can get someone else before lunchtime.' He kept the frown going until Tony Flo had subsided slowly into his chair. Then he said, 'Any debt I owed Minelli was paid in full when I agreed to finance this movie for him.'

'I don't think so,' Agnelli said. 'Carlo was looking forward to a long and mutually profitable association with this studio.'

Baldock crossed his legs the other way. The creases were still looking great. 'You think I don't know that? You think I don't know that's why he assigned you to the movie, so you could learn the business from the inside? I don't want Carlo Minelli as a partner. I never wanted Carlo Minelli as a partner and as things have turned out there's no way I even need Carlo Minelli as a partner. If he shows his face in this town – in this country – again, he's going down for murder. Carlo Minelli? Who the hell's Carlo Minelli?'

There was a lengthy silence, during which Baldock permitted himself a brief smile of triumph. Then Agnelli said, 'Okay, let's assume you're right. Let's assume Minelli's out of the picture. Do you really think nobody's going to take his place?'

Baldock shook his head. 'Of course not. But whoever the new guy is, I can keep him out of here. Any arrangement I had wasn't with the mob, it was with Minelli and only Minelli and whatever that arrangement was it didn't include him taking over my studio. If I'd known from the start that he was placing his own men on the movie I'd have put a block on it. But I didn't know. I was too busy, I guess, to be paying full attention.' He glared bitterly at Tony Flo. 'And people who should have been giving me information weren't doing it.'

Flo rubbed a hand agitatedly across his forehead. Baldock noted his worry with satisfaction and said, 'It could have been a bad situation but with Minelli and you two out of the way the danger's over. As of now, this studio starts again – clean.'

Agnelli took a deep, slow breath. We were standing there, he and I, like a couple of menials who had just been given the old heave-ho, which, I suppose, is precisely how Baldock thought of us. 'All right, I hear what you're saying,' Agnelli said. 'But here's something you should bear in mind: right now, and wherever he is, Minelli is still in charge. His instructions are the ones I follow, not yours. If you fire Bobby and me your movie could run into very serious union problems.'

Baldock was ready for that. He just shrugged. 'Fine. That happens, I close the picture down.'

Tony Flo said, 'Jesus, you can't do that. We'd have to pay everybody off. People will sue us. We'd lose millions.'

'So would Minelli.' Baldock glanced at me. 'And so would your boss. Would they be happy about that? I don't think so. Listen to me all of you, listen carefully: here's the deal – either Agnelli and Lennox walk away quietly and keep the unions off my back or the movie's dead, whatever the cost.' He shrugged. 'If I keep it going with you people out of the way, Bill Charleston can run the production on his own. If he needs help we'll find him some. One thing he certainly doesn't need and I don't need is you two guys. You're about as much use as a wet fart anyway.'

Tony Flo was holding his head in both hands. He had slumped so far down over his desk that his nose was only a few inches from the glass top. Agnelli stared thoughtfully at the ceiling and lit a cigarette.

'Put that out,' Baldock said sharply. 'I don't like people to smoke in my presence.'

'Well, gee,' Agnelli said, taking a deep drag, 'I'm all cut up about what you like and don't like, Charlie.' He flicked ash on the carpet, took another pull on his cigarette and nodded. 'Okay, we do what you say – for the moment. But if you think this is over you're making a very big mistake, my friend.'

Baldock smiled contemptuously. 'Are you threatening me?'

'No,' Agnelli said. 'I'm just telling it like it is.' He stubbed the cigarette out on the desk right in front of Baldock, who started back with a little grunt of disgust. 'See you around, Charlie. You too, Tony. Bobby, come on, let's go.'

I followed him out of the room, probably looking as sheepish as I felt. It had all happened too fast, too unexpectedly for me. I wondered how Donovan would take the news and wondered, too, whether Minelli's plan to use *Death's Head Dangling* as a way to muscle in on the studio itself had also included him. If it had, Donovan was going to be spitting mad.

'What do you make of all that?' I asked.

Agnelli shrugged. 'I think, unless something happens fast, Tony Flo ain't gonna last the reel. There'll be a new head of production in there by Monday. Come on, I'll buy you a drink.'

We left the studio and walked to the bar across the street, Agnelli looking a great deal calmer than I felt.

'You knew that was going to happen, didn't you?' I said.

'Pretty well. Something like that anyway, though maybe not quite like that.' He ordered drinks from the pretty waitress, who was on duty for the lunchtime crowd. 'That Baldock is a piece of work, isn't he? Ballsy bastard, you have to give him that.'

'I'm not going to give him anything. I've nothing left to give. He's taken it all. What do we do now?'

The drinks arrived, a Mexican beer for me, a dry martini for Agnelli. He took the olive out of his glass and chewed it, looking at me thoughtfully. 'What was that heavy night you had, the reason you slept late? Somebody nice, was she?'

I said, impatiently, 'Never mind about that now. We've got more important things—'

'No, tell me. I'd like to know.' He sipped his drink, smiling at me over the edge of the glass. It occurred to me that if he could be as cool as this at a time like this he would make either a very valuable friend or a particularly unpleasant enemy. Maybe both.

'Tell me,' he said again.

In fact, the events of the morning had pretty well pushed last night out of my mind but now it all came back to me and, rather to my surprise, I found I was quite eager to share my knowledge with him, with anyone really.

Agnelli listened thoughtfully, nodding seriously when I told him about recognising and following Darren and chuckling over my run-in with Virna and the reaction of the police lieutenant when he found a 'private party' in progress. I didn't tell him that I knew the police lieutenant; explaining how would have been just too complicated.

When I'd finished, he said, 'So Darren is Lou's boy? Well, well, that's something I didn't know. And he says he didn't kill Harrison?'

'I didn't ask him. I didn't get the chance. But Lou says he didn't do it.'

'Yeah, right, well she's his momma. What do you expect her to say?' He finished his drink and signalled for a refill. 'What are you gonna do now, Bobby?'

'About Darren? Nothing. It's police business, not mine. Come to think of it, it always was police business, I suppose. I was an idiot to go after him last night.' The waitress came back with Agnelli's second martini and another beer, which I didn't want, for me. I waited until she had gone and then, 'Rico, forget last night. Darren is somebody else's problem. We have more urgent things to discuss – like, what do we do now?'

Agnelli swallowed half his drink, sighed contentedly and lit a cigarette. 'What do we do now? Well, unless you got a better idea, I think what we do now is get Carlo Minelli back.'

# 23

BACK AT THE hotel there was a message for me from Donovan. I went to one of the pay phones in the hotel foyer and called him.

'Where you speaking from?'

I told him and gave him the number.

'Good boy. Stay there. I'll call you back in five minutes.'

I stayed by the phone until he rang, watching a couple of elderly millionaires going into lunch, each with a young, long-stemmed Californian blonde on his arm. In this town money could buy you anything and anyone. For a moment I felt like asking the two old goats where they had bought their companions but then I realised I probably knew the answer already. The chances were they'd been shopping at Lou's.

When Donovan came on the line he said, 'All right, Bob, long as nobody's eavesdropping at your end this line's safe so tell me everything – like what's been going on out there? I mean, Carlo on the run, stupid bloody actors getting themselves murdered, you in hospital with a broken head. Papers over here are full of it. It sounds bad.'

'It gets worse,' I said. 'I've just been fired.' I took him through the events of the last few days and when I'd finished I could hear him sucking his teeth reflectively at the other end.

'Dear, oh dear,' he said. 'You've really ballsed this up, haven't you? Reckon I should come over, sort things out?'

'No. You don't know the scene here, you don't know the people. You'd only get in the way and someone like you charging around looking for trouble is just what we don't need right now. Anyway, what do you mean – I've ballsed it up? What could I have done to make anything diff—?'

'Never mind that now,' he said, impatiently. 'You know what really burns me up? That fucking, devious Carlo. He never said a word to me about moving in on the whole studio. How was he planning to do that?'

'No idea. It makes sense, though, when you think about it, for a man with money to launder.'

'Yeah, right.' There was a pause while Donovan did a bit of thinking. 'You say Agnelli's planning to bring Carlo back. How? You reckon Carlo might give himself up, cop a plea or something? You know, plead guilty to a misdemeanour instead of murder and do six months inside?'

'Shouldn't think so,' I said, 'though after the O.J. Simpson trial I wouldn't be surprised at anything that happened in a Los Angeles court. But, no, I fancy Rico's got something else in mind.'

'Yes, well, keep me posted.'

'You want me to hang on here then? I mean, I'm probably banned from the set and the studio by now but you still want me to stick around?'

'Of course I bloody do. I want you to keep close to Agnelli, find out what he knows.' He hesitated, then, 'Mind how you go, Bob, take care of yourself.'

I was touched at his concern for my well-being. Coming from Donovan this was almost a declaration of affection. I would have thanked him for it but he'd already hung up.

By the time I returned to my room there was another message waiting for me, this time from Jane Baker, the girl from the late Greg Harrison's publishers.

I called her. She said, 'I just thought you would like to know, Mr Lennox, that the police say they found no tapes, no tape recorder, nothing in Greg's room. Interesting, don't you think?'

'That's the end of the Harrison book then, is it?'

'I'm afraid so. Unless, of course, when the police finally track down this Darren person they find he still has the tapes with him.'

'I wouldn't bet on that,' I said.

'Curiously enough, Mr Lennox, neither would I.' There was a kind of thoughtful silence between us. Then she said, 'Is Virna Newport a particular friend of yours?'

'Actually, she's no kind of friend at all. You, of course, will find this almost impossible to believe but I really don't think she even likes me.'

She laughed, more of a snort really. 'We women are strange creatures, aren't we? But has it occurred to you that with Greg dead and the tapes gone, the only person who really benefits is the ultra-glamorous Ms Newport?'

'The thought had crossed my mind.'

'Then I hope she burns in hell,' she said. 'I hope she fries alongside her friend Darren.' And she hung up even more abruptly than Donovan had done. She had a point, too, I thought: that Darren had killed Harrison not out of jealousy but at Virna's bidding, to get rid of the rival autobiography that would knock the sails (or sales) out of hers.

I'd hardly put the phone down before it rang again. Well, that's the way it goes. Some of us are more or less permanently in demand. It's a matter of personality, I suppose, charisma even.

This time it was Lucy on the line. 'Do you know what day it is?'

'Yes,' I said, 'it's Saturday. Is it a particularly significant Saturday – your eighty-fifth birthday or something? I only ask because unless you're counting days instead of weeks even, I don't think you and I are celebrating an anniversary or anything, are we?'

She gave a dramatic, exaggerated sigh. 'Listen up, lover-boy: it's Saturday, right, the end of the week, right? And tonight, on account of we're not shooting tomorrow, Richie goes up to Montana to do some location scouting and he's asked me to house-sit for him. Now bearing in mind our conversation last night I wondered if you'd like to come and sit with me.'

I didn't hesitate. 'You're on,' I said.

'No, wait. What I had in mind was that we could spend a little time together, get to know each other better. Nothing more.' She paused, gathering her thoughts together. 'I like you, Bobby, I really do. But our relationship, if that's what it is, seems to have got off to an overheated start. I mean, the way we met – taking Richie home drunk and comatose. And then all that stuff in the hospital. It was like circumstances took control and maybe what we need is a chance to stand back and just kind of look each other over.' She stopped. 'Hello?'

'I'm still here,' I said.

'And?'

'You're still on. For the house-sitting. On whatever terms you like.'

'Thank you,' she said. Then, 'We'll be wrapping early today so do you want to come out to the set this afternoon and then, when we break, you and I can go off together?'

'That'll be okay, will it – me turning up at the set, I mean?'

'What are you talking about?' she said, puzzled. 'You're the so-called associate producer, aren't you? Why shouldn't you visit the set?'

'No reason.' I said, hastily. 'No reason at all.' Clearly the news that Agnelli and I had been given the boot had not yet filtered through to the production unit. Why should that be? Three hours had gone by since the meeting with Baldock – ample time for Tony Flo to spread the word. In a community as tight-knit as a film crew all it would have taken was one phone call and word of mouth but apparently that phone call hadn't been made. Curious.

After our talk in the bar Agnelli and I had both returned to the studio, I to get my car, he to go back to his office. Well, that's what he'd said but maybe he didn't go to his own office; maybe he went to Tony Flo's instead and persuaded him not to make any announcement just yet.

Why should Flo agree to that? If Agnelli was right, which he probably was, Tony Flo himself was only clinging on to his job by his fingertips, so he'd be unlikely to risk offending Baldock any more by not carrying out his edicts, unless …

Unless both he and Agnelli were confident that Carlo Minelli would soon be back in the country and that his return would restore the status quo. I had the feeling that the next few days might be very interesting.

I said, 'Fine. I'll see you at the location then. And, er, one other thing ...'

'Yes?'

'I really like you, too.'

She sighed. 'God, you English are so passionate.'

# 24

THE FILM UNIT was still shooting at the Santa Monica location, an exterior scene this time. You may remember it – the big confrontation between Michael Rialto and Virna Newport after he has learned of the murder of his girlfriend in that same house and believes Newport was involved. It's probably the best scene in the film, crackling with anger and hatred. Newport was terrific in it and even Rialto came as close as he ever did to acting true emotion, but maybe that was because he wasn't really acting.

The house was at the end of a private road, which had been cordoned off to keep the public away and was lined with trucks and vans and cars. I had no difficulty getting past the security men on the makeshift barrier at the end of the road. They said there was still some parking reserved for privileged honchos like me up closer to the house. I drove slowly along the road, past the huge generator truck and the location catering set-up, around which a group of electricians and construction workers was eating giant hot dogs to keep their strength up, and left my car in an area dominated by two enormous Winnebagos. One of them was for the use of Michael Rialto, the other for Virna Newport.

The door to Rialto's was open and I glanced into it as I went by. It was like a five-star hotel room inside – lush carpeting and curtains, a double bed, a polished table and chairs, a fridge, a TV set and a

VCR recorder, two or three armchairs. A girl was arranging sliced fruit on a platter on the table.

She sensed somebody watching her and looked up at me.

'God, they really rough it on location, these movie stars,' I said.

'Yep,' she said, nodding. 'And all for a lousy ten million a picture.'

'Plus points, of course. We must never forget the points.'

'That's right. Heaven forbid that we should ever forget the points.'

'You don't happen to know where I might find Lucy Lane, do you?'

She nodded again. 'Yeah, she went by a couple of minutes ago. I think she was heading for the honey wagon.'

'The what?'

She grinned. 'It's what you guys call a portaloo, it's where people go to make pee-pee.'

'Right, got it. I don't think I'll follow her there.'

'Not advisable.' She turned back to her fruit arranging.

'Pretty exotic fruit he's got there,' I said, watching her. 'Got expensive tastes, has he?'

'Oh yes, indeedy. When he's making a movie he has four different kinds of pasta flown in from his favourite restaurant in Venice every week. And I'm talking Venice, Italy, not Venice, California.'

'And of course the studio pays for all that.'

'Who else?'

'Good stuff, is it, this pasta?'

'I've tasted better in Beverly Hills but what do I know? Me, I just have my donuts trucked in by location catering.'

I looked down towards the swimming pool. Michael Rialto had detached himself from the group that appeared to be holding an earnest discussion around the camera and was heading up the long expanse of lawn towards his Winnebago.

'Better hurry up with that fruit,' I said. 'He's on his way.'

'Oh, shit,' she said. 'Thanks for the warning.'

I'd just started off towards the pool when Terri Chin, coming from the parking lot, appeared from the other side of the trailer. She didn't see me but she certainly saw Rialto. She stopped for a moment, smiled, waved, yelled, 'Michael, darling!' and ran down the lawn towards him.

She was wearing a very short, navy blue skirt and a sleeveless blouse with the top buttons undone and, looking at her as she ran across the grass, all long legs and tousled black hair, I thought any man would appreciate an enthusiastic greeting like that from a girl like that.

Rialto didn't.

As she went to hug him he pushed her away so hard that she stumbled and almost fell. His face was tight and ugly with fury.

'What are you doing here?' he said.

She moved towards him again, more tentatively this time, but stopped when he raised his arm angrily. She said, 'Michael, I don't understand. What—'

'How many times do I have to tell you, you stupid bitch, you don't come near me when I'm working? My wife's coming here. Get the fuck away from me.'

I was in a difficult spot here. I was already halfway between them and the Winnebago. Too late simply to stop and stand still; too late even to turn back and walk away. So I just kept on coming, glancing around at the garden and trying to look like someone who was totally unaware of what was going on ahead of him.

Terri Chin said, 'Why you mad at me, Michael? Because I was with Rico last night? We just had dinner, that's all.'

'Shut your stupid mouth,' he said, and slapped her hard across the face. She gave a little cry and began to weep. Rialto pushed her away again and looked up at me. 'What do you want?' he said.

'Nothing. I'm just passing through.'

He gave me that look of his, the hard menacing scowl beloved of female cinema audiences, the one that turned big, tough heavies to jelly in all his movies. 'You're Lennox, aren't you?' I recognised the sneer in his voice, too. It went with the hard look.

I nodded, waiting.

'You spying on me? Huh? You spying on me?'

Oh God, I thought, he's doing a Robert De Niro impersonation now. 'Not at all. Like I said, I'm just passing through. I'm on my way to visit the set. That's what associate producers do, or so they tell me.'

He stepped closer to me, turning up the intensity of the scowl. 'You tell anyone about what you just saw, what you just heard and your life's not worth living, you understand me?'

I raised both hands placatingly. 'No problem. Tombs come to me for advice on how to keep silent.'

'What?'

Beside us the girl was snuffling quietly, her head bowed, her fingertips gently touching the vivid red mark that his hand had left on her cheek. Rialto glanced at her irritably and then jabbed me in the chest with his forefinger.

'Just keep your mouth shut and you'll stay healthy. Remember that.'

'Okay,' I said, mildly. 'But here's something for you to remember – keep your hands off women in future and you'll stay healthy, too.'

He looked as if he couldn't believe what he was hearing and I suppose, big star as he was, nobody had talked to him like that in years.

'Are you threatening me? Are you threatening me, you punk?'

I shook my head firmly. 'You got that wrong, you know. I'm not the punk here. The punk is the big, strong man who goes around hitting women.'

We stood there, eyeball to eyeball, barely a foot apart. It was all very stupid, I knew that, but I'd had a bad day. I wanted to take it out on somebody and Rialto was about my size and weight. I half hoped he'd take a swing at me and I think he was at least half considering it when a voice from behind me called his name.

We both turned. Angela Rialto was standing beside the Winnebago, waving to him. Her husband waved back, said, 'With you in a moment, honey,' and turned to me again. 'This isn't the end of it, you know.'

I stepped away from him. 'Now which film was that line from? Don't tell me, let me see if I can remem—'

'Goddamn smartass. You fucked with me, Lennox. I won't forget that. Nobody fucks with me.' He arranged his face into a smile, waved to his wife again, said, 'With you right now, baby,' and walked away.

I turned my attention to Terri Chin. One side of her face still looked sore and there was a fleck of blood at the corner of her mouth but she'd stopped weeping and dried her eyes. 'You shouldn't have interfered,' she said.

'Well, pardon me. I just thought maybe you didn't like being used as a punchbag.'

'We're going to be married,' she said. 'Michael and me, we're going to be married.'

'Oh, right, only he just hasn't got around to telling his wife yet, is that it? Men can be very absent-minded like that.'

She flinched away from me, almost as if I'd hit her, too. The look on her face – fear, doubt, self-deception, all those things – made me want to take her in my arms and give her a brotherly hug.

'He will tell her,' she said. 'Of course he will. It's just a matter of picking the right time.'

'Yes, well,' I said. 'If you say so. Does Rico know about this? I only ask because I happen to know that he's very keen on you, too.'

Now fear dominated all the other emotions in her eyes. 'Don't tell Rico. Please, you mustn't tell Rico. You promise?'

I nodded. She blew her nose one more time, finger-combed her hair and looked around her uncertainly.

'I think I'd better go now,' she said.

'Yes. I think that would be best.'

I watched her as she walked slowly back up the lawn. The girl who had been arranging fruit in Rialto's trailer was now standing outside, lighting a cigarette. There was no sign of Rialto or his wife and the door of the Winnebago was shut.

It would have been bad enough and I would probably have made an enemy for life anyway if that had been my only run-in with Rialto that day, but it wasn't.

Richie Proctor and his crew were making final preparations for the big scene, fine-tuning the lighting with Newport's and Rialto's stand-ins shuffling through the movements, when I wandered up to the swimming pool. I watched for a moment but didn't interrupt them. From the snatches of conversation I could overhear there seemed to be some tension in the air.

The scriptgirl told me that Lucy was in the production office and I found her there, on the second floor of the house, hammering away on her word processor. For once she kissed me as if she meant it but still seemed a little distracted.

'How are things going?' I said.

'Great, till Rialto started doing a number on Richie.' She made a gesture of disgust. 'God, I hate actors. Well, no, it's not actors I hate, it's movie stars.'

'Rarely the same thing,' I said, wisely, bringing all my experience as an associate producer to bear. 'What was it about?'

'I don't really know. I had enough problems of my own without getting involved in that one. But I gather it had to do with the way Richie's planning to shoot the scene between Rialto and Newport. It's not fair. This is the best-written scene in the whole picture and Richie's worked like a dog to set it up just right and then that asshole … Aargh.' She took two cans of diet Pepsi from the fridge, threw one to me and popped the cap on the other.

We both took a drink and then, gazing at me a little anxiously, she said, 'Do you think it's going to be okay? You and me, I mean, this weekend.'

'You're not chickening out on me, are you?'

'No, oh no. It's just that I feel a little nervous, spending time in someone else's house with a man I don't really know very well. I keep wondering, is it going to be okay.'

'It'll be okay,' I said. 'I promise.'

I was just debating with myself whether this might be a good moment to try for another kiss when the door opened and a freckled male face about twenty years old peered in.

It said, 'Hey, Lucy, they're gonna shoot the scene now and I thought maybe you'd want to watch.'

'Thanks, Stu. We'll be down in a minute.'

When the door had closed again I said, 'Who was that?'

'That was Stu. He's the gofer. You know what a gofer is?'

'Sure. Go fer this, go fer that, go fer the coffee, go fer—'

'You're learning fast. Come on, let's go watch the action.'

Down by the pool Rialto and Newport were on their marks and waiting, he all in black and scowling, she demure and classically elegant in some kind of flowing designer dress. A young assistant director clapped his hands sharply above his head. 'Quiet, everybody. Settle down. Real quiet now.'

Everyone dutifully settled down and an anticipatory hush descended on the onlookers and the crew. There was a slight crackle of tension in the air, as there always is at the start of a difficult and important sequence.

'Sound running,' said the soundman.

'Camera running,' said the cameraman.

Richie Proctor leaned forward on the edge of his director's chair. 'Aaaand ... action!' he called.

It was a long scene and both actors were up for it, word and gesture perfect. Watching them at work you could see why Rialto was a star. His delivery was wooden and somehow you expected him to fluff at any minute but still there was something about him, a sense of energy barely controlled, that drew the eye.

You could see why Newport was a star, too. It wasn't just her beauty, though that, despite her years, was still considerable. She was much more understated than Rialto, calmer, enviably graceful, even languid. But her stillness was no less eye-catching than his suppressed energy. And she could act, with a naturalness, an effortlessness, that made you wonder what kind of an inequitable system had only rewarded her with one Oscar. Rialto had the best and the sharpest lines and at least delivered them adequately but, apparently without even trying, she stole the scene away from him.

We all watched, riveted, scarcely breathing for fear of disturbing the players until ...

'Cut!' Rialto said. 'Hold it!'

For a moment everyone was perfectly still. Then Richie Proctor leapt out of his chair, livid with anger. 'What the bloody hell are you playing at?' he roared at Rialto. 'That was perfect!'

'No, it wasn't. It was wrong – it was wrong for me. You were playing it all on her.'

Proctor made an obvious effort to control the rage that was churning around inside him. 'Michael,' he said patiently, 'we discussed all that this morning. We spent bloody hours discussing it this morning and you agreed that this was the way to do it. We all agreed.'

The corners of Rialto's mouth dropped sulkily. He didn't look tough any more, just petulant. 'Yeah, well it doesn't play like I thought it would. I'm the star of this fuckin' movie and you're giving the biggest scene in the picture to her.'

Proctor took a deep breath. 'No, I'm not. This is the master shot. It works best the way I've set it up. But later ...' He raised an index finger in the air. He was speaking so quietly and deliberately that you might have thought Rialto had never been in a film before and had no idea how things worked. 'But later we do the close-ups and then in the cutting-room I put the whole thing together and—'

'Don't patronise me,' Rialto said. 'I know what's going on here and I don't like one little bit of it. You better watch yourself, Proctor. My last movie made more money in fuckin' Bolivia than all your pictures put together will make all over the world if they play for ever. Don't you forget that. I'm the star of this movie. You're just the director. I want it that way, we could have a new director tomorrow morning.'

From her position beside the camera Angela Rialto said, 'That's right. You tell him, honey.'

Everyone else was silent. Among the crew the embarrassment was almost tangible. Proctor looked around him, searching for support, but none was forthcoming. Nobody would meet his eye.

'Godstrewth,' he said. For a few seconds he just stood there, staring at the ground. Then he sighed, shook himself like somebody emerging from a nightmare and said, 'Okay, Michael, what is it you want?'

Rialto flashed his famous teeth, those pearly white monuments to the orthodontist's art, in what was not so much a smile as a snarl of triumph. 'I want the camera on me – not on her, not on the two of us but on *me*, that's what I want.'

Proctor looked stunned. So did the cinematographer and the cameraman. So did the soundman, and soundmen don't usually give a damn what's happening in front of the camera so long as the noise in their headphones is right.

'Michael,' Proctor said imploringly, 'hey, come on. It works beautifully the way it is. Trust me. It—'

'Are you listening to me, Proctor? You know what I want, so do it.'

Virna Newport, who had been attending to all this with an air of slightly amused detachment, now contributed her twopenn'orth. 'Tell me if I've got this right, Michael,' she said quietly. 'You want the camera on your face and the back of my head, is that it?'

'That's exactly what I want,' Rialto said.

'Well, I've got a better idea,' she said sweetly. 'Why don't we do the whole shot as a close-up on you? You'd like that, wouldn't you, your face all over the screen? And I wouldn't need to be there at all. Somebody could stand beside the camera and read my lines to you and I could go home. Of course, I probably wouldn't come back – ever. But you'd have the scene all to yourself.'

'Oh, Jesus,' Proctor said. 'This is all I need.'

And as Rialto stood there doubtfully, not sure whether Newport was being serious or quietly sending him up, I decided it was time for the associate producer to take a hand. I stepped forward from the little throng behind the camera and stopped in front of Rialto. 'What you want won't work,' I said. 'It'll ruin the scene.'

He gaped at me, his face registering disbelief better than it ever did in any film. 'You!' he said. 'What the fuck do you know?'

'Not a lot,' I said. 'But from where I was standing that scene was working like a dream until you ruined it.' In my peripheral vision I was aware of the production crew nodding agreement, though still not catching anybody's eye. I lowered my voice so that nobody else could hear. 'And it worked like a dream because Virna Newport can act the socks off you. You're just a movie star, she's an actress. You have the best lines but she gives the scene its impact. Take the camera

159

off her and put it on you and all you've got is simply another macho hunk delivering a monologue.'

Again I thought he was going to hit me; again I hoped he would. But instead he glanced behind him and beckoned to a pair of large hulks who'd been sunning themselves in deckchairs on the far side of the pool. They got up obediently and lumbered over. They wore baseball caps and sunglasses but what I noticed most about them was that they were big.

As they approached, Rialto shoved me to one side and started shouting at Proctor. 'Hey, you, Richie! You think you got a movie here? You haven't got a movie. You got nothing, because I'm walking – now. I'm outa here.'

He started back towards the house and I walked with him. The goons were getting closer. 'You're out of here, too,' he said. 'By the time those two guys have finished with you, you'll be carried outa here.'

'Maybe. But I'll still be better off than you.'

He stopped and looked at me. 'What?'

The goons were closing in fast. I was confident that in an open space I would be fast enough and clever enough to handle one of them but I wasn't so happy about coping with two. 'Tell your apes to stay where they are,' I said.

'Why should I?' he said, giving me his snarling grin.

'Because if you don't I won't be able to explain why you're about to make the biggest mistake of your life.'

He frowned uncertainly but held his hand out towards the two minders who obediently stopped where they were, about twenty paces away. 'You got ten seconds to grab my attention,' he said.

'All right. Your pride is hurt because you've been upstaged by someone who's forgotten more about acting than you'll ever know.' He growled at me but I ignored him. 'Okay, fine. You want to walk away from the picture. Understandable perhaps. Nobody likes to be shown up. But have you forgotten whose movie this is? It's not Proctor's movie, it's not Virna Newport's movie, it's not even your movie. It's Carlo Minelli's movie. Carlo has a lot of money riding on this film. More than that, a lot of his future plans are dependent on it. Now if you screw it up by walking out, if you even waste time and money by throwing tantrums on the set, he's not going to be happy with you.'

'Carlo's not around,' Rialto said. 'Wherever he is he's got other things to think about than this movie. I'm the one has to worry right now because it's my career we're talking here.'

'Carlo's not around today perhaps but who knows what the morrow may bring.'

He studied my expression thoughtfully. 'You know something? About Carlo? You know something?'

I smiled, shrugged, said nothing.

'What?' he said. 'What do you know?'

I carried on smiling enigmatically and saying nothing.

'The hell with it,' he said. 'Doesn't matter what you know. I'm in the clear anyway. I'm family.'

I shook my head. 'You're just a nephew-in-law. That's not real family. If someone like you gets in the way you're expendable. Let me spell it out for you: when Carlo comes back and finds this film is way behind schedule and therefore over budget or, even worse, that it's shut down completely, I'll tell him who's responsible. I'll tell him that Proctor did his job and was doing it well but you behaved like an arsehole, in other words like a movie star, and ruined everything.'

Rialto considered this. 'You said *when* Carlo comes back. Who says he's coming back?'

I shook my head sorrowfully. 'I thought you were a member of the family. I thought you'd know these things.'

One of the goons cleared his throat noisily, doubtless to attract his boss's attention. Rialto turned on the pair of them. 'Get the hell away from here,' he said. The goons looked at each other, shrugged and trundled back to their deckchairs.

I started to say something but Rialto waved an irritable hand at me. 'Shut up, I'm thinking.'

As we stood there in silence, Proctor came up to us, none too confidently. He said, 'Michael, can you let me know what's happening? If you're really going to quit the film I'll send everyone home now. But if you're not and if we're going to shoot this scene the way we agreed we'll have to do it soon or we'll lose the light. On the other hand, if you insist on doing it another way we'll have to wrap for now, have a rethink and shoot it on Monday.'

Rialto was silent for a moment, considering the options. Then, 'Okay, okay,' he said. 'We shoot the scene your way, you'll do close-ups on me afterwards?'

'You know I will. If we get the master shot done quickly we'll have plenty of time.'

Rialto drew himself up like a man who had just reached an important decision. 'So let's do it,' he said, as if it had been his idea in the first place. To me he said, 'You got two strikes against you already today, old buddy. One more and you're out. You know what I'm saying to you?'

'I think I get the gist of it,' I said.

Rialto strode back towards the swimming pool shouting, 'All right, everybody, we've wasted enough time here. Let's get this shot in the can right now.'

Proctor said softly, 'Thanks.'

'Don't mention it,' I said. 'Are you going to do what you said – about the close-ups?'

'Am I hell. The one advantage of getting paid peanuts for doing this film is that I get the final cut. It's in my contract. Watertight and lawyer-proof. I'll shoot the close-ups all right but if they do the master shot as well as they were doing it before Rialto started arsing around, that's the shot I'll go with and sod the close-ups.'

On the third take they did it perfectly. Newport was brilliant, looking positively majestic. It was hard to tell how Rialto looked because most of the time you couldn't see much of his face but, as even his sternest critics agreed later, the anger in his voice and body language seemed utterly genuine.

But then, like I said, it probably was. It just had nothing to do with the scene, that's all.

# 25

At 5.30 THE assistant director said, 'Okay, everybody, that's a wrap.'
The grips and gaffers and the others started packing away the
equipment; Proctor took the cinematographer aside to discuss their
location-scouting trip to Montana; Lucy went to her office to tidy up
odd bits of business; and Rialto and his wife headed away towards
his trailer.

He didn't say goodbye to me but he looked happy enough.
Exhausted, too. Proctor had spent a lot of time on Rialto's close-ups,
making him go through take after take while murmuring, 'That was
good, Michael, that was very good. But I think you can do it even
better. It's important we get this absolutely right, for your sake.'

This was sadism of a high and subtle order. As Proctor said to me
in a quiet moment when Rialto had been sent away to get his make-
up renewed, 'You know what I'm going to do? I'm going to take all
those shots, all those close-ups, and put 'em in a showreel for him.
Then he can play them to himself in his private screening room
because he sure as hell is never going to see any of them in the
movie.'

As the crew cleared away I strolled round to the other side of the
pool and sat in one of the deckchairs recently vacated by Rialto's
minders. I'd only been there a few minutes when Virna Newport
approached me.

'Don't get up,' she said. She stood in front of me, the setting sun right behind her so that I had to squint to look up at her and she was so close that I could only have risen from my chair by pushing her out of the way. 'What did you say to Michael?'

'I told him there was only one actor in that scene and it wasn't him.'

She smiled, pleased. 'And that persuaded him to change his mind?'

'Well, not that perhaps. I said some other things as well.'

'You mean you leant on him a little?'

'You could say that.'

She stared down at me quizzically, her head slightly to one side. I shielded my eyes with my hand to look back at her. Backlit by the sun she made a dramatic picture as, of course, she knew. She hadn't stood there by accident. 'Who are you, Mr Lennox? Are you one of Carlo's men? I think you must be. You know nothing about the movies and yet you exercise an awful lot of muscle around here.'

'I work for Minelli's partner. Man named Donovan.'

She nodded. 'Ah, I see. Well, I still don't like you, Mr Lennox, but I felt I had to thank you. That was a good scene we shot today but it would have been nothing if we'd done it Michael's way. So thank you.'

She turned away. I said, 'What did Darren do with the tapes?'

She hesitated, glanced back. 'I beg your pardon?'

'You know what I'm talking about. Harrison's autobiography. That's what the row was about that day, wasn't it? The tapes he was making. What did Darren do with them? You sent him to get them, didn't you, so Harrison's dead because of you.'

'That's not true! I did know about the book and the tapes and I did tell Darren but I didn't ask him to do anything. I loved Greg. I would never have done anything to hurt him.' She sounded convincing but then, as she'd been proving all afternoon, she was a hell of an actress.

Lucy came round the side of the pool. She and Newport glared at each other and then Newport hurried away.

Lucy said, 'Is that woman still hitting on you?'

'No. She doesn't like me any more. She just said so.' I stood up and hugged her. 'You still like me, though, don't you?'

'Yeah, I guess,' she said. 'Come on. Time to house-sit.'

We got the house keys from Proctor and then Lucy and I drove in a two-car convoy to Encino. On the way we stopped at a Thai restaurant on Ventura Boulevard and while she was ordering a take-away meal I walked to the liquor store on the next block and got us some wine.

The house was cool and secluded and welcoming. We put the food in the kitchen and the wine in the fridge and when we'd finished with the domestic business we stopped and looked at each other awkwardly.

'Now what?' I said.

She shrugged, looking as uncertain as I felt. 'I don't know. This is ... this is a new kind of situation for me.'

'Me, too. I mean, shacking up like brother and sister with a woman for whom I feel a lot of things but nothing remotely brotherly. Do you think somewhere in the house Richie might have a book of etiquette that covers this set-up?'

'I don't think that book's been written yet.' Lucy said. 'Let's have a drink first, then eat, then talk and see what happens. Bobby, I don't want to seem all coy and bashful; I'm not like that, really I'm not. But how often have we met? Two, three times? I just don't want to rush into anything. I do like you. I like you a lot and I don't feel remotely sisterly about you either. But what I don't want, what I don't need in my life right now is a quick, casual, empty affair.'

I thought it over. 'I don't think I want that either. Well, all right, if that was all that was on offer I'd grab it because I'm a man and, alas, men are like that. But it's not what I really want.'

She nodded. 'How do you feel about a relationship?'

'A relationship would be good,' I said. 'A relationship would be better.'

She nodded again, more vigorously this time. 'That's what I think, too. Shall we try for one of those?'

'Deal,' I said. 'Can we seal it with a kiss?'

'Just one.' It was a very nice kiss, warm and friendly, and it banished the awkwardness from the atmosphere.

We had a drink or two and dinner and after that, because the evening was gloriously warm, we swam and later, wrapped in bathrobes, we sat beside the pool with a bottle of wine between us and filled in all the more intimate and private stuff about our backgrounds that we had left out the last time we had sat in this same place.

But we also discussed the movie and I remember asking her why Virna Newport was in it. It had never seemed to me to be her kind of film, any more than it was really Richie Proctor's kind of film. In my mind Newport was associated with heavy dramas or historical epics set in the Deep South in which she swanned around, hot and sultry, in hooped crinolines.

Lucy said, 'I don't think anybody knows why she's there. By the time Richie and I came aboard she was already part of the package. I know Richie didn't really want her. He had someone else in mind because he thought Newport would be, I don't know, just too rich for the movie. But when he mentioned that to Bill Charleston he was told to forget it – Newport was there and Newport was going to stay. So,' she shrugged, 'the lady obviously has friends in high places. It's a mystery.'

It was just chit-chat as we lay there in our reclining chairs, looking up at the moon and holding hands because, yes, we'd reached that stage at least; we'd even kissed a few times.

And yet I was intrigued. I knew, of course, why Rialto was in the movie – not just because he was related to Carlo Minelli but because he was currently hot. His name alone was enough to guarantee that the film would 'open', that it would attract a box office take of around twenty million dollars on its opening weekend in America. That was why he was being paid ten million dollars and a percentage of the gross receipts.

Most of the casting around him was understandable, too. Annie Klane, the leading lady, was Hollywood's latest sexpot-in-waiting, an eventual successor to Basinger, Stone and Moore, all of whom were just as voluptuous but at least ten years older than she was. That she couldn't act any better than they could was unimportant: the only relevant fact was that cellulite was further away from her than it was from them.

Martie Culper, the heavy in the film, was a sound choice, too. For the most part Hollywood preferred the bad guys in big-budget movies to be played by British actors, presumably because their smoother English accents and speech patterns, sometimes going so far as to include complete sentences, made American audiences uneasy and therefore more willing to hate them. But, as Lucy explained, Rialto had been consulted about the supporting cast and though he was arrogant he wasn't stupid. He knew that a British performer, with his classical training as well as the fancy accent, would have acted him off the screen, while Culper, though also a better actor than Rialto could ever hope to be, was as American as he was and therefore would not offer such a sharp contrast.

Virna Newport, however, was a wild card. She was a *grande dame* of the American cinema, more associated with screen adaptations of Eugene O'Neill and the like than with violent thrillers.

I've never liked wild cards. Wherever they crop up they make me uneasy. I'm a simple man. I like everything in its place, neatly explained.

Lucy said, 'Yes, right, *why* is Virna in the movie? I hadn't thought about it much before but, yeah, now I'm curious; I'd really like to know.'

'Let's see if we can find out,' I said and called Rico Agnelli on his cellphone. He picked up on the third ring.

'Rico,' I said, once we'd gone through the identification bit, 'matter of interest – who cast Virna Newport in the movie?'

'Carlo,' he said, surprised. 'You didn't know that? Carlo's a fan from way back. When he was a kid – fourteen, fifteen, in there – he had the hots for Newport. Every kid had the hots for her. Ask me, he still has. So when he was putting the picture together and he heard she needed the money it was like all his wet dreams come true. He's revived her career, so she owes him.'

'He's not …? You know. He's not …?'

'Fucking her? Who knows? Old as she is she's still his boyhood dreamboat so, like I said, who knows? Far as he's concerned she pees eau de Cologne. Why do you ask?'

'Just curious.'

'Yeah, well, I'm surprised nobody told you the score going in. Anything else you want?'

I said there wasn't and hung up. To Lucy I said, 'Virna Newport is in the film because Carlo Minelli wants to get into her knickers.'

Lucy said, 'He can't! She's older than God.'

'I know but apparently he doesn't care. He's lusted after her since he was a boy.'

She shook her head sadly. 'Jesus, these Mafia people are sick.'

# 26

AROUND MIDNIGHT AS the air grew cooler I said, 'This relationship of ours. How d'you reckon it's going?'

'Pretty good,' she said, 'for a first date.'

I groaned. 'Come on, don't pull that on me. This has to be the equivalent of, oh, at least a third or fourth date. We've been through a lot together, remember. I think we …' And then I looked across at her and I knew that this wasn't the time; that for whatever reason – something in her, or something missing in me – she wasn't ready yet.

'Okay,' I said, 'which bedroom am I sleeping in?'

She reached across and stroked my cheek gently. 'Thanks,' she said and a little later, after a chaste goodnight kiss, we went to our separate beds.

The mood between us had been good that night; the next day it was even better, as if by not rushing her I had passed some kind of test. We swam a bit, shopped a bit and then, finding ourselves close to Sunset Boulevard, decided to go for lunch.

Lucy wanted to eat at Morton's but I fancied soft-shelled crabs, fried in butter, at Le Dome. We tossed for it. She called tails and I called heads. It came down heads and she said, 'Okay, let's go to Morton's.'

'No way. I won the toss.'

'Yeah, right, but nobody was taking that seriously.'

'I was. There's no point in doing it otherwise.'

'There's no point in doing it. Period. I want to go to Morton's. I thought that was understood. You get beautiful people at Morton's. Like, stars hitting on other stars' wives. What are you gonna see at Le Dome? Just a bunch of old guys making deals. Besides, if you were a gentleman—'

'Nobody has ever accused me of being a gentleman,' I said. 'What a gentleman might do is of no interest to me at all. I won the toss and we're going to Le Dome. Who knows, we might get lucky, the place might be full of old guys hitting on other old guys' wives.'

She sank lower into her car seat, grumbling. 'You know what my mom told me? All guys are the same, she said. They're just after one thing and the only way you can get them to do what *you* want is to make sure you tape your knees together.'

'Well, we know that doesn't work, don't we?'

'Yeah.' She grinned. 'You reckon that's what I did last night – taped my knees together?'

'That's what it looked like to me.'

She was quiet for a moment and then she said, 'Yes, I guess it must have done. Maybe I shouldn't have done that.'

'Better you tape your knees together,' I said, 'than go to bed with me as an act of charity. Besides, who says I want to go to bed with you anyway?'

She looked at me curiously, unsure whether I was serious or not. 'You mean you don't?'

'I'm thinking it over,' I said. 'Maybe I'm going off the idea.'

'I'll remember that, my friend,' she said darkly.

We were on Sunset now and as we approached Le Dome a dark Rolls-Royce pulled into the kerb ahead of us. A uniformed black chauffeur sprang out, hurried to the nearside back door and helped a woman to alight. Virna Newport dressed for brunch in an emerald green silk shirt, designer jeans and diamonds.

'Oh, God,' said Lucy.

Newport eased the chauffeur aside, turned and offered her hand to the man who was following her out of the car. A man in an immaculate grey suit with trouser creases like razor blades. They walked into the restaurant, arm in arm.

'Oh, God,' I said.

A parking valet loomed up beside me and started opening my door. 'What's the food like at Morton's?' I said to Lucy.

'Great.'

'Good. Let's go there.' I gave the valet a dollar for wasting his time and drove away.

Lucy said, 'That was Charlie Baldock with Virna, wasn't it?'

'It was.'

She gave a little puff of relief and lay back in her seat. 'Boy, that was a close one. If we'd got there a couple of minutes earlier ...'

'Doesn't bear thinking about,' I said. 'I hate eating in the same restaurant as the man who's just fired me.'

She sat up, her eyes huge with indignation. 'What? He did what?'

I told her what had happened.

'You never thought to mention this before?' she said. 'Like last night?'

'Well, I did think about it but I decided not to. In the first place, I'm hoping Baldock might be persuaded to change his mind. And in the second place, I didn't feel it would help the mood last night if I'd suddenly said, "Hey, honey, I've lost my job." Bit wimpish when you're trying to impress a girl.'

'You can be such a macho idiot sometimes,' she said and then, more gently, 'but I'm truly sorry, Bobby.'

'The problem is,' I said, 'that there could be repercussions all round. Virna's in the film because Minelli insisted on it. So, theoretically, with him out of the way, she should now be in a rather precarious position herself, but in practice ... well, in practice if she's hooked up with Baldock she's stronger than ever. Did it look to you as if she'd hooked up with him?'

She nodded. 'Yeah, Charlie stroked her ass as they went through the door.'

'Well, if he's stroking her arse before lunch, God knows what they'll get up to afterwards. I think we'd better assume the worst. I think we'd better assume that before today is over Virna's position on the movie is going to be just about inviolable, which means she'll be able to get rid of all the people she hates. Can you think of anyone she hates?'

Lucy nodded glumly.

'Thing is,' I said, 'if Virna has you fired and Richie threatens to go, too, Baldock will probably accept it. He doesn't have any real commitment to this film, not in the way Minelli did. Dear, oh dear, why didn't somebody warn me about movie-making? Is it always as fraught and complicated as this?'

'It's always fraught and complicated but not usually like this.'

We drove the rest of the way in silence. What I was thinking about was the immediate future and I imagine Lucy was doing the same. Somehow the bright edge had gone off the day.

I was about to say that, the way our luck was running, we'd probably not be able to get a table at Morton's and would end up eating a BLT at Ben Frank's diner when a phone rang. We looked at each other with the unspoken question: yours or mine? Then we started scrabbling around for our respective phones, Lucy in her handbag, me in my pockets.

It was mine.

A female voice said, 'Mr Lennox? This is Lou.'

'What? How did you find me?'

'I called your hotel. They gave me your number. I have somebody here who wants to talk to you.' Before I could interrupt she added hurriedly, 'Don't mention any names. Anyone can eavesdrop on these damn mobiles. Will you come? Now? Please?'

'Well, it's kind of difficult at the moment. I have somebody with me and—'

'Please.' There was a hint of desperation in her voice.

'All right.'

I switched off, pulled into the kerb and stopped the car. Morton's, with its promise of food, drink and Sunday lunchtime bonhomie, gleamed invitingly on the other side of the street.

I said, 'Do you fancy going to a brothel?'

'What? Is this a joke?'

'No.' I started the car again and headed back towards Sunset. 'You're going anyway.'

Lucy tapped me sharply on the leg. 'Hey, what's going on here? I thought we were going for lunch and now you're planning to deliver me into a whorehouse? What are you – some kind of white slave trafficker?'

'If you'll just listen for a minute, I'll explain,' I said and I did that as we drove up Laurel and onto Mulholland, telling her how I'd followed Darren to Lou's and how the police had raided the place.

'Wow,' she said. 'Why didn't you tell me all this stuff before?'

'Because ... well, I didn't want you to know that I'd been to Lou's again. I didn't think you'd understand.'

'Did you sample any of the candy?'

'Of course not. I didn't even have the time.'

She took in a sharp, hissing breath. 'What? You're telling me that if you'd just had more time you'd—'

'No! What I'm saying is that even if I'd wanted to there wasn't the time and anyway I really didn't want to. Honestly.'

But she wouldn't let it go and she was still nagging accusingly at me and I was still protesting innocence when we reached the gate at the end of Lou's drive. This time I had no problem getting in. The guard, the same guard as before, smiled and nodded and said, 'Go right up. Nice to see you again, Mr Lennox.'

'He seems to know you very well,' Lucy said darkly. 'Are you sure you've only been here twice?'

Lou, who was waiting for us on the verandah, was alarmed to find that I wasn't alone. I made the introductions and vouched for Lucy's discretion. Lou still wasn't convinced.

'I wish you hadn't done this,' she said. 'I don't know how Darren will react. He's very nervous. He ... he's not expecting anybody else, just you.'

Lucy had drifted a little away from us and was peering, fascinated, into the big white room where even at this time on a Sunday a small crowd of masculine buyers and female vendors was milling about. But I knew she was listening as Lou said, 'Do you think she'd mind waiting for us while you talked to Darren?'

I said hesitantly, 'Well, I ...' I glanced into the room. The men in there suddenly seemed more predatory than ever.

173

Lucy said, still with her back to me, 'You'd really do that? You'd leave me in there with all those rich horny guys? What if one of them … Oh, look who's over there!' She pointed across the room towards a tall, blond and strikingly handsome young actor, who was fast building himself a reputation as a stud in the exalted class of Warren Beatty and Ryan O'Neal. 'Okay, I'll stay here. I'll go talk to him.'

I grabbed her by the arm. 'No, you won't. You're coming with us. She's coming with us,' I said to Lou. 'Either that or we both leave. I've made up my mind.'

'My, you're so masterful,' Lucy murmured, fluttering her eyelashes at me in a parody of female submission.

Lou said doubtfully, 'Oh God, I don't know. But … oh, all right. I just don't want Darren scared.'

'I won't scare him,' Lucy said. 'I'm only a woman.'

'What are you talking about?' I said. 'There's nothing so scary as women.'

Lou led us along the verandah towards the back of the house. Lucy, pointing towards the big room, said, 'Ah, can't we go through there? I've never been in a whorehouse. I want to know if it even smells of sin.'

'It smells of sin,' I said. 'Take my word for it.'

'Well, you're the expert,' she said sweetly.

At the rear of the house we went up a flight of wooden stairs to another verandah and a big, solid door which Lou unlocked with a couple of heavy keys. Inside, a narrow corridor took us to the long minstrel gallery which led, in turn, to the office in which I had last seen Darren. Lou gave that coded knock again, said, 'It's okay, dear, it's me,' and waited. After a second or two the door was opened and we all went in.

Darren looked better than he had the last time I saw him; cleaner, more rested, though there were still dark smudges under his eyes and he had certainly lost weight in the last few days. He wore jeans, Nike trainers and a grey sweatshirt. No gun this time.

He nodded warily at me, glanced suspiciously at Lucy. 'Who's she? What's she …' A gleam of recognition. 'I know you. You're the girl works with Richie Proctor. What are you—'

'She's a friend of mine,' I said. 'It's all right, you can trust her.'

Darren moved past me to shut and lock the door. Lou motioned to us all to sit down and when we did much of the tension went out of the room. Not out of Darren, though. He half-perched on the edge of the desk, as taut as piano wire, giving the impression that if there was any sudden move he'd be out of there before the rest of us could get to our feet.

He looked at me and said, 'First off, I want you to know whoever hit you it wasn't me. Whoever killed Greg Harrison it wasn't me.'

I said, 'All right. But what's this about? What do you want from me?'

Lou started to speak but he motioned to her to keep quiet. To me he said, 'I think, I'm not sure but I think, somebody wants me dead. So I've decided to turn myself in to the police.'

'What are you talking about? Who wants you dead?'

He shrugged. 'I don't know. I don't know why either. That's what scares me. I … Look, I've had a pretty lousy time these last few days, right? Just laying low …'

I wanted to correct him. I wanted to say, 'You mean lying low,' but sometimes even I am wise enough to suppress my pedantic instincts and keep quiet.

'Just laying low,' he said, 'and doing a lot of thinking.' He made a frustrated, almost petulant, gesture with one hand. 'Thing is, I'm scared. But if I tell you about it it probably won't sound like much. You'll probably think—'

'Why don't you just try me?' I said.

What it boiled down to was this: on the day Greg Harrison was murdered Darren met a casting agent for a drink in the Polo Lounge at the Beverly Hills Hotel to discuss a possible role in a TV mini-series. At about one in the afternoon he returned to the Bel Air Riviera, later picked up some mail at reception and was starting back towards the bungalow he shared with Virna Newport when his cellphone rang.

He stayed there on the path while Newport, calling from the film set, asked him to go to Robinson's, a department store near the Beverly Hilton Hotel, to pick up a certain brand of mascara. It was more of a command than a request but Darren wasn't surprised. Running little errands was part of a toy boy's job.

He switched off the phone, turned back towards the car park and, from the corner of his eye, noticed a man, well-built and maybe in his late thirties, coming towards him from, it seemed to him, the direction of Newport's bungalow. It struck him as odd, no more, but as he reached the car park the man was following and gaining on him.

Darren hesitated, thinking the man – whoever he was – wanted to talk to him. But then a girl he knew, one of the hotel receptionists wandering by, called to him and while he paused to chat to her the man veered away towards a dark green Mercedes with tinted windows and got into the front passenger seat.

The receptionist walked Darren to his own car and waved him away as he drove out onto Sunset Boulevard. The dark green Mercedes followed. He thought that was odd, too, and wondered about it until he turned into Robinson's parking lot and the Mercedes went on past. He didn't know why but he felt a sense of relief.

He was able to park quite near the main entrance and went into the store. His errand didn't take long because they were all out of that brand of mascara and, since there was nothing else he wanted to buy, he decided to go back to the hotel and put in a bit of pool time.

He was just about to step out of the shop when he saw a man breaking into his car. The same man he had seen at the Bel Air Riviera. At first Darren was too shocked to do anything, even yell. He just stood there, watching. It didn't take long. An accomplished car thief can get into almost any vehicle in comfortably less than thirty seconds and this man knew what he was doing.

But when he had opened the driver's door a strange thing happened. Instead of just climbing in and driving away, as a car thief might be expected to do, he reached in, opened the rear door, closed – and, as far as Darren could see, re-locked – the driver's door, climbed into the back of the car and hunkered down, out of sight, on the floor. All of this had taken under a minute and if anyone else had noticed what was going on they gave no indication.

Darren, concealed just inside the store, watched for five minutes. In all that time there was no sign of life or even occupancy in his car. He looked around carefully and spotted the green Mercedes parked a couple of rows behind his own vehicle. After a couple of minutes another burly, strongly built man got out of the Mercedes' driving seat and yawned and stretched. As he did so his jacket opened briefly and Darren saw the shoulder holster and the bulge of a gun under his left arm.

That was when Darren turned, walked quickly through the store, went out of a side entrance, hurried to the Beverly Hilton and took a cab to his mother's house on Mulholland.

I said, 'Why didn't you call the police?'

He brushed the question aside impatiently. 'Right then I didn't want anything to do with the police. A matter of a parole violation, no big deal, happened a long time ago and in another state but it could have caused complications I didn't need.'

So he had gone to his mother's house and spent the rest of the afternoon trying to call Virna Newport, the only person he could think of who might be in a position to help him. It was seven o'clock before he finally tracked her down at the Bel Air Riviera and by that time he was wanted for murder.

'It was Virna who told me,' he said. 'She said Harrison was dead and the police had me down for it. She was mad as hell at me, kept asking me why I'd done it and where was her money. I didn't know what she was talking about.'

'Not even about the money?' I said.

He hesitated. 'Well, yeah, okay I took the money. I'd have paid her back, one way or another, she knew that. I often took money she left laying around. Not usually as much as three thou but if I was going to audition for this mini-series I needed some clothes. I could have explained but she never gave me the chance, kept asking me why I'd killed Greg ...'

Anyhow, after that he lay low, watched television, read the papers and worried as he saw himself presented as a kind of Public Enemy Number One. The following night he took a chance and decided to accost Newport in person to see if, by talking to her face to face, he could straighten matters out. That was when I had seen him leaving her bungalow, although, more accurately, he wasn't so much leaving as being thrown out. She had accused him again of murdering Harrison, had refused to believe his denials, had even blamed herself – indirectly, of course, for there was a limit to the self-criticism of which Virna Newport was capable – for having caused Harrison's death by leading Darren to believe that it was what she had wanted. His protestations of innocence made no impression on her.

'When you left her,' I said, 'did she know where you were going?'

'Well, yeah. I mean, I guess so. When I first got there she asked me where I'd been and I told her. So when I left I imagine she assumed I'd be coming back here.'

'And then she tipped off the police,' I said. 'Anonymously.'

'What?' He seemed horrified at the thought. 'You really think she did that?'

'Who else?' I appeared to have been appointed to the role of Mr Interlocutor because neither Lou nor Lucy had said a word. 'Now what's the position?' I said. 'Are you staying here?'

'Close by.'

I thought over what he had told us. 'You've no idea who those men were and yet you're sure they wanted to kill you. Why?'

'What? You think they were gonna give me a surprise birthday party? There was one guy with a gun and another guy hiding in the back of my car, plus a couple of hours later I'm set up for murder. What am I supposed to think?'

It was difficult to argue with his logic, especially as his car had disappeared. The TV news bulletins had been issuing descriptions of it – a standard Chevvy, hardly worth the attention of a self-respecting car thief – along with pictures of Darren, asking for people to report sightings of either vehicle or driver. If the car had stayed where he left it, in Robinson's parking lot, someone would surely have spotted it by now.

'What do you think happened?' I asked.

He said, 'I think those two guys took my car and drove it way out in the desert somewhere between here and Las Vegas. And I think that, if I hadn't been paying attention, when it was found what was left of me would have been sitting in it.'

Lou made a small anguished sound. Lucy reached over and patted her hand, comfortingly.

I said, 'Why are you telling all this to me?'

Darren looked at his mother, who said, 'We couldn't think of anyone else. If those men really want to kill Darren he'd be safer in police custody but the police seem so convinced that he murdered Greg Harrison they probably wouldn't listen to him unless ... Well, unless he surrendered himself to Lieutenant Brown personally and you went along to ... to ...'

'To make Harry listen?' I said.

She nodded. 'Would you do that? Please? It's a lot to ask, I know but ... If Carlo Minelli had been around we'd have approached him. He has good contacts with the police but he's not here.' She made a small, shrugging gesture. 'So I thought of you. You seem to know Harry Brown pretty well and ...' Her voice tailed off but she looked at me with a kind of desperate hope.

I didn't want to get involved. I didn't want the LAPD, even Harry Brown, taking an interest in my life again. The way I saw it, I had enough problems already.

But then Lucy said, 'Do it.'

'What?'

'I believe him. Darren there – I believe him. So do it. Call this cop you seem to know so well and be there when Darren gives himself up.'

I looked around at them – the mother, the son and Lucy, this young woman who had suddenly become rather an important part of my life. They were all leaning earnestly towards me, willing me to say yes.

So I sighed and said, 'Okay.' I had Harry Brown's telephone numbers in a small address book that I carried with me. My American address book. It was a pretty slender volume because I didn't know too many people in the USA but I had the home number Harry Brown had given me a couple of years ago and I called that.

No reply. I checked it with the operator, confirmed I'd got it right, tried it again. Still no reply. So then I called the precinct where he worked. The phone rang for a long time before someone, not Harry Brown, picked up irritably. 'What?'

I asked for Harry. The voice said he wasn't there, he'd taken a couple of days off and wouldn't be back till Monday. No, the voice said, he didn't know where Lieutenant Brown was. San Francisco somewhere, that's all he knew and would I care to leave my name and a message.

I thought not. I said I'd call again, hung up and explained the situation. 'What I suggest, Darren, is that you go back to wherever you're hiding out. Then tomorrow I'll call Harry Brown, arrange a time and a place for a meeting and give the details to Lou so she can pass them on to you. After that we'll see what happens.'

Lucy and I left a few minutes later. Lunch at Morton's was long forgotten by now and the thought of BLTs, or maybe even corned beef hash, at Ben Frank's had begun to seem strangely attractive.

As we headed in that direction Lucy looked at me appraisingly and said, 'My, my, you're quite a guy, aren't you? Mob-connected, police-connected and you don't even live here.'

'Well,' I said modestly, 'I try to lead as full a life as possible.'

# 27

IT WAS AROUND eight o'clock that night when the phone rang. Lucy disengaged herself from my arm, shrugged ruefully and went to pick up the receiver.

The evening had been going very well. We'd rented a video of *The English Patient* and had argued energetically about it as we watched. I liked it; she thought it overlong, overrated and oversentimental. But at least it made for a more interesting discussion than our conflicting views on Brussels sprouts and somehow, as the talk warmed up, we'd moved closer together on the couch in Richie Proctor's den and by the time Willem Dafoe arrived, thumbless, in Italy she was snuggled up against my shoulder and we both knew that soon we'd be going to bed though not, this time, in separate rooms.

And then the phone rang and Lucy got up to take the call.

She said, 'Yeah? ... What? ... What is this – some kind of sick joke? Get off the line, you creep, or ...' And then for a long time she listened and when she spoke again her voice was different, softer, more hesitant. 'Mickey, I don't know what ... Yeah, okay ... Right ... Right.'

She hung up and looked over to me, her eyes huge with shock. 'I don't believe it,' she said, 'I still don't believe it.' She sank, almost collapsed, into an armchair beside the phone. 'That was Mickey.'

'Who?'

'Mickey. Mickey Meo?'

It took a second or two for comprehension to dawn. 'Your old boyfriend?' I said. 'I thought he was dead.'

'So did I. But it was Mickey all right. He's ... I think he's hiding out somewhere. He was calling on a cellular.' She gave a mirthless little laugh. 'It sounded like he was in a bathroom. There was a shower running, I think. It was all, I don't know, kind of furtive.'

'What did he want?'

'He wants to see me. Tonight. He said he'd call again to arrange it and then he hung up.'

'Do you want to see him?' I said watching her.

She shook her head. 'No. It's over, Mickey and me. I told you – for me it was over even before I thought he'd been killed.'

'But it's obviously not over for him.'

'No. Bobby, if he calls again I'll have to go meet him. I don't want to but I'll have to. I feel I owe it to him. He ... he sounded so desperate.'

I hoped he wouldn't call again. I said, 'How did he know where to find you?'

'He called my home, got my answering service. They gave him this number. Oh Jesus, this is a mess. What I do not need right now is Mickey Meo back in my life.'

I went over to her, knelt beside her chair, held her in my arms. 'What on earth is it all about?' I said.

She stroked my cheek gently. 'Dumb question, Bobby.' And, of course, she was right. The whole thing was too sudden, too inexplicable to be susceptible to guesswork. The only thing that was certain was that Meo's call had destroyed the mood of the evening.

We watched the rest of the film, this time from separate chairs, neither of us paying too much attention. Every now and then we would glance at the phone as if it was some kind of bomb timed to go off when we least expected it.

But when it did go off, half an hour later, it was just Richie Proctor calling from Montana.

He said, 'Christ, Bobby, what's going on? I've just had a call from Tony Flo. He says Charlie Baldock's fired you, you and Agnelli. You're both off the picture. What the bloody hell's happening?'

I sighed. 'It's too complicated to go into now. But yes, you're right, I've been fired.'

'But …' He hesitated. 'Where does that leave me?'

'Pretty much in place, I should think, so long as you don't do anything daft. I didn't hire you, after all.'

'No, but Bill Charleston tried to get rid of me and now he's the only producer on the picture. That doesn't sound too healthy for me, does it?'

'If you want my advice, Richie, I'd say keep your head down for a couple of days, don't make waves and see what happens. Hang on – Lucy wants a word with you.'

I handed the phone to her. She and Proctor talked about the next day's shooting schedule; she didn't mention Mickey Meo.

The call we'd been waiting for came around eleven o'clock. In the interim the film ended, I made coffee and we sat and waited, not talking much. For most of the time Lucy prowled about, restless and preoccupied, never far from the phone.

When, finally, it rang she snatched it up and once more all I could hear were her responses, mostly monosyllabic. Like the first call it didn't last long and when she put the receiver down she wore that shellshocked look again.

'Well?' I said.

'There's a place on Sunset, opposite the Beverly Hills Hotel, a piece of open grassland. That's where he wants to meet me. At the bench there.'

'What time?'

'He said midnight, as close to midnight as he can make it but I might have to wait.' She flopped into an armchair, hunching forward, her chin on her hands. 'God, this is going to be awful.'

I wanted to go to her again but there was something about her posture that said: Keep off. I said, 'What is?'

'He wants me to go with him, to live with him.' Her voice was flat, bereft of emotion. 'He says he's figured out a way. He says he loves me, he's missed me terribly and can't go on without me. He said if I knew what a risk he was taking just getting in touch with me, then I'd really know how much he loves me.'

'What do you want to do?'

'I don't know.' She shook her head, staring at me and yet beyond me. Then she sat up and took a deep breath. 'Yes, I do. I'll go see him and I'll tell him that what he wants is impossible because I don't love him. I'll tell him … I'll tell him there's somebody else.'

'Well, I sincerely hope there is,' I said, softly.

'Do you?' She grinned wryly. 'Yeah, well, if all this hadn't happened we might have found out about that.' She sighed, grinned again. 'I'm sorry, Bobby. One way and another I turned out to be a really lousy date, didn't I?'

Now I did go over to her and hold her. 'I'll come with you tonight,' I said.

She started to protest but I put my finger on her lips to quieten her. 'Several reasons. One, I won't have you hanging around Sunset Boulevard at midnight on your own. It's not safe. Two, if you're alone with the guy he might sweet talk you into doing what he wants and I'll never see you again. And three, well, if he cuts up rough when you give him the Dear John message I'll be around to quieten him down. I'm rather good at that.'

She did make the protest but not with any great conviction. I think she'd been hoping that I wouldn't let her go by herself.

We took Lucy's car. She drove; I sat beside her making a lot of use of the rearview mirrors. She said, 'What's the problem?'

I shrugged. 'Nothing really. It's just that, after Darren's story about the green Merc, I want to be sure we aren't being followed.'

'And are we?'

'No,' I said. 'Not as far as I can tell.'

We got to the Beverly Hills Hotel just before midnight and parked in one of the streets running south of Sunset. From where we were we had a clear view of the stretch of grass that was like a tiny, open park and the bench that Mickey Meo had specified. There was nobody on or near it. Not then, nor at midnight, nor fifteen minutes later.

Lucy said, 'Maybe I should go sit on the bench. Maybe Mickey's hiding somewhere nearby, doing what we're doing – waiting to see if anyone turns up.' She started to open her door, then hesitated. 'Bobby, why do I have such a bad feeling about all this? It's going to be tough telling Mickey but ... but it's not just that. There's something else, something—'

'I know what you mean,' I said. 'I feel it, too. That's why I'm coming with you.'

'Don't come all the way,' she said. 'Stay back a bit, out of sight. It's better I talk to him alone.'

'Okay.' We waited as a small truck went by and we were still not out of the car when she said, 'There he is. That's Mickey.'

A tall, strongly built man had emerged from a small cluster of trees on the other side of the green. He strolled over to the bench, looked carefully around, glanced at his watch and sat down. There was a wariness about him, a tension as if he were poised for flight. He hadn't seen us.

Lucy got out of the car, hurried across the road and started running towards him. I followed a few paces behind. When she was about twenty, thirty yards from Mickey Meo she called to him and he glanced over his shoulder in her direction ...

And then everything seemed to happen at once.

Whether the car parked near the intersection moved before Mickey did I cannot now be sure but, as I recall, it seems to me that when he stood up and turned towards Lucy the car started forward, slowed as it drew level with him and almost came to a halt as the rear window nearest to us slid down and some dark, unidentifiable shape pointed a machine pistol at Mickey Meo, squeezed the trigger and blew him away.

I threw myself at Lucy, hurled her to the ground, lay on top of her and covered her head with my arms. I could see Meo's body jerking as the fusillade of bullets struck home, could see the mess his head had suddenly become, could see the blood gushing from his wounds. A line of stray shots kicked up grass and dirt a few feet in front of Lucy and me.

And then it was over. The gun was withdrawn, the window was wound up and the car accelerated away. Meo had fallen forward and was sprawled, perfectly still, across the back of the bench, blood leaking from a dozen places on his head and body.

Beneath me Lucy was shivering uncontrollably, making small,

anguished, whimpering noises. I got up, lifted her to her feet. She was in shock, hardly able to stand, so I picked her up and carried her back towards the car.

Now the shooting had stopped the night was suddenly very still but I knew it wouldn't stay like that for long. Even in Beverly Hills, an area whose residents held a particularly strong belief in the adage that the secret of a long, healthy life was to mind your own business, curiosity would eventually prevail. Any minute people would be peering cautiously from their houses to see what was going on. This was a good time to be somewhere else.

I bundled Lucy into the car, found the keys in her handbag and got behind the wheel.

She said faintly, 'Mickey ...'

'There's nothing we can do for him.'

Just before we reached Santa Monica Boulevard a couple of police cars raced by, sirens screeching, heading in the opposite direction towards Sunset and the body that was lying there, waiting for them. If they'd asked me I could have told them there was no need to hurry. Mickey Meo wasn't going anywhere.

# 28

LIEUTENANT HARRY BROWN CAME to see me the next morning, not long after I'd got back to the hotel.

It had been a very bad night, with Lucy at first almost stunned with shock and then, as that wore off, raging helplessly at the cynical, cold-blooded callousness of the killing we had witnessed. I lay beside her on the bed, both of us still fully dressed, and held her and did my best to soothe her. Neither of us had slept much and I'd tried to persuade her not to go to work that day, to call in sick.

She had refused even to consider the idea. 'I'll be better at work. Other things to do and think about. I couldn't just sit around here all day going over what ... what happened last night. I'd go crazy.'

In the end I'd watched her drive away on this clear, warm, sunny morning. There were kids going to school, humming birds hovering around the feeders on the porch, lawn mowers starting up in the gardens around. Death seemed far away on a day like that.

When she had gone I tidied and locked the house and drove back to the Bel Air Riviera. And then Harry Brown arrived, neat and elegant in his designer sports coat and slacks but not looking too friendly.

'I was going to call you this morning,' I said.

'Is that right?' He stood in the middle of the sitting-room in my bungalow, hands thrust into his coat pockets. 'Something you wanted to tell me, maybe. About last night perhaps.'

I felt the first twinge of alarm. 'What are you talking about?'

He perched one buttock on the dining table and folded his arms across his chest. 'A man was shot to death last night right opposite the Beverly Hills Hotel. A couple of minutes later another man was seen carrying a woman away from there. We have a description, not a great description but it could fit you.'

'Hey, come on. There must be hundreds of—'

He gave me a nasty grin. 'Cut the bullshit, Bobby. You spent the weekend with a young woman named Lucy Lane. Yesterday a certain Mickey Meo called that same Lucy Lane on a cellular phone. You know about Mickey Meo, don't you, Bobby?'

I just stared at him, waiting.

'Thing about Mickey,' he said, 'until a little while ago he was banging your Miss Lane on a regular basis. You knew that too, didn't you, Bobby? And what we think – no, what we're pretty damn sure of – is that he called her to set up a meeting. We know he called her because we checked with the phone company. And we reckon that she was there and you were there last night when somebody passed by and blew bits of Mickey all over Sunset Boulevard. You care to tell me about that?'

I shook my head.

He sighed. 'Okay. Right now people from the murder squad are talking to little Miss Lucy Lane over at the studio. Far as I know they're being nice and polite, same as I am to you, but if you won't help, well, I'll just have to call and tell them to take her down to the precinct where a couple of guys will play good cop–bad cop and maybe, just for the hell of it, charge her with accessory to murder. That okay with you?'

I thought of all the thrillers I'd seen in which the protagonists landed themselves deeply in the shit because, perversely, they either failed to contact the police or lied to them. You know the kind of movie – people wading about knee-deep in corpses and you're silently screaming, 'Come on, *now* call the cops!' but the hero shakes his head and, without bothering to offer any explanation, says, 'We must keep the police out of this.' Why? Because if he called in the police they'd take over and he wouldn't be the star any more, that's why.

Well, I wanted – desperately – to keep the police out of this but it was too late for that. The police, or anyway Harry Brown, were already in it. And Harry Brown was still perched on the edge of my dining table and looking as if he wouldn't be entirely averse to beating me about the kidneys with a rubber truncheon if it would serve his purpose.

'Can I make a deal?' I said.

Harry Brown shifted his weight from one buttock to the other. 'What are you saying – you shot Mickey Meo and want to plea bargain?'

'No! Look, I'll tell you exactly what happened but on one condition – that you and your mates go easy on Lucy. Do we have a deal?'

'Try me,' he said, and since that was clearly the best offer I was going to get I told him everything. He listened very carefully and without interruption and when I had finished he nodded, as if satisfied.

'Yeah, well, that's pretty much what your girlfriend told us,' he said.

'You knew? You came in here with all these threats and you knew already?'

'Just checking,' he said. He looked around him. 'Do you have a cold beer anywhere in this fuck-pad?'

I got him one. I got us both one. It was a bit early in the day but, what the hell, I needed a beer.

'Tell me about Mickey Meo,' I said. 'Like, why LA's finest should be so upset that someone blew him away. I thought he was just a small-time gangster.'

We poured our beer into tankards. We weren't yuppies; we didn't have to drink straight from the bottle to show how tough we were. Harry said, 'He was a hit man, killed three people that we know about. On the first two we couldn't touch him but on the third we got him – eye witnesses, you name it. Sooo … He made a deal, turned state's evidence and the FBI offered him the witness protection programme.'

'Let me guess,' I said. 'In return for all this consideration he put the finger on Carlo Minelli.'

Harry nodded. 'Right. All the hits he did, and a lot of other stuff, he did for Carlo. He spilled the whole lot, gave us Carlo on a plate.'

'Uh-huh.' I took another swig of beer. 'So when Mickey was supposedly killed—'

'—they buried some other guy. Right again. The Fibbies arranged it all, sweet little set-up but not quite sweet enough. The funeral director, would you believe, actually knew Mickey so he also knew the body he was stuffing in the box wasn't Mickey's. Just bad luck really.'

'And the funeral director told Carlo?'

'Boy, you're hot today. That's exactly what he did and Carlo's people have been looking for Mickey ever since. Last night they found him.'

'How?'

'Through little Miss Lucy, I guess. Mickey was hooked on her. The FBI guys knew that – he talked about her all the time apparently – so I guess Carlo's people did, too. My bet is they've been watching her ever since Mickey disappeared, figuring he'd try to contact her sooner or later.'

'Yeah, but why now? Why did he wait till now?'

He shrugged. 'Opportunity maybe. The FBI had him stashed away in an apartment in West Hollywood, no phone, no fax, nothing. But … Saturday, one of the babysitters got careless with his cellular.'

'Deliberately?'

'I don't think so. Mickey had been no trouble, nice company, real grateful for all the protection, never even suggested that he might want to pass a message to anyone outside. So I guess the boys eased up on the vigilance a little.'

'How'd he get away from them?'

'He started complaining of sickness, barfing every hour on the hour – or so he said. Anyway, he spent a lot of time in the bathroom and I guess he made his calls on the cellular from there. Last night he's in there again, making these distress noises, so one of the babysitters goes in to see he's okay, Mickey coldcocks him, takes his gun, disarms the other babysitter, handcuffs the two of them to the bedpost and takes off.' He held up his hands to forestall any interruption from me. 'I know, I know – what was wrong with those guys? Well, all I can tell you is their first priority was keeping other people from getting at Mickey, not stopping Mickey going out. They never even figured he'd want to with Carlo's people looking for him.' Harry Brown drank some beer and shook his head. 'The chances some men will take for a piece of ass.'

'You know the irony of all this?' I said after I'd thought about it for a bit. 'I suspect Mickey was going to ask Lucy to go into witness protection with him. But he was never in there with a chance.'

'Why? Because she's so crazy about you?'

'No, though it would be nice to think so. But actually she'd stopped being crazy about Mickey even before that first time he was supposed to be dead.'

Harry Brown raised his beer glass to me. 'Women,' he said. 'God bless their fickle little hearts.' Then he said, 'So what were you going to call me about?'

'Ah, yes, that. I think I know where Darren Carmody is.'

# 29

As it turned out, I was wrong.

I called Lou to tell her that I'd spoken to Harry Brown and that he was happy to meet Darren any time, any place. But before I was halfway through the message she said, 'I don't know where Darren is any more.' She sounded desperately worried. 'He's ... he's left the place where he was staying and he hasn't been in contact.'

He'd been hiding out, she said, in a house just off Mulholland Drive. It was the home of one of Lou's girls who, thanks to Lou, had married well a couple of years ago and was now retired. The husband was in the travel business and three weeks earlier he and his wife had taken off for a protracted business-cum-pleasure trip to Europe. The wife had given Lou the keys to the house with a request that she keep an eye on the place.

When Darren had turned up with, figuratively speaking, the sheriff and the posse on his heels, Lou had installed him in the former hooker's quiet, respectable home in its quiet, respectable street with instructions to keep his head down and make sure the neighbours didn't know he was there.

And that, pretty well, was what Darren had done, except yesterday when he had taken a chance and sneaked out in order to meet me. Later, when it was dark, Lou had driven him back, dropped him off at the end of the road and had not heard from him since.

She had called but got no reply; had even driven to the house and knocked on the door but with the same result. And she had been unable to go in and check the place for herself because Darren had the keys.

'Where might he have gone?' I said.

'I don't know. I don't know too much about his life these days. Maybe he has some friends, people I don't know about ...' Her voice trailed off, the tone somewhere between hope and despair but edging towards despair.

She gave me the address, a house in Westwood Drive, just off Mulholland. Harry Brown drove me there in his car, his siren screaming most of the way, though there hardly seemed much need for it.

'Gooses the other bastards awake,' he said with satisfaction, as motorists scattered frantically to give us room. Then, 'Do you believe him? Darren? Do you believe he's innocent?'

I shrugged. 'I dunno. If you take their word for it they're all innocent, aren't they? His mother believes he's innocent but then she would, wouldn't she?'

'And she thought I'd believe him, too, because I'm supposed to be a friend of yours?'

'That's right.'

He glanced sideways at me as we turned left on a red light at Linden on two wheels, oncoming traffic slewing about the road as the drivers stood on their brakes. 'Hell, I don't even believe *you*,' he said.

We turned right at Mulholland, then left onto Westwood Drive, a street of pleasantly attractive houses, way below the league of the movie star pads in Beverly Hills, but looking expensive enough anyway. Harry had turned off the siren by now and we coasted gently to a halt outside the address Lou had given me.

We got out and walked around the house. It had a quiet, deserted look about it, venetian blinds pulled down at every window. At the back were flower-beds, a lawn and a fair-sized pool. There was no dead body floating in it.

Harry Brown knocked and rang at the front door and again at the back. No answer.

'Guess we'll just have to go in,' he said, went round to his car and returned to the back of the house with a huge ring of keys. The fifth one opened the back door, which was the good news. The bad news was that the burglar alarm went off, too.

'Lou give you the code for the alarm panel?' Harry asked.

'I didn't think to ask for it.'

'Then let the fucker ring.'

The kitchen looked tidy enough, so did two of the three bedrooms and their en suite bathrooms, but the third showed signs of recent occupancy. The bed hadn't been made, men's clothes were strewn on the chairs and in the bathroom we found a shaver and various toilet accessories. There was a certain amount of mess, too, in the living-cum-dining area: the remains of a congealed pizza and a couple of empty cans of beer on a table and two upright chairs lying on their sides on the floor.

But there were no dead bodies inside the house either.

We were looking at the overturned chairs when the neighbours turned up. Four men, two women, all middle-aged and from their attitude torn between trepidation and indignation.

Their spokesman was a burly, totally bald man of about sixty who looked as if he had just come off the golf course. 'What the hell's going on here?' he said in the loud, hectoring tones of a (presumably) retired captain of industry or at least some kind of studio executive.

Harry Brown said, 'We have reason to believe somebody broke into this house.'

'Yeah – you. You just did. We heard you. I don't know who you guys are but you might care to know the police are on their way.'

'I am the fuckin' police,' Harry said and showed them his shield. 'Anyone know how to turn this alarm off? It's giving me a headache.'

Nobody did.

'Fuck it,' Harry said. 'Okay, you people, go on home now. There's nothing to see here.'

They went, reluctantly, whispering to each other, and a few minutes later a squad car turned up. The two uniformed occupants came bounding round the side of the house, guns in hand. 'Freeze!' they said when they saw Harry Brown leaning against the door jamb.

I was some distance behind him, inside the house. I don't like guns, especially in the hands of eager young American cops. They have a habit of going off and hurting people before their jumpy owners have realised that what they thought was an offensive weapon aimed in their direction was just a pointing index finger.

Harry held up his shield again. 'Either of you ever seen one of these?'

The leading cop, crouching, aiming his gun at Harry's belly with both hands, said, 'We can't see it from here. Just toss it to us – slowly.'

'Okay. Which one of you can read?' Harry said and then, making an arbitrary decision, threw it to the second cop, who caught it, studied it and looked impressed.

'It's okay, Terry,' he said. 'He's a cop, a lieutenant.'

We didn't stay around long after that. Harry searched the rest of the house but there was nothing to find. A couple of monogrammed shirts more or less confirmed that the recent occupant had indeed been Darren Carmody but there was nothing to indicate where he might have gone.

'I'll leave you boys to clear up, secure the place,' Harry said as we left.

'But, sir, what do we do about the alarm?' Terry asked.

'You figure it out,' Harry said.

# 30

THE FILM UNIT was shooting at the studio that day – one of Virna Newport's scenes, the one in which she squares up to Martie Culper, playing the cop who turns out to be the surprise villain of the piece. Maybe I shouldn't have revealed that last bit but I imagine most people who want to have seen the film by now, if not in the cinema then on video, television or even an airline. It doesn't play so well on TV or airlines because they took out a lot of the violence and cleaned up all the four-letter words. Michael Rialto isn't nearly so menacing when he's saying 'shoot' instead of 'shit' or 'frig' instead of 'fuck'.

The man on the gate wouldn't let me in at first; indeed, he wouldn't have let me in at all if I hadn't been with Harry Brown.

He said, looking embarrassed, 'Mr Lennox, I'm real sorry but I have instructions from Mr Baldock himself to deny you admittance to the premises.'

'What?' Harry said.

I said, 'He means I can't come in.'

'The hell you can't.' He thrust the trusty shield into the gateman's face. 'Mr Lennox is with me, understand? Where I go, he goes. He's a material witness in a murder investigation. Now open the fuckin' gate.'

'Gee, thanks, Harry,' I said as we drove through. 'I'm supposed to be a respectable movie producer. Do my reputation a lot of good, that will, being known as a material witness in a murder case.'

'In this town? Listen, in this town they think you're rich or powerful you could be a convicted child molester and they'll still love you. So what's with you and Charlie Baldock?'

'Long story. We had a falling out, that's all. I'll straighten it out.' But I said this with rather more conviction than I felt.

Actually, Harry Brown had no urgent business at the studio. He was there to see the cops who had – the ones investigating Greg Harrison's murder – and fill them in on what we had found at the house on Westwood Drive. These two, a young brunette and her male Hispanic partner, viewed me with some suspicion until Harry said that I'd had no idea Darren was in the LA area until Lou phoned me that morning when, by chance, he, Harry, was with me. True, he did me no great favour by adding that the reason Lou had turned to me was because I was a highly valued customer.

The Hispanic seemed rather impressed. 'That right? Pretty nice there at Lou's I bet.'

The brunette merely looked at me coldly and said, 'Nice friends you have, lieutenant.'

They were there, she and her partner, to talk to Newport, see if she had any idea where Darren might be, and it was taking time. Newport was on the set, doing good work, and Richie Proctor wasn't about to interrupt the process. The cops could, of course, have insisted that they wanted to see her *now* but the police around Hollywood and Beverly Hills are always reluctant to upset movie people. Movie people have clout and money and connections, commodities which outrank mere policemen anywhere in the world.

I wandered away to watch the filming and after a while, when Proctor had called a break, the brunette came over to grab Newport and I joined Proctor and Lucy behind the camera. She looked pale and tired but said she was okay.

Proctor said, 'What's going on? There's a rumour floating about that Tony Flo's been given the boot and we've had more police round here than you'd find at Scotland Yard.'

'Well, Harrison's been killed, Darren Carmody's missing. You'd expect the police to—'

'Yeah, yeah, but what's going to happen to my film?' Proctor was a man who'd got his priorities sorted out.

Newport came back and the brunette and her partner left. Harry Brown had already gone. Shooting continued until after six o'clock and while I waited for Lucy I was thinking about going to my office, see if there were any messages, when Newport came up like a small storm.

'You!' she said venomously. Venom was always a strong feature of her repertoire. 'I have you to thank, don't I? It's because of you that the police keep asking me about Darren. Why should I know where he is?'

'He was your toy boy. And it looks as though he probably killed your lover. Don't you think the police have a right to be a little curious?' She started to interrupt but I said, 'Tell me about this autobiography Greg Harrison was writing. How many people knew about it?'

That stopped her. 'You really think it's all to do with that? Don't be stupid. Nobody would kill Greg because ... Oh, my God. You really think that?'

'It seems likely. So who knew about the book? And what was in it?'

'Oh, my God,' she said again. 'Greg said he was going to tell everything, stuff I wouldn't tell, that I wouldn't want known, that ... that other people wouldn't want known. I was worried, really scared. I told ... I told a few people about it.'

'Like who?' But by now I'd lost her. She was staring at me and beyond me, gazing from the look of it at some awful predicament visible at that moment only to her. 'Jesus!' she said and hurried away.

I was about to go after her but then Lucy appeared. She had put some make-up on but it couldn't hide the dark smudges under her eyes and the drawn look around her mouth.

She grinned ruefully at me. 'I look great, don't I?'

I took her in my arms and held her.

'It's been like a nightmare all day,' she said. 'I keep remembering what happened and sometimes I can't believe it. I mean, I know it happened – I was there, for God's sake! – but I still can't believe it.'

I held her away from me and gently brushed back a lock of hair that had fallen over her right eye. 'There isn't any cure for that,' I said, 'except time. But I do have a prescription that might help.'

'Yeah?'

'It's complicated but I think I can handle it. It involves my bungalow at the hotel, room service, a good meal and maybe a spot of liquor.'

She nodded thoughtfully. 'Does a bed figure anywhere in that prescription?'

'Could do,' I said. 'But only if that's what you want.'

She took hold of my hands and smiled. 'Why don't we try the first part of your prescription and see what happens about the bed?'

And by that time I'd forgotten all about Virna Newport.

# 31

THE WAY THINGS turned out the bed did figure largely in my prescription.

There are lots of reasons to have sex, love and lust being the most obvious. Lust was certainly there that night but so, on my part anyway, was love or something very like it. What Lucy felt I really don't know. At the very height of intimacy we both murmured protestations of devotion but words spoken at moments like that should never be held in evidence against you. So lust and maybe love, yes, but that night I think most of all she wanted sex for companionship, for comfort and as a means of washing away the horrors of the previous night, as a reminder that in the midst of death there is life. What we did together was not rutting; it was warm, gentle, solicitous, the fulfilment of a need that was as much emotional as physical.

Later, as we were drifting into sleep, she murmured, 'You know something, Lennox? You're a very nice man.'

I grunted. 'Just realised that, have you?'

'Yeah. I suspected it before but ... You know such awful people that I did begin to wonder. Not any more, though. Not after the last couple of days.' She made contented, sleepy noises.

'Nice,' I said, dissatisfied. 'That the best word you can come up with?'

She sighed languorously, snuggling against me. 'Don't knock it. When a woman says a man is nice it's a real compliment, trust me.'

Later still, as she prepared to go to work in the morning, she said. 'This relationship of ours?'

'Yes?'

'I think it's going very, very well.'

Carlo Minelli came back that day. He flew into LAX on a private jet chartered in Rio de Janeiro and the media were there, mob-handed, to greet him. I watched the arrival on the afternoon television newscast along with Harry Brown.

We were in the hotel bar because Harry had asked me to meet him there on account of I owed him a drink. He liked drinking in company because, the way he had matters arranged, the company always seemed to pay and on this occasion I didn't mind. I did owe him a drink after all; without his protection the local cops could have made things a lot tougher for me over the business of Darren Carmody's recent whereabouts.

He ordered a double Chivas Regal and asked the barman to switch over to the newscast. Nobody objected because Harry and I were the only people in the bar at the time.

The news was presented, as it usually is in America, by an avuncular older guy with silver hair and a bimbo. Sometimes it's an ethnic bimbo, sometimes a blonde WASP bimbo. This time it was the blonde WASP, all eyes and teeth and hair down to her shoulder blades, who introduced the item with the same face-splitting smile with which she would have announced a new attraction at Disneyland, the outbreak of World War Three, or the second coming of Christ.

'Watch this,' Harry said. 'You'll like this.'

We saw the jet come in and we saw the massed ranks of the media waiting to greet it.

I said, admiringly, 'You've got to hand it to the news people. I mean, this is a private plane. How did they know Carlo would be on it?'

'Because the FBI told them.' Harry signalled to the barman that his glass was empty. 'Those people,' he gestured towards the excited mob of newspaper, TV and radio reporters currently filling the screen, 'couldn't find their own assholes in a darkened room without a flashlight and a helping hand. The Fibbies wanted them there because they know they've lost Carlo now and the best they can do is embarrass the hell out of him by giving him maximum publicity. It's the one thing that really pisses him off, publicity.'

Minelli got off the plane. His face was impassive but the zoom lens of a camera caught the hard, angry look in his eyes. Harry Brown was right: Carlo was seriously pissed off.

'How'd you like them apples, motherfucker?' Harry murmured softly to the TV screen.

Minelli elbowed his way through the crowd. Questions were being yelled at him, most of them inaudible in the general hubbub, and he ignored them all except for one. A TV reporter stuck a microphone in his face and asked for his comments on the FBI warrant for his arrest on charges of murder.

Just for once Minelli stopped to speak. 'Warrant? What warrant? There was a warrant out for me wouldn't the FBI be here to arrest me?' He held out his arms as if beckoning the FBI to step forward. 'So where are they? Look, me and my associates here, we been in Brazil on a business trip. We know nothing about any warrant.' Then he turned away and flanked by his 'business associates' – a trio of hard-looking men in dark suits who thrust intrusive microphones back into the faces of their owners – he walked to a black limo with tinted windows and was driven away.

'Shit,' Harry Brown said. 'Zarak has foiled us again.'

'I saw that movie,' I said. 'Victor Mature and Anita Ekberg. It was crap.'

'Just like this whole lousy set-up with Carlo. I really thought we'd nailed him this time.'

'Forgive me if I'm wrong,' I said, 'but I was under the impression that you weren't entirely averse to doing the odd favour for Carlo.'

'That was then, this is now.' He signalled to the barman again. 'I remember you asking me once if there was any part of me wasn't for sale. It turned out there was. There was just a small part of me that had "cop" written all the way through it and there came a day when Carlo wanted me to do something and this part of me stamped "cop" said, "Hey now, wait up. There are some things you do and some things you don't and this is one of those things you don't do." So I told him to go screw himself and somehow we haven't been such good friends since then.'

I gazed at him with admiration. 'Harry! You resigned on a point of principle! Nobody does that any more. The last government we had in Britain didn't even know what the word meant. I'm proud of you.'

He grunted. 'Yeah, great. But I gotta tell you, financially I'm hurting bad.'

And by the time he left me, so was I. Chivas Regal is very expensive in American hotel bars.

That night Rico Agnelli called on me. I was in my room, finishing a corned beef sandwich on rye and watching *The Battleship Potemkin* on a video. Lucy was with the film unit, shooting a night scene, and I'd decided to stay in and summon room service. Usually I'm happy enough to go out and eat alone in a restaurant so long as I have a good book with me but I didn't feel like it that evening.

The pram was just bouncing down the Odessa Steps when Agnelli came in. 'Fuck is that?' he asked, looking at the screen.

'This? It just happens to be one of the most influential movies ever made. It's called—'

'It's in fuckin' black and white, for Chrissake. It's that good, why didn't they colourise it? God Almighty, look at the lousy quality of that picture. It's gotta be a hundred years old.'

'Close,' I said. 'What do you want?'

'Get your coat. Carlo wants to see you.'

'Really? Well, I don't want to see him.'

Agnelli shook his head sadly. 'Bobby, why are you such an asshole? You always try to pull this independent shit when Carlo calls. But you know and I know that if he wants to see you, you get your coat and go. So get your coat and let's go.'

I got my coat and went quietly.

The two goons in the front of the dark blue Eldorado ignored me as I got into the back seat with Agnelli and he didn't bother to introduce us. To him they probably didn't exist as people, just as muscle.

'Drive,' he said and we headed down to Sunset and turned right towards the ocean.

'Has Carlo moved house?' I said. 'Last time I looked he was living in Bel Air.'

'Shut up,' Agnelli said and there was silence in the car as we reached the coast and turned right and then, a little later, right again into the hills of Malibu. The houses up there, their grounds brightly lit to scare off burglars, were palatial enough but, frankly, I wouldn't live in Malibu if you paid me. When it rains hard in California, which it does more often than you might suppose, the houses in Malibu are under such threat from landslides that any morning you could wake up and find yourself living in the middle of the Pacific Coast Highway.

The house we stopped at was more palatial than most, set in a lot of ground and surrounded by a high wall with electronic gates and a gatehouse. Two other cars, their lights out, were already drawn up outside the gates. We pulled up alongside them and the driver doused our lights, too. The gates, the gatehouse and the area in which we were parked were brightly illuminated by the big lamps on the gateposts.

Agnelli opened his door. 'Come on,' he said. I followed him out of the car and walked behind him to the dark limo parked nearest the gates. As we approached, the rear window was slid down and Carlo Minelli looked out at us.

'Good evening, Bobby,' he said. 'Good of you to come.'

# 32

GOOD OF ME to come. As if I had a choice.

Minelli didn't get out of the car, nor did he invite Agnelli and me to join him inside it, though since he was by himself in the back there was plenty of room. The front seat was occupied by two more goons and there were another four in the car alongside us.

'You know who lives here?' Minelli asked. I shook my head. 'Charlie Baldock. I invited him to my house this evening, discuss a few matters pertaining to the studio, but he seemed to think he was too busy.' He sighed. 'I can't help feeling that was a mistake.'

He nodded towards the men in the front seats, who got out of the car. Immediately, those in the second car got out, too. The six of them, led by Agnelli, walked up to the gates. Agnelli spoke into the voice box beside the buzzer on the gatepost.

'It's Mr Carlo Minelli to see Charlie Baldock,' he said, then listened for a bit. 'Yeah, well, we happen to know he is home and, like it or not, we're coming in.' He listened some more. 'The cops? Well, you got a cellular, give 'em a ring. Otherwise have you *tried* calling the cops lately? Have you tried calling anybody? Give it a shot, see what happens.' He leaned back against the wall, grinning and looking up at the telephone wires. I looked up, too. The wires had been cut. Agnelli spoke into the box again. 'Charlie didn't give you a cellular, did he? I didn't think so. So now are you going to open up?' He listened, shook his head impatiently. 'Okay, you want it that way.'

He stepped back and gestured to the men beside him. One of them threw a rope ladder over the gate and, when the hooks on the end caught hold, tugged to make sure it was secure and started climbing up. Another man held it steady for him while two more approached the gate with guns in their hands.

Suddenly an enormous man with a ginger beard and a shaven head came out of the gatehouse and pointed a double-barrelled shotgun in our direction. 'Freeze!' he said. Either he'd once been a cop or he'd been watching too much TV.

The man on the ladder stopped climbing, shrugged and glanced back enquiringly at his companions. Suddenly they all had guns in their hands, each of them pointing at the bald man with the beard. Agnelli lit a cigarette and peered through the bars of the gate.

'Look at it this way,' he said reasonably to the bald man, 'you got one chance, we got six. You shoot, we shoot. One of us dies – maybe – you die certainly. We blow your heart out, we blow your head off, we blow your dick off. What did you say just now – "freeze", was it? Good advice. Why don't you take it? Put your gun down, slowly, and freeze.'

The bald man hesitated only a moment then did as he was told, one hand going instinctively to his crotch.

The man on the ladder carried on climbing, settled himself astride the gate, pulled up the ladder, re-hooked it, climbed down the other side and vanished into the guardhouse. In a moment the gates swung open. Two of Minelli's men stayed behind to babysit the gatekeeper and the rest of us drove up to the house.

It was wide, white, two-storeyed, floodlit and palatial. Agnelli put his finger on the buzzer beside the huge front door and kept it there. A couple of minutes passed before the door was opened by an anxious-looking Vietnamese butler in black trousers and a white jacket.

Agnelli didn't introduce himself or anyone else. He brushed the butler aside and held the door open while Minelli and I got out of our cars and went into the house. The gunmen hung around on the long, wide porch and lit cigarettes.

We were halfway across the parqueted hallway, which was no bigger than a basketball court, when a door at the end opened and Charles Baldock leapt out.

'How dare you!' he yelled. 'This is a goddamn outrage!' He was in shirt and slacks, his hair ruffled, a smudge of lipstick beside the corner of his mouth.

Minelli said, 'Good evening, Charlie,' and walked past him, leading us all into a vast split-level living-room that gave on to the patio and, beyond that, the pool.

Virna Newport in something loose and gold and low-cut was curled up, catlike, on a sofa near the open french windows. On a table in front of her was a huge pot of Beluga caviare with all the trimmings and beside the table a magnum of Moët et Chandon nestled in a bucket of ice. The dent in the cushions beside her indicated the recent occupancy of some other party. Baldock would have been my guess but then I'm quick at picking up on these things.

Minelli stopped when he saw her. He didn't exactly look surprised – I imagine very little would have made him look surprised – but he didn't look pleased either.

Beside me Agnelli murmured, 'Oh boy!'

Newport said, 'Hi, Carlo,' and smiled. In one of her movies it would have been the confident smile of a woman totally in control of the situation, however unexpected. But in one of her movies she would have had the advantage of a script to guide her. Here she had only her instincts to rely on and her instincts were clearly telling her that she was in the wrong place at the wrong time. Consequently the smile was a long way from confident.

'Virna. What an unexpected pleasure,' Minelli said in a flat voice. 'Unfortunately, you'll be leaving us now.'

Newport said, 'Carlo, what are you—'

Then Baldock chipped in, his voice straining for righteous indignation but not getting much further than anxiety. 'Who the hell do you think you are? Miss Newport is my houseguest. I won't have you—'

'Send her to her room,' Minelli said. 'You and I have things to discuss, Charlie. We don't want to bore the lady with our business talk.'

Newport, swiftly realising that she'd have to write her own script, put her champagne glass on the table and rose gracefully from the sofa. 'I'll leave you gentlemen to it,' she said, 'gentlemen' coming out as 'gennulmen' in the impeccable Southern accent she had used in her Oscar-nominated role in *Atlanta!* 'Charles, you'll find me in my room.'

'You want my opinion,' Agnelli whispered in my ear, 'her room is the master bedroom. Somehow I don't think Charlie will have too much trouble finding her.'

When she had gone Minelli unbuttoned his jacket and sank into one of the armchairs facing the sofa Newport had just vacated. He waved grandly to Agnelli and me to sit beside him, which we did. Only Baldock, the master of the house, and two of Minelli's minders remained standing.

Baldock said, 'The fuck do you think you're doing?' You had to hand it to him; the guy had balls. His voice still hadn't found its way to righteous indignation but at least it had gone appreciably past anxiety.

'Sit down, Charlie,' Minelli said. Baldock glowered at him for a bit then reluctantly did as he was told. 'That's better,' Minelli said. He beckoned towards one of his minders. 'Ernesto, why don't you pour us all some of that champagne there, keep everything friendly.'

Ernesto found glasses, poured, handed them round. Minelli sipped appreciatively. 'Nice stuff,' he said. He put the glass down carefully, not wanting to spill anything on the seventeenth, eighteenth, whatever century table top. 'I told Miss Newport we had a business discussion here but I lied. We have nothing to discuss, Charlie. I'm gonna tell you things, you're gonna listen, okay? First off, the movie continues just as it was before my, ah, unscheduled trip to South America. That means Bobby's still the associate producer and Rico still hangs around looking after my interests, right?'

Baldock said, 'No way. I don't want either of those hoods anywhere near my studio.'

'Charlie,' Minelli said gently, 'Charlie, what you want doesn't amount to a hill of shit here. We do it my way. Or … there are accidents, maybe fatal, either on location or in the studio. Or … the studio burns down one day. These things happen; they're regrettable but they happen. And … I can stop them happening. Are you following me?'

Baldock summoned up every vestige of his courage – and his courage was considerable. I didn't like the man but I had to admire him, the way he tried – to the end – to stand up to Minelli. 'Get out of my house,' he said. 'You think you can come in here, come into my own house, and kick me around? What? You think I don't know people, you think I don't have influence with the police around here? You think I'm going to let you walk all over—'

Minelli shook his head sadly. 'These people you know, these people you have influence with? These are people I own, Charlie. They live in good houses because of me. Their kids go to good schools and colleges because of me. Sure, you can go to them and complain about me and they'll listen sympathetically. But the next day I turn up with …' He clicked finger and thumb in the general direction of his second minder. 'Petey, show him the pictures.'

Petey took a wad of photographs from the inside pocket of his jacket and handed them to Baldock, who flicked swiftly through them. He didn't seem at all worried. Indeed, a faint smile touched his lips as he looked at them and laid them down, one by one, on the table in front of him. I picked up the discarded pictures and examined them for myself. They showed Baldock *in flagrante* with a stunningly pretty young black woman.

'So,' he said, 'what do you think you've got here? Okay, I screwed her. Well, anyone can see that. And I'll tell you something else: I'd screw her again, any time, anywhere.'

'Really?' Minelli said. He looked at the pictures himself, nodded almost enviously a few times and made approving noises. 'Yeah, I can see how you might feel that way. But, see, I think maybe you might change your mind when you learn how old the girl was when you fucked her.'

Baldock grinned. 'God, Carlo, you must be desperate. She was eighteen. She told me.'

Minelli shook his head slowly. 'I guess she did at that, because that's what I told her to say. But the fact is, Charlie, she was only fifteen. She still is only fifteen. I have her birth certificate and a sworn affidavit to prove it.'

The grin faded from Baldock's mouth. He glanced swiftly, fearfully, from Minelli to the pictures of the girl and back to Minelli. 'You set me up? You bastard, you set me up with this chicken, this jailbait?'

Minelli smiled, the small satisfied smile of the victor. 'Water under the bridges, Charlie. You screwed the girl, we got the pictures, the *National Enquirer* would pay a fortune for them. The cops might be kind of interested, too. They're still not crazy about statutory rape around here. Look at Roman. Roman Polanski? Poor bastard's still in exile in France because he porked a young girl. Okay, his girl was only thirteen, yours is all of fifteen but thirteen, fifteen, it's still statutory rape. You know what I'm saying?'

Baldock glanced briefly at the photos again, then turned them face down on the table top. 'Okay. What do you want?'

'You know what I want. Just keep your nose out of my business, out of my movie. Take a vacation. Hell,' Minelli pointed towards the photographs, 'take the chick with you, what do I care? Just be absent, be scarce, till the picture's finished.' He paused. 'Then we'll talk again.'

Baldock said warily, 'Talk again? What do you mean?'

Minelli raised both hands, a placatory gesture. 'Charlie, relax. I like the movie business, I like your studio, I think we could work together. We'll talk about it, okay?' He stood up. We all stood up except Baldock who still sat there, slumped, holding his head in both hands. 'Don't worry. We'll come to an arrangement.' Minelli chuckled. 'Believe me, Charlie – one way or another we'll come to an arrangement.'

For the first time Baldock looked genuinely apprehensive.

Minelli smiled down at him, shaking his head slowly. 'Charlie, Charlie,' he said softly, 'it's not that bad. I'm talking a future deal here, a profitable deal for both of us. I'm not planning to kill you.' He sighed, the sigh of a man who was doomed always to be misunderstood. 'Not unless you force me to.'

Then he clicked his fingers again and set off towards the front door and the rest of us followed him.

There was a little anteroom attached to the living area we had just left. It was in darkness but the door was ajar. Minelli stopped, pointed and said, 'Rico.' Agnelli went into the room and came out a few seconds later leading Virna Newport by the hand.

Minelli nodded. 'Miss Newport. You've been eavesdropping. No, it's okay. I understand. Women do things like that. It's not always wise but what can I say? At least now you know how things stand.'

She said desperately, 'Carlo, please. It's me – Virna. We—'

'Miss Newport.' He spoke her name coldly, formally. 'If you're smart you'll forget anything you heard here tonight. Also, if you're smart, you'll give a little more respect on set to my friend Michael Rialto. He tells me you belittle him, make like he can't act. He doesn't like that – I don't like that. I think you shouldn't do that any more.'

She said, 'Carlo, don't be like this ... We're friends, we—'

'You appear to have a new friend now, Miss Newport,' Minelli said, talking to her with such deliberate politeness that they might only just have been introduced. 'He's waiting for you in there. I believe he might appreciate a little comforting.'

He turned away and again, dutifully, we all followed him out of the house. Newport watched us go, her hands clasped tightly together under her chin.

When the door closed behind us, leaving her standing alone in the hallway, she must have longed for a director to say, 'Cut. Print it.'

But this wasn't the movies; it wasn't make-believe. This was life and she had just made an enemy of Carlo Minelli.

# 33

AGNELLI AND HIS minders drove me back to the hotel. The minders murmured occasionally between themselves but there was little conversation in the back of the car. Agnelli indeed dozed for most of the journey, which suited me because I had a lot on my mind.

As we pulled up in the hotel parking lot Agnelli yawned, stretched and grinned at me. 'Good night's work,' he said.

I nodded. 'Have you got a few minutes? Couple of things I'd like to talk to you about.'

He shrugged, a little surprised. 'Well ... Yeah, why not?' To the minders he said, 'Wait here.'

On the way to my bungalow he said, 'Carlo handled that pretty good. If he hadn't, things could have got tricky.'

'How d'you mean?'

'Like I told you, some of the other families aren't too happy with Carlo right now. Okay, he's got the FBI off his back but a lot of people are still very nervous about him. Certain parts of his business, the drug business, aren't doing too well. Another screw-up and there could be some interesting changes around here.'

I led him into the living-room. 'Drink?'

'A beer would be fine.'

I got a couple of cold Miller Lites from the fridge and handed him one. He grimaced slightly – it wasn't a designer enough beer for him

– but took it anyway and drank straight from the bottle. 'So okay, what do you want to talk to me about?'

'Mickey Meo,' I said. 'Tell me about Mickey Meo. That was your doing, wasn't it? Tracking him down, blowing him away?'

He took another swig of his beer, wiped his mouth on the back of his hand. Standing there, grinning at me, pleased with himself. 'Of course. When we learned Mickey wasn't really dead we had guys trailing Lucy around, night and day. We knew how he felt about her, figured he'd try to set up a meet sooner or later and when he did we'd get him.'

My beer still stood, untouched, on the table beside me. We were both standing, Agnelli leaning comfortably against the edge of the table.

'But you didn't think to tell me about any of this,' I said.

He shrugged. 'You weren't one of us.'

'So you set us both up?'

'If you want to put it like that, yes. Look, there was nothing personal in this. Mickey was a big problem. He had to go. Okay, I set up the surveillance on Lucy, I arranged the hit, but you think I did all this on my own account? Get real. I did it for Carlo.'

I watched him take another swallow of beer. 'You were just obeying orders?'

'Right.'

'We were followed – when I took Lucy to meet him, we were followed? I looked but I didn't see anybody.'

He shrugged. 'You wouldn't. We had three cars on her, day and night. It's hard to spot three tails. It cost plenty but it would have cost a lot more if Mickey had got to testify.'

I lifted my beer bottle, then put it down again. The glass was still icy cold and sweating in the warmth of the room. 'Lucy and I could have been killed last night. Was that all right with you?'

'It wouldn't have been ideal,' he said. 'A mob hit is one thing, civilians getting wasted is something else again. That can cause real trouble. But look on the good side – you weren't killed, either of you. You weren't even hurt. A little shook up maybe but you'll get over that.' He grinned at me again over the top of his beer bottle.

So I hit him. Twice. A left uppercut that started at hip level – my hip level – ripped into his lower abdomen and as he moaned and doubled up a right hook slammed into his jaw. He went down, as I knew he would, and stayed there, twitching slightly, his eyes glazed. I stepped across and took his gun from the holster under his left arm. It was only a little gun – a .22, I think – but big enough. I cocked it and pointed it at him as he began to sit up just in case he had another .22, or even a .45, concealed in his sock or his underpants.

'Jesus Christ,' he muttered, 'is anything broken?'

'No,' I said, 'my knuckles will probably be a little sore but nothing's broken.'

'I'm not talking about your fuckin' knuckles, I'm talking about my jaw.' He waggled it tentatively, winced, then held his face gently in both hands. 'I think I'm okay.'

'Pity,' I said.

He pulled himself shakily to his feet and leant against the table again, looking interestedly at the gun in my hand. 'What you gonna do now, hotshot? Shoot me?'

'Not unless I have to.'

'You ever done that before? Shot anyone?'

'Once.'

'Yeah? What happened?'

'The man died.'

He raised one eyebrow, impressed. 'You're full of surprises, Bobby. The way you coldcocked me there ... I wasn't expecting it.'

'You once warned me that you fight dirty so I thought I'd better do it first.'

He moved away from the table and sank into an armchair, still holding his jaw. 'That's a hell of a punch you got there. Right hook, was it? I wasn't paying too much attention.' He looked at the gun again and waved his hand. 'You can put that away. You won't need it tonight.'

I lowered the gun so that it was pointing at the floor. 'But maybe some other time, huh?'

He stroked the side of his face. It was already swollen and the first angry red signs of a bruise were beginning to show. 'This one maybe

I had coming. You're right, you could have been killed last night. It's better you weren't but if you had been I wouldn't have lost any sleep.' He took a deep breath and got up slowly, gingerly from the chair. 'What you have to understand is I don't need you, Carlo doesn't need you. Don't step out of line again, Bobby.'

He walked to the door, held out his hand. 'Do I get my gun back?'

'Tomorrow maybe.'

He nodded. 'Right,' he said, and left me.

# 34

THE NEXT MORNING I phoned Greg Harrison's publishers in New York. Jane Baker came on the line, sounding more like the Ice Maiden than ever. 'Do you have good news for me, Mr Lennox? Have you found the missing tapes?'

'No,' I said, 'and frankly I don't think anybody ever will.'

'I'm afraid I'm inclined to agree with you. So why this call?'

'I'm looking for more information. Harrison was going to tell all about the horny life and times of Virna Newport, right? But was the book just going to be about that or would there have been something else?'

'Oh, yes,' she said. 'It was mostly going to be about Newport – and himself, of course – but he promised a lot of other stuff, too. Salacious stuff about various Hollywood stars and executives. Who bedded whom and when and where. What happened at a number of Beverly Hills orgies. Who used what kind of drugs and how often, who provided them, how much people were spending on them. Oh, it would have been a very spicy book.' She didn't sound as if she, personally, approved of spicy books.

'Any names mentioned?' I asked.

'Not too many, not in the outline he gave us. He was a very cagey man; I don't think he wanted to give too much away up front. But there were one or two names as topical examples. The idea was to get the book out just as Newport's latest film – well, this film of yours, I guess – was about to open. So he said he had things to tell about people like Michael Rialto and Martie Culper – they're in your movie, aren't they? – and someone called Bill Charleston. I don't know who he is.'

'Did he give any idea of what he might say about these people?'

'No, he just said that he would mention them. The usual hype, really, to try to secure a bigger advance – promises that his revelations would blow the lid off Hollywood.'

'His words, I imagine, not yours?'

'Quite,' she said.

'Pity the way things have turned out. I'd have liked to read that book.'

'Yes, Mr Lennox,' she said. 'I imagine you would.'

And that was more or less the end of it.

After I'd hung up I called the studio and talked to Lucy. She sounded much better, much livelier. Even a little too lively at first.

'I'm really mad at you,' she said. 'You didn't call me last night.'

'I know. I'm sorry. I was going to but then I got involved in something else.'

She said, suspiciously, 'You went back to that whorehouse? What is it with you – you can't leave hookers alone?'

I sighed. 'No, I did not go to the whorehouse. This was something else. Business.'

'Business or, like they say in the mob, bidness?'

'Better you don't know.'

'Bobby,' there was no hint of banter in her voice now, 'what are you getting yourself mixed up in? Whatever it is, be careful, do you hear? I don't want anything happening to you.'

'Yeah, yeah,' I said. I didn't point out that I wasn't *getting* mixed up in anything; that I seemed to have been mixed up in something distinctly murky from day one. Instead I asked her again how she was and she said, more soberly now, that she still had waking nightmares about Sunday night and even felt guilty about Mickey Meo's death. I tried to tell her that it wasn't remotely her fault, that she was in no way responsible for Meo's obsession with her.

'I know,' she said, 'I know you're right. But … it was me he wanted. I just wish it had been some other girl. I'd still feel bad about him but not quite so bad. Does that sound very selfish?'

'No. It sounds normal to me.'

'Yeah, that's what I keep telling myself. Oh hell, look I'll get over it, I'm getting over it already. It'll just take a little more time, that's all.'

'You're sure?'

'I'm sure.'

'Good,' I said, told her I'd collect her from the studio that evening, exchanged kisses over the line, hung up and went to the whorehouse again.

# 35

At this time of day there were no bruisers on the gate. Lou's privacy was protected only by an elderly man perched on a chair and reading a James Lee Burke novel with his lips moving. He didn't seem pleased to be interrupted and took his time phoning the house on his cellular, giving my name and finally, grudgingly, telling me to drive on up.

In daylight the house looked less grand than it did by night and the interior, when lit by the sun rather than by strategically placed lamps and wall lights, was a little shabbier, the deep chairs and settees showing slight signs of wear and a few stains caused by God knew what human activity.

Lou was waiting for me in the big main room, an opened bottle of Chardonnay and two wine glasses on the table beside her chair. She looked as elegant as ever in a navy blue, calf-length shirtwaister and high-heeled shoes to match, a single string of obviously expensive pearls around her neck.

But when I got closer and bent to kiss her, Continental-style, on both cheeks, the signs of strain and worry were evident in her eyes and the new, faint lines on her face.

'You have news of Darren?' she asked at once, thus making my first unspoken question redundant: she clearly had no news of Darren either.

'I can't think what can have happened,' she said. 'I keep thinking something must have scared him off and that he's left the state, left the country. Oh, God.' She was agitatedly rubbing one hand with the other. 'He is all right, isn't he? You think he's all right, don't you?'

I didn't tell her about the upturned chairs and the other signs of struggle that Harry Brown and I had discovered in the house where Darren had been living. I liked Lou; why should I add to her distress? 'Sure,' I said. 'I've no reason to believe otherwise.'

I poured us both a glass of wine. 'He'll turn up,' I said, 'trust me.' Easy to say, harder to believe. I didn't even trust myself on that. 'How many people know Darren is your son – Hollywood people, I mean?'

She thought about it, frowning into the glass she held in both hands. 'That woman, I guess. Virna Newport. That evil bitch. He probably told her. I've no way of knowing if she told anybody else.' A pause, then, 'Carlo knows. Carlo Minelli.'

I nodded. Since Minelli was Lou's protector against the police and presumably other gangsters who might fancy muscling in on her business it was logical that he should have known. 'I imagine he knew a long time ago.'

'No. I only told him when I heard from Rico Agnelli that Carlo was backing this *Death's Head* movie. I thought maybe Carlo could fix it so Darren had a part in the film, give him the break that was all he needed. I knew Newport wouldn't do anything for him. To her he was just a toy boy, somebody to run errands and screw her whenever she felt like it. Carlo promised he'd see what he could do but nothing came of it. He's so unlucky, my poor Darren – always on the verge of something good but somehow nothing ever quite seems to happen.'

I made sympathetic noises. 'How about Agnelli? Did you tell him?'

She shook her head. 'I don't like Rico. I don't trust him. Besides, I'm not sure he's going to be around too long. The way he's playing around with that Chinese girl – Terri Chin, you know? – that's going to get him into serious trouble one day because she's Michael Rialto's girl and …' She hesitated. Then, 'You know who Michael is, do you?'

'Minelli's nephew-in-law, but I didn't think it was common knowledge.'

'It isn't. Carlo told me one night, right here in this house. We go back a long way, Carlo and I. You know what I'm saying?'

I looked at her. She may have been getting on in years but she was still a very attractive woman. 'I think so,' I said.

'Yeah, well, we were in bed upstairs. It wasn't one of his better nights, he'd had too much to drink, which was very unusual for him, but he told me stuff then, like about Michael being married to his niece. The next morning I don't think he remembered a thing and I certainly didn't remind him but I've never forgotten.'

'Does he like Rialto?'

'I think so, yes. Michael's a whoremonger, just like Carlo, and I think some day he wants to get into the business, Carlo's business, and I get the impression that's okay with Carlo.'

'Really?' Worth knowing, I thought, and filed the information somewhere on the hard disk in my brain. 'Tell me about the drug scene in Hollywood. Was Darren involved in that?'

She sat up indignantly, spilling a little wine. 'Darren? What are you saying? Darren isn't a user. He doesn't smoke, he doesn't even drink much. He ... What? Are you suggesting he might be a *dealer*?'

'No, no,' I said hastily. 'I just wondered whether he might know anything about the way drugs are circulated in Hollyw— No, forget it. I'm sorry I mentioned it.'

'Well, I should hope so!' She glared at me, bristling with outrage, and I reckoned it was probably time to go. I finished the wine, stood up, thanked her prettily and assured her that Harry Brown and the LAPD were doing their best to find Darren and keep him safe. I thought it kinder not to remind her that they wanted him safe so they could charge him with first degree murder.

She softened a little and walked me to my car. She said, 'Believe me, Darren really doesn't do drugs. Oh, he may have smoked a little, I guess we all have, but ... She does. Newport. She's a user.'

'A serious user? Hooked?'

I think she wanted to say yes, but honesty overcame her obvious dislike for the woman. 'I don't think so. No, she's not, I guess. She does it, like they say, socially, always has a little coke on hand for, I don't know, parties or when friends call by. But I don't know where she gets the stuff. Certainly not from Darren.'

As I was getting into my car I said, 'Is there anything else I ought to know? Anything ... unusual that's been happening around here lately.'

She gave it some thought, started to say no, then paused, hesitated and said, 'Well, yeah, a couple of the guys on the gate said they'd seen a car hanging around once or twice. Like parked down the street, you know? They said they probably wouldn't have noticed only it was always the same car. It didn't bother us any. We just thought it was a couple of off-duty cops trying to rustle up some action. A few of them do that sometimes, they need a little money. They'll stop one of my clients when he's driving home with a girl, harass him, ask him where he lives, is he married, does his wife know where he is right now. Then money changes hands and ... no more problem.'

I said, 'Has anyone seen this car lately?'

She shook her head. 'No. I think it first turned up the night Greg Harrison was killed, then a couple times more, but not for a while now.'

I smiled. 'Yes, well. Nothing to worry about there, I imagine.'

But somehow I did worry about it all the way back to Hollywood.


I arrived early at the studio. Lucy was in her office, busy on two phones. She carried on talking into one of them while she frowned, glanced at her watch and mouthed 'I'm not ready yet' at me. I went over to her, nuzzled the back of her neck and whispered, 'No hurry. I'll be back.' She put her hand over the mouthpiece and kissed me hard while a male voice on the line squawked on, unheeded, about some actor client of his.

Lucy broke away from me and said into the phone, 'Why, that's just too bad, Mr Sobretski.'

'Whaddya mean it's too bad?' the voice squawked. 'You crazy? It'd be great.'

She waved me away as she tried to get back on the man's

wavelength and I backed out of the office, blowing her kisses all the way.

Down on stage one Richie Proctor was directing a fight scene between Michael Rialto and Martie Culper. It wasn't going too well. They were already on take ten and Culper, who was no athlete, was still swinging punches like an old woman trying to swat a fly with a handbag.

'Fucking actors,' Richie said as they were re-setting for take eleven. 'Can you believe this bloke? Couldn't hit a cow on the arse with a shovel.'

I left him to it and went back to the office block. Agnelli wasn't around, which was probably just as well. I wasn't scared of him – wary, yes – but I wasn't looking forward to our next meeting very much either. He wasn't the kind of man who would take lightly to being knocked about and I was pretty sure that somewhere, some day, somehow he'd come looking for a reckoning.

Margaret my secretary made no mention of the fact that she hadn't seen me in days but brought me, unbidden, a cup of tea and said there had been no messages for me.

'None at all?'

'No,' she said. 'The phone hasn't even rung.'

'Is this usual for associate producers?'

She hesitated. 'Not really,' she said. But then, no doubt seeking to cheer me up because I probably looked a little downcast, she said, 'Tom Hanks was in the studio again yesterday.'

'Who?'

'Tom Hanks?'

'Oh, yeah, the nice bloke. Asked after me, did he?'

'Well, no, Mr Lennox, he didn't actually.' She added, tactfully, 'Perhaps he already knew you weren't here.'

I finished my tea and looked at the day's call sheet on my desk. Virna Newport had been called for make-up at two o'clock to shoot a scene with the villain Culper – after, of course, he had been badly beaten up by the hero Rialto – at 4.30. Since it was now nearly five and there was a fair chance that Culper was still swatting flies on stage one, I reckoned this would be a good time to approach her.

Because Maestro Consolidated was an old studio that hadn't been much affected by the passing of time it still had some of the sumptuous dressing-rooms that had been built for its contract stars back in the thirties and Virna Newport occupied probably the biggest of these, a lavish suite full of plush furnishings, subtle lighting and great baskets of flowers.

The door with the big golden star and her name in big golden letters on it was closed but through it I could hear her giving a bollocking to some hapless assistant director who'd been sent to ask if she would mind hanging on for a few minutes because they weren't quite ready for her yet.

'Who does that goddamn Proctor think he is?' she was yelling. 'You tell him he's got just ten more minutes. You hear me? Ten minutes and then I'm outa here.'

The door opened and the AD, who looked about fifteen but was probably in his twenties with a degree from the New York film school, tumbled into the corridor, white about the mouth and sweating heavily.

When he'd scuttled away I walked into the dressing-room without bothering to knock. Newport was standing by the make-up mirror with her back to me and pouring herself a generous vodka and tonic. 'What is it now?' she asked without looking up.

I shut the door behind me. 'I just thought we might have a little chat,' I said.

She stared at me in the mirror. 'Oh dear. You again.'

'Yep, me again,' I said cheerfully. 'And no, though it's kind of you to ask, I won't have a drink right now, thank you very much.'

'Get out of here,' she said, but this time there was no sign of the snarling imperiousness with which she usually addressed me. I'd been around when she had the run-in with Minelli at Charlie Baldock's house and to her, no doubt, that meant I was close to Minelli and therefore a much more important player than she had assumed. Her attitude now was uncertain, even a little afraid.

'I won't take up much of your time,' I said. 'I expect they'll want you on set soon. So just tell me where you get your drugs and I'll be on my way.'

For a moment a touch of the old hauteur came back. Her eyes and nostrils flared with rage, or at least a pretty good simulation of it. 'Are you accusing *me* of using drugs? How dare you!'

'Oh, shut up,' I said wearily. 'Everybody knows you snort a little from time to time. It was all going to be in Greg Harrison's book.'

Now she looked scared. 'There is a book then? You've seen it?'

'No, but I know what was going to be in it and I think it was the stuff he had to say about drugs and their distribution in Hollywood that got him killed.'

She sat down, slowly, in the chair in front of the mirror and took a big slug of her vodka. 'Have they found Darren yet?'

'What's that got to do with anything? Or are you suggesting that he was your supplier?'

'No, of course not. But he killed Greg and—'

'Did he? You know that for sure, do you?'

'No, but the police—'

'Ah, yes, the police,' I said. 'Maybe I should call them in on this. I'm sure my friend Lieutenant Brown would be very interested to know where you get your coke from.'

'Oh, for Chrissakes,' she said.

'Exactly. But you have a choice – either you talk to me or you talk to him and I have to tell you that unlike the average cop around Hollywood and Beverly Hills he really doesn't give a shit for movie people. So tell me: who do you get your drugs from?'

'What do you think?' she said.

'I think Carlo Minelli,' I said. 'Or, rather, it used to be Carlo but now it's someone else. What do you say?'

She said nothing.

'Okay,' I said. 'Then tell me this. How does it work? How do you order up new supplies?'

She sucked at her drink again and walloped some more vodka into what was left in the glass. 'Look, I don't know who the end supplier is. I deal with a middleman. Greg arranged it for me. I call a number and say, "I'd like a repeat order of my favourite candies, please" or "I'd like a repeat order times two" or whatever and some guy brings it round all tied up in fancy wrappings like it was a box of chocolates. Then I give him the money in a sealed envelope and that's it till the next time.'

'Neat and simple,' I said. 'And when you call who's on the other end of the line?'

She hesitated. 'I don't know and I've never tried to find out and that's the truth, so help me God. These are not people you mess with.'

I believed her. I said, 'Okay, give me the number.'

More hesitation. 'What are you going to do?'

'Never mind what I'm going to do, just give me the number. Or, if you prefer, you can give it to Lieutenant Brown.'

For a moment I thought she would refuse and if the knock on the door had come a few seconds earlier she might have done. As it was she glared at me defiantly for a moment or two, but when it came to that kind of stuff I was more than a match for her. So after a little intensive cold, hard staring – the best and, maybe, the only trick I have in my acting repertoire – she was the one who glanced away.

'Oh, what the hell,' she muttered uneasily and told me the number. 'But, please,' she added, 'don't ever tell anybody, not anybody, who gave it to you. Will you promise me that? Please? These people scare me.'

I promised and wrote the number down and then the knock came on the door and the assistant director said, 'We're ready for you now, Miss Newport.'

# 36

I WENT BACK to my office and called the number Newport had given me.

After three rings a male voice said, 'Yeah?'

'Good afternoon,' I said brightly. 'I'd like to buy some cocaine please.'

There was a startled silence at the other end of the line.

'Cocaine? Are you crazy? What is this – some kinda joke?'

'Not at all. I was given your number by a very satisfied client of yours, who said that—'

'Who? Who gave you the number?'

'That's neither here nor there. I was simply given your number and told that if I called you'd be happy to supply me. But clearly there's been some mistake. Who exactly am I talking to?'

'Eat my shorts, motherfucker.' Then the line went dead.

I hung up and sat looking thoughtfully at the phone. I wasn't surprised at the way the conversation had gone; broadly speaking it was much as I'd expected. I'd only made the call to check that the number Newport had given me was the right one and now I was pretty sure it was.

The giveaway I thought was that 'Who gave you the number?' line. An innocent householder, shopkeeper, whatever, would either have been outraged or amused, would have treated me as a lunatic or a practical joker, would have wondered whether I was a friend pulling his leg. But somehow, it seemed to me, his first consideration would not have been how I'd got his phone number. That was the question of someone protecting his own back.

I mulled this over for a bit and then called Harry Brown. He didn't say hello, how are you, any of that stuff. What he said was, 'What do you want?'

I told him I was wondering whether there was any news of Darren. He said there wasn't. I asked if he knew who was the main supplier of social drugs to the movie community. He said, 'Why?' I said I was just curious. He said, 'Bullshit.'

'No, come on, Harry. I'd really like to know. It might be important.'

'How?'

'Well ...' It was a good question. How might it be important? I really didn't know. I was just following a hunch, at best a vague theory. 'Well, maybe it's not important but I would like to know.'

'Among the bottom feeders the situation changes all the time,' he said. 'We close one guy down and another springs up. But at the top ... Hey, why don't you ask your friend Carlo Minelli? If anybody knows these things, he does.'

'Yes, well, I might do that. Thanks. Oh, by the way, if I gave you a telephone number could you find the address for me?'

'What for? Does this have anything to do with the other stuff we been talking about?'

'I don't know. Maybe, but equally maybe not.'

'You're not holding out on me, are you?'

'No. I could just be chasing my own tail.'

'Take my advice, Bobby. Leave the police work to us. Stick to chasing tail, doesn't matter whose. Okay, gimme the number.'

I did that. 'When will I hear from you?'

'When I get around to it. We're kinda busy here right now. I don't know whether you're aware of this but there's a lot of homicide in this town and most of it lands up on my desk. You'll hear when you hear, okay? Oh, and you owe me a drink.'

'Don't I always?' I said, and we hung up.

Down on stage one Newport and Martie Culper, strikingly made up to look as if he'd just taken a terrible beating, were going through their paces, pretty smoothly it seemed to me. Newport was a great old pro and Culper was a very solid actor when no physical action was involved. Lucy was sitting beside Richie Proctor and making him deal with paperwork between takes.

I was settling down comfortably to wait for them to wrap when I realised I'd left my pen in my office. No big deal, you might think, but I have a thing about pens. When I find one that suits me, I like to hang on to it, and this one suited me. It had only cost a few dollars but it had a nice feel to it. So I went back to get it.

It was now past six o'clock and most of the offices were empty. Margaret had gone home, leaving me a note to say that there were still no messages. Big surprise. I found my pen and walked back down the deserted corridor to return to stage one.

As I passed Rico Agnelli's office I heard Terri Chin say, 'Rico, honey, I can't. I simply can't. Not tonight.' Then there was the sound of movement, of a slight scuffle and she said, 'Rico, don't! Not here – someone might come in.'

I stopped to eavesdrop, pressing my ear to the closed door. Pretty tacky, I know, but would you have done otherwise?

Agnelli said, 'Jesus, Terri, what's going on? You're giving me the runaround here.'

'No, I'm not, believe me I'm not. I'm … Rico, I didn't know you were gonna be here today. *I* wasn't even supposed to be here today. They called me in for wardrobe fittings and now I have to go home and prepare. I have my big scene with Michael tomorrow and I'm not up for it yet. I can't see you tonight, I just can't. I have to be good tomorrow, I have to be really good and—'

'Michael,' Agnelli said. 'You're fucking Michael Rialto again, aren't you? He got you this part in the movie, right? What did you do – suck him till his ears popped?'

There was the sound of a slap, then she said, scared, 'I'm sorry, Rico. I didn't mean to do that. Please don't hit me.'

Oh, shit, I thought, I'm going to have to burst in and save the damsel in distress again. But it wasn't necessary because Agnelli said, 'Christ, baby, I would never hit you. I leave that to Rialto. He's the one likes to beat up on women. Ah, honey, come here, let me hold you—'

'No, not now. Please, Rico, not now. I have to go.'

And then, taking me totally by surprise, the door burst open, she rushed out, I stumbled in and Agnelli punched me hard in the face. I think it was a reflex action, because he was as startled as I was. Probably he didn't even know who he was hitting – just lashing out at an intruder. It was a good punch, though, that straightened me up and slammed me back against the wall. I stood there, slumped and holding my jaw, and as he came towards me with his fists up I mumbled, 'One more shot.'

He stopped. 'What?'

'You have one more shot, Rico. I hit you twice, so you can hit me twice but after that I fight back. It's only fair. You had it coming, now I have it coming. Two shots each and we're quits.'

He shook his head slowly but he didn't hit me again. 'You are something else, Lennox, you know that? What were you doing out there anyway?'

'Do I really have to tell you?'

'I guess not. So, did you hear anything good?'

'Nothing I didn't know before except that Terri's in the movie. Nobody told me that but, what the hell, why should I be privy to these matters? I'm only the associate producer, for God's sake.'

'Yeah. Terri. I guess it's too late to catch her now.' He moved to the window to look out on the parking lot and I went with him. As we stood there side by side, apparently on friendly terms, it was eerily like one of those John Wayne movies in which the Duke and the other big feller can only bond after they've knocked each other about a bit. Except that I knew that bonding was never going to happen between Agnelli and me.

Down in the parking lot Terri Chin was getting into the passenger seat of an open Porsche. In the driver's seat, urging her to hurry up, was Michael Rialto.

'Michael,' Agnelli said softly. His face was tight with anger.

'Maybe they're just going off to rehearse the big scene together,' I said.

'Whatever big scene they get into tonight it won't have a lot to do with acting.'

'Yeah?' I said. 'Look on the bright side. Whatever they do, Terri might be acting.'

He turned his anger on me. 'Butt out. I don't need your sympathy.'

I shrugged and walked away. He said, 'Hey,' and I stopped and glanced back.

'Your jaw hurt?' he asked.

I touched it gently and nodded.

He passed the fingers of his left hand lightly over the knuckles of his right. 'So does my fist. But, boy, does it feel good.'

And so, once again, I went to Lucy's office. This time Proctor was with her, flopped into a chair, rubbing his eyes and holding a cold beer in his other hand.

'Hard day?' I said to him.

He nodded. 'Yeah. Good one, though. We're getting there.'

Lucy kissed me on the mouth and linked her arm in mine. 'So, all ready for the party tomorrow?' she said.

'What party?'

'Richie's party. It's his birthday tomorrow. He'll be—'

'—a hundred and eighty-three the way I feel now,' he said.

Lucy said, 'You didn't know about the party? The one Tony Flo's giving for him? You didn't get an invite?'

'The word is invitation,' I said, 'and no, I didn't get one. I don't even get any bloody messages. I went to my office today for the first time in God knows when. Not a single message. Would you believe it?'

'Ah, poor baby,' she murmured. 'Never mind. I expect Tony sent your … invitation to the hotel.'

'I hope so. I mean, as the associate producer I ought at least to be invited to the bloody parties. Why this one though? Why's Tony Flo suddenly so generous?'

'I guess he's very pleased with Richie,' Lucy said. 'Way things are going we'll come in ahead of schedule and under budget. Maybe he's celebrating that.'

'Or maybe,' I said, 'what he's really celebrating is the fact that his own job's safe again.'

'Yeah, I heard that,' Proctor said. 'I also heard that you've been reinstated and Charlie Baldock's pissed off out of town. What happened?'

'Carlo Minelli happened.'

'Ah, yes. Why doesn't that surprise me?' He finished his beer and heaved himself to his feet. 'Well, I'm off home, have a think about tomorrow's pages. I'll leave you lovebirds to it. But don't forget, Lucy, you've got a hard day tomorrow, too. Don't keep her up too long, Bobby.'

'I certainly won't,' I promised.

He paused at the door. 'I think I'll rephrase that. Don't keep her *awake* too long is what I really mean.'

'Hey, Richie, tell me something,' I said, 'when did Terri Chin get to be in the film?'

'Couple of days ago. Michael Rialto suggested it. Normally I hate actors trying to tell me who they want in the movie but there was a part for her, not big but not bad, and she looks right for it so I took her on. Saved the bother of looking at a whole bunch of other people. But if you're going to ask me why Rialto was so keen on her, the answer is I don't know.'

I said, 'According to Agnelli it was because she sucked him till his ears popped but I couldn't actually say whether that's true.'

Lucy narrowed her eyes thoughtfully. 'Probably is, though,' she said.

# 37

I WAS TRUE to my word. I didn't keep Lucy up too long; I didn't even keep her awake too long though God knows I tried. But before midnight she snuggled up against me in my big double bed, kissed my chest a couple of times, murmured, 'I'm sorry, Bobby, I'm absolutely pooped,' and promptly fell asleep like a baby.

I lay awake for a while holding the lithe silkiness of her, enjoying just having her there almost as much as I had enjoyed the things we'd been doing earlier. There hadn't been anyone in my life for some time; not since Linda Kelly had dumped me to become a movie queen. Well, no, that wasn't fair. It was her career, not Linda, that dumped me. The chance she had been waiting for suddenly came along and she took it. I couldn't blame her for that. In her place I'd have done the same. But the result was that she went out of my life for good, leaving a gap so big that I hadn't even tried to fill it.

Well, until now, and now there was Lucy. Her breath was soft and sweet on my throat and her thigh firm and equally sweet beneath my hand and I could think of Linda without nostalgia or regret.

There was no word from Harry Brown the next day; there was no word from anybody except Margaret who rang to say that an invitation to Tony Flo's party that night had finally arrived in my office.

After Lucy had gone to work I went for a long, hard run in Beverly

Hills, used the Nautilus equipment in the hotel gym for a couple of hours and in the afternoon I phoned Donovan to give him a progress report.

As before it was a complicated business. I phoned from my room, he gave me the number of one of a series of public call boxes near his home, then we both hung up and I went to the hotel lobby and rang the call box from there.

Donovan was delighted to hear that the film was going well, listened intently to my description of the run-in between Minelli and Charles Baldock, took a professional interest in the assassination of Mickey Meo and didn't seem to care too much about anything else.

'Seems to me,' he said, 'that sometime soon I better come over there, have a word or two with Carlo. If he's thinking of taking over that studio I want a piece of it. As for you, young Bob, I'm not paying you to hang around in whorehouses. Aside from that, you're doing a good job. Things seem to be going very well.'

'Going well?' I said. 'There are two men dead and another man missing and you reckon things are going well?'

'Tell you the truth, Bobby,' he said, 'I don't give a shit who killed Greg Harrison. Never liked him as an actor anyway. And as for Darren how's-your-father, what's that got to do with me? Or you, come to that? I say let the police worry about it. It's what people pay the idle buggers for. You concentrate on the film and watch your back far as that Agnelli's concerned. You understand?'

'Yes, all right.'

'Good. Well, it's all A1 at Lloyd's then, isn't it, or anyway at Lloyd's as it used to be before they all went broke. Now then, how about you – getting your end away, are you?'

'Goodbye, Donovan,' I said.

He was right, of course. None of the other stuff – Harrison, Darren, the death of Mickey Meo – was really any of my business or his, the one proviso being that it didn't interfere with the film. So far it hadn't but that, I thought, didn't mean it wouldn't.

A little later I went to the studio to collect first my invitation and then Lucy and take her to the party. When I got to my office Margaret said, 'Oh, Mr Lennox, you've … er … you've had some messages today.' The look on her face was a mixture of confusion and embarrassment.

'Great,' I said. 'Like what?'

'Well,' she blushed and looked down at her notebook, 'they're very strange. Kim Basinger's office called to say Ms Basinger would like to take you to Acapulco for the weekend. Then there was a call from Michelle Pfeiffer's secretary who said Ms Pfeiffer is missing you desperately and wonders why you haven't been in touch. And ... and Sharon Stone rang to say she wants to have your baby.' She looked at me beseechingly. 'Those were the messages, Mr Lennox. I hope they make sense to you.'

'Certainly they do,' I said. 'Now then, the Basinger offer sounds good. Call back and say I accept. Pfeiffer, well yes, I have treated her badly, I'm afraid. I'll handle that one myself. As for Stone, tell her no way. Okay?' I put the party invitation in my pocket and headed for the door.

Margaret said, 'Mr Lennox, please, are you serious? I don't know how to contact these people. I don't even have their numbers.'

'Let's leave it till the morning,' I said. 'Don't worry about it.'

Lucy was looking terrific in a short, white linen dress, very simple, that perfectly showed off the dark gold of her tan. We exchanged information about the kind of day we'd had – hers had been busy but good – and then she asked innocently, 'Well, did you get any messages today?'

I helped her into my car. 'Just a few. Nothing important, though.'

'Really?'

'Yes, well, you know. Just the kind of stuff I have to deal with every day. Oh, by the way, I'm going to Acapulco with Kim Basinger this weekend.'

She punched me savagely on the arm. 'You bastard. You'd do it, too, wouldn't you? Given the chance, you'd just drop me and go.'

I leaned across and rearranged a stray lock of hair that had fallen over her forehead. 'Nah. I wouldn't do that.'

'Why? Because I'm sexier than Kim Basinger? It'd better be because I'm sexier than Kim Basinger.'

'No, you're not. It's because I know that Kim Basinger, unlike you, doesn't care enough to leave messages to make me feel good.'

She hit me again. 'Are you really telling me I'm *not* sexier than Kim Basinger? Of course I am, you total scumbag.'

I put my hand on her bare thigh and she brushed it away. 'Don't you dare molest me. I will not be molested by men who don't think I'm sexy.'

'I wasn't molesting you. I was just checking for cellulite.'

'What!'

'Good news, though. No sign of any – yet.'

She pressed herself back against the door and studied me wonderingly. 'What am I going to do with you, Lennox? You're an awful man.'

'I know,' I said, 'but you have to admit I have a silver tongue.'

The party was at Tony Flo's home. Bel Air, of course. The predictable movie mogul pad – big colonial-type house, sweeping lawns, near Olympic-size pool. Flo had rounded up all the usual suspects from the picture – the stars, Bill Charleston, who glared at me but kept his distance, Agnelli, the cameraman and a few of the other top production people. Most of them were accompanied by husbands and wives (theirs or somebody else's), girlfriends, boyfriends, whatever.

Agnelli was there unaccompanied. So was Michael Rialto. So was Terri Chin. Chin was schmoozing with Tony Flo, who had rested his hand on her hip. Bit lower than her hip, actually. The other two were watching them from opposite sides of the pool.

Lucy nodded towards Chin. 'She was good today, dammit.'

'Why dammit?'

Her lips formed into a little pout. 'Well, she not only looks great but there's a good chance she can act as well and that's too much for one woman.'

'The feminist sisters would hate to hear you say that.'

'Yeah? Well, sometimes I think screw the feminist sisters. You know what's lousy about this business? It's so hard for us other girls to get noticed when the men are only interested in sniffing around creatures like her. I mean, hey, will you look at that?'

I looked. Flo now had his arm around Chin's waist – bit lower than her waist, actually – while she chuckled deliciously, presumably at some wisecrack he had just delivered. Rialto and Agnelli were still watching.

I said, 'You mean you're jealous? What? You'd like to be standing there with Tony Flo groping your buttocks?'

'No! What I'm saying is that it doesn't hurt a girl's career in this business when the right men notice her and because of girls like Chin they don't notice girls like me.'

'Well, in the first place,' I said, 'if I were a girl, I don't think I'd want Tony Flo's hairy hands all over my bum and in the second place *I* noticed you. I noticed you right off. "My word," I said to myself, "there's a sexy woman. Much sexier than Kim Basinger or …" Who were those other two who phoned me today?'

'Pfeiffer and Stone,' she said.

'Right. Much sexier than any of them.'

'Hmm. You wanna prove you mean that?'

'Later,' I said. 'Right now what I want is a glass of wine and a heaped plateful of whatever's on that buffet table.'

'Christ,' she said, 'you English are so romantic.'

After that we ate, we drank, we mingled. Some time later Tony Flo gathered everyone around the pool to hear him deliver a birthday eulogy to Richie Proctor who stood right in front of him, looking glum and embarrassed and hand-in-hand with his plump, pretty wife, lately returned from her trip to England. Lucy was alongside the wife and Virna Newport was clutching Proctor's free arm with both hands and acting delight and affection. Agnelli was some way behind Tony Flo with his back to the throng while he talked into his mobile phone, and Rialto and Terri Chin …

Well, Rialto and Terri Chin were surreptitiously easing themselves away from the crowd towards the gazebo at the end of the lawn. I waited until they had gone inside, then followed them and took up an eavesdropping position beside the open window. I was getting quite good at eavesdropping.

For a while there was nothing to hear except the wet sounds of kisses delivered to God knew what portion of whose anatomy and, standing there in the darkness, I seriously began to wonder whether it wasn't time for me to take up some nobler calling.

Then Chin said, 'No, Michael, please not here. Someone might come in.' She said it with a convincing mixture of earnestness and regret which impressed me as much as Rialto. I thought that, with all the practice she'd been getting over the last couple of days, she was becoming rather good at delivering this kind of dialogue.

Rialto said, pleadingly, 'Aw, shit, honey, you can't leave me like this. Look at me – this is all for you, you don't wanna waste it.'

'Michael, we have to talk.'

'Talk? At a moment like this? What's to talk about?'

'Us. Her. Have you told her yet? Have you told your wife about us?'

'Angela? Have I told …? Oh, sure.' Rialto laughed. 'Right, yeah. I go home nights, I say, "Hey, sweetheart, you'll never guess who I banged today." What, are you crazy?'

'Michael!' There was real anguish in her voice. 'Don't joke about it. Darling, please don't joke. You said … you promised you would tell her. You said we were going to be married.'

'I said what?' Another laugh, more disbelief than mirth this time though. 'Listen, honey, a guy says a lot of things when his dick's pointing up towards his nose. Terri, let me explain something to you: this isn't the movies, this is Hollywood, this is real life. There's a big difference. There are no happy endings in Hollywood, only in Hollywood movies.'

She was sobbing now, so hard that I couldn't make out what she was saying. I could hear Rialto, though, his voice harsh and pitiless.

'Listen to me, Terri: don't get greedy. I been good to you, got you parts in two movies, given you nice presents, taken care of you. That's enough, hear? Be happy with what you got.'

The sound of her weeping died away. She said softly, 'Michael, you promised. You promised! If you don't marry me I'll—'

'What? Kill yourself? Go ahead.'

'No! I'll tell her about us. I'll tell your wife, I'll tell everybody.'

There was the sound of a slap, a crack almost as loud as a pistol shot, and a scream that was suddenly choked off as if he had put his hand across her mouth.

Rialto said, 'Shut up, you stupid bitch. And don't you ever, ever threaten me. Do you understand? You threaten me and you got no career, you're dead in this town. You hear what I'm saying? One word about you and me get's out and you won't even be able to peddle your ass in Mama Lou's cathouse.'

She made a noise, a thin, wailing noise of sheer grief, and then she stumbled out onto the darkness of the lawn.

Rialto said, 'What? You leaving? Yeah, maybe it's for the best. Somehow I'm not in the mood any more. Have a nice life, Terri.' He sighed, as if at the obduracy, the unpredictability, of women and I heard him light a cigarette and suck in a lungful of smoke.

I was about to tiptoe away when I saw Agnelli coming towards the gazebo and the weeping Terri Chin hurling herself into his arms. They stood together for a few moments, he apparently listening, stroking her hair, holding her close to him. Then they moved apart, he doing the talking now, she nodding until she hurried off, not towards the party but around it, skirting it, towards the side of the house.

Agnelli watched her go and then started walking towards the gazebo.

I thought: My God, now what do I do? He'll kill him; Agnelli will kill him. He'll just pull out a gun and shoot him dead and I can't stop him.

But he did no such thing. He stopped at the entrance of the gazebo, peered inside and said, as if surprised, 'Hey, Michael. What are you doing in here all by yourself?'

Rialto said, 'Rico? Jesus, am I glad to see you. I think I got a real problem with Terri Chin. She says I promised to marry her, can you believe that?'

'I can believe you promised. I can't believe you meant it.'

A hollow laugh from Rialto. 'Yeah, right. Only, women ... You know? A guy says things to make them feel good and they ... She's threatening to tell Angela. She does that, I could be in trouble.'

'You want me to handle it?'

'You'd do that for me? Hey, that would be ... No, no, hold on there. Not like that, okay? I'd like you to handle it but not *handle* it, you know what I mean?'

'What did you have in mind?'

'Well ... I don't know. Could you, could you just cosy up to her, smooth her a little, calm her down? She likes you, Rico, I know she does. If you could just take her off my hands ...'

I could hardly believe what I was hearing. Did he really not know, could he really not guess that there was already something between Agnelli and Terri Chin? But then I thought: well, he's an actor, or anyway a movie star, with a movie star's ego and tunnel vision and it would probably never occur to him that any woman he fancied could have eyes for anyone else.

Agnelli said, 'Okay, Michael. I'll do that for you.'

Then they went back to the party together. And I stayed where I was for a while wondering what the hell Agnelli's game plan could be.

# 38

HARRY BROWN SAID: 'That address you wanted? It's a little store, a shop, on Santa Monica close to Doheny. It's called "Deliveries".'

'What does that mean?'

'What it says, I guess. You want something, they find it and deliver it for you.'

'You mean … for instance, if I wanted a quart of ice-cream they'd go and fetch it for me?'

'Probably, though I can think of cheaper ways of getting yourself a quart of ice-cream. Mostly what they do is they find and deliver more unusual things. Like – how shall I put it? – you wanted a small Indian elephant that played the violin they'd be happy to go look for one.'

'Probably not much demand for things like that around here,' I said, 'although, I dunno, this is Hollywood after all. Do they make money, these people?'

'How would I know? I just found the address for you, I didn't go in with a warrant, demand to see their books.'

'Are they clean?'

'Far as I know. I haven't heard otherwise. Look, I'm a busy man, I don't have time to schmooze. You want the address or what?'

I took the address.

It was early afternoon, the day after Tony Flo's party. That shindig had broken up around eleven p.m. Terri Chin had gone long before then, right after her encounters with Rialto and Agnelli, and Agnelli had followed soon afterwards. Rialto had hung around, flirting with other men's wives and girlfriends, giving them his famous smouldering frown which they seemed to interpret as indicating sexual passion barely controlled and which gave me the impression that a small but vital fuse had blown just behind his eyes.

Richie Proctor had drifted by a little before eleven, muttering, 'Babs and me are pissing off. I've had enough of this schmaltzy bullshit.' Then, 'I'll be in the cutting-room tomorrow, having a look at the stuff we've shot so far. Only a rough assembly, of course, but are you interested?'

I said I was and that I'd be there. He shuffled off, plump and untidy in his shapeless suit, to retrieve his wife from among the clutch of women surrounding Michael Rialto. And soon after that everyone else started heading for home, too.

Lucy stayed with me again that night. She did have a place of her own – a small but pretty apartment, so she said, overlooking the ocean in Santa Monica – but it seemed to suit both of us much better that she should simply move in with me.

In the morning she left early for work. I lay in bed watching her with deep pleasure as she walked naked to the bathroom and came back, still naked but now glowing from the shower, and began to dress.

'What?' she said, as she pulled on her knickers.

I put my hands behind my head and sighed contentedly. 'Nothing.'

'Then stop leering at me.'

'I am not leering,' I said. 'This is in no way a leer. This is a smile of artistic appreciation. Think of me as an aesthete enjoying, disinterestedly of course, a vision of loveliness.'

She shook her head. 'No. I think of you as a dirty old man.' She looked at me appraisingly. 'Well, dirty anyway.'

When she had finished dressing and gulped down orange juice and coffee, she said, 'What are you doing today?'

'What associate producers normally do, I suppose. Bugger all.'

'You're not even going to phone all those glamour queens who called you yesterday?'

'Nah,' I said. 'Sod 'em.'

When she'd gone I dozed for a while, then got up, ran, worked out, swam, ate brunch and talked to Harry Brown.

In the late afternoon I parked my car just off Santa Monica Boulevard, walked to a diner directly opposite the shop called 'Deliveries', took a booth by the window and sat there for more than an hour, drinking coffee and pretending to read the *LA Times*.

'Deliveries' was a narrow, two-storey building made of pale blue breezeblock. The ground floor front consisted mainly of a picture window and a wooden door painted yellow. Over the door was a big black and white sign that said: 'You Want It? You Got It!' From where I was sitting I could just make out, through the picture window, the figure of a man sitting behind a counter.

The whole time I was watching nobody went in and nobody came out. After thirty minutes or so I left the diner, walked down to cross the boulevard at the lights and wandered slowly past the shop front. The man at the counter was thin, shirt-sleeved, wore a dark brown crewcut and was picking his nose and looking bored, as anyone might, since nose-picking rarely leads to exciting discoveries. There was a telephone at his right elbow.

I went back to the diner, reclaimed my booth and called the 'Deliveries' number on my mobile.

Crewcut picked up the phone. 'Yeah?' The same vaguely liquid growl as before.

'Ah, good afternoon,' I said. 'I phoned you a day or so ago but I think we must have been cut off. I was interested in buying some cocaine.'

A sharp intake of breath, a pause, then, 'Who is this?'

'Do you know, I'm never sure how to interpret that question,' I said. 'By "Who is this?" are you asking me to guess your identity, a somewhat formidable task given the absence of any clues, or are you enquiring after mine? If the latter it would be less confusing if you said "Who is that?", don't you agree?'

Dimly, through my window, across the street and through his window I saw him bang the phone down, wait a moment, then pick the receiver up again, dial a number, talk for a while and hang up.

I waited. Nothing happened. What was I expecting to happen? I don't know. Some kind of activity would have been nice; some sign of urgency or anxiety. But there was nothing like that. After a few minutes Crewcut stood up, stretched and yawned, strolled to the picture window and looked incuriously onto the street, then went back behind the counter again and started reading a magazine.

Some thirty minutes later I gave up, retrieved my car and drove east on Santa Monica Boulevard just as a dark green Mercedes sedan pulled away from the kerb a few yards beyond 'Deliveries'. Coincidence? Yes, it probably would have been if the occupants of the car had turned out to be a couple of blue-rinsed old ladies on a shopping spree.

But they weren't. They were two men. Big, hard-looking men like Darren Carmody had described. More than that, there was something vaguely familiar about them although I couldn't think what. They didn't look at me as I drew briefly alongside before dropping back and settling in a couple of car's lengths behind.

The Mercedes hadn't been there at any time while I was watching the shop, so presumably between my leaving the diner, walking to my car and driving back along Santa Monica it had turned up and stopped for a few minutes while ... what? While one of the occupants went into 'Deliveries' on some errand? Maybe. That was my guess anyway.

I had an argument with myself as I followed the car along Santa Monica. That doesn't have to be the car and they don't have to be the men Darren described, right? Right. I mean, there has to be more than one dark green Mercedes sedan in the Los Angeles area, right? Right again. So this could still be a coincidence, couldn't it? Of course it could. But you don't believe in coincidence, do you? Yes, I do. Happens all the time. At certain moments I just don't trust it, that's all. At moments like this, you mean? Yep. You got it.

So when the Merc turned left towards Sunset, so did I. But now there was only one other car between me and it and when we reached Sunset and the Merc and I turned right, the other car turned left. So there was the Merc tootling along in light traffic and me right behind it. I wasn't too bothered. The men in the car seemed to be talking to each other and taking no notice of me. They were going slowly and so was I; but then so was everyone else.

I was still right behind them when we reached the La Cienega intersection and the light turned red. The Merc stopped; I stopped; traffic came out of La Cienega, much of it turning right along Sunset.

And suddenly, with the light still against us, the Merc had gone.

The driver had waited for a small gap in the traffic filtering in from La Cienega, then hit the accelerator, cut in front of a red Volkswagen, swerved round a dirty white truck, nipped between a couple of open sports cars with about an inch to spare on either side and roared away along Sunset.

I couldn't have followed if I'd tried. The driver of the VW had panicked and hit the white truck and the truck had crashed into the side of one of the sports cars. Chaos and cacophony. Screeching brakes and crunching metal; shattering glass, blasting horns and cursing voices raised in anger. By the time some kind of order had been restored and I was able to go on my way the Merc could have been in another county.

An interesting development, though. The men in the Mercedes must have realised I was following them and didn't like it. But did that also mean they knew who I was? And did their appearance at the shop called 'Deliveries' have anything to do with the phone call I had made a few minutes earlier? Or were they, for reasons unknown but probably nefarious, simply people who resented anyone taking a close interest in their activities?

No chance of finding out now. I skirted round the broken glass in the road and made my way to the studio.

Richie Proctor was in the cutting-room with Michael Rialto. Neither of them heard me come in because they were standing in front of the editing deck, yelling at each other.

From where I stood I could see that the film on the machine had been halted at a moment in the scene by the pool at the Santa Monica house, the scene for which Proctor had made Rialto do all those close-ups he never intended to use.

Rialto was saying, 'You bastard! I want those close-ups in, you hear? I want them in *now*.'

'No way,' Proctor said, his stubborn truculence a moody contrast to Rialto's rage. 'That sequence stays like it is. Best thing in the whole bloody picture.'

'The best? All you got is the back of my fuckin' head. Don't you understand, you little Limey shit, I'm the star of this movie. Me. I'm the star – not that beat-up old bitch.'

'Yeah? Well, I'm the director and I get the final cut. It's there in my contract on tablets of stone. So you don't like it, you can piss off.' And then he turned his back on the other man. Big mistake. Because Rialto grabbed him round the throat with his left arm and stuck his knee in the middle of Proctor's spine, arching him backwards. In his right hand Rialto held an open switch-blade whose point was digging into Proctor's cheek, though not quite hard enough to draw blood.

I came up behind Rialto, grabbed a clump of his hair with my left hand and the wrist of his knife hand with my right, tugged him away from Proctor and hurled him across the room. He fetched up hard against the wall, the knife still in his hand.

Proctor gave a yelp of pain and outrage. 'He cut me. The bastard cut me.' From the corner of my eye I could see him wiping blood from his cheek but I had no time to stop and sympathise because Rialto was coming at me, holding the knife as if he knew how to use it.

I backed away, trying to find what open space I could in this machine-cluttered room, crouching slightly, chin tucked in, elbows protecting my ribs.

Rialto said, 'You laid hands on me? Huh? You dared lay hands on me? I'll cut your fuckin' heart out.' His eyes were little slits of hate and there was a thin line of drool trickling from the corner of his mouth. He still looked stupid but very dangerously stupid. He came towards me slowly, moving the knife from side to side.

'What? You gonna box me? You got your fists up, you gonna box me? Get real, asshole. I'm gonna kick the shit out of you.' He made a quick lunge forward and laughed as I took another step backwards. 'Okay, asshole, here it comes.'

Then he threw the knife and as I swayed out of the way, slightly off balance, he suddenly pirouetted on his left foot and kicked, chest high, with his right. A smoothly vicious karate kick which, if it had landed, would have laid me flat. He was fast, I had to admit that – fast, supple, agile, supremely fit. But I was fast, too, and besides I had a slight advantage over him: I knew what was coming. Instead of simply trying to avoid the powerfully lunging right foot I grabbed hold of it with both hands, jerked, swung violently and let go. Rialto arced through the air, crashed his head and shoulders against the door, gave a grunt of pain, slipped to the ground and lay still.

Proctor said, 'Christ, what have you done?'

'He'll be all right,' I said, panting a little. 'Probably have a nasty headache, that's all.'

Proctor knelt beside Rialto, who was now mumbling and groaning, and propped him up against the wall. 'How did you do that? I mean, that kick he threw at you, it was bloody quick.'

I got a paper cup of water from the cooler and handed it to Proctor, who started dribbling it into Rialto's mouth. 'I've seen his films,' I said. 'He always starts a fight with that move. It's a kind of trademark, so I was ready for it.'

'Does he?' Proctor said thoughtfully. 'Trademark, eh? He's got a big fight scene coming up next week. I'll get him to work out some new moves. Don't want any more clichés in this bloody film than we've got already.'

The door opened and Proctor's editor came in carrying a couple of cans of film under his arm. 'What happened here?' he said.

'Michael had a nasty fall,' Proctor said. 'He was showing us one of his karate kicks and lost his balance, knocked his head on the door.' He poured some more water into Rialto's mouth. 'That's right, isn't it, Michael? Had a nasty fall, didn't you?'

Rialto pushed him away and got up unsteadily, one hand pawing lightly at the back of his head. He glared at all three of us for a moment before his gaze settled on me. 'I'll fix you,' he said. 'Believe it – I'll fix you.' And then he staggered out.

The editor said, 'What happened to your face?'

'Cut myself shaving,' Proctor said. 'It's only a scratch. Don't worry about it.'

The editor nodded. 'Pulled a knife on you, did he?' He was an elderly man who looked as if he'd been around the movie industry for a long time, long enough anyway for nothing much to surprise him.

'What?' I said.

'He's done it before when he doesn't like the way a director's putting the movie together. I don't think he's ever actually cut anyone before, though.'

'Probably wouldn't have cut me either,' Proctor said, 'if this silly sod hadn't interfered. His hand slipped when you grabbed him.'

'Well, pardon me,' I said. 'I thought he was going to dig your eye out. I wish I'd let him do it now.'

The editor looked at me appraisingly. 'It was you threw him against the wall, was it? Yeah, you look tough enough. But watch yourself, know what I'm saying? Michael's a very mean guy with some very nasty friends. He doesn't turn the other cheek and he doesn't let bygones be bygones.'

'What about Richie here? Does he have to watch himself, too?'

The editor thought about it. 'Not yet awhile. The picture's too far along to change directors now. Michael has clout but not that much.' He shrugged. 'When the movie's over, though …' He left the rest of the thought unfinished.

'I'll worry about that when the time comes,' Proctor said, though he didn't look as brave as he sounded. He gestured towards the Moviola. 'Now, do you want to see what we've got so far or what?'

# 39

THE FILM, WHAT I saw of it, looked good. Violent, of course, because violence is box office and box office is all that Hollywood cares about. I wouldn't quite go so far as to say that, like the late and largely unlamented Hermann Goering, Hollywood tends to reach for its gun when anyone mentions culture. Hollywood has nothing against art and culture, so long as somebody else – preferably an independent producer – is financing it. What Hollywood says is that art and culture are absolutely vital to the health of the cinema and thank God there are philanthropists out there happy to provide such stuff. But the bottom line is the dollar and culture doesn't earn much in the way of dollars so, given the choice between culture and the gun, Hollywood will always reach for the gun.

*Death's Head Dangling* wasn't art or culture but it was very superior commercial cinema. Proctor, who had the eye and the instincts of a born filmmaker, handled the violence, the sex and the action scenes with easy skill but where he really scored, where his talent was most obvious, was in the more personal sequences, the conversations, the confrontations, the build-up to the sex and the violence. Without ever sacrificing suspense and urgency, he lent these moments a subtlety, a vibrant intimacy that were rarely found in movie thrillers. Newport and Martie Culper, the two real actors in his cast, were as impressive as I'd ever seen them and even Rialto and Annie Klane, who was largely there because of her drop-dead beauty and sensational body, gave performances which I should have thought were beyond their modest skills.

'So what do you think?' Proctor asked later over supper at Morton's.

'Amazing,' I said. 'You could be a latter-day alchemist. You may have found a way of turning crap into gold.'

He nodded, pleased. 'Be nice if I have. I could really use a box office hit right now. What about that scene by the pool in Santa Monica – do you think I'm right, playing it all on Virna?'

'No question. Like you said – best scene in the picture, so far.'

'Annie Klane,' he said. 'What do you think of her?'

'Great. I didn't know she could act that well.'

'Neither did I.' He shovelled Caesar salad into his mouth and munching it, with lettuce on his teeth, mumbled, 'You know who I really wanted for that part? Linda Kelly. She's going to be such a star that one – gorgeous, sexy and seriously talented with it.'

'Yes,' I said non-committally, 'that would have been very interesting, Linda Kelly in the picture.'

He looked up from his food. 'Lucy tells me you know her.'

'Used to,' I said.

We were eating together, Proctor and I, because his wife was out at a baby shower and Lucy was working late making final preparations for tomorrow's location shoot. He was an agreeable enough companion so long as you were content to talk about the cinema because nothing else seemed to interest him much. There are a lot of people like that in Hollywood, people to whom the movies and their own relationship to them are so important that nothing else seems quite real. Things like politics, war, global warming, crime, punishment, homelessness and unemployment – the kind of stuff the rest of us are inclined to worry about – impinge upon them only in so far as they might make subjects for future films. These people might not be able to tell you the names of the White House cabinet but they can – and Proctor did – rattle off a list of which stars are sleeping with whom, which are gay and terrified of being outed, which have entered into lavender marriages, which have serious drug problems and which are on the point of a messy divorce. As the evening unfolded a somewhat depressing roster of familiar and much-loved household names seemed to enter into one or other, and sometimes several, of these categories.

It was getting on for midnight when we left the restaurant. As we waited for the valets to bring our cars Proctor said, 'Thanks for what you did this evening. I hadn't invited Michael, you know. He just heard I was looking through the rough cut and insisted on being there. I don't think he meant to stripe me but he might have hurt me a bit if you hadn't turned up. So watch yourself, eh? Don't go walking down any dark alleys at night.'

Good advice but hardly necessary, I thought as I parked my car in the hotel lot and strolled down the prettily and discreetly lit path towards my bungalow. I would certainly keep an eye out for Rialto and his friends but I was confident I could handle any trouble they might offer.

It was a beautiful night, warm but with a slight, cooling breeze, the moon bright, the stars covering the face of the sky like silver freckles. It was, I felt, a night for romance, a night for champagne and the woman you loved, a night for ...

A man stepped out of the shadows and said, 'Are you Bobby Lennox?'

I stopped and turned towards him. He was a big man, dark and hard-looking. 'That's me,' I said.

'Thought so,' he said, and shot me.

# 40

IT WAS AS if someone had taken a steel railing, as wide as your fist, heated it till the end glowed white and thrust it straight through me, high up on the left-hand side. And it was as if, too, the muscles and cartilage and sinews just above my chest had been ripped apart, the raw nerve endings exposed like so many naked electric wires, touching each other and sending shockwaves of searing pain through my arm and shoulder.

I fell backwards from the path into some kind of soft bush that broke my fall. I could feel the sticky warmth of blood on my neck and face and upper body and I was conscious of the sounds I was making, gasping, breathless, sucking sounds, agonised, moaning sounds.

And as I stumbled and fell I heard another shot and didn't even know whether the second bullet had hit me or not because all sensation had centred on the area around my left shoulder and the burning, screaming mess of torn fibre and skin and ligament and flesh.

And then I heard yelling, a woman yelling, a loud, frightened but angry sound, and soon other people were shouting, too, and I heard footsteps running fast away from there and through it all I could still hear the ugly, stricken animal noises that I was making.

I was conscious, just, my gaze unfocused because of the shock and the blood in my eyes, when a shape loomed up above me, vague and unrecognisable. I tried to strike out to protect myself but my left arm wouldn't move and even my right no longer seemed to have much strength in it and in that moment I knew that I was dead, that the assassin, whoever he was, had come back to finish his work, and even then, through all the pain and confusion and sheer disbelief that such a thing could have happened to me, I wondered why.

What had I done and how could it have upset and scared and angered someone so much that I had to die?

And then the vague, unrecognisable shape was on its knees beside me saying, 'Bobby, oh Christ, Bobby, what have they done to you?' and Lucy held me gently in her arms and now there were other people around her, muttering excitedly, fearfully, about police and ambulances and paramedics and Lucy lifted me gently towards her and with my face pressed against the soft, firm warmth of her breasts I felt the pain ebbing away as I slipped finally into unconsciousness.

# 41

Donovan said, 'You don't have to go back there, you know. Christ, it's only a bloody movie, not worth dying for.'

'Wouldn't you go back?' I said. 'Somebody tried to kill you, wouldn't you want to find out who and why and nail the bastard?'

'Probably. But I'm in a different line of business from you. I know who my enemies are from the start. Somebody shot me, I could finger the bugger immediately. It's not like that with you, you're just an ignorant bloody bystander.'

'Innocent,' I said. 'The phrase is "innocent bystander".'

Donovan shook his big, shaggy Irish head. 'Not in your case. You got involved in something you don't even understand and got yourself shot, so you're an ignorant bystander. And if you go back you'll be just as ignorant and probably get yourself shot again, so if you've got any sense you'll stay here.'

I still don't remember too much about the immediate aftermath of the shooting. The police came and so did the paramedics, who rushed me away to the same hospital I had been in before but I wasn't aware of much except the pain and drifting in and out of consciousness until I finally woke up a couple of days later in the old familiar hospital bed, weak and hurting badly and with about a million tubes stuck in my body, dripping some stuff in and sucking other stuff out.

It was the sound of voices that woke me, Donovan's and Lucy's, hushed voices, Lucy saying, 'So yeah, we've been kind of living together.'

And Donovan, 'Well, he's a lucky bugger then.'

They were sitting side by side on metal chairs beside the bed, heads close together, keeping their voices low so as not to disturb me. I said, 'I've been shot. How lucky does that make me?'

Then they were both up and leaning over me, Lucy kissing me, jarring my left arm and causing me to moan with pain and then apologising tearfully and kissing and jarring me again. Soon afterwards I drifted back to sleep, feeling the coolness of her lips on my forehead, and when I woke up again, God knows how many hours later, she and Donovan had gone and there were doctors and nurses around me.

The doctors, too, said I was lucky. The bullet had gone straight through, making a mess of muscle and tissue but causing no permanent damage and the prognosis for a full recovery, give or take a couple of nasty scars back and front, was good. It would take time, though, along with therapy and hard work to strengthen and rebuild my shoulder and arm.

When the medical staff had gone Donovan came back. He'd flown to LA, he said, as soon as Carlo Minelli phoned and told him what had happened.

'I gave that bloody Carlo an earful,' he said, 'letting this happen to you. I've made him post two of his blokes outside your door, night and day, case the shooter comes back to finish you off.'

'That's nice,' I said. 'Unless it was Carlo sent the shooter in the first place.'

He looked startled. 'What? Carlo? You don't believe that, do you?'

I shook my head. No, I didn't. But then I didn't know what to believe and that's what I told the police and later the media people when they came in to question me. I couldn't even answer the simple questions properly. Could I describe the man? Well, yes, vaguely. He was big and menacing and dark-haired. Right-handed, fit and tough by the look of him. But no, I didn't know the colour of his eyes or whether he had any obvious scars. Did he have an accent? Yes – an

American accent but I didn't know which kind. Would I recognise him if I saw him again? Yes, damn right. The police brought a mass of mug shots to my bedside but the shooter's picture wasn't among them and in the end both they and the media seemed to write the whole thing off as an attempted mugging that had turned sour.

I didn't think Harry Brown believed that but this wasn't his case. He came to see me in an unofficial capacity and helped drink the champagne that Donovan had brought in. I introduced Donovan simply as a friend from London but Harry Brown wasn't fooled. He knew who Donovan was.

'Long as you're not planning to go into business in my town,' he said, as they shook hands, 'welcome to LA.' Then his eye lit on the champagne and, unbidden, he opened it and poured himself a glass and, as an afterthought, poured some for us, too.

'I guess we can talk in front of him,' he said, jerking his head towards Donovan. 'So tell me what happened?'

I did. I told him about the store on Santa Monica and about the green Mercedes and the two men in it. He said nobody had mentioned a green Mercedes near the hotel on the night I was shot but that didn't necessarily mean anything.

And then he said, 'You really think they're selling drugs out of that store?'

I shrugged. With one shoulder, the right. Not a smart move because it still caused shooting pain in my left shoulder. 'I dunno. Go and ask them.'

'I might at that.'

As he was leaving I asked about Darren Carmody. Harry Brown said, 'No news. The guy's either left the country or he's dead.' He looked across at Donovan. 'You wanna come for a drink?'

'Wow,' I said, 'he likes you, Donovan! Of course, you'll have to pay but don't take it personally. When Harry invites his mother for a drink she has to pay.'

It was when he returned a couple of hours later that Donovan said, 'I'm getting you out of here, taking you back to London, soon as you're fit to be moved. Harry doesn't buy the neighbourhood mugger theory and neither do I. If somebody wanted you dead before they probably still want you dead now and I don't trust those low-grade goons of Carlo's to look after you proper.'

'Properly,' I said automatically.

'I don't want any arguments and I don't want any fucking elocution lessons either,' Donovan said.

I didn't want to leave LA; I didn't want to leave Lucy. But when she came in the next day and I told her what Donovan had said she agreed with him. I could recover from my wound as easily and in greater safety in London, she said, and besides there'd be people there to look after me, which was something she wouldn't be able to do in LA because the film unit was moving to Montana in a couple of days for two weeks' location shooting.

'So you want me to go?' I said. 'You'll be really happy if I do?'

She sighed. 'Sure, I want you to go. I want you out of my life. I don't ever want to see you again.'

'Right. You've sucked me dry and now you're throwing me out like an empty Coke can.'

'Assuming you mean the sucking dry metaphorically,' she said, 'and I hope you do, the answer is yes.' She leaned across the bed to kiss me. It still hurt my shoulder but I was tough, I could take it. 'There are just a couple of conditions. One, I don't want any female under the age of fifty or weighing less than one eighty pounds anywhere near you and, two, I want you back here as soon as you're well, you hear?'

So on those conditions I went; the state I was in, there wasn't a lot I could have done in Hollywood anyway. And now, a few weeks later, I was going back. I wouldn't say I had healed but I was healing; my left arm and shoulder were still weak and I wouldn't have been much use in a fight but the physical therapy was beginning to work, slowly restoring the muscles and tissues to something like the shape they used to be in.

Donovan and I had discussed the shooting many times. As he put it, the identity of the actual gunman didn't really matter – 'He was just doing a job; nothing personal.' The important question was who had hired him.

'My best guess?' I said. 'Either Rico Agnelli or Michael Rialto.

Rialto because he's a conceited prick and I've offended his dignity a couple of times. Agnelli?' I shrugged – both shoulders this time; it didn't hurt at all by now. 'I dunno, except that I don't trust him.'

The idea worried Donovan. 'See, if Agnelli hired him,' he said, 'we got to ask: was it his own idea or did Carlo put him up to it? If it was down to Carlo I could have problems, because he might be trying to get at me through you.'

'Have you done anything to upset him?'

Donovan thought about it. 'Not that I know of but who can tell when you're dealing with these Mafia buggers? Maybe he wants to cut me out of the deal.'

'Or maybe you haven't shown him enough respect.'

'Respect?' Donovan said scornfully. 'I'll give him bloody respect! No, if he's trying to get at me it must have something to do with business …' He shook his head. 'No, I really can't believe it's Carlo.'

And so we chewed it over time and again until the evening I told Donovan I was going back to LA and he said, 'You want me to come with you? Bring a couple of blokes along to keep an eye on you?'

'No, if I turn up with a bunch of bodyguards it'll probably frighten everyone off – at least for a time. But if I go back and say I think a mugger shot me, then everybody will feel secure, so secure that whoever tried to have me killed in the first place will have another go. And I'll be ready.'

'Oh, yeah? What with – a couple of right hooks? Because your left hand's useless.'

'No,' I said, 'with a gun. You can get a gun to me in LA, can't you?'

Donovan nodded. 'Yes, I can. But will you use it?'

'I used one once before, didn't I?'

He nodded again. 'Yes, you did.' He hesitated for a moment, worried. 'Bobby, I still think this is a seriously bad idea. Are you sure I can't talk you out of it?'

'Yes.'

'Then you're a bigger bloody fool than I thought.'

'Maybe.' I could have said, and maybe should have said, that I was really returning to LA because of Lucy, because our daily phone calls since I'd been back in London had only served to make me miss her more than ever. But if I'd told Donovan that he would simply have thought me an even bigger bloody fool than he had already decided I was.

# 42

A UNIFORMED CHAUFFEUR met me at the airport, holding up a card with my name and the studio logo on it. The car, a black stretch limo with darkened windows, was parked, illegally, right outside the exit. It wasn't until I started to climb in the back that I saw Agnelli, cool and sharp in a light grey summerweight suit, sitting on the far side, and then I hesitated.

'What are you doing here?' I said.

He shook his head. 'That's cute. I make this dreary, fuckin' trip from Beverly Hills and that's all you can say? Get in.'

'Am I safe with you?'

'What? You think I'm going to blow you away in the back of the car and ruin the nice upholstery? Just get in.'

The chauffeur, a portly, middle-aged black man whom I'd seen a couple of times at the studio, stood behind me, holding the door. I got in.

Agnelli closed the partition between us and the driver and said, 'Let's get something straight: far as I'm concerned you could have walked to the fuckin' hotel. It was Carlo sent me. He had a talk with your friend Donovan last night. Donovan doesn't think it was a mugger who shot you, so he's got Carlo providing you with baby-sitters. Oh, and this, too.'

He handed me a small brown cardboard box, taped around the edges.

'What is it?'

'A .38 Police Special and a couple of spare clips. Donovan said you wanted a gun. You know how to use it?'

I said I did.

The car moved off, heading for the freeway. Agnelli said, 'You really think I had you shot? Listen, if I'd wanted you dead I'd have done it myself and done it right.'

'Well, it crossed my mind.'

He lit a cigarette, ignoring the red no-smoking sign stuck on the driver's partition. 'I don't like you, Bobby. I don't trust you because you don't owe allegiance to anybody, not even Donovan. Nobody knows where you're coming from or even what you're really doing here. That makes me uneasy but it doesn't make me want to kill you, except maybe on a general principle that every public-spirited citizen ought to kill at least one asshole a day.'

'I've already told you,' I said. 'Donovan's my friend. And I'm here to see that Minelli doesn't try to screw him.'

'Why would Carlo do that?'

'Isn't that what he does? I'm sorry, I thought screwing people was how he got to be so rich and powerful. Can I have been wrong?'

'Leave out the irony,' Agnelli said. 'It doesn't work with me. Carlo's not gonna screw Donovan. Why should he? They're in bed together, they do deals together all the time. You think Carlo had anything to do with you getting shot you gotta be paranoid.'

He reached forward and opened the limo's cocktail cabinet. 'You want a drink?'

'What's this – some kind of peace offering?'

'No, I'm just asking if you want a drink. I'm being polite, like a good host, but frankly I don't give a shit whether you want a drink or not.'

I had a Scotch on the rocks, he had a bourbon. Actually, by the time we reached the Bel Air Riviera we'd each had a couple. When we arrived at the hotel and a couple of bell boys were carrying my luggage into reception, Agnelli said, 'Want me to stick around, escort you to your room, case a couple of boy scouts on crack try to steal your watch?'

'Fuck off,' I said.

'You, too,' he said.

The hotel made a big fuss of me, grateful probably that I hadn't threatened to sue them for allowing me to be shot on their premises. The bungalow they allotted to me was even bigger and more luxurious than the one I'd had before and they'd stocked it with flowers, chocolates, a huge bowl of fruit and a magnum of Krug on ice. On the table there was more champagne with 'welcome back' notes attached from Tony Flo and Richie Proctor, a tub of caviare, purportedly from the cast of the movie, and a bottle of not very good Chardonnay from Bill Charleston. There was nothing from Agnelli.

Lucy turned up just after I'd shaved and showered and was hanging around in a bathrobe wondering whether to get ready for dinner just yet or simply put on a T-shirt and chinos.

Her first kiss was unexpectedly cool, almost perfunctory, not at all what I wanted. Then she moved away from me and looked at the goodies on the table.

'I didn't send you anything,' she said.

'I'd noticed.'

I was puzzled. While I was in London we'd talked every day on the phone and followed the calls with letters, long letters full of amorous nonsense. And now she was behaving as if we'd only just been introduced.

She looked gorgeous – tanned and lightly, deliciously freckled, her hair streaked even blonder by the sun. She was wearing no make-up but she needed none. She looked even more desirable than I'd remembered.

'I brought you something instead,' she said, 'something I thought you might like more than' – she waved her hand at the accumulated loot – 'champagne and candy. But now I'm not so sure.'

I said, 'What—'

She put her finger to her lips. 'Ssh, hear me out. I left work early today to come here and all the way over I was like a kid on her first date. I couldn't wait to see you again. And then ... I saw myself in the mirror as I came in and' – she gestured down at her blue denim work shirt, her faded jeans with a rip at each knee, her scuffed white trainers – 'and I thought, who the hell are you kidding? Do you really think the guy wants to be welcomed back by something that looks like Pippi Longstocking on a bad hair day?'

I nodded gravely. 'I see what you mean. So what are you saying?'

'I'm saying that all of a sudden I'm very shy and very unsure of myself and I wish I'd waited and gone home and done my hair and put on my make-up and my tightest little dress and my fuck-me pumps and … I think it was a big mistake coming here in my work clothes. I should have sent you a present instead.'

'A present would have been nice,' I said. 'What did you bring me?'

'What?'

'You said you brought me something. What was it?'

She was standing with her head down, her hands clutched together at about crotch height, her feet turned inwards. 'Just me,' she said softly.

'What – Pippi Longstocking on a bad hair day? And you thought I might like that?'

She nodded ever so slightly.

I looked at her in silence for a moment. She still had her head down and was peeping back at me through the tousled fringe that had fallen over her forehead. The whole posture, almost a caricature of coyness, would have had me fooled if I hadn't noticed the glint of amusement in her eyes.

'Yes, well, you were right the first time,' I said. 'You should have gone home and changed.'

Suddenly she stood up straight, blowing the hair out of her eyes, her hands on her hips. 'Why, you sonofabitch,' she said. 'And after I went to all that trouble to look soft and appealing and clinging. Have you no better nature?'

'None at all,' I said. 'Come here, Pippi Longstocking.'

'I don't think so. I've gone off the idea.'

So I went to her instead and several minutes later she drew away from me and said, 'Let's take a shower.'

'I've just had one,' I said.

'Yeah, but I haven't.'

'Well, now you mention it,' I said. 'Of course, being a gentleman, I wouldn't have brought the matter up myself but—'

'I hate you, Bobby Lennox,' she murmured. 'I really hate you. Now come and take a shower.'

# 43

I GOT A BIG welcome, pretty well a standing ovation, at the studio the next morning. Richie Proctor greeted me with a bear hug, Martie Culper shook my hand with both of his, Annie Klane threw her arms around my neck and gave me a big wet kiss on the mouth and I daresay even Newport and Rialto might have nodded grudging acknowledgement had either of them been there, which they weren't.

Lucy came over and tucked her arm possessively into mine, looking pleased. 'Hail the conquering hero,' she said.

'Hey, look,' I said, 'I know I was pretty good last night but you didn't have to tell everybody.'

She looked at me appraisingly. 'You were okay,' she said. 'I guess. But why would I tell anyone? Who'd be interested? No, you win the ovation because you're the guy who got shot in LA and survived. That's pretty rare.'

Shooting on the film was nearly over; a couple more scenes and a few pick-up shots and it would be finished. Proctor was pleased with it. It wasn't the movie he would have chosen to do if he hadn't needed the work but he reckoned it would be pretty good of its kind. 'High-grade commercial shit is what we're talking here,' he said.

He'd had a little bother with Rialto, he told me, since the incident in the cutting-room but nothing too serious, nothing he couldn't handle. The usual movie star bullshit, only a little more so, was the way he put it.

I hadn't arrived at the studio till about noon. I had lunch with Proctor and Lucy in the commissary, then hung around the set or my office for the rest of the day, not that there was much for me to do and what there was Margaret could have dealt with perfectly well.

'Any calls while I was away?' I asked her. 'You know – Pfeiffer, Basinger, people like that?'

'No, Mr Lennox,' she said and smiled. 'I guess they just gave up on you when you didn't call back.' She seemed to be developing a sense of humour. 'Tom Hanks didn't call either.'

'No, well, I don't talk to him any more.'

I was on the point of leaving and going back to the hotel when Harry Brown phoned and asked me to meet him in the bar across the street. 'Got a couple things to tell you,' he said.

What he told me, once we were settled in a booth and the waitress had brought him a large shot of Chivas Regal, was that Darren Carmody had finally turned up. Dead. Shot twice in the back of the head.

Just as Darren had predicted they had found his body in the desert. Not a pretty sight, Harry Brown said. Coyotes and other creatures had been snacking off him on a regular basis and there wasn't all that much left, but it was Darren all right.

'Lou took it badly,' Harry Brown said. He shook his head. 'Well, how else would she take it? Her only son gets murdered? The cops who broke the news say she aged like ten years when they told her. I feel for her. She's a nice woman Lou, honest, too, for someone in her line of business.' He summoned the waitress for another drink. 'Here's a weird coincidence for you. One of her bouncers also got himself shot, similar m.o., a while back when you were in London. What do you make of that?'

I said I couldn't make anything of it and asked what else he had to tell me.

'Oh, yeah. We found the green Mercedes. Well, *a* green Mercedes, abandoned and burnt out in South Central LA. My hunch is it's probably the same one, for what it's worth, which ain't much. Phoney LA plates, otherwise no prints, no nothing. Car was reported stolen in Nevada some months back.'

I thought about these things for a while. 'Well,' I said, 'I suppose all that's the bad news. What's the good?'

He grinned. 'I don't know whether it's good or bad but I checked out that store for you on Santa Monica.' He took a notebook from his pocket. 'Owner's a guy called Horace Wilkins, aged thirty-nine, married once, divorced eight years ago, no kids, no siblings. Parents both dead, died in a plane crash fifteen years ago. Horace lives in the Valley – house in Tarzana – sometimes with a lady, sometimes without. The business does pretty well. Clientele are mostly movie companies or individual movie people looking for exotica, erotica, something out of the ordinary anyway.' He closed the notebook and put it back in his pocket.

'That's it?' I said, disappointed. 'No criminal record, no history of drug dealing?'

'Nope. Clean as a whistle, not even a traffic violation. Couple of interesting points, though.' He took a sip of his drink. 'Horace Wilkins is Bill Charleston's nephew.'

'What?'

'And ...' Another sip. 'He went to high school right here in Hollywood with Michael Rialto.'

I let all this sink in for a moment, feeling a small stirring of excitement. 'But it's perfect,' I said. 'If Wilkins is dealing drugs in the movie community Charleston or Rialto – or both – would be ideal contacts.'

Harry Brown nodded. 'Yeah – if. Only, we got no reason to believe that, do we? All we know for sure is he's running this cockamamie store on Santa Monica and making a decent living out of it.'

'Yes, but ... Ah, come on, Harry, it fits, you know it does. Virna Newport said—'

'I know what she said and it doesn't mean shit unless it's backed up with evidence. What she said, she said to you and very probably under some kind of duress. Do you think she's gonna repeat it to the cops? "Oh, sure, I use drugs, use 'em all the time, give 'em to my friends. Now you can read me my rights." Come on, Bobby, think about it.'

I did and while I was thinking about it, Brown said, 'You want to know what this guy looks like, this Wilkins? Here.' He took a coloured photograph and passed it across the table to me.

The picture had been taken outside the shop, apparently without the subject's knowledge. It showed a big man, who could have been anywhere between thirty-five and forty-five, tough and fit-looking, nondescript features.

I said, 'That's the man who shot me.'

# 44

SOME TIME LATER I said, 'You knew, didn't you? You knew Wilkins was the man. That's why you had the photo with you.'

'I didn't *know*,' Harry said, 'but I thought there was a chance. Your description of the shooter, vague as it was, seemed to fit old Horace pretty well so I drove by the store one day and took the picture with my trusty little Pentax.'

I looked at the photograph again. 'You can see why my description was vague, can't you? Apart from being a bit bigger than average there's nothing distinctive about him. He's the one, though, I'm a hundred per cent sure of that. He stood ten feet away and fired a bullet through me while I looked at him. I'll never forget that face.'

We were in my bungalow at the hotel, the congealing remains of a room service meal on the table. There were just the two of us because Lucy had gone back to her apartment that night to pick up some fresh clothes before moving in with me.

A lot had happened in the hours since Harry Brown had first shown me the photograph. As soon as I'd identified Wilkins, Harry had called the cops who were investigating the shooting and told them to join us in the bar.

It was the same pair, the brunette and her Hispanic partner who had been looking for Darren Carmody. They spent a lot of time taking me through the night of the shooting again and thrusting the photograph at me, asking insistently if I was sure that was the guy. In the end Harry said, 'He's sure. Okay? He's sure. Now go collar the bastard.'

So the two cops went to Tarzana and Harry Brown and I returned to my hotel and waited. And while we waited Harry told me some more about Horace Wilkins: a man who'd had several jobs – in public relations, freelance journalism, photography – and failed at all of them. Eventually Uncle Bill Charleston had fixed him up at the Maestro Consolidated Studio, working in Tony Flo's office. A sinecure, really, a favour from Flo to Charleston. Wilkins had become one of Tony Flo's numerous assistants, ostensibly there to learn the business. But towards the end of last year Flo, like all Wilkins's other employers, had fired him, saying he was useless and idle.

Soon after that Wilkins set up the store on Santa Monica Boulevard.

'Where'd the money come from?' I said. 'How did a loser like that get the money to go into business?'

Harry shrugged. 'How much could it cost, small store like that on Santa Monica?'

'The store itself? Probably not a lot. But what about the operating costs? All right, once the business was up and running it would probably pay for itself. But at the start, when he was searching around finding unusual things for people he'd have needed a fair amount of seed money. Where did that come from?'

'Who knows? Maybe Uncle Bill made him a loan. Maybe Tony Flo gave him a handsome pay-off just to get him out of his hair.'

The latter seemed unlikely. Uncle Bill was my best bet – Uncle Bill setting himself up, at one remove, as Pusher to the Stars. A nice little earner that could be.

Some time later there was a call for Harry Brown. Maureen, the brunette cop. Harry listened intently, frowning, said 'Shit!' a couple of times, then put the receiver down.

'Wilkins has gone,' he said. 'House is all locked up and empty. The neighbours think he's on vacation, somewhere in Europe. But since he doesn't talk to them much they don't know when he left or where he went or how long he'll be away.'

'What about Charleston – good old Uncle Bill? What does he have to say?'

'He doesn't know anything either. Maureen and Juan have just left his house. They're on their way over here.'

Charleston lived in Beverly Hills, on Coldwater Canyon Drive, so the journey didn't take them long. I poured them drinks – vodka because they were on duty and vodka left no trace on the breath – and they told me pretty much what I'd already heard from Harry Brown.

When they'd finished Harry said, 'Now tell them what you think.'

So I did: I told them about my conversation with Virna Newport, my calls to the shop on Santa Monica, the green Mercedes I'd tried to follow and about Wilkins's connections with Bill Charleston and Michael Rialto.

When I'd finished Maureen shook her head sceptically. 'That's all you got? There's nothing we can use there. The only suggestion of drug dealing comes from Newport and she'd deny everything. As for Charleston, okay, he's the guy's uncle. So what? And Rialto? He and Wilkins went to the same school. Big deal – I know a dozen people went to that school. You figure they're all dealing drugs with Rialto? Look, all we can do is try to find Wilkins, check with travel agents, airline companies, see if we can discover where he went and then pick him up. As for the other people, we can't touch them, we can't even approach them. There's no cause. We start talking to them about drugs and we'll have every hotshot lawyer in town on our ass.'

Harry Brown said, 'She's right, Bobby. Sooner or later, one way or another, we'll get the guy who shot you but otherwise we can't help you.'

'Maybe not,' I said. 'But I think I know a man who can.'

# 45

Rico Agnelli shovelled half a fried egg into his mouth, swallowed it noisily, wiped away the yolk that had dribbled down his chin and said, 'Okay – what?'

We were having brunch in my bungalow. It wasn't a comfortable occasion; he was wondering what I wanted of him and I was wondering whether I had been right to call him in the first place. He was a crook and a killer, hardly my concept of an ideal partner, but I couldn't think of anybody else.

I'd phoned him at eight and invited him for breakfast and he hadn't wanted to come.

'Breakfast?' Agnelli had said. 'What are you, some Rip Van Yuppie left over from the eighties? No sensible person, conscious of his health, goes to breakfast conferences any more.' I could hear him lighting a cigarette, sucking down the smoke, being conscious of his health.

I told him he should come anyway because I had a proposition that he might find interesting, something I couldn't discuss over the phone. Eventually, reluctantly, he agreed.

'Make it brunch,' he said. 'I have to see Carlo first.'

So now it was midday and he was eating steak and eggs and he said, 'Okay – what?'

I laid it all out for him, just as I had done for the police last night.

And when I'd finished he said, 'So why are you asking my help? We don't even like each other.'

'I know that. But the police can't do anything because they have to play by the rules. You and I don't. Besides, you have a vested interest in this, too.'

He nodded, seeming to find that reasonable. 'Look, I'm not saying I'm entirely sold on what you told me,' he said. 'Could be you just have a wild hair up your ass.'

'The police didn't seem to think so,' I said. 'But whether I have or not we'll never know unless we do something.'

Agnelli pushed his plate to one side and refilled his coffee cup. 'Bottom line,' he said, 'you want me to help you get back at the guy who shot you, right?'

'Yes, but there's more to it than that. If I'm right there's a little revenge in this for you, too.'

'True.' He hesitated, then shrugged as if he had come to a decision. 'All right. I told you I had to see Carlo? Well, he's hurting a little right now. Nothing serious, not yet. But what's happening, the custom drug trade has been falling off lately. You know what I'm talking about? The Beverly Hills trade, the Hollywood trade. Carlo had it all sewn up. No big deal but nice money coming in, regular. Now there's not nearly so much of it, so either the movie people have all cleaned up their act or they're buying cheaper elsewhere. Carlo thinks they're buying cheaper. What do you think?'

'I'm with Carlo,' I said.

He nodded. 'So maybe, just maybe, there's something in this cock and bull story of yours. And if there is, you know what I think? I think Wilkins and Uncle Bill arranged the whole thing.'

'No,' I said firmly. 'Or rather yes and no. Wilkins and Uncle Bill, fine, I go along with that. But there's got to be somebody else too, somebody well-known. I believe Greg Harrison was killed – and not by Darren Carmody; he was just the fall guy – because he'd threatened to name names, the names of people not just using but dealing drugs in the Hollywood community.'

'So? Bill Charleston's in the Hollywood community.'

'Yes, but he's not even a household name in his own street.

Nobody outside the movie business has ever heard of him. He's an old Hollywood hack. He could be dealing drugs or selling Webster's Dictionary door to door and nobody outside this town could care less. My bet is that Harrison had somebody much bigger than Charleston in his sights.'

'Like Michael Rialto? It's a nice idea. Jesus, I'd love to see that motherfucker brought down. But ...' He shook his head regretfully. 'The guy's rich, he earns ten million dollars a movie. Why would he need to deal drugs?'

'People think Virna Newport's rich, too. She's been earning big bucks a lot longer than Michael has but according to Greg Harrison she needs money. Think about it: how does Michael live?'

He thought about it. 'As high on the hog's back as you can get. He has a big house here in Beverly Hills, a ranch in Texas and a duplex in New York – Upper East Side. He has full-time servants everywhere, a car for just about every day of the week ... yeah, he lives well.'

'In other words he lives like a movie star. Okay, he earns like a movie star, too, but how many people have a part of him? Never mind all the servants, how many agents, business managers, lawyers, PR people and personal trainers does he have to support? And on top of all that he'll be paying taxes at the highest rate. You really think some extra money, just for him, undeclared to the IRS or anyone else, wouldn't come in handy?' Another thought occurred. 'Does he have a drug habit?'

Agnelli shrugged. 'He snorts a little coke but I don't think it's a problem. He's a social user, like a lot of people in this town. You go to his house for a party, there's always plenty of stuff around if you need it. I see where you're heading, though – that can be expensive, too.'

'But not so expensive if you're also your own supplier.'

'Right,' he said, nodding. 'So what do we do?'

What we did – for openers – was we went to see Virna Newport.
She was at the studio, re-shooting a couple of close-ups that hadn't quite worked the first time around. Richie Proctor had brought the

film in sufficiently under schedule and under budget to be able to afford such a luxury. Fine-tuning, he said; the original takes had been good but by changing a word here and an emphasis there they could be made even better.

We approached Newport in her dressing-room, just as she was pouring herself a post-prandial vodka. She didn't seem concerned to see me there but Agnelli's presence bothered her.

'Rico!' she said. 'What are you ...? Is Carlo still mad at me?'

'Carlo?' He grinned wolfishly at her. 'Carlo doesn't even think about you. Whether you live or die he doesn't care.'

She blanched, even seemed to shrink a little. Her familiar arrogance appeared to have vanished since that night at Baldock's house, though she recaptured a little of it as she turned sharply towards me.

'What are you smirking about?'

I said, 'Me? I'm not smirking. This is an ironic grin playing about my manly features. I'm wondering what made a smart woman like you throw over someone with the clout Carlo has for Charlie Baldock.'

She fiddled with the make-up on her dressing table. 'Charlie is in the movie business, Carlo isn't. Simple as that. For this film I took less than half my usual fee because I needed the work. If it bombs, I could be finished. Charlie was insurance against that. He promised to find more pictures for me, whatever happened. He might even have married me.'

'And now Carlo's scared him off,' Agnelli said. 'Tough shit. How do you order your drugs?'

'What?' The abrupt change of attack unsteadied her. She needed vodka to recover.

'When you want more stuff what do you do? You call a number and say "This is Virna Newport. Send me some cocaine, heroin, whatever." Is that how you do it?'

'Of course not. I call a number, yes, but I have a pseudonym. Greg told me what it was. I just say, "This is Mrs Miniver and—"'

'Mrs Miniver!' I said. 'You order drugs in the saintly name of Mrs Miniver?'

She gave me a sour little grin. 'Cute, isn't it? I just say, "This is Mrs Miniver. I want my usual order", something like that. I told you this already.'

'Not the Mrs Miniver bit, you didn't.'

She shrugged. 'Yes, well, then the stuff is delivered.'

'Who by?' Agnelli said.

'Big fellow. Late thirties maybe, in pretty good shape.'

I took out the photograph of Wilkins that Harry Brown had given me. 'This the man?'

She looked at it and nodded. 'That's him.'

As we left her Newport said, 'Maybe it wasn't very clever to ditch Carlo for Charlie but I'll tell you something: Carlo would never really have done anything for me. You know what he is?'

Agnelli nodded. 'Yeah. A star-fucker.'

'Right,' she said.

Bill Charleston's secretary said he was out to lunch. Agnelli said, 'Guy's been out to lunch since the day he was born but I know he's in his office right now,' and we went straight in.

Charleston was on the phone, giving some menial a hard time, but he looked up in alarm and cut the call short as we walked in. He stood up and tried a little bluster.

'Hey, what is this? You can't just burst into my—'

Agnelli strode across and shoved him and the bluster back into his chair. Then he perched on the edge of the desk and lit a cigarette. Charleston glanced at the 'Thank You for Not Smoking' notice on the wall but wisely chose to say nothing.

'Horace Wilkins,' Agnelli said. 'Your nephew. Tell us about him.'

'Horace?' Charleston said and then said it again, 'Horace? I haven't seen him in months. I damn near broke my ass getting him a job here and then he screwed up. I haven't even talked to the piece of shit since the day Tony Flo fired him.'

'He's running a business of some kind on Santa Monica Boulevard,' I said.

'So they tell me.'

'So where'd he get the money to start it?' Agnelli asked.

'How would I know? He certainly didn't get it from me. The guy's a loser. I did my best for him because he's my sister's kid. I got him more jobs than you could shake a stick at but there's a limit, you know what I mean? He fouled up once too often. Now I wouldn't give him a dime if he was begging in the street.'

'He's gone a touch lower than that,' I said. 'He's pushing drugs.'

'Is he?' Charleston shook his head. He didn't look shocked or horrified; he just looked sorrowful.

'You're not surprised?'

'No. Nothing about Horace could surprise me. He's a worthless piece of trash and always was.' He looked from one to the other of us. 'You guys going to blow the whistle on him?'

Agnelli tossed his cigarette butt out of the open window. 'Could be.'

Charleston nodded. 'Good.'

I said, 'What if Horace isn't in this alone? What if he has partners and he, in turn, blows the whistle on them?'

'Then they have it coming, wouldn't you say?'

Agnelli glanced at me. 'What do you think?'

'I think I believe him,' I said.

'Me too. Let's go.'

So we went.

# 46

THE SIGN ON the shop door said 'open' until Agnelli turned it round. The place became even less open when he then turned the key in the lock and slid home the bolt.

The crewcut man behind the counter said, 'Hey, what are you guys doing?' He started scrabbling around in a drawer beside him.

Agnelli said, 'If you got a gun back there I bet this is a bigger one.' He pointed the one he was holding, a Magnum, at Crewcut's face.

'What do you want?' Crewcut stopped scrabbling and put his hands where we could see them. 'You want money, take what there is but I can tell you there's not much here.'

I pulled down the blinds on the shop door and windows and joined Agnelli by the counter. The name tag on Crewcut's red and black plaid shirt said JOE. 'We don't want your money, Joe,' I said. 'All we want is a little information.'

'Yeah? Like what?'

'Like,' Agnelli said, 'we want you to tell us exactly how you sell drugs from here.'

Unexpectedly Joe started to laugh. 'Jesus, not you, too. I had another guy call me up and ...' He turned abruptly towards me, pointing his finger at my chest. 'It was you, wasn't it? You're the guy who called and asked for cocaine. I recognise the accent. Australian, isn't it?'

'No, it bloody well isn't,' I said.

'Well, whatever it is it was you. And now you've brought a friend.' He laughed again. 'Are you guys crazy or what?'

Agnelli said, 'You think it's funny, Joe? See if you think this is funny, too.' And he hit him sharply across the side of the head with the gun barrel. Joe reeled back into his chair, his expression dazed and shocked, one hand clutched to the cut that was squirting blood just above his ear. 'Do we have your attention now?'

I said, 'For God's sake, go easy.'

'That was going easy,' Agnelli said. 'It's when I start going hard he has to worry.'

I leaned across the counter towards Joe, who was trying to staunch the blood with a handful of paper tissues.

'Joe,' I said, 'listen to me: all you have to do is answer our questions and you'll be all right. I promise you that. Okay?'

He nodded.

'Right. Now, I called you twice. What did you do?'

He looked at his handful of blood-stained tissues, gave a little whimper and pressed them back on the cut. 'He didn't have to do that,' he said.

Agnelli said, 'You're not answering the question. You want me to fix the other side of your head, too?'

Joe looked at him sullenly, then turned his gaze back to me. 'First time I did nothing. I just figured you were some kind of nut. Second time I got a little worried, so I called Horace. Horace Wilkins? The boss? He sent a couple of guys. I don't know why, just to look around, I guess, see everything was okay.'

'You find things for people here, is that right? What kind of things?'

'Anything. It's not that difficult you got the right contacts. I mean, a movie producer wants a dozen tarantulas, like tomorrow, I know who to call. Or some executive's having a stag party, wants a girl who can fire hard-boiled eggs out of her twat, I know where to find one of those, too. More difficult requests I leave Horace to deal with but we don't get too many of them.'

Agnelli said, 'How about somebody calls, says "This is Mrs Miniver. I want my usual order tonight." What do you do then?'

Joe tossed his blood-soaked tissues into the waste basket and pressed a fresh handful against his cut. The wound was just oozing now, the hair around it wet and stiff with blood.

'Yeah, well, we get quite a few of those; more than ever these last two, three months. Mrs Miniver, Mr Deeds, Mr North, Mr Blandings, Dr Dolittle – names like that. You ask me, they're pseudonyms.'

'You reckon?' Agnelli asked dryly.

'Yeah. We even got a Dr Strangelove. And what I do, when one of them calls, and Horace isn't around, I phone him, tell him there's a special order and he deals with it. He always deals with the phoney names.'

'Did he ever tell you what these "special orders" were?'

Joe shook his head and winced. 'I'm getting a headache,' he said. 'You shouldn'ta hit me so hard.'

'Only way to concentrate your mind,' Agnelli said. 'So what did you *think* the special orders were?'

'Hey, I don't know. Horace just said certain very famous people had special tastes and didn't want them known, so I figured maybe sexual preferences you couldn't always get at the average whore-house. Like, when Dr Strangelove calls and says he wants his usual order, well, it could be two Korean faggots, a chicken and a German shepherd dog, something like that.'

'Or maybe an ounce or two of heroin,' I said.

'No. Horace hinted it was sex things and that made sense, as much as anything makes sense in this town. If I'd thought he was pushing drugs I'd have been out of here fast. No way I want to get involved with that.'

I said, 'But pushing kinky and maybe illegal sex was okay with you?'

He shrugged. 'I guess. I don't know. Since I never had any idea what these special orders were I didn't worry about it.'

We didn't seem to be getting very much further. I felt, and I was pretty sure Agnelli did, too, that Joe was telling us the truth as he knew it. I said, 'What happens at a time like this, when Horace is out of town and, I don't know, Miss Firecracker calls in with a special order that she wants urgently?'

Joe said, 'Hey, we got a Miss Firecracker. How did you know that?'

'I watch a lot of movies. So what happens?'

'I just leave a message on Horace's machine and I suppose somebody else picks it up and handles the order.'

'If you call that machine can you get the messages played back to you?'

'I guess – if you know the code to punch in, which I don't.'

I glanced across at Agnelli, who just shrugged. He looked very disappointed, probably about as disappointed as I felt. He said, 'Let's get out of here.'

I held up one hand. 'Give me a moment.' I thought back over what Joe had told us and said, 'Those two men Horace sent round the second time I called. I saw them and they looked vaguely familiar. Do you happen to know who they were?'

Joe laughed, for the first time since Agnelli had hit him. 'Sure. They're a pair of overweight body builders, pure muscle between the ears. I think they're Michael's bodyguards.'

Agnelli and I looked at each other. He said, 'Michael?'

Joe grinned, a small glint of triumph in his eyes. 'I thought you guys were supposed to know everything, all that stuff about drugs and all, but I've surprised you, haven't I? You don't know about Michael, do you?'

Agnelli reached across the counter, grabbed Joe's hair, forced his head back and stuck the gun into his mouth. 'Yeah, you surprised us. Now are you going to tell us who Michael is or do I have to pull this trigger and surprise your brains right out the back of your head?'

I put a restraining hand on Agnelli's arm and he took a step backwards. Joe coughed and spluttered and said, 'Jesus, give me a break. I was going to tell you anyway. Rialto. Michael Rialto. The movie star? Him and Horace know each other. They were at school together or something. Michael's been in here a couple times. Him and Horace go into the room in back and chew the fat about old times or how the Lakers are doing or whatever they find to talk about and the musclebrains hang around out here, waiting for their boss.'

Now Joe had identified them I remembered the two men from the swimming pool at the house in Santa Monica. I had seen them but not seen them because I wasn't much interested in their faces then. They had been a potential threat and it was not their looks but their size and possible mobility that had concerned me. Besides, most of my attention had been fixed on Rialto.

Agnelli said, 'Is Rialto a partner in this business?'

Again Joe laughed, the idea clearly striking him as preposterous. 'Michael Rialto? Why should he bother with an outfit like this? The guy's a big movie star, for Chrissakes.'

'And therefore rich,' I said.

'Right. I don't know what kind of money this business makes but Rialto probably spends as much in tips in the Polo Lounge at the Beverly Hills Hotel.'

I nodded and looked across at Agnelli. 'Heard enough?'

'Yeah,' he said. He grabbed hold of Joe's hair again and this time tried to shove the muzzle of the gun up his nose. I shook my head, sadly, as Joe snorted and whimpered.

'One last thing,' Agnelli said, 'and it's very important you should remember this: we were never in here, okay? Doesn't matter who asks – your boss, the cops – you never saw us, you never even heard of us. You got that?'

Joe nodded frantically and yelped as the gunsight tore the skin inside his nostril.

'Good,' Agnelli said.

As we walked to the door I said, 'What did you want to do that for? He was being as helpful as he could.'

'I didn't like his haircut,' Agnelli said.

I pulled up the blinds on the door and the windows and turned the sign back to 'open'. Joe said, snuffling, 'Hey, are you guys gangsters? Are you connected?'

Agnelli turned and pointed the gun at him. 'In your worst dreams you never met anybody as well-connected as we are. Just keep that thought in mind and you might live a little longer.'

I closed the door behind us, the quiet of the shop giving way to the bad-tempered roar of traffic on Santa Monica Boulevard.

'God, that last line was so corny,' I said. 'Even Bruce Willis couldn't get away with stuff like that.'

'Yeah, but I'm a hell of a lot tougher than Bruce Willis,' Agnelli said.

# 47

'WELL,' I SAID, 'what do you think?'

We were back in my hotel room, sinking a couple of early evening beers.

'I think we got zilch,' Agnelli said. 'I also think you're right and that Michael's involved in Wilkins's drug business. But there's no way we can prove it.'

'To the police, you mean?'

'The police? What? I look like a stool pigeon to you? No, Carlo's the one we have to convince and there's no way we can do it with what we got now. Jesus, give me fifteen minutes alone with Horace Wilkins and I guarantee we'd have all the proof we need.'

'Yes, well that's never going to happen, is it? The minute Horace sets foot in this town the police will nab him. But all they can charge him with is trying to kill me.' I took a moody sip of my beer. Like Agnelli I was drinking straight from the bottle. Hell, I can be as macho as anybody when I feel like it. 'Couldn't you just go and talk to Carlo, tell him what we know?'

Agnelli shook his head decisively. 'He wouldn't listen. One, Michael's family and I'm not. Two, he knows Michael and I don't get along. Carlo would just assume this was personal on my part, a vendetta against his nephew by marriage. Unless I could discredit Michael I'd be the one Carlo stopped trusting. I'd probably wind up dead.' He tossed his empty bottle into the waste basket. 'You got anything stronger than this ant's piss?'

I pointed towards the cabinet. 'Help yourself.'

While he was mixing bourbon, ice and a splash of soda I opened the envelope that a hotel messenger had left in my room. In it was a fax from Margaret telling me I'd been invited to the film's wrap party at the studio the next night.

'Have you got one of these?' I read it to Agnelli.

'If you've got one, I got one.' He made an irritable, frustrated sound. 'You know, that's a sweet little deal Michael and Horace have going. Bold but simple.'

'Bit dangerous, though, out in the open like that.'

'How out in the open? There's probably only two people know about it – Horace and Michael. Horace probably supplies the drugs, gets them from the Colombians, because if he was dealing with any of our people Carlo would know about it, and Michael provides him with the customers. Nobody's in a better position to know who's likely to be interested.'

'You mean Michael approaches them himself? Surely not.'

'No. If I was Michael I'd just give Horace the names, let him make the approach. Okay, that would be the danger point – the approach. But he's dealing with people who already use. Are they going to blow the whistle on him? They wouldn't want to get involved with the cops any more than he does.'

I thought about it. 'What if they were already buying from Carlo's people and told them about the approach, out of loyalty or something?'

Agnelli looked at me derisively. 'You know anybody that loyal to his dealer? So loyal he'll pass up a better offer? Besides, even that's not difficult to handle. If I was Horace I'd give out a free sample, good stuff, guarantee that anything they bought would be the same quality and quote a price maybe twenty-five per cent less than they pay Carlo's boys. That still returns a big profit, the money there is in this business. And then I'd make it very clear that whether they buy from me or they don't it wouldn't be healthy to tell anyone, and I mean *anyone*, about it.' He shook his head admiringly. 'No, it's a really sweet deal. And there's not a damn thing we can do about it.'

'Right.' I said. 'We can't touch Wilkins because he's not here; we can't touch Michael because Carlo wouldn't like it; and we can't even do anything about Michael's bodyguards although they probably killed Darren and Greg Harrison, too.'

Agnelli mixed himself another drink. 'Know who I blame? Newport. She hadn't gone around shooting her mouth off about what Harrison was planning to write, he'd still be alive, the book would come out, the finger would be pointed straight at Michael and then, sure, Carlo would take care of it himself. One thing Carlo won't take from anybody is disloyalty, family or no family, and anyone disloyal enough to steal his business shouldn't even start planning what he'll eat for breakfast tomorrow.'

I considered what he had just said and the main point that occurred to me was that Newport had not in fact gone around shooting off her mouth. Which left the question ... 'Who did she actually tell about the book? You? Minelli? Who?'

Agnelli held up his hands. 'Hey, not me. And not Carlo either, far as I know.' He put his glass down on the table. 'Damn, I gotta take a piss.'

He was in the bathroom when Lucy arrived. This was always a good moment, for we were still in that stage of the relationship when a reunion after only a few hours was a big event So we clung to each other as though we hadn't met in weeks and then she pulled away from me and said, 'Have you heard the great news? One more shot, one more retake and the movie is oooover! Boy, am I looking forward to that wrap party.' She stretched languorously. 'I am planning to be taken very seriously drunk. You'll probably have to carry me home but I'll be safe with you, won't I? You wouldn't take advantage of a defenceless, intoxicated girl, would you?'

'Damn right I would,' I said.

'Good. I hoped you'd say that.' She hugged me again and when once more she drew back she said, 'What I need immediately is a shower. You want to take a shower?'

'Love to but perhaps we should wait a while. The bathroom might be a little crowded right now.'

On cue, Agnelli came out of it. He said, 'Hey, Lucy.'

She said, 'Oh, shit, it's you. What are you doing here?'

Agnelli shook his head in mock admiration. 'Gotta hand it to you, Luce. You want to ooze charm, you really ooze charm. Whatever happened to "Hi, Rico, how's it going?" stuff like that?'

She said dully, 'Hi, Rico, how's it going?'

'Great, now you ask.' There was an uncomfortable pause during which Lucy stared at Agnelli, freezing him out. He looked at me and shrugged. 'I guess we're just about through for the moment.'

'Just about.'

'Right. Well, I figure you two would like to be alone and I got other things to do, so ...' He swigged down the remains of his bourbon and went to the door. 'I'll be in touch, Bobby. Look after yourself, Luce.'

When he'd gone she said, 'What are you doing with that sleazebag?'

'Good question,' I said, 'to which the short answer is that we're rather important to each other just now. It's a complicated story. I'll tell you all about it one day.'

She looked at me suspiciously. She despised Agnelli – for God's sake, the man had caused the death of her former boyfriend – and I certainly couldn't blame her for that. 'I warn you, Bobby,' she said, 'I, personally, will kill you if you start telling me he's not as bad as I thought he was.'

'I wouldn't dream of saying any such thing. He's quite as bad as either of us ever suspected, probably worse. But right now he's rather useful to me. So, what about that shower?'

We had the shower, went out to dinner, came back, did some private things together and were just dropping off to sleep when the phone rang.

Agnelli.

From the background noise I assumed he was calling from a phone booth in a disco or at least a particularly rowdy restaurant. He said,

'That business with Michael? I think I've figured out how to nail the bastard.'

'Are you drunk?'

'Probably. Just a little. Will I see you at the wrap party?'

'Sure,' I said. 'Why?'

'Fasten your seatbelt, kid. It's gonna be a bumpy night.'

# 48

THE WRAP PARTY on sound stage one at Maestro Consolidated started slowly, the way these things do. Everybody sober, everybody dressed to impress, the employers distributing kind words to the employed (or in many cases, as of tonight, unemployed) and the recently unemployed schmoozing with the employers in the hope of landing another job. Tables laden with booze, others with a variety of salads and finger foods. A small combo, tucked away in a corner, played dance music, not too loudly, but at first nobody danced. People broke up into groups, discussing the movie they had just made and the one they hoped to make next or swapping information on who was hiring at which studio.

Lucy and I got there early. As associate producer I felt I should, even though most of the people present knew me only by sight, if that. Lucy was wearing a simple midnight blue shift, matching blue shoes, a thin gold bracelet and necklace, her hair carefully brushed and teased to look slightly, casually dishevelled. A little lipstick, a little eyeshadow, not much else in the way of make-up.

She had spent forty-eight minutes getting ready; I timed her as I paced up and down waiting for her to emerge from the bedroom.

'What took you so long?' I said.

She glanced at herself in the mirror, touching an errant curl back into place. 'How do I look?' she said.

I examined her carefully. 'Edible,' I said.

She nodded, satisfied. 'That's what took me so long. Beautiful, of course, comes naturally, adorable needs a little work, but a girl really has to go for it to reach edible. You don't look so bad yourself.'

After a while the party warmed up. People ate and drank and began to dance. Voices rose higher, laughter grew more raucous, the employed or recently unemployed stopped kissing arse and either paired off or formed little groups with their peers.

Tony Flo was there, so were the stars – Newport with a new toy boy she had found somewhere, Rialto with his wife and mother-in-law. It was the first time I'd seen her – Carlo Minelli's sister, Maria, a slim, dark woman in her mid-forties, still good-looking. Her daughter would probably be exactly like her in twenty years' time. The three of them sat at a big round table with Flo and the other stars, Rialto and Flo dominating the conversation, the rest laughing helplessly at their jokes, though Maria, I noticed, didn't laugh much.

Lucy and I ate a little, drank a little, danced a little. When the band stopped playing for a moment we walked, hand in hand, back to our table where Richie Proctor and his wife had joined us, Proctor greedily tackling a huge plate of assorted meats and salads.

I said, 'Has anyone seen Rico Agnelli tonight?'

Proctor said, 'No, thank God. Bloke gives me the creeps. I reckon he's a killer.'

'He is,' Lucy said. She looked at me curiously. 'Why do you care whether he's here or not?'

'Well, he said he'd be here, that's all. I think he wants to tell me something.'

'Mate of yours, is he?' Proctor asked. Now they were all staring at me.

'No,' I said. 'I don't think he likes me any more than I like him. It's just that we're … well, we're working on something together.'

'Oh,' Proctor said, 'and I thought you were one of the good guys,' kind of echoing something Lucy had said to me many weeks before.

'I am.' I squirmed a little under the threefold disapproval of their gaze. 'Only sometimes the good guys have to work with the bad guys to bring down the even worse guys.'

'What's that supposed to mean?' Lucy asked.

'Fuck all if you want my opinion,' Proctor said, turning his attention back to his salad.

There was an awkward silence, during which I felt quite friendless. Then Lucy leaned across and kissed me on the lips. 'He is one of the good guys,' she said to the Proctors. 'I guess we'll just have to trust him.' I gave her a grateful kiss in return.

'Do you mind not making those sucking noises?' Proctor said. 'It's putting me off my grub.'

So the mood lightened, we ate and drank and then the two women went off together to the loo.

'Well, thank God that's over,' Proctor said, his mouth full of pastrami.

'The movie? I gathered it had gone rather well.'

'So it has. I reckon it's about as good as it could be, for what it is. But for what it is, I wouldn't want to do it again. It's not me, you know, all this cops and robbers, bang-bang you're dead stuff. Give me a good, meaty drama any day. Know what I'm going to do next? A modern version of *The Cherry Orchard* set on a citrus farm in California. Low budget, cast of unknowns, really tight script. Lucy's going to produce it for me.'

'I know,' I said. 'She told me.'

The women came back, people passed by – mainly to let Proctor know they were available whenever he started work on his next movie – we drank a little more and the band played on.

Then the music stopped and Arthur, the studio PR man, climbed onto the platform set up at the back of the sound stage and craved our indulgence for the speeches. We indulged him. We indulged Tony Flo when he got up to tell us all how marvellous we were.

'This studio,' Flo said, 'and the people who work in it mean everything to me.' He spread his arms wide, a plump but still impressive figure in his habitual white suit. 'Without you I am nothing, the studio is nothing. But we need each other, we need to pull together. Think of the great names of the past, the legendary Hollywood moguls – think of Louis B. Mayer. L.B. *was* MGM and what happened to him? MGM fired him.' People laughed uncertainly, not sure whether Flo was making some sort of joke. Flo shook his head. 'And what happened to MGM?' Now nobody laughed. Nothing very good had happened to MGM. 'What happened to the great individuals, the great studios can happen to all of us. We have to look out for our studios, we have to look out for ourselves, we have to look out for each other and one way, the best way, to do that is to make great movies.' He paused. 'I truly believe that in *Death's Head* you guys have made the great movie this studio needs.' Another pause and then, with a smile so that everyone should know he was only kidding, 'You might just have saved my ass.'

The audience – except those on our table – rose to him as he pranced off the stage, blowing kisses.

'Oh yeah,' Barbara Proctor said sourly, 'he's really looking out for us. Thanks to the deal he offered Richie we might with luck be able to keep our home, while good old Tony has just sold his own house and moved to a bigger one in Beverly Hills. We saved his arse all right but what about ours?'

Then Proctor himself got onto the stage and we indulged him as we had indulged Flo while he mumbled his own thanks to the crew and after that we indulged Virna Newport and Martie Culper and Annie Klane and Michael Rialto.

Midway through all this, and pretty well unnoticed, Agnelli came in. Terri Chin was with him. They stood, unobtrusively, just behind and slightly to the left of the platform while first Klane, then Rialto made their pretty, eulogistic speeches to all the wonderful people who had made this wonderful movie so wonderfully possible.

Rialto came to the end of his paean, took his ovation and returned to his companions at the big round table. Arthur bounced towards the platform, presumably to tell us that that was the end of the speeches and we could all carry on getting smashed out of our minds, but Agnelli stopped him.

He stepped in front of him, put his hand gently but firmly on the man's chest and shook his head. Arthur froze. Agnelli nodded towards Terri Chin and, after a moment's hesitation, she sprang up onto the platform. The PR man started to protest, then looked into Agnelli's face and walked away.

I don't know how many other people observed all this; probably very few. I only noticed because I'd been looking for Agnelli all night.

As Chin ran onto the platform and approached the microphone I got up and started walking towards the table where Tony Flo and the stars were sitting.

The partygoers, thinking the speeches were over, had begun talking among themselves again until Chin said, 'Hey, everybody, can I have your attention please?' The chattering stopped; everyone turned to look at her. This caused no pain, for she had clearly dressed to attract attention. She was wearing something gold and form-fitting that seemed to have started out to be a cheongsam then changed its mind and plunged from the top down towards her navel and at the same time soared up from the hem towards her crotch. High-heeled gold shoes, jet-black hair gleaming in the lights, no stockings. The gold was echoed in the colour of her skin and there was a lot of that on view.

She said, 'Look, I know I'm not a star, right? Not like all the others. And I know I don't have any right to be up here but, like, I have something *soooo* important to say and because we've all worked together and I love you all so much I want you to be the first to hear it.' She took a deep breath, summoned up a dazzling smile, turned towards Tony Flo's table and said, 'Ladies and gentlemen, I want you all to know that Michael and I are going to be married.'

There was a moment of total, shocked silence, followed by a buzz of excited chatter. A whole flock of emotions that he couldn't have acted if he tried passed across Rialto's face – amazement, horror, anger, fear. He leapt up shouting, 'Hey, what is this? Is this some kind of shakedown? Will somebody throw that crazy bitch out of here?'

He looked about him wildly, presumably in search of his minders, but they weren't around; minders didn't get invited to parties like this. Agnelli was there, though, standing right behind him.

Rialto said, 'Rico, for Chrissakes, do something.'

Agnelli pushed him back into his chair. 'Be cool, Michael. Hear the lady out.'

I looked at the women with Rialto. An interesting contrast. His wife was staring at him with a look of horror, his mother-in-law with cold hatred.

Terri Chin said, 'Angela, I know how hurt you must have been when Michael told you about us and I wish we could have spared you that. But from the day we met there was nothing either of us could do about it. You remember that first day, Michael? On the set of *Forked Lightning*? We made love three times in your trailer. You were so marvellous, so exciting and we both knew then that this had to be for ever.'

The lines may have been corny but she was delivering them well. She turned to look at the audience, goggling at her from their tables with rapt, salacious attention. 'I want you to know it all because Michael and I want to start our lives together with no secrets from anybody, with everything in the open. We've been an item ever since that first day. Michael found me an apartment and we made love there, oh so many times. And, Michael, do you remember when Angela went to visit with her mom in Canada? That glorious month when we were together all day and all night? And now, darling, it'll be like that for always.'

I thought she'd begun to overdo it a bit but everyone else was still lapping it up. Well, not quite everyone. Angela had her face in her hands and was weeping, great convulsive sobs of humiliation, I imagine, as much as anything else. Her mother was holding her in her arms but still glaring at Rialto, who was squirming frenziedly, trying to break free of the grip Agnelli had on his shoulders. Agnelli didn't look happy either. From the expression on his face I gathered that even he was unaware of the full intimacy of the Chin–Rialto relationship.

Rialto, pinned in his chair, started shouting. 'Will somebody stop that bitch? She's lying, for Chrissake. There's never been anything between—'

It was his mother-in-law who shut him up. First she threw a glass of red wine in his face, then she hit him in the mouth. As a pro I had to admire the punch – plenty of shoulder in it and a good, smart snap of the wrist. Blood spurted from Rialto's torn lips.

Terri Chin carried on as if Rialto's outburst had never happened.

She was an actress and this was her moment. Nothing was going to stop her.

She held up her right hand and said, 'Everybody, do you see this ring?' It was hard to miss: a chunky diamond on a platinum band. 'Michael gave this to me. He said it was our unofficial engagement ring but I wasn't to wear it properly until everyone knew about us. Well ...' A dramatic pause and then she switched the ring from the third finger of her right hand to the third finger of her left. She waved that hand triumphantly above her head, smiling up at it, on tiptoe, her head arced back, all the curves of her body accentuated by her pose and the tightness of her dress. 'Now it's official!'

At last Rialto struggled free and rushed towards her, his face and shirtfront crimson with blood and wine. He didn't get far. Agnelli stepped up behind him and chopped him down with a thump to the side of the neck.

Lucy had come to stand alongside me. She said, 'What the hell was all that?'

'That,' I said, 'was the sound of the shit hitting the fan or maybe,' I added, looking thoughtfully at Terri Chin, 'the fan hitting the shit.'

Terri bounced off the stage and was immediately lost in a voracious crowd, eager for more of the good stuff she had just given them.

Angela Rialto got up from the table, still weeping, still with her hands over her face and half ran, half stumbled towards the exit. Her husband rose to his feet, a dazed, hunted look on his face, stared around, spotted Angela and started moving towards her.

Agnelli stood in his path. 'Forget it, Michael. It's over.'

'Over?' Rialto said. 'Over? It's over for you. It's over for that bitch. You think you can set me up like this and get away with it? You're dead, both of you.'

'I don't think so, Michael.'

They glared at each other for a moment. Or, rather, Rialto glared. On Agnelli's face there was an expression almost of pity.

'You'll see,' Rialto said and moved away, only this time in the opposite direction from the one his wife had taken.

Maria Minelli, or whatever her married name was, finished

gathering together her and Angela's belongings and started off after her daughter, hatred and anger still visible in her eyes and the set of her mouth.

As she passed us she said, 'Rico, I haven't talked to my brother for many years. But tonight I would like you to call him.'

Agnelli nodded. 'I'll do better than that, Maria,' he said. 'I'll go tell him right now. In person.'

We all watched as the crowd parted to let her through, festooned with handbags and evening shawls.

Then Agnelli turned towards me. 'Got him,' he said softly. 'Got him.'

# 49

AGNELLI PHONED ME the next morning, about an hour after Lucy had left for work. The shooting of the film was over but now came the post-production, the editing, the dubbing, the addition of music and titles. This was the stage in which everything that had gone before could either be enhanced or ruined.

I was in a good mood when I took the call. A couple of things had been bothering me slightly all night but I'd sorted them out by the time I spoke to Agnelli.

He said, 'I'm at Carlo's. Michael's here, too. A couple of the guys picked him up at the Beverly Wilshire around six o'clock this morning. We had a little talk in a quiet room here, Michael and me. Carlo was there, too. He heard some interesting things.'

'Yes, I imagine he did. How's Michael holding out?'

'Not so good. I think he's broken a few ribs and a couple of fingers.'

'Well, I suppose he fell down some stairs.'

'Something like that.' A pause. 'Carlo says you can come up to the house if you want. He'd like to thank you, all the help you've given.'

'Is this a genuine invitation – come if you can, pretty please, that sort of thing?'

'Sure. Or, put it another way, Carlo says come up to the house.'

So I went. As I walked to my car I passed Virna Newport's bungalow. She was checking out that morning, her work on the movie over, to return to her apartment in Manhattan. When I went by a squad of bellboys was carrying her luggage through to reception.

Newport was standing at her door. We nodded to each other but didn't exchange greetings. We'd already spoken that day.

The men on the gates at Minelli's place were expecting me and waved me through. Agnelli met me at the house. He looked tired but happy.

'What a night,' he said. 'What a morning. I haven't slept.'

'Where's everybody else?'

He gestured down the hallway towards the big living-room. 'Michael's in there with two of the boys. Carlo's upstairs talking to Angela and Maria on the phone. You want coffee? I think we got time. Nobody's in a hurry any more.'

We went into a small room off the hallway and an elderly, Italian-looking woman brought us coffee. I said, 'Okay, bring me up to date. What's happened?'

'Jesus, what hasn't happened.' Agnelli leaned back in his armchair, scratched his head, stretched and yawned. 'Boy, am I bushed.'

'Get on with it,' I said, irritably.

'Okay, well, first off Michael's two goons turned up at Terri's apartment about two a.m., loaded for bear. But I'd figured this might happen so I had some people waiting for them. Terri wasn't there, anyway. She was way out of town by then.'

'And where are the two goons now?'

He shrugged. 'Who knows? They seem to have disappeared.'

Maybe I should have been shocked and outraged but I wasn't. After all, there was a kind of poetic justice in operation here, since the same two goons had almost certainly killed Darren Carmody. Whatever had happened to them wasn't going to break my heart.

I said, 'How did you persuade Terri to do what she did last night?'

'No persuasion necessary. Michael had made her all those promises about marriage and happy ever after. And then he walked away, no goodbye, nothing. He hadn't even bought the apartment for her, just leased it, and the lease runs out end of the month. The other night after I left you when Lucy turned up? I took Terri to dinner and she'd just heard about the lease. Talk about a woman scorned. You never saw a woman as scorned or as good and fuckin' mad as Terri was that night. All she wanted was to get even. So I just suggested that maybe the wrap party might be a good place to do it.' He grinned smugly. 'Was I right or was I right?'

'Where does all this leave Michael?'

'Michael was dead in the water as soon as Terri opened her mouth last night. With Carlo it's a matter of honour. Screw as many whores as you like but bring shame on your family, on your wife, on *Carlo's niece*, for Chrissake, and you're finished. Plus when Michael admitted the drug scam with good ol' Horace, well, you can imagine he's not exactly Carlo's blue-eyed boy any more.'

I poured myself some more coffee. 'He just came out with all that, did he? About the drugs? Just decided to confess, to clear his conscience.'

'Yeah. After he'd bust a couple of ribs and fingers, yeah, that's what he did.'

'Did he say why?' I sipped coffee, staring at him over the rim of the cup.

'Money, what else? It's like you said: he earns a lot but he spends a lot. You're a star in Hollywood, you have to live like a star and that costs plenty. On top of that there's a woman in Texas had his kid last year. He had to buy her a house, pay her off, send her money every month. There was another woman in New York apparently had the world's most expensive abortion. Then there was the lease on Terri's apartment. The way Michael explained it, however much he earned he could never get ahead of the game. So that's why he listened when Horace came up with this drug deal.'

'It was Horace's idea, was it?'

'So Michael said.' Agnelli suddenly sprang up. 'Hey, there goes Carlo. You better come say hello.'

We caught up with Minelli in the hallway. He shook my hand and thanked me gravely for the help I had given him. 'But I have to say,' he added, 'that indirectly you have caused me a lot of emotional pain. I believed in Michael. He's been a very stupid boy.'

We went on into the living-room. The two minders who had been watching over Rialto got up and left as soon as Minelli, Agnelli and I walked in. Rialto was sitting in an upright chair, his arms clasped around his body as if he were in considerable pain. Two of the fingers on his left hand stuck out at curious angles. His expression was both sullen and fearful.

Minelli waved Agnelli and me to easy chairs and sat down in one himself. He said, 'Okay, Michael, I've talked to Angela and my sister and here's what's going to happen. The divorce will go through immediately. Angela's lawyer will be in touch with you and you will agree to everything he says. You won't like the deal but look at it this way: if Angela was a widow she'd inherit everything. As it is, you play ball, Angela doesn't end up a widow and we may leave you a little something for yourself. You have any problem with that?'

Rialto actually looked relieved. 'You're not gonna kill me?'

Minelli shook his head. 'No. You're lucky there were so many witnesses last night. I'm not happy about that but it worked out well for you. If you died now it could cause a lot of embarrassment for people I care about.' He paused, clicked his fingers, pointed to the drinks cabinet. Agnelli got up and brought him a glass of champagne. Well, it was eleven a.m. and champagne is always a pleasant morning drink. I wouldn't have minded a glass myself but Minelli wasn't offering.

Minelli said, 'But there's a weird kind of statute of limitations operating here, Michael. As time goes by your death would become increasingly less embarrassing to the people I referred to. Understand?'

Rialto nodded eagerly.

'You're a lucky boy, Michael. Remember that. You leave this house, I never want to see you again. Angela never wants to see you again. All she wants to see is your signature on the divorce settlement her lawyer draws up. If you need a lawyer of your own, for appearances' sake, I'll provide one for you. But bear this in mind: if you ever do or say anything to cause me or anyone close to me the slightest problem you are dead.'

For a moment they stared at each other. Then Rialto looked down, nodded his head fervently, mumbled something.

'Okay,' Minelli said, softly. 'You can go now. The boys will drive you back to the hotel.'

Rialto got up slowly, groaning with pain.

I said, 'Just a minute.'

Rialto stopped, glancing towards me. Minelli frowned at me, annoyed at a mere outsider muscling in to top his lines. 'What?' he said.

I motioned to Rialto to sit down again and, after a brief hesitation, he did. Minelli looked even more annoyed. I didn't care.

To Rialto I said, 'This drug deal. Horace Wilkins brought it to you, right?'

He nodded, eagerly.

I said, 'You're a liar.'

Now I had everyone's attention.

I said, 'A couple of things have been bothering me for a while. For instance, the other night Rico said he blamed Virna Newport for all the trouble that has happened and he was right. If Newport hadn't shot her mouth off because she was scared that Greg Harrison's book would pre-empt her own autobiography there'd have been no trouble at all. But who did she shoot her mouth off to?'

They were all watching me – Minelli frowning, Agnelli just interested, Rialto a little scared.

'She knew what Harrison was going to put in his book because he'd told her when she dumped him and he wanted to hurt her. And she was terrified, not because Harrison would name the dealers but because he would name her and everyone would know that she, the pristine Queen of Hollywood, sniffed candy up her nose. The problem was: who could she tell? Not you, Carlo, because she reckoned you'd just have Harrison killed and she didn't want that. She wanted him stopped but not dead. Can I have some of that champagne?'

Minelli waved irritably at Agnelli who poured me a glass and brought it over. It was good: crisp and dry and chilled just right.

I said, 'So she went to the one man she felt she could trust, the man who had the right kind of clout in the right kind of area to buy Harrison off. I'm not talking money here, though undoubtedly that would have come into it; I'm talking work, acting roles, the opportunity for Harrison to resurrect his tired old career.'

I sipped some more champagne.

Minelli said, 'You're talking about Charlie Baldock?'

'No, I'm not. She didn't even know Baldock very well at that time.'

Rialto looked even more anxious. The other two stood around frowning for a minute or two. I thought that for a couple of high-ranking hoodlums they were really rather dumb.

'You don't …' Agnelli shook his head. 'You don't mean Tony Flo? Not Tony Flo, for Chrissake.'

I nodded. 'The very same. I had a chat with Virna this morning, that's how I know all this stuff. You see, there was something – a very little something – that had always struck me as odd. Do you remember, Rico, that first party in the studio about a hundred years ago when we'd just started the film?'

He grunted.

'Well,' I said, 'when Harrison broke in and created a scene, who did Virna turn to for help? Not you, not Darren, not me, even though she was trying to suck my tonsils out at the time. No, she turned immediately to Tony Flo. "Do something, Tony," she said. Well, okay, he was the studio boss. But this wasn't a studio matter – this was a domestic. She was being hassled by a former lover in the presence of Darren, her current lover, the bloke – me – who she seemed to think might become her next lover and the right-hand man – you, Rico – of, to put it delicately, her patron or protector. If it had come to rough stuff Darren would probably have been useless but you or I, Rico, could have thrown Harrison out with one hand. She must have known that. And yet she turned to Tony Flo.'

'So?' Minelli said.

'So I wondered about that at the time. Later I wondered about it even more and I also started wondering where a loser like Horace Wilkins would have found the money to move into the drugs business. He could have got it from Michael, of course, but I didn't think Michael would have had the bottle to set up in competition with you, Carlo, with only Horace as a partner. There had to be somebody else, somebody with a bit of weight. And then I remembered that Horace's last regular employment immediately before he opened his shop on Santa Monica was as an assistant to ...' I paused expectantly.

'Tony Flo,' Agnelli whispered.

'Give the man a coconut. Yep, good old Tony Flo, who apparently fired him. Only I don't think he did fire him. I think he recognised someone who would do anything for a quick buck, made him an offer he couldn't refuse and gave him the seed money. And around then, I imagine, was when Michael was co-opted, possibly because Tony needed more capital than he could raise on his own. Tony knew, obviously, about Michael's connection with you, Carlo, so he knew Michael had no difficulty living cheek by jowl with organised crime. He probably also knew that Michael was interested in making some extra money that he didn't have to tell anybody about.'

Now we all turned and looked at Rialto.

'Well?' Minelli said.

Rialto glanced at him, then glanced away again. 'Yes,' he said, mumbled rather.

Minelli slapped him hard across the face. 'What?'

Rialto glanced up at him again. The slap had left a red mark on his cheek but it also, for a moment, brought a flicker of anger to his eyes. 'Yes. I said yes. Okay? That's pretty much what happened. I needed money, Tony showed me a way to make some. End of story.'

'And Tony?'

'He needed money, too. He gambles, what can I tell you? Look, Carlo,' the anger had died and he was pleading now, 'it seemed like such a little thing, a small specialised market. I didn't think it could hurt you.'

'You took the bread from my mouth, Michael,' Minelli said gravely.

I went over and refilled my champagne glass. I didn't offer any to Minelli.

Agnelli said, 'Michael, why didn't you tell us about Tony before? It could have saved you at least a broken finger.'

Rialto drew himself up in his chair. The movement made him

wince as his broken ribs stirred but the man had his pride. 'I don't rat on my friends,' he said.

Minelli stared at him pityingly for a moment. 'You asshole,' he said. Then he turned towards Agnelli. 'Go tell Tony Flo I want to see him. Now.'

# 50

Carlo Minelli was merciful: he let Tony Flo live.

As Agnelli explained to me later, although the money Rialto and Flo had skimmed from Minelli's drug operation was a lot by most people's standards – enough anyway to enable Flo to pay off his gambling debts and move to a bigger house – it was, in the general scheme of things, merely nickels and dimes. Rialto and Flo were not big enough to kill; besides why waste a man when it's more profitable to make him pay heavy compensation, which is what Rialto and Flo did and, as far as I know, are still doing.

Flo was gone from the studio by mid-afternoon that day. Minelli had ordered Charlie Baldock to fire him at once but with a handsome pay-off, which pay-off immediately found its way into Minelli's possession.

Lucy came home in the evening, all excited by the news. 'Have you heard?' she said. 'Tony Flo's gone. He quit a couple of hours ago. Health reasons, he said.'

'Good way to put it.'

I sat her down and told her what I knew. She was interested enough to delay our communal shower for more than an hour.

'So when Virna went to Tony Flo and told him about Harrison's book she didn't know what names he was going to mention?'

'No,' I said. 'She just knew they were Hollywood hotshots. It was Harrison who told Flo that he was in the frame. He called him the

305

night of that start of shooting party with an ultimatum – "Get me on the movie and I'll leave you out of the book." I think he was pretty drunk at the time.'

'So Flo told Michael and Michael told—'

'Horace Wilkins. Right. And that was the beginning of the end of Greg Harrison. They could hardly leave him roaming around with all the knowledge he had.'

She said, 'Let's eat in tonight. I'll call room service.' She did that and then she said, 'But how did Harrison get to know all this stuff?'

I shrugged. 'Search me. Even I am not privy to every secret. But perhaps, as the guy who ordered Virna's coke, he got curious about where it was coming from at such a competitive price. Maybe he followed Wilkins one night after he'd made his delivery, found out exactly who he was and dug a little deeper into his background. I just don't know. But you can find out almost anything if you really set your mind to it.'

She topped up our wine glasses. 'What about Darren?'

'Well, he was just unlucky. The murder of someone as well known as Harrison was sure to create a stink but things would be a lot more comfortable for Rialto and company if there was an obvious suspect. Everyone knew that Darren and Harrison hated each other, so Darren got elected. The idea was for Rialto's goons, or Wilkins's goons because he provided them, to snatch him the afternoon Harrison was killed, take him out to the desert and shoot him. Nobody would go looking for him there because the police, not unreasonably, thought he was on the run from a murder charge. Not a bad idea. It just took a little longer to put into operation than anyone anticipated. The goons bungled the first attempt to grab Darren but it didn't really matter. Tony Flo knew from Virna Newport of her toy boy's connection with Lou, so they watched Lou's house for a while, not looking for Darren particularly but working out which of her bouncers might be open to a deal. Not particularly difficult – this is a factory town, after all; everyone's for sale. So they bought the man of their choice and he tipped them off the day Darren turned up to meet me. The goons followed Darren to his hideaway and grabbed him there. Then when they'd got rid of him they came back and shot the bouncer. Just covering all the angles. Very neat, really.'

She thought it all over. 'So who did kill Harrison and hit you on the head?'

'According to Rialto and Flo it was Horace. He got into Harrison's room, did the deed, snatched Harrison's audio tapes and was on the way out when I turned up. Rialto says it was also Horace's idea to kill me. Rialto was happy to go along with that because I'd hurt his pride when I knocked him about a bit in Richie's editing suite. Besides, Horace had got it into his head that Harrison and I were buddies and that I knew what was going to be in the book. He reckoned that explained why I went to Harrison's room that day.'

Lucy nodded. 'Always a mistake when assholes start thinking too much,' she said.

About then the food came and we ate it and showered and went early to bed. A perfect ending to a very odd day.

# 51

So what else can I tell you?

*Death's Head Dangling* opened in America in December that year and was an immediate hit. It took twenty three million dollars at the box office on its first weekend and just carried on climbing from there. Even the critics liked it. They gave Rialto the best reviews of his career, raved over Newport and were unanimous in declaring that Richie Proctor had brought the freshest eye to the crime movie since Quentin Tarantino. (The fact that a lot of them had originally hated Quentin Tarantino was conveniently forgotten.)

A few weeks later the film gathered six Oscar nominations – best picture, director, actor, supporting actress, cinematography and editing. In the end only Newport and the cinematographer actually won awards but on the whole everyone was pretty happy. I was sorry that Proctor missed out again but secretly rather glad the movie hadn't won best picture because if it had Bill Charleston, as the producer, would have gone home with an Oscar, and though an Oscar isn't everything it's too good for a prick like him.

I was there at the ceremony, sitting next to Lucy. Bloody boring event, if you want my opinion. It lasted about three and a half hours, largely because it just stopped every twenty minutes so the TV company which was transmitting it could bung out a few more commercials.

Marvellous, isn't it? Film is supposed to be the art form of the twentieth century – well, not in Hollywood perhaps but almost everywhere else – and yet the celebration of the industry's biggest night of the year had to go on hold at regular intervals while a bunch of bimbos of both sexes tried to sell America all kinds of crap nobody really needed.

There was a good party afterwards, though, and then we rounded things off at Morton's in Beverly Hills. Apparently all the winners and most of the also-rans go there on Oscar night to show the assembled TV cameras outside how modest they are in victory or how gallant in defeat.

The studio paid, of course. The studio paid for everything because *Death's Head* was the biggest hit Maestro Consolidated had had in more than ten years.

I spent most of the evening with Lucy and the Proctors. At Morton's Newport, hugging her newly acquired golden bauble, was queening it over the other side of the room, with Annie Klane and Martie Culper in her retinue. Of all the principal people involved only Rialto wasn't there because the studio boss had let him know he wouldn't be welcome.

Well, what else could he have expected from Rico Agnelli?

Oh, I hadn't told you, had I? Charlie Baldock doesn't own Maestro Consolidated any more; Carlo Minelli does – or, at least, Minelli's nominees do. I think Donovan has a piece of it, too, but I'm not sure. Donovan doesn't tell me everything. Anyway Agnelli runs the place now. I don't know how grubby the money is when it goes into the studio but I bet it looks newly minted when it comes out.

Tony Flo had set himself up as an independent producer, making vacuous movies for TV. According to the trade papers he seemed to be doing all right, even though he had had to sell his new house in Beverly Hills and move into a comparatively modest apartment in Santa Monica. I imagine he'll be okay financially once he's finished paying off whatever Minelli reckons he owes him.

Rialto's career, thanks to the Oscar nomination, was on a high, which was just as well for him. The divorce had left him pretty well skinned. Angela had got the house in Beverly Hills, the duplex in Manhattan, all the stocks and shares and whatever was in the bank.

True, she had let Rialto keep the ranch in Texas, though since that was already double-mortgaged it wasn't much of a bargain. But at least he was still alive and I expect he was grateful for that.

Lucy and I left the post-Oscar revelries about midnight because she had to be up fairly early the next morning to work on her new film. It was the one Proctor had been so keen on – *The Cherry Orchard* updated, retitled *Oranges and Lemons* and set on a California citrus farm – only Proctor wasn't actually directing it, Lucy was. She was producing it, too.

Proctor himself had ducked out when an alternative offer came his way, another bang-bang, you're dead, shoot 'em up crime thriller, only this time with a seventy-five-million-dollar budget and all the stunts and special effects in the world.

I asked him about that at Morton's. 'Correct me if I'm wrong,' I said, 'but somehow I got the impression that you'd had your fill of Hollywood commercialism, that you were desperate to make an honest film, something real, something artistic even.'

'Yeah, well,' he said, grabbing another Jack Daniels from a passing waiter, 'but that was before Warner's offered me all this bloody money, wasn't it?' Ah, these artists. Who can ever understand them?

Lucy and I were still seeing a lot of each other, or as much as two people can whose homes are separated by the continent of North America and the Atlantic Ocean. Her career was in and around Hollywood, mine – such as it was – in London, but we spent all the time we could together. And if that meant that I was in California a lot more often than she was in England, that was okay by me. I'd lost Linda because the Atlantic lay between us and I didn't want to lose Lucy the same way. In any event, if you earn your living by wheeling, dealing and speculating all you really need is a phone and a fax machine. Besides, there's a lot to be said for California – the climate's great and the people are okay, too, so long as you always remember that most of them came originally from Mars.

For that Oscar trip the studio had put me up in my old bungalow at the Bel Air Riviera and that was where we went after we left Morton's.

As we lay in the bath together Lucy kissed the scar just under my left shoulder, the place where Horace Wilkins's bullet had entered my body before passing through on the other side. The exit wound left a bigger scar but neither is too unsightly and my arm is as good as ever now.

Incidentally, Wilkins never did stand trial for trying to kill me. He was arrested and charged as soon as he returned to LA. But his lawyer got him out on bail, which wasn't really doing him any favours because two days later he was discovered, shot dead, in his kitchen, his face resting in a congealed bowl of spaghetti bolognese. Nobody ever found out who did it and though I suspected I knew I thought it wiser not to ask. Besides his death would have had nothing to do with me. Some businessmen who make the wrong move simply go bankrupt; Wilkins made his wrong move on Carlo Minelli's territory and so all his accounts were terminated.

Lucy said, 'If you carry on doing that with your foot I'm getting out of this bath right now.'

'Sorry,' I said. 'I was thinking of other things.'

'Oh my, isn't that so utterly goddamn English? If you were doing stuff like that you might at least have paid me the compliment of keeping your mind on the job.' She took my foot and rested it between her breasts where she could keep an eye on it. 'Anyway, what were you thinking about?'

'Well, I was reading in *Variety* today that *Death's Head* has so far taken three hundred and five million worldwide.'

'So?'

'So I was wondering whether all my points might actually make me some money.'

'What kind of points – nett or gross?'

'Nett.'

'Forget it,' she said. 'Right this minute a whole army of accountants is working out foolproof ways to make sure you never see a penny.'

'Why don't they award an Oscar for best creative accountancy?'

'They will. Just give them time.'

'Hoorah for Hollywood,' I said.

She got up on her knees and moved towards me. 'Shut up about your money,' she said. 'I've just had an idea and I want to see if it's possible in a bath. Bear with me for a minute.'

So I did. And it was possible.

'Hoorah for Hollywood,' I said again, only a lot more enthusiastically this time.